Summer of the Cicada

Will Napier was born in West Virginia and now lives in Fife, Scotland with his wife and two sons. *Summer of the Cicada* is his first novel. He is at work on a collection of short fiction and his second novel.

Summer of the Cicada

Will Napier

JONATHAN CAPE
LONDON

Published by Jonathan Cape 2005

2   4   6   8   10 9   7   5   3

First published in Great Britain in 2005 by
Jonathan Cape
Random House, 20 Vauxhall Bridge Road,
London SW1V 2SA

Random House Australia (Pty) Limited
20 Alfred Street, Milsons Point, Sydney,
New South Wales 2061, Australia

Random House New Zealand Limited
18 Poland Road, Glenfield,
Auckland 10, New Zealand

Random House South Africa (Pty) Limited
Endulini, 5A Jubilee Road, Parktown 2193, South Africa

The Random House Group Limited Reg. No. 954009
www.randomhouse.co.uk

A CIP catalogue record for this book is available from the British Library

ISBN 0-224-07357-5

Papers used by Random House are natural, recyclable
products made from wood grown in sustainable forests; the manufacturing
processes conform to the environmental regulations of the country of origin

Typeset by Palimpsest Book Production Limited,
Polmont, Stirlingshire
Printed and bound in Great Britain by
Mackays of Chatham plc, Chatham, Kent

For

Elaine, Ethan and Zac
The Three Muses

Willy Maley
A Mentor and a Friend

Jim and Denise Napier
They made a Writer

Summer of the Cicada

Chapter One

First swing almost missed me. Fist came over his shoulder and I swayed back. Knuckles grazed the bridge of my nose and chin before digging into my chest. When I swayed again my foot didn't follow back the way I'd practised. I went off-balance. Lost focus when the second punch came. A left that landed like a brick on my right temple. A good shot that made a hollow sound inside my head. Sparks flashed behind my eyes. I went down, but not all the way. Something kept me up even while my mind told me to drop.

Let yourself go, Joseph. He's gonna hit you again. Fall! What are you think . . .

Third punch came down. A line of knuckles pushed into my scalp. Reflex brought my jaw closed. Somewhere in all of the flashes of light – colours that played on my eyelids like a movie reel – I sensed my mouth going wet. It went real hot. Before I could react the floor met my knee, then my shoulder. My chest pulsed hard. There was a sharp pain opening up under my arms. It moved between my ribs. It was growing. Then another pulse landed against my head with more pain.

This is it, my boy. Should have gone down the first time. You've made him mad. Ain't nothing stoppin' him now.

1

There was a moment when everything went still. I couldn't hear any sounds. The taste of pennies was soaking into my gums. The hot sensation had escaped from my mouth and started running down the side of my face. When I swallowed I felt a piece of something large and heavy move against my teeth. My eyes opened even though I tried to keep them shut. There was my old man standing over me, his stance telling me not to get up. His hands, clenching tighter and tighter, dared me to move. Just an inch's all he wanted.

I stared at his bare feet, wide apart. Just over shoulder width. He was rocking from side to side. It's how he learned to fight, first from his father and then in the navy. I learned from watching him swing at me. Behind him Mother held her chin in a steady hand. Her eyelids looked thick and pink. Her shoulders rose up on a slow wave. Then they fell. I think she was breathing deep. She may have been signalling me. She stood behind a haze – like she was on the opposite side of a hot, blacktop highway in summer. My eyelids tried to blink the haze away, but it wouldn't go.

Her mouth moved but I couldn't hear what she was trying to say.

Stay on the ground, Joe. He'll hit you again. Stay still.

'What the hell is wrong with you?' my father said. His voice was calm. He was barely out of breath.

I tried to talk, but could only manage a wet sound that spilled onto the wooden floor. I looked at my mother whose eyes widened. She disappeared into the kitchen. My old man pushed his foot against my shoulder and rolled me over. Mother was out of sight, shuffling through the keys on the rack near the back door. They rattled and fell and made crashing sounds each time another set hit the linoleum. The lump in my mouth was falling back into my throat. I tried to swallow it, but it wouldn't go. My throat filled up. I coughed. I had a fit of coughs and closed my eyes. The pain in my chest jumped tempo and started hammering away. When the fit was over I rolled to the side.

Father slid backwards. The hard soles of his feet skidded against the wooden floor. He was clearing out of the room – his way of letting me know he'd finished. I opened my eyes and caught him standing in the doorway Mother had passed through. She kept dropping things. Father didn't look mad any more. His eyes were calm. His shirt now looked too small against his swollen muscles. I blinked and my right eye saw clear. His arm was specked with dark drops. There was a coating of red around the soles of his feet.

'Help me get him in the car,' Mother said when she floated back into the room. She had on her long blue dress that made her look like a teenager. I felt dazed and disconnected. To keep from passing out I stared at her dress and tried to figure out if it was denim. She liked that and linen. She was always in the stuff.

'Put a towel on the back seat. Make sure he doesn't move too much.' Father's voice rocked me. I tried to turn my head to look at him, but a shot of pain jammed in my neck. I closed my eyes again and swallowed at the blood. It started filling up my mouth. When I opened my eyes my old man was out of the room.

Mother looked down at me for a minute. She just stood there sucking at her lower lip. It's like she was trying to figure out where to touch me. She gave me one of her sideways looks. It was a quick thing – just a glance. Eye to eye. Tender enough to forgive her for not stopping him. Then she straightened up. The pain came in like a strong wind but I got up on my own. I brought my arms in close to my sides to keep the pain from escaping. It worked to a degree, but then over the years I may have forgotten how much it didn't help. Mother passed through to the hallway and I followed as quick as I could. She reached into the closet and pulled out two of my winter coats. One she pushed roughly under my chin.

'Don't say anything until they fix that tongue. Hold it together if you need to,' she said. She kept the other coat tucked under her arm.

I got in the back of the car with one coat covering the side I was sitting on. I had the other coat covering my head. Mother refused to open the garage door before I had nodded an agreement to keep out of sight till we were well away from Westchester Drive.

'Let's keep the neighbourhood out of this, huh?' she said. Her face twitched like she didn't know if she should smile a little.

She drove fast. Mother never drove like that. With the coat over my head I started to worry I was in bad shape. I had lost a lot of blood. From the way Mother looked at me I could tell I was real messed up – sitting in silence in a fast car with half a tongue. I felt around my mouth with sore fingers and found a couple teeth that were shaped different than before. They were sharper and smaller. But at that point I was still dazed. I had a light head. A medicine-head, Mother used to call it. Even with the music that was playing on the radio – Hughey Lewis and the News, I think. 'Back in Time' maybe – I started wondering if this was the beating that would do it. If this was the one that knocked me out for good.

I was still hoping for the worst when Mother slammed the car into a stop. The wheels skidded. I slid the coat off my head. Mother was looking at me in the rearview mirror. I turned to the window to find she had pulled over to a roadside parking space off State Road Nine. The picnic tables just past the trees were empty. The trash barrels overflowed from the weekend of visitors. They were under the trees. Just further down was Wild Lake. I waited for laughter. I waited for a dog to bark. Maritime never sounded so deserted.

'You got in a fight with some boys in the woods,' Mother said. She set her right elbow on the top of the bench seat and gestured with a closed fist. 'You don't know them. First time you'd ever seen them before. They chased you and were too fast. You gave up.'

I nodded my head and started to pull the coat over again. Mother let out a heavy breath.

'You always give up,' she said.

I nodded and pulled the coat tight against my head.

'They never attack the strong ones, Joseph.'

4

She turned the radio off and drove the rest of the way slowly. I heard cars honk as they flew past. She'd figured things out. Everything fell back into place. At the hospital she parked in a space far away from the entrance. She opened my door and pulled the coat away. While I got out she folded the coat and placed it on the floor mat. With her purse tucked under her arm she started walking. I followed her.

'What happened, Joseph?' she asked.

My father just beat the living shit out of me. Are you fucking blind? I shrugged. She'd told me not to speak. It was a test.

'Did you get into a fight?'

I nodded.

'With who?'

Shook my head. She wasn't looking at me. A red BMW rolled by and slowed up when they got close. Mother stared at the couple in the car. The young couple were looking at me. I took advantage of the attention and spit a wad of blood. I'd been swallowing up to that point and my guts had filled with the stuff.

'Did you try to run? Did you even try to get away?' she continued, when we'd made it past the car.

I nodded again.

'You didn't try hard enough, Joseph. Not nearly hard enough.'

We were at the door. It opened when I stepped on the rubber mat and inside rushed a quiet calm. The women at reception were dressed in white cardigans over green vests. One of the women wore a white cap. The other had small, tight braids that, when she turned round, I saw reached to the centre of her back. They both stopped talking when Mother and me made our way to the desk. The one in the cap looked down and shuffled through a stack of papers. The other just stared, first at me, then at Mother. It made me feel uncomfortable so I looked away. Down a corridor I saw a metal gurney with a ruffled sheet on it. Beyond that there was an empty wheelchair, half-folded and pushed up against the wall.

'My son's been in a fight. He needs some stitches I think.' Mother could put on a soft and sweet voice when she needed to. She must have thought this was a good time for it.

'Should we have an officer come in to take statements?' the nurse with braids asked.

I kept my eyes away from her. The nurse was an attractive girl. Maybe mid-twenties. I always felt nervous around nice looking girls anyway, but with a face like a broken melon I became even more introverted.

'We've already spoken to the police. Our neighbour brought him home. Her husband's a policeman. He'd spoken to Joe right after the . . .' Mother waved her hands in the air. 'The thing. The fight. I think he even chased the boys who did it. God love him. I'll be calling him when I get Joseph back home. See if he caught up with them.'

Mother had a gift for elaboration. The story had even convinced me. The boys who chased me began to materialize in my mind. One of them wore a New York Giants jersey and kept checking it to make sure it wasn't marked with my blood. Another had taken his shirt off when he started punching me. He had muscles that looked too big for his age. The third kid hadn't come up clear yet. Listening to Mother speak I figured she'd been right about the whole thing.

I hadn't tried hard enough. I never tried hard enough.

Mother kept talking so I went and sat down. The waiting room was large with rows of chairs all lined up like they were there for an audience. I suppose they were. All of the chairs faced the reception desk so everyone could see the lame freaks that came in with busted bodies. I was thankful that the audience hadn't showed up for the matinée. An old woman sat slumped on a seat in the back row. Her chest swelled and shrunk otherwise I may have thought she'd given up the ghost. On the far wall a young woman with a little boy huddled up to one another. The boy's skin looked too yellow. When he pulled away from his mother he caught sight of me. Wasn't but a minute before he buried his face in the woman's side again. She smiled at me – not a happy smile, just one to apologize for either her son or my misfortune – and looked away. Other than those few people the place was empty.

Are Tuesdays slow for trauma?

Mother came over and sat down next to me with a clipboard the nurses handed out. She went back to being the silent woman who floated round our house. The room remained silent. The only sounds coming from the nurses tapping at their keyboards. Pages rustling as Mother read through the forms. Then her pen started clicking against the board under the sheets of paper. The sounds came like gunshots. My nerves were edgy.

It seemed a long wait. Mother finished filling in the forms. An old guy came in with his wife. He held his hand in a dish towel that looked stained with rust. They went up to the desk and got their own clipboard. Then they sat a few chairs away and ignored us. A black couple came in after them. The woman was heavily pregnant. She held the weight of her swollen stomach with one hand. She gripped the man's shoulder with the other. The guy was frantic. Orderlies came and put the lady in a wheel-chair and pushed her down the hall. I'd started to stiffen up when a nurse came and touched my shoulder – nice shot, one of the few places I didn't hurt.

'Come this way, Joseph.' She didn't have to call my name in a questioning way. Although there were others who came in I was the only one looking like I needed immediate attention – other than the old guy with the rusty towel. But he didn't moan any. His wife touched his knee as they talked in whispers. Once up from my seat I found that I was the only one leaking on the linoleum. I looked at the small circle of red and wondered where it came from. Mother stood but the nurse shook her head.

'You just sit tight and we'll see to Joseph. If you'd like a coffee there's a vending machine down the cast corridor. Just over there.' The nurse didn't even motion to my mother as to which direction 'over there' really was. Instead she touched my shoulder with the delicate hand of a person who knew how much pain I was in. She knew how much people could take before they just gave up.

We went down the hall without talking. When we passed doors I tried to look in, but I couldn't see anyone. The nurse

7

showed me into an examination room on the right. I took a seat on a bed that was just high enough to make me strain – even after she lowered the thing by pushing some fancy buttons. My ribs felt like they were coming apart and readying themselves to break out of my skin.

'Well, soldier,' the nurse said with her hands on her hips. 'What in God's name happened to you?'

I opened my mouth to speak. My guts turned like a cement mixer and rolled out a line of blood and saliva. It came in a steady stream that hit the floor and curled a good way up the wall. The nurse stepped aside. She must have heard the gurgled belch that came before the explosion. It wasn't until I was telling Dean Gillespie what happened a few weeks later that I remembered the belch.

The nurse helped me lay on my side and gave me a kidney-shaped basin to hold on to. She left the room. I started feeling faint again so I closed my eyes. I think a few people came in and out of the room while I was in that phase – dropping out of wakefulness and into that heat-haze thing. There was a black man in an aqua-coloured uniform who came in. He had a mop and a smile that he used in equally skilled measure. I remember him because he spoke to me.

'Y'all right, bud?' he asked as he sloshed his mop around on my blood.

I nodded and felt my neck seizing up.

'Have an ax'dent?'

I nodded again.

'Car?'

I tried to shake my head, but couldn't lift it well enough to make it happen.

'Fight?'

I closed my eyes.

'Musta been some big dude.' He went quiet for a while. I listened to his mop slashing against the floor. Then he'd rinse it and start the process again. When he finished he dropped the mop in the bucket and went for the door. The rollers on his mop squealed like a pack of hungry mice. He leaned in close and tapped the pillow my head lay on.

'Hang in theya, kid,' he almost sang to me. 'It's all good.' Then he left. I listened to his whistling fade down the hall.

I kept my eyes shut and the door opened and closed a few more times. People came in and out. Some spoke. I heard papers being flipped when the door opened another time. But whoever came in to look at me didn't stay for long. I had almost found sleep when the first nurse I saw came back in.

'Here we go, Joseph.' She had a tray that she wheeled in on a silver cart. The tray was covered with a towel the same aqua blue as the janitor's uniform. It's a hospital colour, a calm colour. The shapes under the sheet didn't look friendly.

She helped me sit up. I tried to blink the tired feeling out of my eyes. She took my hand and placed two fingers on my wrist. She watched the clock on the wall and counted without making a sound. When her lips stopped moving she smiled at me. She rolled up my left sleeve and found the bruise from a few nights before. It had turned purple and yellow. She spent a few seconds just staring at it, checking it from different angles.

Nice work, huh? I wanted to say. Instead I closed my mouth up tight and felt the blood squeeze out of my split tongue.

She ended up taking my pressure from the other arm. When she uncovered the tray I saw an assortment of silver tools and some needles wrapped in plastic sleeves. She pulled two small bottles from her shirt pocket. She must have seen that I was wondering how much of the stuff she had intentions of using on me.

'We're going to make you good as new, hun,' she said.

I smiled. It must have looked like an odd gesture. My left cheek had swollen into a nice lump. My lip on that side didn't move on account of its own swelling. On the other side I couldn't feel a thing. When I smiled the lip seemed to shoot up fast from the sensations in my cheek. I felt like I had to control it before it jumped off my face completely.

Before she could lift a needle the door opened and a doctor

9

entered. He seemed young. The hair stood up from the front of his head in short strands and gradually fell in the back until it was flat. His face was hairless except for two over-thick eyebrows. He winced at me and smiled at the nurse. The nurse handed him a clipboard and he flipped through a few pages.

'Hey, Joseph. Looks like you've had a bit of trouble.' His voice had a soothing tone. It was heavy, but didn't have the malice I'd got used to over the years. He took a flashlight from his breast pocket and shined it into my eyes, one at a time. After replacing the light in his pocket he took my head in both of his hands and tried to turn it gently to the left.

'Ah!' I cried. More fluid leaked from my mouth. I'd been swallowing gulps of the stuff since vomiting the first time. My stomach had filled up again. I'd been storing it, desperate not to swallow, but having no choice.

'Get that for me, Lynn,' the doctor said. The nurse moved quick and touched my face with a towel. She wiped up what leaked without making the pain flare up.

The doctor moved close and took a hold of my chin with his thumb and index finger. Without warning he pulled my mouth open slowly.

'That hurt?'

I shook my head the best I could. The pain kept me from moving much.

'Nasty cut on his tongue,' he said to the nurse. Then to me: 'You remember biting your tongue, Joe?'

I shook again.

Yeah you do. You tried to swallow it. That dead piece of meat. Remember?

'Might need to sew that.' He took gauze and pressed it between my tongue and lower row of teeth. 'Needs to see a dentist too. Chips all round.'

The nurse made some notes on a clipboard. She'd write a few things down before pulling at her rubber gloves to keep them tight against her fingers. Each time she pulled the gloves she'd let them snap against her skin. Sometimes she'd look at me and

10

give a timid smile. I wanted to smile back, but couldn't bring myself to make one.

'This the year those bugs come?' the doctor asked.

'I'm sorry,' the nurse said with a hint of a laugh in her voice.

'The cicadas I've heard about.'

'Couldn't tell you,' the nurse said. She looked at me like she wanted me to hear what she had to say. 'I'm from Florida.'

For some reason that connected us. There was something more to it than coming from the same state. Still my head was full of hot lead and I wanted everything to go quiet and dark.

'We don't have them where I'm from either. I've heard enough to know when they come you know they're here.' He pushed a thumb over my eyebrow. I could feel the swelling skin roll under his touch. He frowned when he caught me looking in his eyes.

'You know about the cicadas?' he asked me.

I shook my head.

'Fair enough.'

'Do you want to get him to X-ray before the sutures?' the nurse tried to say it quietly. When you say things in a low voice they sound less threatening. I couldn't have cared less.

Shout it out, lady. Let the world know. This kid's got holes that need closing!

'Better close him up first.'

I listened to a lot of this sort of thing in the exam room that day. They found a cut in my head where my father's knuckles caught me good. On the right side of my head there was another cut. They didn't give me any stitches for that one, but put a couple of heavy butterfly tapes on it after shaving away some hair. Over my left eye they cleaned off the blood and found a mess. The skin broke off and a quick heat broke open again. They sewed that one too. That's my Frankenstein wound. Shoots out over my eye like the long half of a broken wishbone.

I went to X-ray. My ribs were bruised, but there were no breaks. I felt disappointed. With the lack of internal injuries I couldn't be admitted without my mother's approval. They wanted to keep me in for observation. Mother came into the exam room they'd wheeled me to after the X-rays. She'd been crying and the sight of her puffed-up face shocked me. She looked pale and small. I wanted to think she'd been crying for me, but I knew those times had passed long before. Now she cried for herself.

It could have been this time – the last of the beatings. She'd been broken down and told what really went on. She spent so much time mending me before and this one had been too much. She didn't want the neighbours involved. *It's a new neighbourhood, for chrissakes. Can't make that kind of first impression.* Now we had a steady flow of hospital staff asking again and again what happened. The signs could have been undeniable. I lay watching her with a face like a crash victim and still Mother had me convinced of the three boys. They'd been faster than me and I gave up too fucking easily.

When the police officer walked in the room behind her I went cold.

This is it. Here we go.

The cop stepped past my mother. He knelt by my side. His hair had been blond once, but the wiry steel strands showed he was close to finishing his career. I looked at his name badge. Officer Rich Benn. It was almost enough to make me want to laugh.

'We'll get the boys who did this,' he said to me. My heart skipped. 'Your mother has been through all that happened. I've got the report right here.' He tapped at a closed folder. 'Your mother's glad to see you're alright, son.' He paused. I just stared at him. He sucked at his lower lip and then stood straight. He grew like a cloud of smoke from a fire. Before he left my mother thanked him and shook his hand. I think the young doctor had come into the room by then. It's hard to remember. They'd doped me up for the pain in my ribs. If the doctor had been there he stood behind me. I knew there was someone back there but I couldn't move to see who it was.

The nurse standing by the door asked my mother to sign the form to admit me. Mother broke down then and cried. She cried and told them that she only wanted me home. She wanted to take care of me. She wanted to make sure I was alright. There was a debate. Voices grew loud as they tried to convince my mother to let me stay. The nurse kept her cool and Mother touched her hair with shaking hands. There was another voice coming from behind me. It was a man's voice.

'He needs to be in for observation, Mrs Pullman,' he'd said, sounding angry and concerned.

Why don't you come out from back there? Come out and stand up to her.

'I'll sign nothing,' Mother said quietly. 'He's leaving this hospital now.'

After that I dropped away. During that moment – with all the excitement – my blood must have pumped through me quickly with my heart pulsing hard. The drugs made their way through my system fast. When I came to, a nurse and an orderly helped steady me on my limp legs. I fell into the back of the car. There was no coat under me this time. The orderly reached over and put a lap belt over my waist. Mother spoke to someone, but I couldn't tell who. I couldn't find a reason to care. For a few seconds I listened to the voices speaking – first Mother and then the other voice. The words didn't matter. The coats weren't on the floor any more. Mother moved them. Must have thrown them in the trunk. Two red-soaked coats. Evidence.

But I'd been seen and all of those people had done nothing. Mother drove me home.

She pulled the Diplomat in and closed the garage door behind her. She stood outside the car and stared at me while I sat in the back seat – leaned against the window. I looked back, but didn't offer an expression. She switched the overhead light off and went in the house. It was quiet in the car that night. The air held a chill, but it was a good feeling. I slept with the drugs running through me.

If I dreamed I can't remember.

Chapter Two

Mick Drexler's dogs got a hold of a stray cat. They barked and yelped in their excitement to tear the damn thing apart. At first the noise blended in with the sound of my bare feet slapping on the pavement. My father panting while chasing me down the road. The sun burned through the canopy of tree limbs, swords of bright light that I ran through to get away. I couldn't scream. Not enough air left in my lungs. Then the noise of the dogs filled my head. Louder and louder. It grew with the pulsing thumps inside my head. He was getting close. Breathing close to my shoulder. Feet slapping. Pounding away. A final wail from the cat before Zeus broke its neck.

My body jolted. My head thumped against the side window of my father's Diplomat. I pressed my face to the window and held it there for a few seconds. The glass felt cool. Mixed with the damp smell in the garage it was comforting. Gasoline and old cigarette smoke moved round the inside of the car and slipped into my head. The pulsing slowed to a thump. The rhythm kept time with thick pumping in my chest. I breathed deep and it all slowed down.

My ribs felt stiff, but the pain was less than expected. They fought back when I shifted in the seat. My reflection in the rearview mirror slid into view like I'd come in contact with a stranger. A dull shock hit. Gauze pads covered the stitches over my left eye. The white patches soaked up some blood. Small round shapes of red and yellow marked the gauze making them look like abstract Japanese flags. Even in the low light that snuck in under the garage door the bruising showed in brown and purple clouds. In the few places that escaped bruising my skin looked pale. Almost looked dead. The bridge of my nose had swelled out. I tried to open my mouth, but my jaw held strong. I didn't fight it.

You don't try to fight it, Joseph. You never try to fight it.

I'd been out cold for a long while. The drugs they'd pumped in me at the hospital made my head spin. When I closed my eyes the spinning stopped. Don't know how long a time it was, but I'd woken to complete darkness during the night. Must have fallen asleep when it was still warm outside. When I woke the garage held a midnight chill in the air. Sitting in the car I thought about the coats in the trunk. Soaked in blood, but still good to keep heat in. But there was no way to get to them. Stiffness had set into my joints so I didn't try to move. Gave into the darkness and the cold and fell asleep again. Next thing I knew Drexler's dogs welcomed a new morning with a fresh kill.

With my head pressed against the window I took things in. A bright strip of light cut under the garage door. It was enough to see the shapes of boxes. The long handles of rakes and brooms stuck up in the corner. Looked round the garage. Made sure there wasn't a shape that could've been my old man waiting for me. Standing guard until his busted son got the hell out of his car. Holding back to see if I'd dropped blood on his cloth interior. My mouth felt dry and I needed a drink. Needed something to stop the burn cutting through the centre of my tongue.

I got out of the car and took my time opening the door to the house. Didn't want to wake my parents if it was still that early. The clock in the car had been busted for months. The sidedoor entrance to the house came open. I'd half expected it to be locked. Figured Mother would want me to stay put until

15

she was ready to let me in. She must have figured I'd have had to open the garage door if I wanted in earlier than that. That would make it so I'd have to go outside to get inside. My parents never liked the neighbours to see the day after effect.

I'd pressed myself half in the house when the scream came. Frozen in place and balanced on one foot. My other foot hovered over the threshold and I stayed like that and listened. The pulsing took speed in my head. My ribs gripped at my heart that thumped and pounded away. That next sound didn't come. No scream to match the first. I moved fast as I could up the stairs, keeping my arms close to my chest. Each step felt like it was pulling bones out of place. Squeezed my arms in tight against the bandages holding my ribs in line.

Inside my bedroom I waited. Chest pounding. The cuts on my head pulsing with fresh blood. The gauze felt heavy.

Stripping off had never been harder. My ribs came alive and tried to break free. It felt like they were spreading out from one another. Even with the bandages holding them in tight as can be, they felt loose. After I got my shirt off I pressed my arms into my sides. The pain got worse, but eased off again. Then I dropped my jeans and the pain came back. Took a few minutes to pull the elastic bandages they gave me in the emergency room. Found a better fit and breathed small breaths until the pain went again. Dropped my jeans and shirt on sheets of newspaper in the corner. Didn't want to find more trouble without looking for it.

Where'd those stains on the carpet come from, Joe?

'Shut the fuck up, old man,' I breathed.

Even with the blood dry I couldn't help but worry. I'd get caught out for screwing things up. From the bottom drawer of the dresser I took out the fatigues Aunt Penny gave me before we left Tallahassee. Penny had lived next door and didn't have any relation to my family, but she watched out for me. When the police came that last time she stood in her yard with her arms crossed. She cried and kept waving at me. Then she'd hold a hand to her mouth and shake her head. While dressing I wished

16

I could see her again. Maryland to Florida seemed a world apart. Too long a haul for a kid my age.

Dressed and out of breath I stood holding myself together. After a few minutes I opened the door and looked down the hall. Found nothing but closed doors. The only sound filling the hall was a struggling breath. Some poor sucker searching for air. I pinched my lower lip between an index finger and thumb. The sparkles of pain helped sometimes. Stopped me from daydreaming when I couldn't help it. Got me outside of my head and back to reality. Reminded me that all the things I should worry about were real. Made me think about the pain that comes when I got caught out. A cut opened up inside my mouth. I sucked at the blood while I listened to the breathing coming from the back room.

Remember the days, Joseph.

The gulping sounds came and then a quieter scream. Someone was rolling round on the sheets. Then there was no breathing. Nothing more than the soft rub of a body over sheets. The numb crunch of weight pressing down on a mattress. Then a deep, wet cough.

Mother had her bad days. As a kid I listened at the door to my parents' bedroom. My mother would be screaming until she found herself caught in a struggle for breath. At first I'd been afraid she'd come to the door and give it to me as bad as my old man. Didn't want her to catch me out again. I'd seen her half naked when I wasn't more than knee-high to a puddleduck. She came round the corner, pulling up her towel to cover her breasts. Her hand was warm and hard. Her thin arms were enough to knock me down then. Once she'd started she found a taste for it. As much a taste as my old man. Only she didn't find a need to keep it a regular thing. It was just that once. Couldn't figure she'd be able to do it again.

The more I listened to her bad spells the more I learned about her. Realized early on that she didn't move when she had what my father called *a fit*. The fits lasted for days. She'd be in that bed when I went to my room at night. She'd be there when I got up the next day. It'd last a while. Longer closer to the end.

First off I felt frustrated. Knowing there wasn't a damn thing I could do for her. I took up post outside her door – listening for some kind of sign. She gave me permission to eavesdrop by ignoring my being there. From early days I became a member of an audience at her solo concerts. As a small kid still feeling a sense of closeness to my mother I imagined I was somehow helping her cope. When I learned to write I took notes. What words she screamed. How long she lasted. The fits grew longer in a slow progression. I sat with my journal propped against my knees. These were lonely times. Waiting for her to make a sign. Hoping to find some reason for her madness.

Even with my scars – 'your father's marks', as she called them – Mother's blindness continued. She couldn't see my old man's rage. When it came she locked up. Didn't say a freaking word. Went all glazed over and blind to the whole thing. Never raised her hands to stop him. I pitied her for that at times. Guess it's bad to admit that I hated her for it most often. There remained a part of me still wanting to know why the fits came. But before long, seeing her fits grow more frequent, I just wanted to get away.

That was the first of her bad days since the move to Maritime. I listened for a while, but she wasn't speaking. She cried and breathed. When she screamed it just came in a burst of noise. Short and dead before it really started. My head pulsed. To get away from it I packed up my gear and set off for the open space. There was a moment that morning when I considered staying inside. *Listen to her, Joe.* I could have made notes. It could have been the day she revealed it all. Where the pain came from.

I carried my bag downstairs and set it by the front door. Listened out for my father while walking through the house. He didn't make any sound sometimes. Those quiet days were when I feared him most. He'd just be sitting in a room. Nothing happening. Lights out and quiet like a burned-up church. You'd come up on him and he'd be locked on your eyes. It's like he followed your eyes everywhere you went. Even when he wasn't around I figured he knew what I was doing.

18

Going through the hallway and into the living room cold hairs stuck up on the back of my neck. The wood floor where I'd bled looked clean. The room had a lemon smell. The ficus I'd knocked over was gone. That damn tree. Just a freaking plant. *Clumsy sonofabitch. You think you can go around here tearing up my things, Joseph? What's going on in your head, son? Not like the things I put in here? Watch where you're going. Can't stand up when your old man shoves you? Better learn, son. Better take a lesson. Better find your footin'.*

My father sat at the kitchen table. He'd been sitting there with his hands clenched into one large fist. He looked a few years older than usual. When Mother had the fits my old man clammed up. He aged while he waited for her to snap out of it. His head bent forward with his chin almost touching his chest. At first I didn't realize he'd even been in the room. It was a frightening feeling when I thought of the meeting later that day. I'd opened the refrigerator searching for a can of soda. Figured all that time that I was alone.

'I guess you hear her.'

His voice rammed against the pulsing in my skull. I tried to catch my breath. Looking at the cartons of juice lining the top shelf. I turned to look at my father and felt my knees lock. My hip fell against the counter before I regained my balance. He must have seen the worry clouding my face. He looked away without saying another word. My body still felt winded and I took a deep breath. It stretched my ribs against the bandages. But this time the pain wasn't there. Instead there was this hot rush that filled me up. The refrigerator door swung shut on its own.

'I heard her when I woke up,' I said.

'Yeah. The neighbours'll be able to hear her too.' His words were rubbery and moulded into one another. An empty glass container sat in the centre of the kitchen table. My mother once kept fresh flowers. Next to that was a plate. It was crisp with dried yellowed bacon grease and egg yolk. On it sat a knife and fork.

'I'll be out today,' I said.

'If somebody asks you 'bout your face?' my father asked.

'Three guys.'

My father didn't respond. He made a rumbling sound deep in his throat. If he'd been thinking of what to say I didn't give him time to come up with anything.

'I never run fast enough.'

I slipped out of the room, lifted my bag from the wicker mat and went out. Made it through the front door when I heard my mother scream. It sent a charge through my legs and without thinking I shut the door and ran for the open space. If I hadn't needed to collect my bag I would've used the straight line from the back door. I didn't mind as long as I'd gotten away. I turned the corner of the house and yanked the bag over my arms. My ribs pulled in tight. I ached, but ran for the twin oaks. Once through I slid down the hill on the seat of my trousers.

Before my ass hit the ground at the bottom of the hill I felt out of breath. Still I kept moving. I made myself climb the tallest tree until I reached a height that felt safe. Pulling myself up brought on new pain. *Leave it, Joe. He ain't coming after you. Give yourself a break.* Still, I climbed. I sat on the limb for a few minutes taking in air and peeling away the bark from the crook where the branch met the trunk. When I felt my stomach ease up I took out the telescope. Focused it on the back of my father's house. It was the only house on that side of the hill so there wasn't any fear of being seen. I'd used that perch so many times before.

Although I was high in the tree I could only see the top of my old man's head. Still, it seemed always enough to know he hadn't left the room. More importantly it meant my father hadn't left the house. He wasn't looking for me. I'd got away.

I didn't stay in the tree long after that. Once on the ground I ducked into the heavy shrubs and started making my way toward the sound of running water. Held my right hand in front to push branches to the side. I kept my left hand over the gauze pads that covered the stitches. The burning coming from my face reminded me to watch out for branches. Along with the burning there was the itching. It made me think of ants and millipedes. All the while I walked along that day I imagined stray branches snagging a single stitch and unravelling everything that held my head together. I got to thinking so much about it that I had to stop and check my reflection. Used the blade of a survival knife. The gauze was falling away at points. Too much blood to keep a good hold on my brow. Each time I stopped to check I had a mix of emotions. Both pleased and disappointed after finding the wetness on my face wasn't anything more than sweat. I placed the knife back inside the sheath. Took the time to hang it from my belt before continuing the walk to the water.

At the creek I looked for tracks animals made in the sand. Each day I'd taken the time to look. I'd found new prints all the time. Occasionally I came across markings of a snake that had slithered by. They looked like etchings in glass. They cut smooth shapes in the moist ground.

'Hey,' I heard a voice call out.

I twisted round and grabbed for something, anything. Nothing but air. I stumbled away, but kept my footing. Then I looked upstream and saw him.

There, in the middle of the water, stood a boy. He'd waded in knee-deep and now stared at me. He had a net in his hands. The net looked battered and was obviously handmade. A ragged looking thing made from a broom handle, a coat hanger and an onion bag. He hadn't even taken the time to tear off the label from the red mesh of the bag. Vidalia Onions it said. *Just like being home in Tallahassee.* The bag had faded, but you could still make out the cartoon of the red-onion man logo. As for the boy, he wasn't wearing a shirt and his slender body looked extremely pale. Even in the forest shade he almost glowed.

'Hello,' I said.

'What are you doing?' the boy asked.

'Just looking around.'

'For what?' he sounded annoyed.

I shook my head and touched the gauze over my left eye.

21

'Why are you wearing camouflage?'

'Sometimes I hide,' I answered. My face pulsed with a fresh flow of blood. I felt myself becoming angry at the way the boy asked questions. Like shooting tin cans. He seemed random but to the point. Recreational conversation had never been one of my strengths. I wanted to walk away and find a tree to climb and be alone. There had to be a tree I could sit in and see him without being seen in return. Instead I stood there and kicked the heads off large mushrooms that grew from a fallen tree trunk.

'Whatcha do to your head?'

Stick to the plan, Joe.

'I fell and cut it on the stairs at my father's house.'

'Must've fallen a lot,' he said.

'Fine,' I said feeling worked up for a fight. 'I got jumped by three guys. I took two of 'em down and ran. They caught up with me. Wasn't fast enough.'

'Bummer,' he said. He looked into the water. I couldn't tell if he didn't believe me or if he didn't trust me. Maybe I'd jump him too. Maybe I'd beat his head in and take his shitty net home with me.

Either way he seemed to lose interest in the conversation and stared at the surface of the pond. He caught sight of something moving beneath the surface. He stepped farther into the water, sinking in above his knees that seemed too thick for his thin frame. Poised with the net in front of him looking like he was aiming a blowgun. The net pointed at the crooked base of the tree that overhung the pool. I crept forward and looked into the water. Could only see the reflection of the leaves high above me with small cracks of sunlight. Blue sky bleeding through. After a few seconds my eyes adjusted and as the sediment settled into the floor of the pond I could see his target.

On the rocky bottom a group of crawfish crawled like giant bugs toward one large flat rock. It was like watching a nature programme about the deep seas that showed footage of huge creatures walking on and off boulders on the ocean floor.

The kid looked at me for a second and smiled out of the side of his mouth. It's the kind of smile I expected poker players would give to their opponents when bluffing a hand. Then the boy looked back to the settling water. With a quick motion he speared the net through the slow moving surface. He twisted the broom handle around. Pushed it farther in and dragged the net-head along the rocks before struggling to pull it up. The water took a few seconds to drain through the holes of the onion bag. The weight of its contents made the coat hanger bend madly. The silver duct-tape that secured the hanger to the wooden broom handle looked frayed. I began to wonder how long ago the boy had taken to this hunt.

'You get anything?' I asked knowing already the net held nothing living.

'Don't think so.' When the water drained the boy sifted through the rocks and branches he'd scooped from the bottom of the pond. Instead of looking disappointed he assumed the position of a hunter once again, aiming the net at the bent tree trunk. He stayed in that position while he waited for the water to settle.

'You'd have better luck if you put the net behind them,' I told him. 'Then you can scare them with a stick.'

The boy eased up his stance and set the broom handle against his shoulder. He frowned at the debris that floated slowly by him. When he looked up his face troubled me. I couldn't read his expression. Then he began sucking air between his lips. He screwed up his eyes at me before looking back into the water.

'Why would I put the net behind them?' he asked.

'Crawfish swim backwards.' I didn't make an attempt to stifle the laugh. 'Haven't you been watching them?'

The boy wasn't amused and again I began to consider making an exit farther into the forest. When he aimed the net at the trunk again I stood still awaiting the spearing motion. The kid's face crumpled up like he'd just figured on something important. His thin arms tensed and he crouched slightly. Then all of a sudden he straightened his back and raised the net. I anticipated, as he used one dirty finger to push the heavy-looking glasses back up the bridge of his nose, that he wanted me gone. Then he pointed the net at my face.

'Come down here and show me what you mean,' he said.

I took off my pack and tossed it to the sand on the opposite side of the pond. There was an area where the creek ran in a narrow stream. I jumped across and hit the sand hard. The pain shot through my ribs, but I gritted it away. Walked to where the boy stood in the water. My body ached, but I held it in. Not knowing this kid I couldn't afford him thinking me weak. I took off my shirt and set it on top of the bag. The boy watched me as I untied the laces of my black boots. He made a long whistling sound as I set them away from the water's edge. Socks stuffed inside.

'Beat you up good,' he said.

'What do you mean?' I asked.

'The guys who chased you.'

'Yeah,' I said standing up. Ran a finger over the purple and red bruises that crept out from under the bandages. Looking at the colours brought the pain back. I tried not to flinch, but couldn't help it. 'You should see the two I got hold of . . .'

'They from around here?' he asked me.

'Don't know,' I said walking to the edge of the water. 'Just moved here with my parents a few weeks back.'

'What'd you do to them?'

I shook my head.

'To start it all off. You must have done something.' He smiled at me. I could almost feel that snap on the inside. The one that sends everything into slow motion. The snap that turns my head hot and makes it hard to stop.

'You never jumped anyone?' I asked.

'No.'

'Don't need a reason for it. Best if you don't have a reason.'

I walked away and found a long stick from a pile of fallen branches. Rolled my trousers up past my knees and waded into the water with the stick in both hands. I felt like I'd gotten a hold of a sword. The kid watched me with what I hoped was a look of amazement. The scars and the bruises made me tough. They kept him short of words, and that was good because I didn't need them.

'Let the water settle,' I said. We walked into the deeper water. 'After we know they're crawling on the rocks you need to cover the hole under the trunk. Put the net right over it. That's where they live. They'll try and get back in there. When you have it covered I'll scare them with the stick.'

'What's that gonna do?' the boy asked.

'Makes them swim backward into your net.' I heard my voice taking that cynical tone. The same tone my father used when he had to tell me something he thought I should already know. The boy gritted his teeth when he looked at me. I felt myself beginning to blush again and turned my face toward the surface of the water. Had to escape his little black eyes.

Neither of us said anything else for a long while. In that time the water cleared enough to see the rocks on the bottom. A large black crawfish walked toward the flat rocks at the centre of the pool. I nodded my head slowly. Without saying a word the boy lowered the net into the water. As it broke the surface the craw-fish stopped and the boy froze. I stayed still as I could manage. Bending over made my ribs hurt, but I kept steady. We were like that, still as ever. The crawfish started his march again. The boy went back to sinking the net to the bottom of the pond. It took a long time, but the net fell into place over the hole. I nodded again before shoving my stick into the water at the head of the crawfish. It shot backward, kicking up a line of mud that spread through the water.

'Pull it up! You got him!' I yelled.

'Did it go in?' he called out.

'Pull it up!'

When the boy got the net out of the water he didn't find debris. There were no rocks or branches or even a decaying leaf. Instead he had in his net a large, flapping crawfish.

'Man, it's huge!' the boy yelled.

'Yeah. It's the biggest there ever was.'

25

We touched heads when we bent in and a bolt of pain shot through me. Still I couldn't help but look into the net to catch sight of the crawfish flip and twist. We kept it in there for a while and just stared. When it slowed down and lost its liveliness the boy gave me the net to hold. He walked up the bank and into the wood. He went through the leaves and trees with his head down. I gave him a while, just watching him peck around the place like a crazy chicken.

'What the hell?' I called to him.

He flapped a hand at me and kept at it.

'Looking for a bucket. A can maybe,' he finally said. 'Just something somebody may have tossed.'

He found nothing. Washington Pond's a difficult place to get to unless you walked the creek bed or didn't mind passing through dense thicket and briars to get there.

'Might as well throw him back.' He hopped down into the creek bed. 'I can't find anything to put him in.'

'Alright,' I said. 'I guess we can come back and catch him again.'

The boy must have thought that idea was sensational. He broke out in a smile and nodded his head like one of those plastic dogs people put on the dashboard of their cars. He pulled the net away from my hands and turned it over. The crawfish fell to the sand and landed with a cracking sound. I used my stick to flick it into the centre of the pond. It hit the water and sank like a stone. When the crawfish touched the rocks on the bottom I half expected it to flip over and swim off into the hole. Instead the current turned it over and over and pressed it down the stream. I walked away from the water and dried myself off with my socks before rolling my trouser legs down. Then I pulled on my boots and shirt.

'I'm going to a deeper pond farther down the creek.' I lifted my bag and wiggled both arms through the harnesses with my ribs yelling out in protest. 'You want to come along?'

The boy stood with bowed shoulders watching the crawfish getting bounced. It'd made it to a miniature rapid where it thumped against a large rock. Over and over again. When its body eventually got tossed through and into a fresh tide it moved like a torpedo downstream.

'No. I'm going home now.' He watched the water without changing the look on his face. 'What's your name anyway?' he finally asked.

'Joseph Pullman,' I told him. 'What about you?'

'Dean Gillespie.'

'You be back here tomorrow?'

'Yeah,' the boy said. 'About the same time too.'

'See you.'

I walked away and placed a hand over the gauze patch before pulling aside a stray branch I thought looked sinister. The burning had died away. Got deep into the forest before I looked back. I couldn't see the boy and I didn't spend much time trying to find out which way he'd gone. While I walked on my own I couldn't help wondering how long he'd been trying to catch crawfish. Couldn't help but imagine him on his own with a home-made net and his awkward way of using it. So many days with nothing happening and still he'd kept trying.

I stopped walking when I got to the sandbank. Standing next to the water I looked upstream and could see Washington Pond through a space between sloping trees. The boy had gone. I watched the pond anyway almost hoping he would reappear. When I finally looked down I saw that the black crawfish had been swept downstream. The water had lodged it against a fallen tree limb where a sponge of discoloured foam had taken shape. I lifted the limp body and dropped it inside one of the pouches I wore on my belt. Then I jumped across the creek and started to walk away from the sand banks. Went back into the forest.

I headed for the place where the Killing Tree grew and the dead animals slept.

Chapter Three

Dean and me connected somehow. We had problems in our heads that we didn't like people to know about. So we kept quiet. Most times people don't understand that kind of thing. Dean and me had it all figured out – first for ourselves, then for each other. So we walked to school every morning. Two quiet kids unsure about the world and our place in it. We had a certainty within our awkwardness. We met in the open space at the bottom of the hill behind my father's house.

On wet days I waited at the kitchen window until I saw Dean round the circle of oak trees. Before the warm weather came I could see him far off, through the scattered branches, heading down the path. His red slick-looking jacket gave him away. Each week the forest sprouted more green. The leaves grew too thick for me to see past the edge of my father's property. Dean would stand near the path where I could see him. He'd wait there, staring at my father's house like he could see me. The path leading from my father's house to the main road stayed quiet. Not many people knew about it. It wasn't paved and it wound through the trees – close to the stream in parts.

The mouth of the path entered onto Grant's Road near a deer crossing sign. The trees made a canopy over the path, hanging low at the entrance. With all of the leaves surrounding it, the head of the path always stayed dark. It didn't look like it would lead anywhere. Dean named the path 'The Angry Snake' and we didn't like people walking it.

The path didn't go all that far. It was long enough for Dean and me to stoke the conversation before we reached the main road. The branches of some trees came down and touched our heads at parts of the trail. The thin grey branches looked like long, dead fingers reaching for one another. I pointed this out to Dean one morning. He grunted and refused to speak to me for a few minutes. Our conversations were dependent mainly on the time of year. Sports played a big part in Dean's life and he wanted me to know he'd kept up to date on all the statistics. I listened to him most of the time trying to get him to warm up to my topic – when I had one. While he spoke I waited for my chance to pick a subject. My interests were far different from Dean's. To him they may have been abstract.

'You think there's a connection between twins? You know, one you can't see?' I asked one morning. This was Dean's baseball season. He wanted to talk about the Orioles. Then he wanted to get my take on the Redskins' future prospects. Even Dean was tired of speaking about the last season, but he'd played that to death before it finally got buried.

'Don't know,' he said. He tried to push a branch out of his way. It escaped his hand and swatted him in the face. 'Dammit.' He kept touching his lip and looking at his fingers.

'It's one of those mental connections,' I said. 'Kind of like ESP, only between two people.'

'What's the big deal if there is?' he asked.

I wanted to break his lip. It was turning red from his fingers rubbing at it. He couldn't stop touching the place the branch caught him.

'If one of them gets hurt the other one feels it,' I said. 'If one's in trouble the other one knows it. Even if they're not around. Can't even see what's happening and they still know.' I was calming down again.

29

'Dad says that's all a bunch of horse. It's just a load of stories to freak people out.' He forgot about his lip. His hands were in his pockets again. Steam pulsed from his mouth. Even with the days growing warmer the early mornings bit at your skin. Dean's breath came out in white bursts that matched his stride.

'It's not going to freak anyone out. Besides they've done studies on it. Doctors and universities. The Germans did a bunch of tests on it. World War Two, remember?'

'Wasn't there.'

'Don't you read about this stuff?'

'No,' he said. Then paused. 'You don't think the Germans would want to freak people out?'

'What?' I asked.

'Scare tactics, dumbass. The Germans were always doing that stuff. It's called propaganda.'

'This is for real, Dean. What they did was real and there were a lot of people that died when they were getting . . . studied.'

'Twins?'

'Yeah.'

He didn't speak for the rest of the walk. I don't know if I got him thinking about it or if he just got tired of hearing me go on. He could talk his talk, but if you got onto something he couldn't understand he shut you down.

The Angry Snake passed close to part of the creek near a fallen tree. The roots were exposed and stuck in all directions. The tree lay across the creek. Once in a while we'd stop there. We would walk out onto the tree. From the middle of it you could see up the creek to where the viaducts flowed under Grant's Road.

Dean knew the kind of stuff that got me fired up. The questions that stuck up under my skin and got me boiling. Usually he left it alone, but sometimes he wanted to see me riled.

'You afraid of the jocks?' he asked.

The jocks were guys on the sports teams. They played everything. Football, baseball, basketball. Never picked up a book, but they were all going to college. Eventually, when they'd finished knocking around the geeks and freaks clogging high school gymnasiums. That was another of their sports – a kind of pre-requisite for high school athletic stardom.

Dean's was a straightforward question, but I still felt a bubble burst inside my stomach. The muscles in my back strained. My bag pressed against my shoulder blades seemed heavier than before. I adjusted the bag by shrugging my shoulders. Snapped my arms out in front of me and made a laugh I hoped sounded confident.

'No,' I told him and laughed again. 'I can handle what they bring my way.'

'Mookie Carlyle's a tough guy.' Dean's voice sounded shallow. He'd been watching the path with too much interest. I could tell he'd gotten himself worried about asking me the question. He kicked at an acorn that lay in the path. His sneaker sent it tumbling ahead of us.

'I'm a tough guy too.' I said this more to myself than to Dean. Looked at the side of his head and wanted to knock it hard with my knuckles. Sometimes I felt a need to show him how tough I could be. Throw a kick to his nuts and follow it with a left to his jaw. A hard something to make him aware of the power in my hands. Holding back I watched him rub at his nose with the sleeve of his shirt. It left a wet line.

We walked a while without talking. A squirrel crossed the path in front of us. Although we both watched it go by neither of us said a word. The squirrel picked up an acorn and jumped onto the trunk of a tree. It disappeared around the other side. I saw Dean taking more of an interest in the animal than he usually would.

'Give it up, Dean.'

'He's got friends that like to fight,' he said.

'He can bring 'em all with him.' I squeezed my hands into fists.

'That's what I'm worried about.' He made a motion like he was going to throw something. There was nothing in his hand.

'You're not involved, Dean.'

'I don't want to be.'

'Everything's alright then, huh?'

'Yeah, I guess.'

We made it out of the canopy and turned right at the deer crossing sign. We kept close to the side of the road. That length of Grant's Road didn't have sidewalks until the following year. Some young racer took out a middle-aged jogger one fine weekend. Tragedy makes things happen. Sets the wheels of change in motion. We walked side by side until we heard a car come along. Then we'd go single-file on the emergency lane until it passed. The high school kids drove some of the cars. They almost always yelled something at us when they passed by. We never made gestures back, just kept our heads down and took the taunts.

Hey, faggots. Queer boys!

When they were long gone Dean would sometimes get tough.

'Bet they wouldn't do that if they were on their own,' he'd say. 'Bet they're all pussies.'

'That's the way it always is,' I told him.

'Why'd they have to do that? It's stupid.' Pause. 'Pointless.'

'It's just ego. Something that doesn't come natural to everyone.'

'They'll never have enough.'

The road bowed up into a hill and we would often take a breather halfway up. It was more so we could prepare for the day ahead than from the fatigue of the walk. The tree we chose to stand by was dented on one side. The bark had been peeled away by a car or lightning, or something. The city workers had come out and painted the bald patch with a thick black substance. It was more than paint and less than tar. Me and Dean took turns peeling it away with rocks.

At the top of the hill the road evened out and on the right was a veterinary office. Farther down stood a convenience store. Just past the store was the elementary school. The parking lot was always half full of teacher's cars. The buses never arrived before we were in our own classes. Then the buses were always cleared away, along with the younger students, before we were allowed to leave.

On the left side of the road sat a large field. In the centre of the field stood the Mormon Church. J. D. MacFarlane and his brother Ernie would sit on the steps in the morning. They smoked and laughed. If I waved they looked away, just like they didn't catch the gesture. Sometimes they'd extend a middle finger in our direction. We never showed them one in return. I never would've expected a fight if I had. They were tough enough that they never had to show it. Every time they got in a fight they did fine. They came out tops – bruised knuckles and pearly whites flashing. But they never started things off. I didn't give them the finger. It was out of respect, understand. They gave it to me out of instinct. The brothers were of a different breed and it made me ache that I wasn't one of their kind.

No matter what Dean and me had been speaking about the conversations ended at the same point every day. We went quiet when we got to the apartments that bordered the grounds of Hampden Academy. Ahead on the cement path leading to the school stood four benches. They'd been spaced out to border the path leading to the school entrance. The benches were always taken. Six students to each. I recognized each of the faces, but none of the faces were accompanied by names. Farther up the path stood a group of jocks. They watched us as we marched on. Dean slowed.

'Keep up, Dean. They'll kick your ass if you look weak,' I said. He stayed at my side.

When we got close heads turned and voices were raised. Then came bursts of laughter and urges for a fight. I moved the bag around on my shoulders until it felt like I could move my arms where I wanted them to go. Dean started to fall behind again. This happened every morning. To that point nothing had kicked off past the exchange of words and the occasional shove. Still I prepared for the worst. It's what I'd always done. It's the way I was brought up.

'They won't fight now. Too early.' It was hard to get the words out the side of my mouth, but we were too close to say them loud. Dean came up on my side again. I didn't feel any better having him there. But with him moving up close I knew he'd heard me.

A few more steps and a bottle exploded at my feet. Sprayed shards of glass and Mello-Yellow cross my shoes and blue jeans. I kept walking. Dean jumped back, but kept pace soon enough. To my left a group of students from a few years below stood against the metal fence to the baseball diamonds. They laughed and must have felt triumphant. I stared at them. None of those fuckers had what it took to stare back. They felt safe in the group. Two still had their bottles of soda. The third had his hands in his pockets. With my eyes on him he went red and stepped behind his friends. When I had the chance I'd pull him away. I'd see how much his personality changed when my anger got vented against his smug little face.

'Pullman.' The voice was familiar and when I turned my head I saw Mookie Carlyle standing ahead of the pack. They blocked the cement path, arms folded and legs far enough apart to make them look relaxed. Over the years Carlyle had built a crew of misfits. The group had moulded themselves to his image. Tracksuits with fake snake skin stripes. Fila sneakers and ball-caps worn with the bills to the side.

Push the first man down and they all tumble, Joe. Like a freakin' pack of dominoes.

The New York Yankees hat Mookie wore set him apart from the others. Still the crooked bill dropped a black shade from the sun that fell over his left ear. He squinted to keep the rays out of his eyes. Thick lines cut impressions into the wide bridge of his nose.

'Least you got one friend,' another voice called out.

'Not much of a friend.' There came laughter. Laughter that was too excited to be fuelled by anything less than anticipation.

'Bitch more like.' Laughter came from everywhere.

I could imagine at that moment Dean's confidence breaking up like small rocks under a sledgehammer. His legs would be filling with a wicked and burning energy. Without looking at him I knew he had readied himself for flight. Inside his mind and body there existed no fight. The only problem lay with the pack of wolves ahead of us. If he ran they would catch him and tear him apart. Just like Mick Drexler's dogs took that cat to pieces. If he stayed close the bark would be big, but the bite wouldn't follow. This confrontation set the stage for things to come. Every main event comes with full promotion. The stand-off acted as advertisement. The audience started to gather with mounting interest.

'Yeah, looks like a pair of bitches to me,' Mookie said walking up to Dean. More laughter.

We kept walking. I did my best to keep the same pace. When we met the group they didn't move. I'd expected that much. It'd happened time and again. If it ever changed I would've wondered what powers of the world had shifted. There began the moment of dread when I started the walk from my father's house in the morning. There came a sense of urgency. I felt a need to try something different that would make my life better. Only, there was nothing presenting itself as another option. From tragedy comes strength. I'd been building an empire inside my mind, but in the beast of the outside world everything remained unchanged.

'Let us by,' I said.

Mookie moved away from Dean and grabbed at my neck. His fingers scraped the skin, but I moved back before he got a hold. The crowd behind him made a sound. Excited and shocked that I'd slipped him. Mookie hadn't got his way. He'd been defied. They'd come to expect people they confronted to submit. I had no intentions of hitting the deck.

Drop, Joseph. Just go down.

I'll light my place in hell before I give up to this asshole, I told myself. Just go down. There's an idea. Then the laughs would fall down on me along with Mookie Carlyle's punches. Laughs that haunt more than the pain.

'You want by, bitch?' Mookie yelled in my face. 'You gonna have ta go through me, mothafucka!'

35

'Don't expect me to stand here all day,' I said.

Mookie's left hand moved like a flash. Thumped into my stomach. Felt like a hole opened up inside me and filled up with pain. His knee came up and landed on my falling chin. There came a buzzing sound that started deep inside my head. Then it surfaced and overcame the cheering of the crowd. My face felt hot and my body boiled with energy. The pain sunk in deep and what came up in its place made me want to fight. His punches scraped off my head, but slipped aside. More buzzing.

I straightened fast. Carrying with my weight I brought in an uppercut. The two centre knuckles of my right hand jammed against Mookie's chin. While he fell back I aimed a kick at his crotch. It missed and dug into his left thigh. Before he hit the ground two of his crew grabbed his shoulders and pushed him up. Once standing again he looked untouched. Hovered in place and held two loaded fists in front of him.

Blood dripped from my mouth. Pulsing from the old scars in my forehead matched the thumping of my chest. Then Mookie came at me. Fists swinging with his practised finesse. His shoulder rolling out punches that connected like his hands were magnets and my head was a tin can. Before I went hazy Dean split. I caught sight between punches of him breaking off for the football field. I'd taken too much of a hammering to care that he'd jumped like that. No one followed him. Eyes stayed on the kid with all the scars.

Eyes watching the kid no one knew. The freak who didn't have a name, but bore a mark. Pullman. The kid with a scar over his left eye. A weak scar that always broke open – always made an easy target. The one from where the blood now came. Streaks of blood running from his face. Same fucked up kid getting more carved open by the second.

I'd hit the ground somewhere in the mass of students. A runner went on to the school and called the alarm. May have been Dean, but he never said either way. Must have gone early 'cause the staff came and broke up the crowd. Two teachers lifted me up and took me inside. I sat in the health room for a while. The nurse's aide sat drinking coffee and eating a thick bagel. She looked up from her book once in a while to make sure I hadn't left. When the nurse came back in she had Mr Cunningham with her.

'Joseph Pullman,' he said. 'Got yourself into another altercation I see.'

'Yessir,' I said. I touched my cheek where the swelling came through worst. It felt stiff, but moved over the bone.

'We need to nip this in the bud before real trouble starts,' he continued. He pulled up a chair and sat next to me. Kept it personal and sat on my side of the nurse's aide's desk. The chair made a moaning sound when he shifted his weight.

'That wasn't real trouble then?' I asked.

'No need to be a smart-ass, Mr Pullman,' Nurse Gene said.

'I got worked over for walking to school,' I said in a slow and calm voice. I'd figured this conversation would take place. I'd run a few options over in my head before Cunningham showed. 'He grabbed my neck and started punching me when I moved away.'

'Let's not get all excited again,' Mr Cunningham said. His years as a guidance counsellor made him a nervous man. His hands never stopped moving. His hairline had fallen back and now it exposed a large shining forehead. Couldn't have been more than mid-thirty. Reminded me of the car salesman who was never quick enough to reach the customer first. He looked more beaten every day I saw him.

'What should I do?' I asked.

'Find a different route to school,' he said. 'That's one option.'

'Ignore what just happened?' I asked.

'If you don't you will find yourself in more of a mess than you can handle,' Nurse Gene offered. 'I'm tired of cleaning cuts and icing bruises for people like you, Mr Pullman. Why do I only see a select few people coming through here? The same. Day in and day out.'

'Guess I got a face for it.'

Just like she didn't hear me she said: 'You'll have to get that cut of yours fixed at the hospital . . . again.'

'I wouldn't put you out to ask,' I said.

'Let's take it easy,' Cunningham said.

'Well,' Nurse Gene moaned. 'I can't understand why it's just the same kids. Every day. Every week.'

'Because we give up,' I muttered.

'Excuse me?' Mr Cunningham asked.

I looked at him. Squared off with his small eyes.

'We're not fast enough.'

Chapter Four

Not all the residents of Westchester Drive would hide from me. But some did. Mick Drexler and his wife Valerie came out when they saw me walking near their driveway. They even caught me at the side of their house a few times. Neither of them said anything more than a quick hello. They spoke to each other and laughed when I didn't acknowledge them. For some reason that felt okay. Even when they'd point at me and make their faces like they didn't understand it was alright. Next door to them Helle Bishop would come out and drink from a steaming mug. She watched everything I did. But she never spoke a word to me.

Some, like Gilbert and Beatrice Stapp, sat on their front porch and waited for me to approach like they were watching a grazing deer. Each time I walked close to the Stapps' front yard Beatrice would stand and lean against one of the columns supporting the porch roof. She looked like she wanted to throw me a piece of meat and lure me closer.

'Dammit, Beat!' I'd heard Gilbert Stapp hiss at times. 'Sit yourself down. He's not going to come close if you keep standing whenever he starts this way.'

Hearing him speak as loudly as he did made me feel uncomfortable. It's like he was talking about someone who lived a hundred miles away. It's the same voice he used when he spoke to the players on the Baltimore Orioles when their game was being televised. I stood a few feet outside the border of his lawn and his voice reached me as if I stood at his side.

'Well, he's not going to come close if he hears you cussing up a storm.'

'Just relax.'

They went real quiet when they watched me march to their neighbour's house – my right hand clutching the red journal. They lived next to the Rosenthals – an old woman and her husband who only came outside when a van arrived to pick up the old woman and her wheelchair. It wasn't very often. The old guy never left the house. He'd wave from the front porch and go back in without even taking a breath of fresh air. I stopped at the wall of the house and lowered to one knee. I used the other to brace the journal while I wrote in it. Everyone who saw me must have had a different idea kicking about in their heads. *Now, what was that kid writing?* Whatever it was they came up with they missed the mark. None of them were close to target. Of that I am almost certain.

After a while Gilbert Stapp usually became impatient and if there was a ball game on television he'd head back into the house. He'd sink into his oversized reclining armchair. In the evening I could see him through the front window. He left the seat only during commercials. He always returned before the programme had continued. I never watched Gilbert if Beatrice was outside. Sometimes she'd go around the house and sit on the wicker bench they stuck in a corner of boxwood hedges. But if Gilbert went inside Beatrice usually stayed out on the porch, watching me. Sometimes she watched with too much interest. She must have considered herself lucky for having raised normal children. When we moved to Westchester Drive all her kids were grown and gone.

Being a mother may have given her reason to like the idea of having another young boy on the street. That may have been why she sat and watched me each time I walked round checking every-thing out. It may also have been the reason behind her holding

Gilbert back when he made a motion to walk into the house that day. After hearing a voice from the television announce the 'Sports Center' was due up after another commercial break he stood up from his plastic chair. I had my face aimed in the journal, but watched the two of them out of the corner of my eye.

'Stay where you are, Mister.' Beatrice continued to look straight at me. I looked up and saw her. She didn't make a motion to look away. She wanted me to know she intended to find out what the new kid was like. Her large features made it easy to see that she had applied to her face a look of stern force. She held a look I'd later see her use frequently to keep her husband on the straight and narrow. In some relationships it's plain to see where the power lay. With the Stapps, Beatrice possessed an arsenal.

'I think it'll be best if we met him,' Beatrice said looking at me, but speaking to Gilbert. 'Just have a little talk and see what he's all about.'

'Beat, come on now,' Gilbert sounded off with a long sigh and sat back into the chair. It creaked against his weight and made a sound as if the thin white shine was readying itself to bust apart.

'The kid's riding on his own little trip,' he went on. 'When have you ever seen someone his age walking from house to house like that? He's got a freakin' book with him, Beat.' Gilbert pointed at me. Thankfully I'd looked away by then and could act like I didn't know they were talking about me. Leaning against the vinyl siding of the Hathaways' place I started to feel ill. I felt cornered.

'He's not all there, Beat,' I heard Gilbert say. 'Walking around like he does. He doesn't take to people. He doesn't look anywhere but at the ground in front of him. He doesn't even make any sounds.'

'Just what are you going on about?' Beatrice asked.

'The kid's a retard, Beat. He's thick as a wall of pig shit and I'm missing a sports show watching him do his goofy things. I've got no time for this.'

41

'Well, then. Let's see if you're right.' Beatrice stood from her chair and leaned her hands against the wooden rail that ran the length of her porch. 'Excuse me, darling,' she called out.

I remained still. The only part of me that moved was my hand. Just kept writing in my journal like something possessed. Words. Words. Words. One after another. Not even thinking about what it was coming out of the pen.

Fat man and his wife . . . NumbR. 95.
Always on poRch. Watching oveR me.
Waiting foR a mistake. Think I'm
RetaRded. May tRy to speak with MotheR.
May appRoach FatheR when he is outside.
Wife likes to watch me. Calls out to me.
Thinks I can't heaR. Fat man dRinks
beeR duRing the day. House is bRick.
PoRch made of timbeR. Old wood.

When Beatrice Stapp called out again I turned quickly, looking in the opposite direction. I knew she'd call me again. Expected her to walk down the porch steps and onto the lawn. If I walked away I knew somehow she would be compelled to chase me down. When she called me again I wanted to run. Had this sudden urge to find a tree and lay myself under it. Hide away in its shade. But I knew I wouldn't get away from her.

'He's either going to start counting the grass again or he's going to run like a cat on fire,' Gilbert said. He made a grunting sound with his throat that passed for a laugh.

'Don't be so horrible. You don't know if he's retarded or if he isn't. It might be nice if he knew he could come to us to talk.'

'Yeah, that would be a good thing, wouldn't it?' Gilbert said. 'I can't wait for football season to start so I can have kid-freak here come around to watch a game or two with me.'

'Hello, darling,' Beatrice said again. This time her voice came out much louder than before. I stopped in mid-step and turned around. 'See there. He hears us just fine.'

'I'm going in,' Gilbert said.

'Like heck you are. Sit yourself down and put your nice face on.' Beatrice continued to smile and cleared her throat before addressing me. I'd turned to face her. 'Would you please come here for a moment, dear?'

I started to walk toward her. Gripped my journal tight and pulled it to my side as I made a slow progression toward the house. Gilbert remained seated. He looked too large for the thin plastic chair to support him. He started checking the tip of his thumb while he watched me get closer. Through the wooden slats of the front porch I could see his legs. He was wearing shorts and his knees were large and pale and bald. I could see thick blue veins cutting close to his skin. There were hundreds of them and they all looked just like they were ready to burst open and spill something blue and purple. He shuffled his feet as if he was getting himself ready for a quick exit. I looked away fearing he knew how amazed I'd become by his grotesque limbs. Beatrice straightened her back and brushed her hands over the front of her trousers where a few small flakes of paint had collected from the porch rail.

'Yes?' I asked. My voice sounded hollow. My hands started to sweat like cold faucets on a hot summer's day.

'I just wanted to be introduced,' Beatrice said. Her smile stretched too wide to be more than show. 'I am Mrs Stapp. Beatrice is my first name and this is my husband. His name is Gilbert.'

I nodded my head looking first at Beatrice then at her husband. Gilbert made a polite smile and nodded his head back once, a bit too quickly. When I returned my stare to Beatrice she'd started brushing the white flakes away from her trousers again. Only this time she did it without looking down.

'It's nice to meet you,' I said. My voice came out strong and the sound of it surprised me. Without thinking I heard myself continue. 'I'm Joseph Reginald Pullman.'

'My, that is a fine name.' When I didn't respond or show

interest she clicked her fingers as if she had remembered something she had forgotten. 'Where did you move from?'

'Tallahassee.'

'Oh, you're a Floridian. That's nice, isn't it?' Beatrice tilted her head slightly to the right.

'I suppose, yes.' I bit my lower lip hoping she would see my disinterest.

'Did you come here with both your parents?'

'I'm sorry?' I said.

'Are your parents still . . .' she paused. Watching her at that moment no longer seemed a difficult thing to do. She'd started something she didn't want to finish. She'd backed herself in a corner.

'For God's sake, Beat.' Gilbert pushed himself up in his chair. 'Are your parents divorced?'

'No,' I said.

'That's not what I was going to ask, Gil,' she said. Her face turned red.

'Oh, like hell it wasn't. 'Sides the kid doesn't give a damn.'

'Stop that swearing.' Beatrice touched her cheek. Before I could walk away she started again. 'Where are they now?'

'They're inside the house unpacking.' The excuse seemed lame. Although we'd only moved into the house a couple months before, the boxes had all been emptied, crushed and taken away in the last garbage collection. I wondered if the Stapps would pick up on the lie. Maybe they'd seen the flattened boxes leaning against the trash bin. I'd resigned myself to using the statement in case someone asked. It seemed safer to lie than to let them in on the secret of what my parents really were. We had a workable façade going and it wasn't going to be me who screwed it all up.

Beatrice had been one of the few people in the neighbourhood to speak to me since the move. People had knocked on the door the day we were moving in, but my parents never answered it. I kept to myself – opening boxes in my room. Felt pleased with myself for not crumbling under the pressure. Breaking open and telling the Stapps what my mother was doing.

Yeah, folks. She's back at it. Should really let you all in. Charge you for having a look-see. Best do it soon. Never know when this here fit'll end.

I looked directly at Beatrice, but she looked back at me strangely. She had a look on her face like she had a cold flush wash over her. The sun stayed positioned in the centre of the sky and dropping with its shine a stream of heat.

'I'll make a cake or a roast and bring it over to them,' she said absently.

'It'd probably be best if you stayed away for a while,' I said. It came out before I could hold it in. 'The move's been tough on my mother. She's still trying to recover.'

I don't know where the words came from. They were mine. I recognized my voice. Felt the vibrations rattle inside my throat, but I'd never spoken of my mother before that moment. Never came out and made any indication that she was sick. Not to strangers or anyone else. I didn't want people to know what kind of person had given birth to me. Being part of her and being raised by her made me breakable. If people knew about her they would wonder about me. Sometimes I wondered about me.

Are you stable, Joe? When's your fit going to come? Will you even know when yours have started?

'Is she ill?' Beatrice asked.

'No,' I breathed. I made a laugh to cover up my shock. 'God, no.'

'She's just tired then,' she said.

'That's right.' I nodded until I thought my head would come off.

'Long time to be tired. Don't you think, Joseph?'

'Your dad like sports?' Gilbert finally offered. He frowned a deep frown and turned an annoyed eye to his wife.

I turned my head slowly to look at Gilbert. The bones in my neck popped. It must have looked like I was a machine that had been neglected. My bones felt like they needed a good oiling.

'My father keeps to himself.'

45

This brought another bout of silence that I passed by looking at Gilbert's face. He had large pores on the end of his nose that blistered with sweat. They collected and fell in single swollen beads. Stubble had started to grow on his face and turned the skin dark around his thin mouth. His chin stuck out like two knots on an old tree.

'Well, dear.' Beatrice let out a shy laugh. 'It was good meeting you. If you need to you can run along now.'

I spun quickly and marched away as if I was keeping time with a row of other soldiers. The large green bag I wore over my shoulders bounced from side to side like it had been filled with nothing more than wadded up paper. I looked over my shoulder after I'd made it away from their yard. Gilbert Stapp lowered a hand into his lap and sneaked a scratch at his crotch. I saw it through the wood porch slats. After turning my head straight I walked toward the hill that led to the open space.

I could just hear what they were saying.

'I told you the kid's not right, Beat.'

'Yeah, well I guess. I don't think he's retarded though. He seemed bright enough.'

'Smart kids that are overly quiet are dangerous.' There was a pause and when Gilbert continued his voice was louder than before. 'You can ask any psychologist about that.'

'He'll be all right,' Beatrice replied. 'Just needs time to adjust.'

Chapter Five

Couldn't figure that advice from Nurse Gene and Mr Cunningham. They didn't mean for me to get in deeper. But then they didn't mean anything at all from the way I saw it. Fights came my way. With a quickness of both mind and fists I accepted them. They came from fellow students. I came up against punks in the neighbourhood. Didn't matter. Trouble found me. It's not that I wanted the punishment. I took my knocks just as good as I gave them back. I've got to admit there came this amazing burst when I bled. More than the cuts and bruising, I found something inside me. Some kind of primal urge to strike out came to life when my skin cracked open. That kind of thing didn't appear until I got cut. With the blood I fought better – harder and more determined.

The fights gave me a chance to release that power. Let inhibitions fly. Outnumbered and outgunned. The punches I landed could never have beaten the guys I hit. That's the way I figured it. Even if they did the sonsofbitches wouldn't even have hit the deck before someone else knocked me off my legs. The kind of guys wanting to fight me came in teams and fought in packs. Get past one and another stands with tight hands and a jaw of stone. Of course there was still that thing inside me. This burning core of hope that kept me aiming for a knockout. Drove me to shoot for perfection. Flailing my hands to beat a guy until his eyes glazed over. You know you hit him right when his eyes are still open. When he's looking straight out and he's seeing nothing but black.

You get the big guy stunned with a jab and floor him with a hook. That's the combo I went with. Marvelous Marvin Hagler showed me that one. I imagined myself throwing that kind of punch. It'd come out one day, big and beautiful. Watched my reflection in the mirror when I threw them. One after the other. Slow motion swinging to see how I'd look. I flexed my arms in that pose. Without my shirt on my ribs gave away my weakness. I was brittle. The muscles in my arms never looked like they could hold power. But still I hoped for a break that would somehow set me free. I kept ever ready to stand face to face with the punchers and the wrestlers. Didn't matter what they brought. I was ready to match his every move. When the fighting started I swung my arms and kicked my legs anticipating the precious dull thump when I connected.

That moment came while fighting Desmond Walker.

Desmond was a tall boy who wore expensive sneakers and a flat-top hairstyle. He always stayed calm and infinitely quiet. I had some classes with him and he seemed to pay attention for the most part. He answered when instructors called on him and, unlike me, Desmond never got caught out for daydreaming. I thought I liked him. I even raised a hand to acknowledge him when Dean and me walked away from the school parking lot toward the main road. He sometimes raised his oversized hand in return. But, the part of his brain that refused anger got switched off somewhere along the line. A girl came to town. Dez took a liking to this girl and it changed him. The new girl was Naomi Phillips.

The day of the fight I sat in the school hall reading a book. I couldn't concentrate on the words with all the noise in the cafeteria. Too much sound made my mind shut off. At that age the smell of a hamburger could distract me from simple things.

My guts rolled and rolled. But, that book was important – so I went looking for a quiet place. I slid my back down a wall between two rows of lockers. Another page had been read before my ass hit the floor.

I'd found the book a week before in the trunk of my father's car. He'd left the house on business. Mr Moon picked him up early that morning. They'd left on a trip that got my old man out of the house for a few days. Mr Moon drove my father to the airport in his Lincoln Continental – the only car I could ever imagine big enough to hold his personality.

I found the keys to my father's car on the counter top in the kitchen. From the way they were flared out in the centre of the counter I figured my old man had forgotten them. That dark space in the trunk of the car had a draw to it. While I drank a glass of milk I stared at the keys and weighed up my chances. Imagining what I could find in the car came like a junkie's sweats. The more I imagined the more painful it became to hold back. There was this overwhelming need to find something out. Something about my father. Something about me. Was he a bad guy outside of the house? Could I do it? Could I take something from him without him knowing?

I drank another glass of milk and ate some leftover goulash Mother had made before her fits started firing up again. I sat at the kitchen table turning over the bent pages of the newspaper. Then I paced for a while. After the pacing I stared at the trees through the kitchen window. Before long it became too much. Nothing could stop me from looking in the trunk of the Diplomat.

In the garage I found myself standing behind the car with the keys in hand. The key chain felt heavy. It held a half-dozen keys and they wouldn't stop rattling. It was the first time I realized how much my hands were shaking. So I looked at my hand and I looked at the keys. Tried to think about something to cool my nerves.

The ring held the house key and the one for the Diplomat. Then four more silver keys with a bright silver shine. They were all the same – all fresh-cut with small shards of metal clinging along the winding edge. The word 'Yale' was embossed on each. They stopped rattling. Found myself looking down at the keyhole for a few minutes. While I stood there I felt like a crime was about to be committed. Just by thinking about undoing the lock I'd been convicted. *That's you kid. He'll know you been in here now. May as well have something for it.* When I finally put the key in and turned it the trunk popped open with a sucking sound. I took the key from the lock and lifted the lid with two fingers. The thing came up on its own.

Inside sat three neat stacks of hardback books. The stacks were bound together with terrycloth straps that looked like they'd come off new bathrobes. Titles read like a medical library. *Understanding Schizophrenia. Mental Illness. Coping with Psychological Disorders.* Everything you needed to know about human psychology and sickness of the brain. I took a book from the centre of the middle stack. Took it from where it would be less obvious. Something I learned from the times Dean and me stole from Li'l Mel's Convenience. Never take it from where they may notice it's gone missing.

That day I abandoned my plans to meet Dean at Washington Pond. I sat in my bedroom and paged through the book. Couldn't understand the words, but the photographs were revealing. The more pictures I looked at and the more pages I turned the more things became familiar. I began to recognize trends. The words on the pages passed me by without my comprehension even grazing the sides. But the pictures were something else.

All those people in the book had a special look about them. The first few pictures I flicked by without thought. Then I slowed down. Some of the captions had been written in laymen's terms. *This patient (picture above) began suffering from schizophrenia at sixteen. The severity of her illness is still apparent almost a decade on.* I didn't know what schizophrenia was, but it didn't matter. The pictures didn't hold a common bond, not at first. Just a bunch of freaks who looked like they could use an updated wardrobe maybe. But the more I looked the better I understood. The face and the eyes held a clue. The skin looked slack over the cheeks and the bones showed through. The eyes of those people had dropped back in their heads. These people all started looking the same.

Everybody changes when they lose their mind, Joe. You'll change too. Just you wait and see.

I had never seen the face of a person I knew to be crazy before. After seeing that book I always looked at the faces of people I met more closely. There were pictures in the book that made me turn back pages. Over and over. The more I looked the more I realized and at times even recognized. I stared for hours at the black and white picture of this one woman. She was middle aged and wore a man's tweed sports jacket that covered a light coloured dress. I remember wondering for hours about her age. Each time I looked at the photograph I guessed different. She might have been young, judging from the smooth appearance of her skin. There were no wrinkles at the sides of her eyes or around her small, thin mouth. But below her eyes were dark crescent shapes. It may have been medication, I remember thinking. She might have been battling her mind each night and losing terribly. Whatever it was that made the crescent shapes swell aged her otherwise dull face. Most of the hair at the sides of her head had gone. The skin on those patches looked raw. I supposed she'd pulled it out herself. The bald patches held no scars. Tracing the picture with my fingers took up a lot of time. Couldn't help but trace her face and touch the dark patches under her eyes.

The cold, red school wall pressed against my back. This buzzing sound rattled off in my head and I figured it was coming from the fire alarm. The drumming of voices coming up and down the hall and the strings of laughter seemed distant. Once in a while someone passing would kick at my feet. I'd pull them in closer to me, but they'd slide back out on the polished floor. I remember hoping the woman had gotten better. Took time to wonder how old she would be if she'd survived her illness. Somehow I couldn't convince myself that she'd lived.

That damn buzzing sound keeps getting louder.

Then the book slipped from my hands and floated away.

I looked up and there was Desmond and Naomi standing over me. His thick brown forehead creased and his shoulders hunched in a muscular bend. I wanted to look at Naomi's face to see if she was as mad. Something kept me from looking at her. Something made me keep my eyes on Desmond Theodore Walker. From a blurry peripheral I could see Naomi holding a cluster of schoolbooks to her chest. She didn't move. To this day I still hope Naomi looked at me with pity in her eyes. I can't imagine such a beautiful girl hating for the sake of hate.

'Get your monkey ass up, punk!' Desmond yelled.

Pressed my back up against the wall, hoping he'd leave me alone. He leaned forward and grasped at the collar of my shirt. I knocked his hand away harder than I'd intended. In his face I saw the blank suspension of thought. His eyes widened and the whites looked unclean – like they held the flares of a smoky yellow. His nostrils opened in large circles and his lower lip drooped. It became evident at that moment that he hadn't counted on my retaliation. As I waited for his reaction I felt like I had defused the situation by a simple stroke of the hand. All the following events may never have happened if the crowd hadn't formed. Desmond had attracted them in packs of ten when he pulled the book away from me. Those who yelled and pressed into the circle around us were the weak dogs. They came to feed after the prey fell fresh out of breath. The cluster of faces standing behind Desmond looked down at my fading figure. They started to chant for a fight. The energy of their voices fuelled the aggressive machine.

'The hell you followin' my girl?'

I shook my head. My mouth opened, but nothing came out.

'Can't hear you, bitch! Talk up now,' he said.

'I'm not . . . Don't understand.'

'Callin' me a liar? Front of all these people?'

'It's just I never . . .'

'When that last bell ring, boy,' Desmond said.

The crowd cheered and I ground my shoulder blades against

the wall until they burned with pain. Looked up at everyone above me wanting to stand and be at eye level. Sitting on the ground in the centre of a maddened crowd made me feel hopeless. The faces above me were suddenly all people I'd never seen before. I'd been in classes with them just hours before. All of those faces were smiling as if what they were witnessing had been long awaited. They all looked down at me and spoke but I couldn't make out what they were saying. The voices mingled together to form one angry sound. They were chattering – almost chanting – and my thoughts clouded. My chest felt ready to cave in. It became harder to find my breath.

Then amongst the faces I saw Dean emerge between a pair of girls. They wore masks of inflamed acne and crisping mascara. He looked at me without much of an expression. Just like Dean to show now. It's over. He pushed his glasses back onto his thin nose and used the same hand to wipe his mouth. He shook his head just enough for me to see it. He probably never knew I caught the motion. He looked pleased. I expected a smile that never came. There was a sense that he felt glad it'd been me. It meant he'd escaped again. Once more he'd been the lucky one.

That day I bided my time. I watched the clock and lost track of the teachers. They spilled facts and figures over our sleepy, dreamy heads. No one seemed to be listening. They were all waiting and anticipating. An event had been scheduled to happen that day. A prize fight was about to be staged for their entertainment. My stomach had emptied itself into the urinal after I'd been able to get myself away from the gathered students. Even after Desmond had broken through the crowd with Naomi in tow people remained. They'd studied me like a lame pigeon. When the last bell rang I tossed the bag over my shoulder and joined the flow of bodies. We pressed in a loud mass toward an exit door. I didn't make it far.

Two large boys took hold of me, one at each arm. My ushers to a special moment. *This is your life, Joseph Pullman. We'd like you to meet* . . . They'd been afraid I'd try for an escape. With me in hand they walked quickly, my feet skimming over the pavement as we went. In front of me on the football field I saw a circle of students. The circle opened up when we got near. We were swallowed by noise. Desmond stood in the centre – pacing back and forth while biting at his lower lip. He watched me and gritted his teeth. He lifted his hands to his chin while he stared me down. When he saw I didn't intend to look away he started throwing slow punches to warm up his muscles.

My arms went free after the big guys let me go. I looked behind and saw the circle had closed itself up again. A wound healed. The bag slid from my shoulders and dropped to the ground. My knees shook and a burn started up in my thighs. It spread quick and went to my guts. Then it found my arms and my face went numb. While Desmond started hopping around and throwing punches at the air I stayed still. My arms hung loosely at my side. I bent my legs slightly at the knees. The burning kept light and the bending joints heated things up. Desmond hopped in front of me and then danced around behind. Out of sight.

Here he goes, Joseph. Right in the back of your head. He's gonna get you from behind like a coward. Just like a damned . . .

I closed my jaw and clenched my teeth together tight as they'd go.

Right side, kid. Here he is . . .

Desmond took a swing that missed. Fist popped out. Knuckles close by. Then they were gone. Hands back at his sides. He kept dancing. I didn't flinch. *Can't get no satisfaction.*

'Punk ass.'

That's all I heard. There was the rumble of the crowd. The screams and the laughs. Sounds jumping out of chaos.

– *Kill him, Dez.*

– *Fuck him up, Dee.*

– *Going down, Pullman.*

Then there was buzzing. Something almost humming inside my head. Light and cold.

They can't help it, Joseph. You have a face that asks for it.

54

'Fuck off, Mother.'

Laughter rushing in. Voices close by. Holding me inside the circle. Talking. Small conversations. Out in the air. Distant. Close by.

This is the end. This is how the script works, Joey. Your part is here, here and here . . . Don't wait for your cue. Begin.

Stood limp. Burning came from deep inside. Energy buzzing along the bone. The voices fuelled it all. My head spinning with the sound of the voices. Laughing. So many people. Faces floating round. Detached faces smiling and yelling. Laughing and building more layers. Layers I could hear. Voices I recognized tumbling into my head.

Giving him too much time, Joe.

Something burning inside. Burning so hot it made my hands shake. Clenched fingers into fists and shaking. Holding them out so I could see them. See them to stop them from shaking.

Quit watching your hands, kiddo. He's gonna move on you.

And a voice I knew coming from Desmond. Laughing with the rest of the faces. Never moving. Smiling and laughing . . .

– *Get your monkey ass up, punk.*

He came closer. He never moved. Still came closer. So fast and he was there. Face to face. My shaking hands coming into the air. Right hand moving up. Moving out. Fast as a flash. Shooting out and hitting and coming back against me. Then the left. My hands were light and shaking and pulsing. Right again. Left. Moving on their own. Reaching out and touching his floating face. Connecting hard and adding to the noise. Voices calling out.

– *Oh, my god . . .*

– *The hell . . .*

– *Get him off . . .*

– *What's he . . .*

My arms swinging. Burning along the bone. Propelling me forward. Moving him to me. Hands clenched and burning and shaking. Hammering and moving. Guts rolling and nausea coming in.

My hands shooting off and touching his skin. Coming back again. Red. Colliding before I could see them leave. Watching them. Watching hard. Wanting to find them. Keep them back. Out again. Colliding with that face. Eyes looking up. Up at the sky.

– *Somebody stop him . . .*

Knuckles digging in. Soft popping sounds.

Nothing like the movies, hey boy?

Desmond watching something in the sky. Hands moved up to cover his face. My hand moving behind. Catching his jaw. Buzz coming from his jaw to me. Travelling through my knuckles. Sending jolts through my knuckles. His face falling. Coming up to me while he was falling. My hands still moving. Sloppy combinations. Simple. Left. Right. Left. Right. Fists against his ears. Right hook falling down fast.

Boom.

Boom.

Boom.

Rocking his head. Bouncing his head on his neck. Left. Right. His knees hitting the ground. Boom. Left. Right. Keeping him from falling. Red hands like bombs.

Then my head shook, like a TV out of focus. Bad frequency. My legs gave way and I dropped. Landed on top of Desmond Walker. His face lay down in the dirt and I got a hold of his neck with my arm. I did that out of defence. If he came to I wanted control. The fists that knocked me to the ground started digging into my back, one after the other in a litany of revenge. I closed my eyes and thought of the woman in the psychology book. Somehow I knew she had died in her mind and she never had recovered. I squeezed hard on Desmond's neck. More fists hammered me from behind.

'Back it up! Get off, Peterson!' someone yelled. 'I said back it off Peterson!' Gerry Peterson never left Desmond Walker's side. Now he didn't want to leave my back. The punches stopped landing on the nape of my neck. Quit drumming against the back of my head. There was a gulp and the weight on my legs was released.

'Get off his neck, Pullman,' the voice said close to my head.

Mr Kelly lifted me up by my left arm. He stretched all the muscles that had just been tightened up by Gerry Peterson's punches. My back came alive like it was covered with wasps. Mr Kelly pulled on my left arm twice before I could think straight enough to let go of Desmond's neck.

'Had enough, Pullman?' Mr Kelly asked when he got me to my feet.

'Yessir,' I breathed.

There was an expression of disbelief that marked his face. He adjusted his glasses on his nose before he looked down at Desmond Walker. I used my right hand to wipe grass out of my eyes. Wriggled my left arm to remind Mr Kelly he'd got a hold of it. He looked down at me and let go. Then he sucked his teeth and shook his head.

'Clear it out,' he yelled. When no one moved he took a step forward. Swung his arms out to his sides like some huge bird readying itself to take flight. Both of his arms went straight out – the right almost knocking me in the head.

'Get the hell out of here!' His face turned red and the veins in his neck swelled up large and purple.

The crowd started to filter away. I turned and picked up my bag. Didn't have any intention of a clean getaway, but Mr Kelly took hold of my arm. Enforced a sense of captivity. I turned slowly and met his eyes. Reminded me of something you'd see on a smiling clown. Thin, but magnified under powerful corrective lenses.

'You do this yourself?' he asked, not loud enough for the few lingering students to hear. He knew. That was the kicker. The scarred freak got his own back.

'Uh-huh,' I said. 'But he started it. He told me he wanted to fight. I don't go looking for this kind of thing, Mr Kelly. He cornered me in the hall. Ask anybody.'

'Understood,' he said. 'Go to the office. Tell them what happened out here. I'll be in after a minute.'

I walked to the office without incident. There was the worry of Desmond's pals hovering round the place. Setting up ambush to grab a quick shot. Work up the kid that brought down the giant. Couldn't help but wonder if one of them would take a shot if they had the chance. Who would know? All my scars. All that commotion in the fields. I walked through groups and nothing happened. I was a free man that day, but even then I knew it was all just borrowed time.

Feeling good I sat in the chair in the empty waiting room. Then Mrs Nemechek took me in her office. Just me and her divided by a desk. She did a lot of talking that I didn't hear. Kept shaking her head. Then she left me to sit and think while she phoned my father from the reception desk. I just sat tight – waiting for my release. I heard people in the office talking. The walls were thin and didn't reach the ceiling. Still I could only hear the sound of the voices. You couldn't make out what the voices were saying. Couldn't tell if they spoke about me or about the fight or about Desmond's broken nose. Maybe that cut on his right cheek that would take six stitches to close. Somehow I liked the idea of being mean. Suddenly I was more than just the guy who got his ass kicked daily. Sitting in the office of the principal on my own made me feel for the first time like I'd been noticed. It made that feeling sweeter knowing I'd found the spotlight for something almost dangerous.

Mrs Nemechek stood outside her office drinking coffee. Alone. She looked back once in a while to make sure I hadn't decided to stand or look through her things. Her voice still sounded fresh in my head. Her words were spoken like she'd meant to congratulate a student for perfect attendance. Very precise. Very paced.

'You were wrong for fighting,' she told. 'I have no choice but to suspend you. Three days for you and Mr Walker.'

'I understand,' I offered.

'I don't think you do, Joseph. This is serious.' She rolled one of her expensive looking pens round in her hands. 'These are not going to be free days for you.'

58

'Okay,' I said, thankful the days weren't going to be spent at home. 'So it's a detention really. In-school suspension?'

'No,' Nemechek replied. 'I just mean you have something to do on your days off. Along with your class assignments, that is.'

'Right.'

'I want you to write a letter to Desmond apologizing for breaking his nose,' she said.

'No chance,' I said.

'He will be visiting the hospital this evening for that cut as well.' She felt like she was on a roll. In her face she lit up. She thought I was affected by all this. 'I hope you think about the fact that he may be concussed.'

'Forget it. I'll take an extra day.'

'You can expect a letter from Mr Walker in return.'

'What should I say?' I asked.

'That is for you to decide, Joseph. But what you need to remember is that you did a terribly dangerous thing.' She was rubbing hand cream over her fingers now. The pen sat with the others in a silver container. The lotion made a squishy sound that somehow caught me. 'What are you smiling at, Joseph?'

'Just the sound that hand cream makes.'

'I hope you do not consider yourself clever. Do not think you are a tough guy,' she said leaning toward me. One hand twisted into the other. 'There are some angry people out there now.'

'Angry people have always been out there.'

She left again and used the telephone on the desk in the waiting room. After making her calls she came back into her office. She sat looking at me. I set my hands on the edge of her desk and stared at my knuckles. She watched me and we both kept quiet. I understood where she was coming from. The prospect of fighting Desmond again became real. He'd be ready and have people backing him. I'd get into it all again and it'd be bad. It was unavoidable. Before taking Desmond Walker to the ground I'd thought winning a fight would be a good thing. After, I saw that I'd become marked. Each punch I landed put another tick against my name in some other joker's book. My name landed on a dozen other shit lists that afternoon. One lucky shot opened up an opportunity that day. I jumped on the moment and hammered home all the aggression I had inside me. Tossed the sucker punch that set up a flurry for the knockout. Fighting again would be a different story.

I slumped back into the vinyl chair and closed my fists. The bruises had already started to surface on my knuckles. Mrs Nemechek looked at my hands and frowned. When she stood from behind her desk I twisted in my seat to see if my father had entered the office. He wasn't there. No one was there.

'No,' she said. 'Just stay there. Keep seated.' She walked out of the office, careful to shut the door behind her.

I felt good that she didn't want to be near me. Something in me changed that day; something that made me more of a man. Something that had shaped the way my mind processed fear and disposed of it. While I sat there with a sheet of glass separating me from the rest of the world I thought of the fights to come. Thought of the punches I would land and the punches that would land on me. I thought of Desmond and his shattered face. Clenched my fists up tight as they'd go and willed the next one on.

'Brought you down today, punk,' I whispered. 'I'll bring you down again.'

My father walked into the office with a cool stride. He nodded to Mrs Nemechek and straightened his tie before shaking her hand. I stared at him because I found myself tired of looking away. Met his eyes and they glowed with the storm mounting inside him. I saw his hands clench up before they stretched out again. Looking at him I saw through the old man. He was no stronger than Desmond Walker. I had already beaten that sonofabitch.

I shouldered my bag and walked to the door. Looked through the glass and waited while my father spoke to Mrs Nemechek. He stared at me over Nemechek's shoulder, watching my eyes. He could see I'd found pride. He stood there watching me. With my scars and my smile he must have seen it. I'd found something real. I'd had it all along, but it had been deep inside.

60

Today it had surfaced and somehow I already knew how to use it.

I waited for Nemechek to open the door.

I came out of her office whistling.

Chapter Six

The bird would have been large for a sparrow but without the head it was hard to tell for sure. I stared at the thing for a long time, struggling to remember the colour and pattern of the feathers. Stood and looked and felt a need to take it all in. In those days I had this drive for that kind of detail. Needed to keep things vivid. Make them mine. A hand placed next to the carcass gave a scale for length. Wrapping my fingers around it gave the scale for breadth. It became habit to do these things with the animals I found. Looked them up in field guides when I got back home. Couldn't have taken the bird with me when I left the Killing Tree that day. That kind of thing would have broken the storms in my old man. I'd thought about chancing it. Even made a motion to stuff it back in my pocket.

Leave it, kiddo. Your old man'll send you two steps closer to the dead bird if it reaches his place. I put it back. Set it on the pile of dead things.

Dean had been with me that day. It wasn't usual for him to be out of his house so early. The ground was still slick with wet from a morning rain. He was waiting for me in the open space – sitting on the stump of a fallen oak tree. Lightning had hit it the summer before. Dean told me that Paul Felton came from the next street up with his father and one of his uncles. They brought chain saws and cut the thing to small bits. Paul used a rusted wheelbarrow to move the pieces into the woods. He took them just past the tree line. Flipped up the barrow and landed all the pieces in a heap. When they got to the base they cut the stump as flat as they could manage.

Dean sat on the base counting the rings when I met him that morning.

We said our hellos with nods.

'Figured out how old it is yet?' I asked.

'Too old to count. I lose track before I even get started.'

'Not worth it.'

'No.' Already both tired of the conversation. That's the way it went with Dean. He needed someone to hang out with. Conversations were both optional and occasional. He took part when the mood caught him. Dean lived on the inside and liked to be alone. The clouds hung low and Dean must have been thinking of the storm that never completely left the sky. Wading through the thicket on our way to the Killing Tree Dean found a rabbit. It was dead and the side had been chewed open by a fox or a dog.

'It's a big one,' Dean said.

'There's bigger rabbits than that.' I laughed a bit, knowing what he was getting at.

'There won't be enough room if we keep finding 'em like this.'

'Bring it through.' I walked ahead while Dean chose a part of the rabbit's carcass to wrap his fingers around.

Inside the circle of grass that surrounded the Killing Tree I started the survey. It wasn't much more than walking the field and kicking my sneakers through the leaves. Rustling up the grass. Waiting for something heavier than paper to hit the toe of my shoe. Dean started on the other side of the circle after tossing the rabbit onto the roots of the tree. Around the roots we were careful not to knock down the small tombstones placed over each of the graves. They were markers made by Dean and

63

me after we buried the animals. That was our first week placing sacrifices into the ground. We were careful to make sure the dead touched the roots before dropping dirt over them.

I found the day's second offering.

'Got one,' I called out.

'Kind?'

'Bird.'

'You're always finding birds.' Dean had that soft sound in his voice. The kind of soft that kids press into words when they feel left out. It's a sound Dean may have carried into adulthood if he'd been given the chance.

'Keep lookin'. There's got to be a bunch more.'

I ran my fingers over the breast feathers. Started saying aloud the markings that needed to be remembered. The sound of my own voice brought comfort. That morning I'd been speaking to Dean in a way. But, most times I spoke to myself in those days – being careful that I was completely alone when I did so. As I spoke that morning under the Killing Tree I wrapped my fingers around the animal. I had an overwhelming desire to make my palm a fist and crush it. When my fingers started to constrict I watched hopelessly as blood began to seep through opened tubes in the neck. There wasn't much blood. The animal had been dead for some time. Still, enough came out to remind me it had recently been able to fly. That it could even have been tending to hatchlings in a now empty nest. When the ribs crushed under the weight of my index and middle finger I opened my hand. Dropped the remains to the ground.

'Good one, Pullman,' Dean said.

He had a way of making me feel hollow. He watched me with a dead stare, revelling in the anger that it made swarm inside me. It was his way of showing me that he was clever, but not willing to take charge. Dean lacked imagination and confidence. That's why he latched on to me. He knew I had both in abundance. I could take care of him and fill the gaps where he was in need. We were both socially inept, but Dean was almost entombed within himself.

There were a few minutes after Dean spoke that were filled with a heavy silence. I stayed on my knees and started rubbing my hands up and down my thighs. I tried to wipe away blood that had never touched my fingers. The action seemed to come with instinct. I stared down at the bird and stopped my hands from moving by gripping at my legs. As the pain of my closing fingers dug into my thighs I could tell his eyes were still on me.

'Quit it, Dean,' I said.

'Quit what?'

'Watching me, asshole.'

His feet moved him around to the other side of the tree. He picked up the rusted spade that we hid under a stone pile and pressed it into the soil. There was a slicing sound when the spade went in. There was just enough grit in the soil to make a scraping sound on the metal. The more he dug the faster he moved. He got himself all wound up knowing I'd caught him.

I let Dean bury the bird. He did it with haste and in his madness broke one of its wings. The break sounded loud. It came like a thick, dry twig snapped across a knee. The grave had been far too small. It could only have been wide and deep enough for a large field mouse, maybe a young garden snake.

Made up for his mishap days later when I carved a headstone out of a flat piece of tree bark I'd collected on an earlier trip to the creek. On the bark I had engraved the work 'Hawk' using the corkscrew from my army knife. The process had been slow, but I felt it needed to be done. It was both to make up for the desiccated remains of the bird and to commemorate the newest offering to the Killing Tree.

That same day we buried the rabbit. Again, Dean dug the hole and placed the animal inside. Because the rabbit was his find he took more care in sinking it into the ground. He set it in tail-first taking the time to position the head so the never-closing eyes stared at him while he dropped dirt over the top. I stood behind him feeling my patience thinning.

'Finish up.' I kicked his left sneaker. He'd been sitting on his feet and the action threw him off balance. He steadied himself

65

with his hands and let out a breath. It wasn't the kind of breath you let out when you're mad. It was more like the kind you let out when you're concentrating like crazy and someone breaks you in mid-thought. I gave him time to fill in the rest on his own.

'We'll need another ground soon,' Dean said. He brushed the soil off his jeans and stood up. He'd been biting his lip hard. The skin below had turned a deep crescent-shape of red. Through his glasses he scanned around the base of the Killing Tree. I followed his lead. The markers for all of the animals stood just above the blades of grass. They were like a sea of swimmers fighting to keep their heads above water. We had talked about wheeling my father's mower down and clearing the area. But the Briggs and Stratton would never have made it through the thicket. Even if we brought it through it would have taken all day to lift the grave markers before running the mower. The process would be a long one. Most important, the sound of an engine in the middle of the forest would attract attention we didn't want.

'I'll bring the bleach tomorrow. We'll start clearing the place out.' Dean looked sad. The bleach had been his idea. Kill all of the grass and the problem of upkeep ended. Still the green made the Killing Tree look at peace. We had sat and talked about the Tree standing in the centre of nothing and it seemed to fit. It should stand alone.

'Bring your dad's sprayer too,' I said.

'Yeah. I'll bring it.'

We made an effort, like we always did, of staying away from my father's house until the sun fell. When the hourly chime sounded on my watch I climbed a tall tree. There were several in the forest, just past the open space that I could sit in and have a clear view of my father's house. I'd sit myself on a limb and use my old man's telescope to look into the windows. Dean stood at the base of the tree sucking on blades of grass. Once in a while he'd ask for an update. Sometimes I told him what I saw, other times I kept quiet.

There wasn't much movement in the windows that didn't have curtains. When movement came it was nothing more than one of my parents passing through the room. I could tell which rooms my parents were using by the closed drapes. Once in a while my mother would press her eye to the slit between the two pieces of fabric and peer out. During these times I found it hard not to imagine myself as a German sniper during one of the World Wars. I even imagined her head exploding as the bullet made impact.

My father never looked out of windows. He had told me that it was in bad taste to watch people. He had caught me watching Ruth Malcolm. She and her husband lived next door with their two kids. She'd been out sunbathing on her back deck and her chest swelled with every shallow breath she took. I found a rhythm with her that day. My old man's hand met the back of my neck before I knew he'd come up behind me. The hit sent my head smashing against the windowpane. The glass didn't shatter and I felt lucky for that. Not because I would have been cut. There came the fear of him hitting me more for destroying his house. On the occasions he hit me it was hard for him to stop. I didn't like to give him reasons to continue.

Chapter Seven

Mother warned me about my old man's temper. Each time he boiled over with that anger, I felt the weight of his hands. She'd spell it out like I'd never heard her before. Like I couldn't have guessed the old man had a fighting streak in him. Mother's warnings came too late. I'd already suffered from the violence. The punches and the cuts. Still she'd give me what she thought a mother should give. Sat with me after the heavy sessions when I was still small enough to fit her lap.

My old man got her scared a few times. Hit me till I stopped breathing once. She spoke about that one on occasion. Never came out and told me about it, but it was a hot topic on their drunken evenings. I'd caught them thinking it may have been better if Mother had let me choke on my tongue. Got the feeling my old man had convinced her that he'd be able to cover it all up. If she'd let me go I figured that my old man had a plan. Get rid of what was left behind.

'You fixed him more than once, Clarisse,' my old man had said.

'What should I have done?'

'Nothing.'

'Maybe,' she'd told him. 'But where would that have left us?'

68

'Where're we now?'

There were a few of these conversations over the years. Probably a load more than I was aware of. What I knew was that my old man was still aiming for the chance to count me out for good. The one-sided slugfests came without invitation. My father didn't give me chance to think about the moves. Didn't warn me not to run after the last bell. He'd just come out and tag me with a shot. Started it all off when I was just a kid.

My mind was still young and those thumpings I took were heavyweight. I still have a few burned in deep. The memories are vivid. They come playing back time and time again. Like the episode when my father took me down so furious I couldn't remember my name. Even when he'd finished and stood sucking at his split knuckles. Strange I can remember it happening. Laying there holding my arm that felt too heavy and wouldn't move. Looking at the tough guy move left to right. Breathing steady. Staring down. My blood matching his and running off his hand. Red drops falling from his fingers and dotting the cream carpets. Ready to strike. *Where am I? How'd I get to the floor?* Nothing happening. Mind blank as a full moon. My old man looked almost worried. His face started to blur out. Swayed over me. Bent down close to my eyes.

'What's your name?' he yelled. 'Oh, Christ. You did this. You made me. What's your name? What's your name?'

His fingers were thick. They grabbed my face and squeezed. The pain brought me back. In tiny shards of light the pain brought me back. I choked back the blood and mucus hanging in my throat. Coughed a time or two. Felt myself coming up off the floor. Grabbed at my old man's wrist when my neck started to hurt.

Of course, this beating came before I learned to watch out for the expressions. He had a brightness in his eyes. Living the good life kind of thing. I'd seen him speaking to Mr Moon. Same as when he got to drinking with Mother. It was a kind of glimmering happiness. Wouldn't go so far as to say it was a fairytale or anything. But it was a big shift from his rage. All the smiles

69

and that brightness in his eyes clouded over when he got angry. Those clouds were the only way he communicated with me when it came to the summer of the cicada. If his eyes looked clear all felt calm. Sometimes I even felt safe. But when the storms started rolling in I knew there was something bad building inside his head. These times I stayed well away.

Before Mother lost her mind she'd sit with me. She'd hold me real gentle and hum low and sweet. Took that time for me after the worst of sessions with my old man. I'd sit in her arms. She'd rock me gentle as the breeze. When she wasn't humming she'd do this other thing. Made this moaning noise. I'd listen to her chest. Somehow the sound of her voice – the buzz I felt coming from her throat – would numb my wounds. It'd settle me down and make my breathing easy again. She'd wait till I was almost out. Right there near sleep. Then she'd warn me about my father's anger. Just like she was hypnotizing me. The things she told me during those moments still remain. During her warnings she laid the blame for my father's actions on my own shoulders.

'Shush, now. You feel better. Quiet, Joseph,' Her voice was no more than a whisper. 'You understand your father. You're a smart boy. You know he can't stop.'

She hummed. I pressed my head onto her chest.

'You have a face that asks for it, Joseph. He can't hold back when you're around.'

Her hums were beautiful. They were full of life.

'It's your face. He can't stop.'

I heard her words. They sunk in with an acid pain. I remained still and pressed my face to her chest. Feared she would punctuate her remarks with another bout of violence. Matched her hums with my own long breaths. It almost felt safe at times. Felt like I almost belonged to her. I learned later in life that my face tempted more than just the hands of my father.

I took easy to my solo trips into the forest. They introduced me to wildlife, something I'd never come across before. My earlier years growing up in Tallahassee were more confined. The old man's temper kept me holed up in the house. Kids with bruises and scrapes gain a lot of attention. Mother patched me up and kept me in front of the television most days. My asthma kept the schools from asking too many questions. All the doctors' notes Mother wrote out and signed with fake names confirmed I was a sick kid. My file in the hands of principles and councillors released schoolwork. I studied from home till the healing was over. Kept out of sight until the worst of the visible wounds had healed. Then I went back to school with scars that no one questioned. Walked round with the yellowing patterns of old bruises on my neck and arms. Showed off my fresh pink cuts and only got shy smiles from the teachers who saw them.

There was hope that things would change when we got to Maryland. Had these visions of people seeing the trouble straight off. Maybe not to take me away, but at least recognize what I was up against inside my father's house. Behind that façade of a happy family home in American suburbia was some bad shit. Still, no one seemed to smell it when the door came open. The Stapps. Mick and Valerie Drexler. Ruth Malcolm. Even Helle Bishop who was the only one ever to get into the house. No one caught on to the trouble inside 100 Westchester Drive. So I kept outside as much as possible to stay clear of the trouble. Roamed the great wide open where things were different than Tallahassee.

Even the grass that grew in the front yard of the new house was softer, easier to walk on than the hard blades of Saint Augustine grass that covered the ground in Florida. The palms were replaced by maples and sycamore and thousands of oaks. Dean listened to me talk about the difference between Maritime and Tallahassee. He'd nod his head and keep quiet, but it was just to keep me on the line. He didn't care where I'd come from. He didn't even really see what he had around him. Dean just existed and that kind of thing never really sat easy with me.

All the new things in the forest begged for my attention. Couldn't handle the idea of sitting in a classroom. Unable to explore while surrounded by people I didn't want to know seemed like I was being punished for a crime I didn't commit. The days at school were the same as pulling dead weight. At the end of the day I felt burned out and didn't even have the satisfaction of accomplishing a freaking thing. Even when Dean and me got outside after the last bell it wasn't until the air hit my lungs that I came to life. Then we'd run like mad for Grant's Road. We'd head off over the baseball diamonds hoping it was a day when no one would chase us down. Worried all the while that someone had beaten us to the fields.

'Think we're clear?' Dean'd yell at me while we ran.

'Never know until we get there.'

'Get where?'

'Doesn't matter,' I'd tell him. 'Just keep on going.'

After we hit the Angry Snake Dean would ease off his pace. He'd fall behind most days. Other days he'd head off like he needed to be someplace. Either way we split up round that point most often. When we got to the open space Dean went home. I'd head back to my father's house if I didn't have much energy. Drop my book bag on the deck and take out my supply bag from where I'd last buried it. Then I'd go back to the forest. Other days I'd just stay out there. Keep my books with me and sit on the bridge. Or I'd just drop down in the soft sand at Washington Pond. Didn't matter where it was as long as I was on my own.

I spent all of my days and most of my evenings roaming round the bases of the trees. Along the banks of the creek and through the brush and thickets. I'd found the bridge on one of my trips. It became a kind of base. A place I stayed when it rained. Hiding beneath it with my bare feet in the cool flowing creek water. The path leading to the bridge had been overgrown by thorny vines and poison ivy. You couldn't see the bridge from the ground. Never would have found the thing from the maintained foot-paths. I'd only found the bridge after climbing a tall pine tree. I'd been looking for animals through my telescope – tracking this raccoon – when I spotted it. Nothing but a rotting structure. Still, I had to get closer. Have a look.

If it hadn't been for the raccoon I'd never have found the bridge unless I'd walked the length of the creek bed. Dogs and cats would sometimes show up out there in the forest. On their own most of the time. Kind of wild themselves. I'd follow them for a short while to break up the time. Just sat and they'd go by. Sometimes I imagined I was on safari. The domestic dogs were really lions and the cats were antelope. There were times I watched just to see where they would go. If I had the supply bag I'd use the telescope and got so deep in the game I could see the crosshairs inside. The long-range rifle felt heavy on my shoulder. Didn't take much to bring the animals down. Gave them no warning. All of my shots carried deadly aim.

The day I found the bridge I was intent on watching the raccoon. It waddled along the sandbanks, dipping its head close to the water. Felt content to watch silently without my imagination playing up. All of this just so I could see why a night animal had decided to walk the banks of the creek during the day. What was it that made an animal change its clock? Change its behaviour?

But the bridge caught my interest. The raccoon kept on doing his thing and he just kind of faded. That's the way it worked with me. Good for a time. Fine as long as it's useful. When the raccoon caused a commotion down in the water I shifted back to him. He'd pounced on a crawfish. Got the thing in his mouth and shook it like mad.

Come out at light to kill for the night.

Didn't walk to the bridge that day or even the next. Made myself keep away from it. I played my games – allowing my mind to work up what I'd find. All the things I hoped would be there when I finally got round to exploring. Picking at the decaying slats. What hid in the shadow waiting for me? Something down under, waiting. Breathing quiet until I crawled on the sand to test the strength of the supports.

I imagined that bridge so thoroughly I knew what it held, down to the web a family of spiders had made. A web that held an infinite number of mosquitoes and flies. Some half-eaten. Some still struggling to survive. In the few days before I went to the bridge to test my expectations the place became a sort of mystical site. I'd only seen enough of the bridge to know it existed. Through the trees I couldn't see if the bridge even made it across the length of the creek. Knowing so little made it hard to keep away, but I made myself hold back. The days before I went to have a look were difficult. Knowing the bridge was waiting for me.

The evening I found the bridge I returned home to find my mother kneeling on the kitchen floor. Crying into her hands. I stood outside the sliding glass door watching her. As always I'd stopped by the end of our deck to stash my bag. Concealed it in a plastic bag to protect it from rain or the morning dew. Crawled halfway under the deck, pushing the bag in a hole behind a cluster of ivy. Then I'd heard the noise. At first I thought it was an animal. Something wounded and maybe close to dying. I just sat steady and waited. Listened for it to scream again.

I squinted and looked under the space – deeper under the wooden deck. It ran the length of the house. With the sun almost down the darkness under the deck went on forever. Couldn't see any more than a few feet in. There was a depth of blackness behind that I could only imagine. Could have held any number of secrets. Proof of evil things done could have been hidden down there. Dead things buried. I was content to let the maker of the noise die. I'd pull it out the next morning.

When the sound didn't come again I crawled out from the dark. Climbed the slats and dropped onto the deck and brushed at the soil that dusted my legs. When I'd got most of it off I looked at the roof. Thinking a cat might have climbed up one of the trees and misjudged the jump. It could've landed awkwardly against the shingles. But the roof was so high I would never have seen it if that had been the case. That one would have to stay. The wind would bring it down after a while. Then I'd take it to the Killing Tree with the rest of them.

Took my shoes off and slid my feet over the wood. Came up to the door silent as silent could be. Mother never saw me coming up like that. When I got to the sliding door I looked through the glass. Thinking my father may have taken a coffee break at

74

the kitchen table, I didn't want to be seen straight away. I leaned my head forward to look inside, ready to jerk back if I met up with his down-turned head. What I saw made me freeze. My eyes couldn't move away. Just kind of got caught in time.

Never learned what it was that happened that day. What it was that had brought my mother to her knees. But there she was with her feet tucked under her ass. Her hands holding onto her face like she worried it would come away if she let go. Her shoulders bounced. Looked as if an electrical force was shooting volt after volt into her. A gulping sound came from her mouth as her head fell back. Her hands slid from her swollen face to her chest. Then she screamed like a dying animal.

You gonna bury her when she's gone, kiddo? Put her in the ground when she's dead, Joseph?

It was the sound I'd heard alright. While stuffing my gear under the deck, behind the ivy, she'd hit the same note. I stood outside and listened to the gentle rub of the crickets. There was the song of the bullfrogs that sat blurping off in the distance. In an instant I was filled with this strange satisfaction. I've felt it since, but it's come only on rare occasions.

Suppose that was my first realization – the first full-scale confirmation that I was a born voyeur. I liked the idea of seeing without being seen. Watching my mother break down while she had no notion of me being there. Not the slightest sense of me on the other side of half an inch of glass. She watched the ceiling and I watched her fall to pieces. Her body jostled by invisible waves. I watched just like I was dead and no one could see me. It all got too much after a while. The excitement built up fast and furious. Couldn't help it any more.

I opened my hand and went to slap the glass. That anxious fire burning down the length of my spine. *You're gonna react to this one, Momma!* My hand came back, positioned in the air. Ready to strike . . . and then her head dropped. Just like she'd already broken from the trance. Didn't give me the last second I needed. Couldn't even let me have that moment of satisfaction. She twisted on her knees. Came spinning round, squealing through her lips. Her eyes met mine and with the look she emptied me. All of the blood and energy drained. Wounds burned into my guts. Felt the coldness entering as I was sucked dry and the only thing I could do was muster up a smile. A smile Mother didn't return.

'Open the door.' I pointed to the safety bar holding the sliding glass panel in place. 'I need your help to get in, Mother.'

She didn't move. She didn't even blink.

'The lock's in place,' I said too loud. 'You need to lift the lock.'

She mouthed something at me. She looked so pitiful and as I stood watching her my energy started to return. I didn't make any attempt to figure out what it was she'd been saying. That would have broken the game. I wasn't ready to stop playing. The pit of my stomach felt empty when she stood and walked to the door. If I could have lunged at her at that moment I'd have done it. Just as she got to her feet I would have tackled her to the ground. Before she pulled the security bar up. Before she opened the door. I stepped in and stood against the wall. She shut the door and replaced the bar.

'Where have you been?' she asked. Her voice sounded raspy. She had a dry throat. I thought about telling her to take a minute. *Cough if you need to before you talk again*. She coughed just like she was reading my mind.

'I was walking.'

'You're always walking, Joseph.' She looked at me and tried to smile. The weight of her swollen face made it tough for her to get the expression right. Her mouth only just came up at the sides. Looked to me like she'd been pumped full of anaesthetic. Just like she didn't really have control of her own expressions.

'You're always away,' she said.

'You look tired,' I told her. Walked past her and looked into a deep pot sitting on the stove. Inside were the remains of pasta and a red sauce. Reached in and pulled out a pair of noodles, wiped them against the side of the pan to collect the solidifying red paste. Placed it in my mouth. It tasted bland, somewhat coppery like blood.

'I'm going to the swim centre tomorrow to register you,' she said. 'You'll need to be up to leave by eight.'

'I know how to swim.'

She looked confused. She kept her head aimed at the patio doors.

'You'll meet people,' she almost whispered. 'Real people.'

She started swaying. Just the slightest bit at first. Almost like she'd been hearing some old easy song. Felt like dancing, but didn't want anyone to know about it. *You're going to fall, old lady. When you hit the floor you'll be shattered into a thousand pieces. And there ain't gonna be no fool to pick you up again.* Her arms crossed and she held her elbows in cupped hands. I leaned against the counter and waited for her to go down. I could sense some kind of energy at work in her muscles. An energy she didn't even know she had. If she'd thought about that energy, right at that moment, even for a split second it would have failed. She'd fall and shatter. I wouldn't have helped her up.

Stood against the counter and willed her to drop. Down like a cut tree. I watched her bow to one side then the other. She closed her eyes and ran a limp hand over her nose. I thought I'd done it. *She's going down, boy.* She had to take a step to the side to recover, but she never hit the deck.

'I'll make sure I'm up,' I said. Then left.

Walked toward the stairs without waiting for her to respond. Couldn't stop the anger building. *What an idea. What a brilliant fucking concept.* She was telling me when to wake up the next morning. Before she even opened her eyes I was out of the house. Each morning, with my pack of gear over my shoulder sometimes sitting on the limbs of a tree. At the bottom of the stairs I heard the dying animal again. It rose up and spread its wings. That sound filled the house. On the wall of the kitchen stood the shadow of my mother. The shape buckled under the weight of her demons. Watching the black figure suddenly made the woman real. Somehow it made her fragile. All the screams. The weight loss. Those eyes. She wasn't my mother. But the shadow. Somehow that was still her and it was devastating to watch her fall.

There was a moment I thought of going back. Returning to the kitchen. Maybe getting up close enough to place a hand on her shoulder. Stand there a while and let her cry, knowing she had someone near. Reminding her that she had someone touching her. Somehow that was what I thought she needed. Those were serious intentions. May have even taken a step toward the shadow. While it slowly crumbled to the ground I may have straightened the collar on my shirt. Tried to make myself more controlled. To look like a good young man. It's how I thought someone who cared may have acted. But whatever it was that I did, however far I took it, Mother never had the chance to see. Before her shadow had touched the floor – before I was away from the bottom steps of the staircase – I heard my father's footsteps. Boom. Boom. Boom. His feet sounding off on the wooden steps as he came up from his projects in the basement. At the thought of my old man rising from his workshop I headed for my room. Took the steps two at a time and shut myself in. May have pulled the dresser over to keep the door from opening again.

That night I laid in bed and thought about the bridge and the Killing Tree. I thought of the headless bird and my gear. The bag I'd buried under the ivy. Then I thought about the darkness under the deck. All the layers of blackness that were set up one after the other. Each one of them bleeding into the next. Mother was falling into those shadows. She was falling under the deck. She'd stopped screaming. Under the deck she would never scream again. Under the wood planks where the darkness was deep. Deep and for ever. No use screaming.

No one to hear her even if she tried.

Chapter Eight

Oscar Lewiston walked with a limp. He had the kind of body that would beg you to call him husky. He was close to fat but still young enough to lose it through active years. His limp was severe and bent him to the side when he walked. With each step he'd go over, like he was about to topple. Looked like he was hinged at the waist. Put together the wrong way. If he walked fast he looked like he was carrying some serious pain. Must have been a bear for him to deal with it. He got a lot of flak. Picked up a bunch of shit from just about everybody.

At that age most people are straight up with questions. What happened to your arm? What's up with the cast? Where'd you get that scar over your eye? *Wal-mart, you fucking asshole!* Oscar'd get asked all the time about the limp. He'd make this what-the-hell kind of stupid look when he was hit with the question. It was a good look. It brought you down to size. He wanted people to look at him the same way they looked at everyone else. He wanted them to think he was a normal kid. Wanted people to see past the limp.

Only problem with that was once you saw him walk you couldn't imagine him without the bend. While he was sitting down it was even worse. Twice as hard to see him as a normal kid. His legs dangled at different lengths. Like all the times he sat on the bridge with his feet hanging over the side. Feet swaying over the water. He sat with Dean and I'd go off to find stones. I'd look back. Couldn't help but check it out. There they were. Three legs the same and one a good few inches off. You'd see straight away that his right leg was longer than the left. Same length as Dean's. He wasn't built right. Not in his body. Not in his mind.

Me and Dean let Oscar hang out with us. We felt kind of bad for him. If Oscar had made that big a thing about it, about us being his friends, we'd have dropped him. But he didn't. He didn't say anything about being part of our thing. Part of us. He knew it wasn't anything like a group. It was just me and Dean and sometimes the freak with a bad leg. He was just there. Me and Dean would just turn round and there he'd be. Popped up like our shadow. Other times you'd look and he'd have dropped off. Just like he'd disappeared into thin air. It was like walking alone and having a cat come up to you. I've never been a fan of cats. Still, I'd let one walk with me as long as it keeps to itself. Not all cats are happy just to walk. Before long they rub up against you. They ask for something. I've never felt comfortable giving away that something. Never really liked anyone or anything expecting it from me either.

Oz came in handy at times. We took him along some days when we were out for a haul. That's what Dean called it. Took the long walk up the path to Li'l Mel's Convenience. Me and Dean went there to pick up stuff cheap. We'd been at it for a while. Ever since the Yarborough lady got sick. After a few times we figured taking Oscar on would be a safe bet. He'd be there if the brown stuff hit the fan.

This one day all three of us were heading up the path. The sun was out, but it was cool under the trees. Dean started talking to me like he was mafia material. Like he was this crooked conman from the fifties. He hunched himself over and acted like he was smoking a cigar or something. It wasn't like Dean to be so creative. I guess that's why this day sticks out in my head so much. He had this shell that he'd pull over most times. When it was on it was on tight. There wasn't nothing strong enough to shatter Dean's shell. When it came off he really got you.

'You know, Joey. Here we're about to knock off this place and you don't even look hot. You don't look bothered. Why's 'at kid?' Dean had the voice down. It was a wiry thing that he must've picked up from some old movie. Maybe a black and white gangster flick.

Oz laughed and Dean stuck him in the ribs with an elbow. He kind of squealed then went quiet.

'You tell me,' I said to Dean.

''Cause you're good, kid,' he told me. 'You got style and we like that. Listen up, bub. This is the plan. We hit the front of the shop – you first, then me. We got a couple seconds between en-trees. Kapeesh?'

'Yeah.' I was smiling hard by this time. When we walked to school he'd be cut off. I'd try to pull his thoughts out of him, but he wouldn't let go. When he did let go he was amazing. I didn't want it to stop.

'When you're in the store make the move. Hit the magazine aisle. The cashier might look up. Keep cool. Nice and easy, kid. Get a few of them mags. The kind your old man would pull. You know the ones. High-gloss and sexy ladies, my boy.' He'd almost caught himself with this one. His smile got close to breaking out but he held it in. I don't know how he did it. 'Ones with the breastestes 'n bare ass.'

'Right,' I told him.

Oz was howling with laughter, but Dean didn't even give him a glance.

'Taken 'em to the end of the aisle,' he continued. 'By this time I'll hit the door. You'll hear the ratta-tat-tat of the tommy while I pop shots like the Fourth of July.' He made his hands like he was holding a gun. Left hand in front of the right. 'If she's lookin' up I'll mow 'er down.'

'What next, Godfatha?' I asked trying to sound Italian. It was a bad attempt.

81

'Move to the corner. Get up unda the mirror. The security numba. The one the lady tries to spot you in.'

'And?'

'I'll go straight up to that dame. I'll say somethin' to her and drop her on her knees. When she goes down you slip out the door. Don't run, kid. Nice and easy. Rememba that. Always nice and easy.'

It's the way we always did it. Just like Dean said in that Brooklyn accent. But usually Dean wouldn't be so alive on the lead up. He'd walk the path not saying much. He'd have his hands in his pockets watching the path his feet hadn't touched yet. He'd say even less when Oscar was round. He'd clam up and look at me with this real annoyed frown. Whenever Oscar started up on his jokes about fags and blacks Dean'd get real serious. He'd make these sounds in his throat.

'Why's he coming around again?' Dean asked me.

''Cause he can't get away.'

'And that's a good thing?'

'Dean,' I smiled. Maybe I smiled too big, 'cause he looked like he was ready to throw a punch. 'If you're getting chased who do you want with you?'

'No one.'

I kind of agreed with him, but I didn't let on. Instead I tossed another stone from the bridge. It hit the water with a splash.

'You want the slowest fucker around,' I said.

'Why?'

'So the chase ends before it gets to you.'

After that Dean let Oscar come along. He'd still give me the look. He'd still make that noise in his throat when he got mad when Oz showed his idiot side. Bad jokes and politics he'd heard from his dad's mouth. But Dean let things fly. Oscar had a job. Me and Dean both hoped we'd never need him to work it. That day we did it just like Dean's mafia voice said it. It was the way we always did it. Everytime I'd load up and stand under the security mirror. Like I'd heard Mick Drexler say about his old Ford pickup, that mirror wasn't worth a piss in a river. The domed surface was so covered in dust you couldn't see anything through the grey. When I took my place under it Dean came through the door and went up to the counter. Straight up to Yolanda Yarborough. She was shuffling left and right trying to see what I was up to. Where I'd got to.

'Hey, Ms Yarborough,' Dean said. He had this real calm way about him when he was speaking to adults. Even adults like Yolanda. They all seemed to like and trust him. It was all for good reason, I suppose. Good parents, good kid.

'Hi, Dean.' She moved to the right. I could see her just fine from where I was standing. Had a good view from between a couple 2-litre bottles of Diet Pepsi. With her eyesight I could have been in the next aisle. Could've been right in front of the door without being seen. As long as you stayed still she had trouble spotting you. Even though her glasses grew thicker by the month.

'Something wrong, Ms Yarborough?' Dean asked. He was doing his best to hold back a laugh. Yolanda didn't pick up on the vibration in his voice. She stopped shuffling. Kept her eyes on the bottles hiding me.

'You have the papers for my dad?' he asked.

'Ordered papers.' Her head bobbed. Could have been a nod.

'May I have them?' Dean was talking with a hint of shyness in his voice. Guess one part of that voice was genuine, but the other was wickedness. Yolanda was Harris Yarborough's daughter. He sat her on a stool at the counter when he left through the back door to get his lunch. They lived in a house a few hundred yards from the shop. Yolanda sat in the back of the store all day long. Most of the time she knitted. You could hear her needles clicking like a pair of pirates in a swordfight. When she got going she was a machine. Other times she practised reading. She'd sound out the words. Never seemed to get them arranged the way they'd been written on the page.

It was a new thing for Yolanda to take charge of the shop. We'd only started the outings to Li'l Mel's Convenience when Yolanda's old man changed the way he did things. With Harris around we didn't chance any of our raids. He had an eye for thieves. Before you had your hand on the booty he'd have counted the change in your pocket. He had that instinct. Not afraid to confront you and quick to call the cops. He watched the place like a hawk over a mouse. But he changed things and started leaving Yolanda in charge just before springtime. It was only for a few minutes a day and even though he knew a few minutes was all it took to bleed him dry – it was better than the alternative.

Before the change in routine, Harris had been sending Yolanda home for his bagged lunch. She'd skip out and head back with his grub. He'd eat and she'd crack on with her needles. One day she came back just as usual. Dropped his bag on the counter and went back to knitting. Harris finished the afternoon shift and locked up just past six o'clock. He gave Yolanda a bit of extra time to clear her things into her bag. Then he walked her back to the house. They got to the door about the same time. Harris must have followed his daughter, but when he got into the house he pushed her aside hard enough to bash her head into the counter. Out of shock more than anything else. The thump she took cut her scalp open. Good doctors down at Columbia Medical Center stitched her up real nice.

Harris went nutty after seeing his wife on the kitchen floor. He'd also seen the blood – it was all over the place. Ordinarily he took his time with Yolanda. He talked to her in a hushed voice people didn't recognize. Once in a while he just didn't have time for her slow ways. The sight of his wife laid out on the kitchen tiles made him move without thought. Yolanda had been unlucky to be in his way.

Nick Diamond told me he'd heard the blood had splashed up the fridge and on the cabinets too. He said it looked like she'd been whacked around the place with a baseball bat. Then she'd spun round when she was on the floor. Nick Diamond's mom was a paramedic for an ambulance service in Howard County. She'd been on call that day – or so the story goes. She'd gone into the house first. The only people to get there earlier were the police.

It all ended up that Harris's wife Rita Yarborough suffered the first of a series of seizures. When she fell she'd smacked her head on the kitchen floor. Started the blood flowing. Her own convulsions tossed the blood round the room. Yolanda confessed to the police that she knew her mother had been on the kitchen floor. She didn't say anything to her father 'cause she thought it was better to be quiet. Said she was too afraid to tell him or something like that. She thought that somehow she was to blame.

Harris started closing the shop down for lunch during the few weeks following. At first he took Yolanda with him to check on his old lady. The sign out front of the shop read *Back in Half an Hour*. Never said when that half an hour had started. Didn't matter to Harris. He just wanted to make sure things were fine and dandy. But to keep Yolanda from becoming too dependent on others he allowed her to keep an eye on the shop. Before two months had passed Yolanda was in charge. Just a few minutes each day, at midday. But it was all the invite and opportunity we needed.

Most times we'd find J.D. and Ernie MacFarlane kicking at the grass at the side of the shop. They'd hang their heads down and make sure Dean and me were kept out of their conversations. As soon as Harris headed out the back they'd go in and take all they wanted. Yolanda watched them, but she had a thing for J.D. She'd smile and he'd smile back. Sometimes he'd pull something off the shelf for her too. Then the brothers would head off laughing like a couple drunk bums. All they'd stole wide out in the open for anyone to see. Walking along the centre-line of the road.

'That girls got it bad for you, J.D.'

'They all do, Ern,' J.D. would reply. 'They ain't got a choice in the matter.'

Me and Dean would wait by the trashcans at the side of the shop. When Harris was halfway home we'd head inside. Most often we'd wait for J.D. and Ernie to come out first. Dean had this gut feeling that it'd turn ugly if we screwed up their looting. Didn't bother me to wait. Figured they'd appreciate it, even if they never said. Either way it went – with or without the MacFarlanes around – the trips to Li'l Mel's Convenience were the same every time, but it never mattered. Each half-hour was like a new day for Yolanda. Her memory held less than a cracked sieve. Some stuff caught for a moment or two, but it wasn't longer before it was gone with the wind.

'Can I have my father's papers?' Dean repeated.

'Yes. I have them.' Yolanda turned to Dean and placed her hands on the counter. She bit her over-sized lower lip and sucked hard. 'What colour?' she finally said.

'Huh?'

'Which colour are they?' she repeated. 'In what colour?'

She stared at Dean. Like he wasn't even there. Or she was trying to figure out where he'd come from. Then she raised a hand to scratch at her face. Her hands looked incredibly small. Compared to her forearms and wrists they looked like a transplant gone wrong. She had a wide back and a neck that looked too sturdy for her narrow head. All her brown hair was pulled back in a ponytail that sat off-centre at the back of her head. It hung over her left shoulder.

'Hey, everybody,' Oz yelled out. He came in and walked straight up to the magazine aisle. Yolanda watched him with her mouth open and her bottom lip sagging that heavy sag.

'They're papers. Newspapers. Different colours, I guess.' Dean was holding the laugh back.

'They are in a bag. What colour is that bag?' Yolanda was getting frustrated. When she got frustrated she got loud. Sometimes she hit things. Most times it was the counter-top. She'd get riled and slap with an open hand. Brought her palm down hard enough to shake your bones. We'd got her breaking the donations jar on occasion. Whatever was on the counter was a target.

'They're for Gillespie. We live on . . .' he started but didn't get to finish.

The hand landed on the counter with a force that made you wonder how the skin didn't break open and spill out muscle and fat and bone. Dean jumped back. I almost lost the magazines. I'd been trying to shove them down the front of my pants.

'Can't read good. Keep your names,' Yolanda cried out. 'Can't read places. Can't read.' She started shaking. Looking at her I felt this guilt. It didn't come on slow. It just came on. Thought about getting rid of the magazines. Dropping them right there on the floor. Thought about setting the chocolate bars I'd slipped into my pocket back on the shelf. Needed to relieve myself of all that stuff and head out the door. Shifted and caught sight of Oz stuffing a *Playboy* down the front of the pants.

'What colours do you have?' Dean asked.

She ducked under the counter and started calling out colours. Once she was down I went for the door. It was the same way we always did it. The magazines were in the front of my jeans. My shirt pulled over them. When I got outside the feeling of escape came in a rush. Just getting out in the sun felt enough. I even held the door open for Janette Pearsol.

'Thanks, hun,' she'd said passing by. She patted my head.

Yolanda kept reciting colours. Dean stood against the counter waving at me. His smile was so damn wide. He pointed at Oz who was stuffing another skin rag down his Levis. Dean made a face like he wanted the chance to run. He'd got all geared up to leave the gimp behind.

We changed the operation when Oz was around. We could get more stuff. It was both me and Oz stuffing our blue jeans. Oz came along to play the decoy, but it was a bonus when we all came out clear. Best of all, it was a better game then before. More at stake. Me and Dean wanted Oz to get caught. We wanted a running situation. If we had to make a quick dash me and Dean could have made it to the woods. Free and clear. No trouble. From there we could make the trail and be back to the open space in no time. Oz would be lucky to make the front door of the shop.

He never got caught. Neither did we. Rita Yarborough died in mid-May. A sign showed up in the front door one morning. *Closed until further notice. Family bereavement.* It didn't open again.

87

A Seven-Eleven went in at the entrance of Neider Park. Security cameras and three members of staff. Never found the nerve to give it a shot. Even with all the cigarettes and beer the MacFarlanes got out of that place. Dean and me just didn't have the balls.

Chapter Nine

Hampden Academy is built with thick bricks. They've changed colour over the years more times than a chameleon at a traffic light. The walkway leading from the street to the main entrance is covered in corrugated metal. Twelve steel girders hold up the roof. They're now painted a wet looking blue. I stood with Dean each morning by the girder nearest the main door. Back then they were painted yellow. There was always a teacher watching out for trouble. They'd walk up and down on the other side of the glass doors. Coffee mug in hand. The doors were locked until the electric bell rang. Then a warden-like teacher with the coffee mug would use the big ring of keys to open shop. Different members of faculty took turns on morning patrol. Could never figure if they drew short-straws to stand patrol or stay in the staffroom. Most of them got a thrill out of the morning patrol. It was all about control.

Some days Dean got restless. If the weather turned cold, or if the rain fell in at an angle, standing outside could get rough. The roof didn't catch all the rain. Nothing stopped the wind. He'd try to move up close to the doors. It helped with the rain. Some of the wind too. Even when the sun shined standing out there could be uncomfortable. The wind cut under the roof enough to cool you off, but it wasn't enough on the real hot days. Too many bodies in one small space generate a lot of heat. When they'd be bumping up against you to see how much you'll take before you snap the heat mounts up.

What you lookin' at, Pullman? You touchin' my ass, bitch? Wanna piece of this, scarface? That's the kind of thing that came with the shoving. The back packs nudging up against me and Dean. Pushing us into the wall. Shoving us into other angry bodies.

Me and Dean had targets on us. Dean had a target 'cause he was quiet. He was small, easy prey. My target was a different kind. It got bigger each time I fought. If I connected some good shots in a fight my target grew. The more people I hurt the more people wanted a piece of me. Even when I got the shit kicked out of me in a dozen shades of brown the target got twice as big. The number of guys coming after me shrunk when that happened. Of course that made it easier for me to raise up to contender status again.

Catch-22, Pullman. Good ol' Mr Heller told you 'bout that.

Standing up against the girder closest to the main door let Dean breathe easier. The wardens watched us. No matter which one got the straw that day they had their eyes on us. Dean stayed close to my side. I kept eye contact with the member of faculty whenever possible. It was a way for both me and Dean to relax. Someone's watching over you. Of course I never let out that the eyes bothered me.

The electric bell sounded like a fire alarm with a drained battery. It pumped out in high-pitched whines. Short bursts that came in fives. Then a pause. Five more. Pause. It'd scare the piss right out of you. Then it just got annoying. I'm not sure if they've changed it now, but it used to get right up under my skin. The buzzers are mounted above the main entrance doors. It made for a quick entrance after they started whining. Standing under them made your teeth shake out of your jawbone. No one wanted to be out there after they started up.

Some of the faculty liked watching us when the bells started. They'd take their time and enjoy the effects. *How do the animals react to this torture?* When Warden Glenn Shriver had the keys he'd take his precious time. Set his coffee mug down on the display cabinet. Search the big ring for the key. And mosey on over to the doors. Slow as slow can be. All the while the half-dead alarm's ringing overhead.

'Take your time, Mr Shriver.' I mumbled it while going by him most days. Must have heard it all those times and finally he felt that snap on the inside. The snap that makes everything happen in slow motion. His over-sized hand grabbed me. Pulled hard and got me close to him. My feet came off the fresh-waxed floor. He held me against the front door while everyone else passed.

'Good morn'n, ladies and gentlemen,' he said. Groups of smiling faces passed by. 'Keep heading to your classes. I have my hands filled with one smart-ass already. Of course I'll be happy enough to detain more. Give me the option, sweethearts.'

Shriver let me down. My feet hit the floor. His hand still held tight on my shirt.

They stared. All of those bastards coming through the door stared. *Get a good look, assholes.* Faces passed by, slower than usual. Some I recognized. Others just kind of floated past without much of an expression. Nothing for me to recognize. Nothing to catch a hold of. There were the laughs. They came in thick and heavy at times. Jabs got thrown in and hard fingers cut into my ribs. Shriver kept his head turned away. He watched the mass of students herding themselves down the corridor. A smile crept up in the corner of his mouth. He knew about the fingers firing into me. He knew fists knocked into my arm and kidneys. He saw the faces that mouthed warnings. *Gonna get you, Pullman. See you in the locker room, pussy.*

Terry Brewer with his heavy looking nose: *I got you, Pullman.* Lucas Kramer with his expensive Polo shirt: *Poor bitch.* Brent Dreiser, with his premature chin hair, winked at me when he walked by. Brent never spoke because he didn't need to. He'd hit me before. One shot in the back of the head. Thought all my teeth had fallen out when I smashed into the locker.

The flow through the door eased up. Dripped to a single body here and there. Shriver changed his grip. Dropped the wad of shirt and took hold of my arm. Squeezed it until the blood collected around the imprint of his fingers. Pulled me across the lobby with my feet dragging. A member of faculty came out of the glass door leading to the main office.

'Happened here?' the guy asked.

Shriver shook his head.

'You should take it easy on the kid, Glenn.'

Shriver moved faster. Gripped my arm tighter. We walked. I looked up at his face. Caught a good close-up shot of him. Saw he'd nicked himself shaving. He tossed me through the door into his metal shop. Stumbled a few steps and dropped my bag. When I turned to face him he had his legs at shoulder spread. His arms hovered inches away from his sides. In his right hand the keys dangled. Rattled together. They made the sound that only shaking keys can make.

'You got a nerve, son,' he said. 'You have some nerve.'

'Sorry, Mr Shriver. Just wanted to get inside.'

'Bullshit.' He wheeled round and threw the keys to the floor. The metal ring made a twanging sound that resonated for a second. The keys clanged together. Slid along the floor. Disappeared somewhere under the grinder.

'You are a stupid kid, Pullman. You are stupid in the academic sense. You are stupid in the social sense. And what really gets my gristle is your mouth. You keep it shut all the times you need to open it. Then you open it when we all want it shut.'

'Yessir.'

'What is that?' he narrowed his eyes and tilted his head to the side. A thick mound of flesh under his chin touched the collar of his sport jacket. Looked like his head was suspended on an inflatable haemorrhoid cushion.

'You're right. I'm real sorry. Today's been a bad day.'

'It's only just started, Pullman. I could send you into Nemechek's office right now. I can make it the worst day of your life.' The cushion deflated and his head set itself straight on his shoulders.

'Sorry. It won't happen again.'

'Damn right it won't happen again.' He came at me with fast steps. Came right up close to me. Too damn close.

'If you forget about this, just the slightest bit and make a comment like that again, I will come down on you. I will break you into pieces.'

'Yessir.'

'One day, Pullman. One day you will know what respect is. One day you will know the important people. It may take someone to come down on you hard. But when you understand what a little prick you are . . .' He must have used up the rest of his energy holding that fist at my chin. The sound of his voice shut off. *Thank Christ for small favours.* His lower lip shook and looked moist.

He backed off and started looking for the keys. I snatched my bag and shouldered it. Before I'd made it out the door Shriver started talking again. His voice didn't have the same effect. Now it landed on the back of my ears. There was a second I came close to spilling it. Turning round and calling it like it was. Giving it to him straight about the pain in the ass he had become.

Listen up, you fat piece of . . .

I dropped the idea.

The walls of the corridors in Hampden Academy were painted scarlet red. Bare bricks painted with the glossiest paint they could find. I followed the hallway. It led to the guts of a beast. In front of the entrance doors stood the trophy case. Photographs of past athletes and students lined the shelves. A few worn jerseys and pom-poms to make it all seem authentic. The great American dream of stardom – junior high style.

I passed the display case after coming out of the trade wing. It's nothing more than another red hallway. Leads to Shriver's wood and metal shops. Some absurd planning arrangement placed the music suite across the hall from these two rooms. During the day when classes were in motion the sounds that emerged from this wing pulsed. The band saws and wood grinders grunted away. With it came the noise of un-tuned guitars and misplayed trombones.

Like most of the other rooms in the building the main office had been fronted with large windows. The windows of the main office sat on short brick walls. The walls held three large panes of glass. Doors so clear you'd think the word office floated in midair.

When I passed, the secretary looked up. She sat in the centre of the room behind a wide metal desk. She looked small sitting there. A large palm bent in all directions to her left. A mildewed American flag fell limp on a pole to her right. The flag hung on a wooden pole engraved with the name of every American President. The secretary didn't have a nameplate on her desk. All the times I'd been in there I'd listen out for it. People would call out to her, but never used her name. It's kind of like she didn't have one. They didn't think she needed one. As long as she showed up and dug the dirt that needed digging she could stay.

Bring me Joseph Pullman's file. Can you get Social Services on the ringer again? Call Joseph's father. We're all done here. See Joseph back to his classroom.

That's the dirt she dug.

Spent a lot of time in that office. Had trouble staying away. Because of these visits I got to know a lot of things. The soil in the palm's pot was full of tiny white balls. The names of the Presidents on the flagpole didn't have any kind of order. Not alphabetical. Not by year they were in office. Lincoln with Carter. Washington with Taft. That kind of thing. The fish tank with the noisy water pump didn't hold any fish. The ashtray under the No Smoking sign never went empty.

Raised my hand when I passed the main office door. The marks Shriver's hand made on my arm still showed red in places. The secretary didn't raise her hand in reply. I went up the hall. At the row of orange lockers I made a left. The intersection led to different class arenas. That's what the faculty called them. The arenas were large rooms, for the English and Science classes mainly. Some other subjects crept up in the arenas depending on the semester's curriculum. The other arenas were for Mathematics and History.

In the centre of each arena were four classes. English on one side. Science on the other. American Literature and English grammar lectures played along with films on African tree frogs. The films were projected against a white wall. The arenas were large. No partitions separated one subject from the next. The sound of Mrs Bennett's voice carried the writings of Poe and Hawthorne only so far. The chirping of a yellow-spotted frog would suck it straight from the sky.

Like everything else in that place, there was nowhere to hide. Five enclosed classrooms surrounded the arenas. All of these were made of the same half-brick and half-glass walls as the front office. Students made attempts to communicate with one another on the two sides of glass. They used a makeshift sign language. Each group had their own. I never learned any of them.

The classes in the centre arenas caused problems with noise. It was a test of distraction. I was always failing. Before long I was moved to all-enclosed classrooms. Stuck behind glass like a guinea pig. Still, most of the classes breezed by me. Couldn't think straight enough to learn. Didn't see the point in trying. But a few times I made a go. Even in Rhodes' English. I wrote about Poe when we were reading short stories. Turned in a report on *Catcher in the Rye* when she assigned a free-choice report. Christ, I even read four books for a single project. Drew a poster and wrote a report twice the length of any of those stupid assholes in the class. Did she appreciate it? Did it get me anywhere? Not even a second glance. The more I tried the more determined they became to show me I wasn't worth shit. Rhodes blew me out of the water. Every chance she got, she shot me down. They all did. Still, it didn't surprise me. Even when I tried it was a dead effort. If the students weren't bringing me down, Rhodes and her gang of faculty cock-ups came rushing in for a chance.

None of that mattered. I didn't spend much time trying. Never have when there's no point. The forest was still calling me. While the sun cut through the trees, while the stream bubbled with the fast water, I was in a room with people who looked forward to my next public beating. In the forest I was invisible. Indestructible. Under the trees my life was different.

I was in control.

Chapter Ten

The first house on Westchester Drive was owned by the Murtaches. It stood tall and yellow. The paint peeled from seasons of extremes. It looked thin on the front end. On the sides it stretched for what seemed like miles. Early in the morning I'd sit in the bushes beside the Seavers' house. While cars pulled from their driveways – leaving Westchester and Maritime for the city – I watched the Murtache's place. From the Seavers' hedge I saw the whole thing from the side. To me it was incredible.

The place was like it'd been made up of two houses connected by a conference hall. In that middle section there was a pool table. Blue felt and leather pockets. The first pool table I had ever seen that wasn't green. The balls were always racked and set in a perfect triangle. The white ball shined like it'd been dipped in grease. It was lodged against a bumper near a corner pocket. Looked just like it was waiting for someone to come back. Make the break. A black cue-stick leaned against the table on the far side.

Although the paint crumbled in places round the windows, the house still looked like a shrine. Frozen in a moment. Mr Murtache lived in the house with his wife and pet dog. He treated that dog like it was more than an animal. The wide yard that surrounded the house was never overgrown. He was always out in the hottest part of the day sitting on his big riding lawnmower. The days after he cut the grass were the best time to watch the house. Deep in the Seavers' bushes I could smell the cut lawn. I'd pick up clumps of the wet green and mash it in my fingers. When Mr Murtache passed through the room with the pool table I froze up. He almost caught me once. Maybe he did see me, but he didn't stop. Didn't make the slightest motion toward me. He just looked at me and went on like nothing was wrong. Just like nothing was out of place.

By the time my family moved to Maritime the Murtaches had been through some hard years. Found out about it all from listening in. Doing that voyeur bit. Cutting in on the conversations my mother had with Helle Bishop. Helle came round to the house when she saw my father's car pull away in the mornings. At first I wondered if she was just lucky to miss my old man. Each time she visited he'd already headed out to the office. But she was a sly woman. I wrote about her in my journal:

Helle Bishop . . . Nmbr. 101. WCD.
Visits Mother in mornings. Been in
neighbourhood for years. Wants to know
about family. Asks about my father.
Mother cries when she leaves. 101 is
made of wood. Very flammable.

My father shuffled around downstairs. Getting ready to leave. He was yelling and growling about things. *Car's low on gas. Late again. Never have money. Feel sick on Mondays.* His usual start. I sat in the study and held the telescope up to my eye. Watched the windows of the Bishops' house. It was a single storey Victorian that sat directly across the street. Just when our garage door started to go up the Bishops' curtain twitched. Helle Bishop's nose poked out from behind white lace. Moved her head out and looked up and down the street. When my old man's car made it to the street she'd pulled aside the curtain. Stood there in the window like a whore in Amsterdam. Some days she just pulled the curtain tight around her neck and turned into an old Jew or a gypsy woman.

After my father's car was out of sight I'd count out how long it took her to hit the pavement. *One-Mississippi. Two-Mississippi. Three-Mississip* . . . Most I ever got to was sixty-five seconds. She'd have her front door opened and closed. She'd be patting out the creases in her skirt before a minute and a half were up. Waddling across the street with her macramé handbag swaying heavily in her right hand. A saran-wrapped mound of baked goods balanced in her left.

Then she'd ring the bell. Wait. Listening with her head close to the door. Ring again and wait. Sometimes Mother would test her patience. But Helle had plenty in reserve. Mother must have known this too. After a while she'd give in. She never got away from Helle Bishop. No one did. She'd come in and set up shop. Talk too loud and show too much interest in what my father did for a living. Asked too many questions about how we liked the neighbourhood. *How's Joseph doing at H.A.? Isn't it a wonderful school?*

Then the stories would start. It was a tough build-up. Like bad trailers for shit films, but the feature presentation was usually worth the wait.

'The last sixteen years have been a kick in the short pants for sweet old Leo. I'll tell you. God love the man for still breathing.' That was what Helle said to my mother. I couldn't see my mother's reaction to this. I'd sat at the top of the stairs. Sat on the centre of the top step. Never had the intention of being seen. Whenever the conversation stalled I sank my head into the pages of a magazine. Can't remember which magazine it was. Must have been *National Geographic* or *Time*. One my father had left on the desk in his study. They were the only ones my father ever brought home. Sometimes he had boat and car magazines.

There was this fear that my mother would appear at the

bottom of the stairs. Think I'd been eavesdropping. Give me one of those looks. Maybe say something short that would cut deep. *Enjoy the conversation, Joe? What's your father going to think about you snooping around?* Thought about it so much I almost gave up. Almost went back to my room. Maybe would have sat with the radio on. Looked at the books with the madwomen. But I stayed. Somehow it was worth the risk.

Their conversations were one-sided. Mother would respond with a shy laugh. Sometimes she'd throw in an 'Oh, my.' Didn't offer much of her own thoughts. Maybe she figured it wasn't her place to speak about the people of Westchester Drive. Leave it all to those who know. Could have been she just wanted to listen and learn. May have even thought Mrs Bishop was a deviant old bitch who couldn't keep to herself. Same as I thought of her. Still, she came and she talked. Mother listened and brought drinks.

It could have been that Mother kept quiet because we weren't really members of the neighbourhood. Not just then. Not yet anyway. We were new and new people get stuck on a probationary period. Expectations are you settle in and make the house your own. While you're painting and pruning the neighbours are busy with the initiation. People get to figure you out and talk amongst themselves. That's why there's so much curtain flapping. *There's that kid again. Look at him picking through the Bishops' trashcan. Can't his father control him? That mother of his doesn't come out much.* After they've figured us out they move in and ask questions. They find out who was right about what. Only there's no winner in gossip. Just a new family investigated and interrogated, ready to take part in welcoming the arrival of the next poor bastard.

It's something that takes a lot of work. A lot of time. Unfortunately for my mother she never had that much time. Even if she did, she didn't have the drive to adapt. It was almost spring when Helle Bishop started calling in to speak with Mother. The weather was warming up. By April my mother would be taken away.

100

Helle continued to tell my mother about the Murtaches. She'd spoken about every other family on the street. It was from listening to these conversations that I learned the Murtaches once had a son. He'd been in a special military division. Mrs Bishop couldn't remember what branch of the forces he had been in. Still, just the idea that he had been a soldier made him sound daring. A lost hero. A killer of men. Mrs Bishop spoke in a quiet voice. Almost like she knew I was listening in. She told my mother that the Murtache boy had been killed somewhere in South America. He was only nineteen. They didn't bring all of him back home.

'Oh, it was such a shame when Christian was killed. All the street knew about it before Leonidas did. Poor man was away on business. Most everybody on the street was out on the porches that day. It was blistering hot and the sun felt like it was riding your shoulders if you weren't in the shade,' Helle was saying. 'I was relaxing on the tree-swing Alfred had put up in the big oak tree out front. The tree's still there, you know. The swing went weak with all the rain over the years. The bench broke in two when the boys were on it one summer. Thank the Lord above they didn't hurt themselves worse than they did. My Ricky had to get stitches in his cheek. He fell straight through it. Head first. That boy's a crackerjack. Was a crackerjack. Good man now.' Her voice was trailing off. Teacups rustled and clanked against my mother's marble coffee table.

'Would you like some more?' my mother asked. 'I can make a fresh pot.'

'No, dear. I'm fine.'

I felt a sense of guilt while I waited for Helle to start up again. Had this burning sense of urgency. Needed her to keep at it. Go to where she'd left off. There was this need to hear her telling about Christian Murtache. A long silence came. I didn't know what was happening down in that room. Mother would never have sat idle with a stranger in a small space. Helle Bishop was still a stranger. Mother was always moving around and touching ornaments and figurines, forever shifting things from one place to another and back again. She stood near the window looking out at times. Even then you could still hear her moving stuff. Couldn't keep her hands still. She'd get a hold of the leaves of the palm tree while she stared into the street. She'd rub each one of those leaves until you thought the colour would come off in her hands.

'How did you know the Murtache boy was dead?' my mother finally asked. Her voice was soft and cut into the silence like a child's voice coming from a dark room.

'We were all outside when the military men came. They pulled up to give Agnes the news. My Alfred was mowing the yard and as soon as he saw the black car roll up onto the Murtache driveway he killed the engine. He yelled over to me that something was wrong with Christian. He said the military doesn't dress up and make house calls when a soldier gets a medal.'

'Oh, dear.'

'That's what I said, darlin'. Then we all started walking up the street. Not just me and Alf, but everybody. The Jessups were in this house back then. They both came out and met us walking up. Even Sally Rosenthal, she don't show much face now and didn't back then neither, but she caught us up and we all went to the Murtache house together. Back then we knew everyone in all the houses. We were close, you know. It's not like nowadays where people move every two or three years. Most of us were born here or close by anyway.'

'Oh, yes.'

'Don't feel like you don't belong, dear. We're glad as a bunch of monkeys you're here.'

'Did you speak to Agnes that same day?' Mother asked.

'Well, we saw her. We didn't speak to her and I think that was a good thing. She must have seen the car pull into her drive because she came rushing out the front door. Still had on a cleaning scarf around her head. She screamed and hollered. The men in military dress looked stiff getting out of the car. They took a moment straightening themselves when she came out into the yard. Both of those men looked round like they were expecting a war. I suppose they were getting one. Agnes fell into her daffodils and slapped all the heads off that she could get her hands to.'

'How did he die?' I whispered.

There was another moment of silence. A dead lapse in the conversation. This time no cups stirred. My mother didn't offer to make anything this time. There was movement. It was my mother clearing the tray from the table. She excused herself for having things she needed to do around the house. With a loud laugh and an apology Helle Bishop said her farewells and left. That day my mother walked around the house watering all of the plants over and over again. Some were watered six or seven times. The pools of water collected on the carpets. Left dark round patches that she never cleared up.

Helle came back. She was the kind of woman that could never stay away. She'd started on the Murtaches and never got the chance to finish. They were the last family on the street that Helle had to fill Mother in on. From those conversations I learned that Leonidas and his wife had been unable to conceive another child. Christian had been a difficult pregnancy. Tore up a bunch of stuff inside Agnes. Helle didn't seem old enough to know all that she told my mother. Still, she had a bunch of dirt she'd dug up along the way. Must have figured Mother was the best place to dump it.

'Me and my mother, God rest her tired old soul, went down and sat with Agnes after she got back from the hospital.' Helle spoke softly again, but there was a liveliness in her voice. 'She had been admitted after her third miscarriage. At that time Christian was four, I guess. I remember him sitting on the couch watching the television screen. The cartoons were on. He was a fat little thing and I tell you that he was content with the world. Anytime when you left him with Bugs and Daffy he was all giggles and hiccups. But poor Agnes just cried herself sick.'

Helle told my mother that her husband had spoken to Leonidas after Agnes became ill.

'Men don't offer sympathy about that kind of thing,' she said.

'I was so upset with Alf at that time. He spoke to Leonidas almost every day. Whenever Leo was outside or passing in the car, Alf would stop him and have a word or two. But he never did find out what was going on in that house. We all sat and wondered what was happening. Agnes was nowhere to be seen. The garden started to die off. When we went up to the house asking for her Leo would tell us she was resting.'

'It's sometimes good not to know,' my mother said.

'But we're all neighbours. We're all in it together.'

'Things aren't always that simple.'

Helle must have got used to Mother not responding. She went on as if she hadn't heard my mother:

'Alfred did say that Leonidas was worried for Agnes. Told me that Leonidas was talking about quitting his job so he could stay home and look after her. Make sure she didn't do anything . . . you know.' Helle blew her nose and for some reason I was angry she'd paused in the middle of her story. 'He did stay home for a while. But toward the end of that summer he went back to travelling. She seemed like she was all right when we finally saw her. It was less frequent, you understand. But she came outside and stood in the sun. We waved to one another. But we didn't talk all that much. No one seemed to make much of an effort. No one went out of their way to talk to her any more. We watched her when she came out of the house and made sure she seemed normal. Everything was fine until one of the boys found the shells she'd been collecting. They were all strung up with thread. Pushed the needle right through and lined those shells up side by side. Just like you do with popcorn to hang on a Christmas tree.'

'What shells?' my mother asked.

'The cicada shells. That was the last summer they came. 1970.'

'Oh, my.' Mother was quiet for a moment. She cleared her throat. I knew it was Mother because she had this real quiet way of clearing her throat. Kind of like she did it just for show.

'I'm not familiar with cicadas,' my mother said. Like she was frightened of what she was about to be told.

'Oh, darlin'. You'll be seeing them soon enough. They'll be here before you know it. Then you'll be an expert on them little things. Just like the rest of us.'

Mother picked up where I needed her most.

'I don't understand,' she said.

'This is the cicada summer, dear,' Helle said. 'They come every seventeen years.' She let out an excited laugh. 'It's a cycle.'

Chapter Eleven

The brothers always walked round town with a certainty in their stride. It's a prowess that comes when people know what they're doing. They knew they were doing it well. Their motives didn't matter a damn. They moved with style and spoke with confidence. Laughed with the ease and echo of giants. They both had a swagger that aided the other's strut. Didn't seem to care what people thought. They went around with a flair that made you stop and watch. The pair played a cool-show come to life. You couldn't wait for what would happen next when they were around. People tried to stop them, just to talk. Sheriff Wilcox tried to make friends with them, but the brothers wouldn't have any of that. They had each other and that was all the company they needed. They were able to walk with pride in a duo of confidence.

They lived in a house in the old section of town. I think The Lakes is what the neigbourhood was called. The area where the houses were owned by retired people who manicured their lawns on a daily basis. Topiary bushes and garden sprinklers were on constant display. Such attention to detail didn't seem to fit the image of J.D. and Ernie. The brothers moved down the yellow line in the centre of the road. Cigarette-worn voices called from porches telling them to use the sidewalk. The two would nod for show and continue as they were. Tradition had passed those two by. Their elders were people who had been unlucky enough to live too soon. The brothers couldn't give much of a damn about times that had been and gone. It was only now and this was their time.

They had just come into possession of a beaten-up Indian motorcycle when I finally got to meet them properly. All the times before it was just holding a hand up when Dean and me passed by. Never really got much of a reaction from either of the two. Sometimes Ernie would show me his middle finger. J.D. would just shake his head and look away. Dean had a problem with the way they cut us off like that. He didn't like it when people made him feel as insignificant as he really was.

'Just who the hell do they think they are anyway?' he asked me one morning. Ernie was heated about something and when I waved he stood from the church steps and threw a glass Coke bottle. It smashed on the sidewalk on the other side of the road. Didn't even get close to us and still Dean got upset about it.

'Don't get yourself worked up, Dean.'

'Alls you do is wave. They never wave back.' He went quiet for a minute. 'Should just give up.'

'Why?'

''Cause they don't want anything to do with you. What's the point, Pullman? Make yourself look like a dick.'

'They'll remember me.'

'When?' he asked.

'When I need them to.'

That conversation jumped into my head when I saw J.D. and Ernie on the back of that old motorcycle. It was never clear where they got the thing. It had a bad engine. Rust grew over the silver gas tank like lichen on a battered rock. If the engine died while they were stopped it took them hell and all trying to get the thing going again. The bike was covered in dents and smelled of black oil that dripped from it in steady streams. Cobwebs grew between the spokes and the seat was covered in strips of duct-tape to keep the foam pad from falling away.

They ran it up and down Grant's Road. It was the least busy of the streets in town. Although Grant's was the main road that side of Maritime most of the housing developments had gone up across town. Suburbs closer to the Grant's junction with State Road Nine. Up as far as Westchester Drive there was nothing for people to see. Being so dead no one came down that way unless they were heading for Kilverston's Farm. After the farm's entrance there was a spider of dirt roads that eventually made it somewhere. Never really took the time to figure where they all ended up. Young people used the stretch of Grant's Road from the state road junction to the Kilverston place when learning to drive. Late at night you could hear the sounds of car engines revving as the racers took off in competition.

There was always a handful of deaths at the bottom of the hill. The road bent at a right angle down there. The trees had been cut away by out-of-control cars. County crews built a barrier on the curve just after we moved to Maritime. A month later it was being repaired. Another car had run through it. The driver was badly injured, but lived. Lost a limb or something – that's what the word was, anyway. Could have been suburban myth.

Hunting for answers I would walk through the woods with Dean and Oscar. We spread out looking for pieces of glass and metal. Collected anything that had been knocked away during the accidents. We dug a hole that we dropped the found pieces in. Those outings stopped when Oscar found a shoe. It was rimmed with red crust on the ankle support. We all thought it would be best to stop then and there. Quit before we found a head or leg or some such thing.

J.D. and Ernie were the kind that raced the cars that crashed. It was their belief that the crash would never happen that made them shine. It wasn't that they thought themselves to be indestructible. It was much more simple than that. They just never thought about the crash.

If it can't happen there's no point frettin' about it. Nothing at all to worry about.

They were too young to drive the motorcycle legally. But then there was no one trying to stop them either. I'd been coming up Westchester Drive, away from my father's house, when I heard the bike. I'd decided to take Grant's Road to Dean's that day. My old man was mowing the lawn and I didn't want him to see me go off into the forest. So while he was hidden on the other side of the house I took off for the top of Westchester Drive. Thought of my old man's pounding feet working on the road behind me brought chills to my sweating skin. I snapped out of it when I caught the sound of the bike. The engine made a rattling noise like a bomb just before it detonates. I made it to Grant's Road as the brothers shot by in a grey and black streak. J.D. was steering the thing and Ernie was on the back. He held onto J.D.'s waist. Both of them bent into the wind and smiled like they'd beat the world.

I stood at the side of Grant's Road watching them go. They made it to the bottom of the hill, and J.D. saw the bend in time to mash the brakes. The bike skidded and J.D. struggled with it. The beast threatened to go down, but they worked together and kept it up. With the bike stopped J.D. yelled out as he tried to turn it around. He grunted and swore. Even from my distance up the hill and the hammering of the engine his voice was strong.

'Come on you old bitch!' he yelled. 'Move dammit!'

Ernie sat on the back with his hands now on his own hips. Looked into the trees where the crashed cars fell. When the bike was aimed up the hill J.D. twisted the throttle again. Tucked his chin close to the handlebar. Ernie wrapped himself around his brother's waist. The front wheel edged off the gravel. The bike screamed and J.D. dropped it to second. The tyre licked at the gravel and came back up. He had it controlled like a wild horse. They picked up speed while climbing the hill. Moving. Moving. Faster as they roared back up toward me. They made it up the incline in a flash. The engine struggled to keep up.

When they passed I'd got up close to the road. Stood out in the open where they'd see me waiting. Standing with my hands in my pockets. I nodded my head at them. It was a slight movement, one that they would never have noticed with the speed they were going. It made me feel important making the effort. They disappeared where the road bent behind a cluster of trees. The sounds of the bike died out. I could hear cats fighting in the distance. A police siren somewhere on the other side of town. Then the bike roared and made it around the curve of trees. It shot past me again.

Each time they went by they would offer a little more attention my way. They attempted more speed each time they ran the course. The skids at the bottom of the hill stretched longer and blacker. J.D.'s confidence grew with the black lines of burned rubber he left on the asphalt.

There was a liveliness that radiated from the brothers that I couldn't stop craving. I wanted to be like them and do daring things. Wanted to jump before I thought of how far I may fall. Suddenly there was a need to perform uncalculated acts of mischief. Ernie and J.D. were legendary in the school for telling dirty jokes. They would sit on the steps of St Paul's Church on Victoria Street when their brother Russ was home. Visiting from his travels. They'd sit and smoke cigarettes and set fire to their farts with butane lighters. There was a rumour going around that J.D. had almost burned the church down on one of his turns.

I was blown away at their gall. Envious of their self-reliance. They were everything I wasn't and I was desperate to become one of them.

When the bike came roaring down the road toward me J.D. had his head down low. He looked tough, like he was fighting the wind and winning. His curly blond hair bounced spastically on his head and his eyes were smashed into narrow slits. Behind him sat Ernie, clutched tight and grinning. A cigarette was hanging from the side of his mouth. His dark hair floated high and wide. When they got near the wind took his cigarette away with an invisible and lightning-fast hand. Ernie looked back like he thought himself quick enough to catch it. Must have shifted his weight because the bike swerved to the left.

For a second the tyre aimed at me. J.D.'s face grew long. He sat himself straight up. Leaned to the right and Ernie, gripping with locked arms, went with him. The bike shot across the road. The front tyre ate at the gravel emergency lane. When J.D. squeezed the brakes it slid sideways. Dropped a few inches from the gravel and found the soft grass. When the back tyre hit the emergency rail the bike stopped. The front wheel twisted and the two brothers went into the air. The momentum sent them off onto the grassy bank.

J.D. flew out with his hands and feet spread wide. Ernie came off curled-up and flipping all the way over. He spun once and opened up from the curl before he hit the ground. When they landed they made almost no noise. The ground was wet from the rain that had been falling. Both of the brothers lay at the end of muddy streaks and crushed blades of grass.

I ran across the road after looking both ways for traffic. The front wheel of the bike was still spinning slowly. A dull grumbling sound was humming in the engine. I stood by the bike for a minute while I listened for the brothers. Waiting for either of them to make some kind of indication. Give me an idea of the injuries they'd suffered. J.D. was the first to sit up. He swatted at the arm of his leather jacket then ran a finger around the inside of his mouth. When he pulled his finger out he looked at it and seemed satisfied. The high grass where Ernie lay began to move. Then a groan started up. First it came low and almost soft. Then it grew in anger and pain.

'Oh, Jesus,' Ernie finally yelled out. 'Oh, my Jesus!'

'What is it?' J.D. asked. 'Ern?' He had a hint of concern in his voice that may have been full-on worry if I hadn't been there. Still it was hard to imagine. I looked on from the side of the road and felt like I was intruding.

'You guys need an ambulance?' I asked.

'No,' J.D. said.

'Yeah,' came the voice from the high grass. 'I need one quick.'

J.D. got up with a grunt and walked over to the crumpled shape at the end of scarred ground. Ernie rolled one way and then the other. J.D. stood next to his brother and kept bending his knee like he needed to make sure it still worked. Ernie's movements slowed up. Moved more tentative. J.D. kind of surveyed the area around him and kept bending his knee.

'I'm bleeding, Doug,' Ernie said.

'No you're not,' J.D. said. 'C'mon. Let's get out of here.'

'Yeah, I am.' Ernie let out this high-pitched moan. 'Real bad.'

'There's no blood, Ern.' J.D. cleared his nose and spat into the woods. 'I'm lookin' and there ain't no blood.'

Ernie's head popped out of the bushes. His black hair was sprouting long strands of dried grass. A streak of dirt ran from his left cheek to his chin where a clump of mud hung. As J.D. leaned down close to the grass, Ernie sat up farther. He was holding a hand with splayed fingers over his chest.

'I'm bleedin' on the inside!' he cried.

'I'll get someone to call for help,' I yelled. Even turned to run.

'No!' J.D. had a voice that could cut down a buffalo if his mouth was aimed at it. 'He's just bruised. He's had worse.'

'I ain't never had pain like this,' Ernie said.

'Come on. Get up.' J.D. spun on his feet and started toward the bike. I stepped away from the back wheel and positioned myself out of his way. As he passed me I could smell the cigarettes he and Ernie had been smoking that day. The two spent the mornings sitting on the steps of the Mormon church on Merchiston Avenue. They'd just sit and smoke those cheap cigarettes they ripped off from Li'l Mel's Convenience. Without Russ they wouldn't have tried their usual game. In the absence of the older brother they were pretty mellow. Even opted for the Mormon church over St Paul's when it was just the two of them. Still they always left their cigarette butts scattered on the steps for someone else to sweep away.

'Damn,' J.D. breathed, looking down at the bike. 'That ain't good.'

Ernie was slow getting himself out of the grass. He made a lot of noise. Then he rubbed at his jacket like all it was covered in was a few stray lint balls. When he finally stood he had a streak of mud running the length of his back. I fought the urge to tell him. He seemed content thinking he had dusted himself to look like new again.

'The fork's bent,' J.D. said.

Ernie walked around to the front of the bike. They looked down at the wheel and seemed mesmerized at the motion it was still making. Ernie ran his fingers through his black hair. It fell into place and looked respectable. He made a few attempts to stretch out his back. J.D. rubbed his hands together and kicked at the front tyre.

'Who's Doug?' I asked. My voice jumped out of my mouth and seemed too loud.

When the brothers looked up at me I felt just like I'd thrown a low blow and missed. They stared straight at me for a second. Then in unison turned to each other. Gave that questioning look people were always using round me.

'When you was laying down in the grass you said Doug,' I offered.

Ernie looked at me again. He made a popping sound with his tongue and went to scratch his chin. His fingers found the clump of mud and pulled it away. With his other hand he made a hasty pass over his cheek. He had no success at moving the streak of dirt that marked him.

'Yeah. He's Doug.' He nodded his head in the direction of his brother.

'I thought your name was J.D.,' I said.

'Yeah, it is. James Douglas.'

'J.D. for short.' Ernie seemed pleased to clarify his brother's identity.

'I'm Joseph,' I said.

'Yeah, we know.' They did everything together. Even echoed in the same bored voice.

Still I felt good that the brothers knew me. Had heard about me from somewhere along the way. It somehow confirmed that I was something more than a waste of space. I left them at the side of the road that day. They were still looking down at the bike. Ernie said something to J.D. as I was walking away. It may have been something about me. It could have been about the wreck they just had. Whatever it was it set them both laughing. J.D. in his short, deep bursts of heavy air and Ernie with a high-pitched honk. I found I could make the same sound if I sucked in big gulps of air while clenching my throat. I did it while I was alone in the forest because it sounded funny and was some-thing different. Forgot myself once and did it in front of Ernie. He punched me in the arm hard enough for me to remember never to do it again.

Chapter Twelve

I kept my father's psychology book under my mattress. Took it out more often when the spring storms grew heavy. Most of the time I spent looking at the page with that woman. One in the guy's sports jacket. I already had the image in my head. Vivid as I could remember it. Still I kept checking. Just needed to see if I'd missed something all the times I'd looked at it before. After a few weeks of having the book the pages had worn from the sweat of my fingers. By March they were bent and wrinkled from my constant searching. A coloured tab stuck out almost halfway through the book. I'd placed it there to make it easy to flip open to that woman. It gave me reassurance. As the spring moved toward summer I felt the need to make sure it wasn't my mother on the page. Even if it had been I'm not sure I would've known.

Never saw my mother much after the bad fits took hold of her. Spring started and she stayed hidden away. She'd float round the house. I'd hear her feet swishing over the carpet. The quiet creak of the stairs when she went down to the kitchen. Her loud breathing when she made it back up the stairs. The way she shut her bedroom door. She went with almost no sound, like I wasn't supposed to know she'd ever left. Couldn't help but wonder if she was being kept inside that room. Had a feeling that she was a kind of prisoner. Confined to her room by either her own weak mind or by my old man.

He'd keep me in line when he was home. Off at work he was still present. That feeling like he was watching. He knew where I'd been and what I'd seen. There was even a feeling like he knew where I was looking. When I felt safe in the house there would be a reminder. His tennis shoes sitting in the corner of the room. One of his jackets hung over the back of a chair. His leather driving gloves that he never took in the car. The knuckles worn out of both hands.

He was always present.

He'll never stop watching you, Joe.

Mother stayed hidden when he was away. When he came home she'd remain out of sight. Back in that room she'd cry. The screaming stopped, but she'd go to pieces now and again. She'd call out names most of the time. They sounded like names anyway. I couldn't keep hanging round to listen out for them. They never came with any regularity. Kind of like a cough in the summer. Only comes when the pollen gets bad.

When he was home my old man acted as an usher. He'd come out ahead of her like some Indian scout making sure the trail was clear. I was good at keeping away from him. Sometimes he came up on me without warning. Moved at times without a sound. I'd just look up and there he'd be. Feet spread and those hard hands of his dangling at his side. Staring me down with eyes that looked too black.

'Clear the hell out of here,' he'd say.

'Yessir.'

'Leave the shit, Joe. Move your ass.'

I'd leave without a fuss. Sometimes worried I seemed too eager to go.

Sitting in my room reading through a few pages of the newspaper took up the hours. The articles ate through the day a few minutes at a time. I'd stolen them from my father's den. Turned the pages over and listened to my old man while he was speaking. There were long pauses when his voice died. Then it would start

116

up again. The changing of seasons brought heavy rains. The sun didn't come through much and it all started to have an effect on him. His voice got deeper. Once in a while he'd cough real heavy and his voice would smooth out a bit. Most of the time he just talked with a rubbery kind of grumble. Sounded kind of like an old car engine needing a good tuning.

The way his voice stopped and started I figured it was some kind of conversation. Since I could only hear his voice I thought at first it was a telephone call. The office checking up on him, maybe. Mr Moon calling to find out the scoop on the Pullman family. *How's the wife? Coming in today? Still work here?* Then I heard some of what my old man was saying in those one-sided conversations. Knew the person he spoke to didn't have a phone to her ear.

'If you're not going to get on with things . . .' He paused. 'Fuck it then. Just get it over with.' His angry voice had come to town. His storms were building. It was safer to stay shut in behind my bedroom door. Lowered my head to the paper and read with a forced interest. Maritime's Morgan High football team had a new head coach. An arsonist was setting small fires round the town. Wild Lake was closed to swimmers until chemical tests were carried out.

'Dammit, help me out here,' my old man yelled.

Shoved the newspapers under the bed in case my father decided to make a dash for my room. It didn't seem like he'd have any reason to do that kind of thing. But then he did a lot of things around that time you'd figure he didn't have a calling for. He'd emptied the plant pots throughout the house, for one. I'd gone downstairs one morning thinking things were the same as the day before. Gone to the kitchen and found the macramé hanger with no plant inside. The butterfly plant Mother had shined every Tuesday with a swipe of mayonnaise on a piece of paper towel. It was gone. Nothing of it left behind. He'd dumped the plant and cleaned the pot. Mother could never have done it. Never got out of her bedroom long enough.

After seeing the empty pot I figured something was up. Drank

117

my water and went through the house ready to go back up the stairs. Stopped when I got to the bottom step. In the living room the pots all sat on the usual stands. Each pot glowed. Clean as clean can be. They'd all been emptied and wiped out. The ones at the window sat on placemats and looked like something you'd find in a gallery. The pots on the other side of the room were sitting on the end tables. No placemats underneath. It looked good. I thought everything seemed fresh. It didn't hit me that things weren't the way they needed to be. For a minute it just looked like things had got back to normal – if they'd ever been normal before.

Mother's better, I told myself. She's come down and fixed it all like new. Then I heard the sound of my old man's drills. A screaming machine working up from the basement. My fear set in. The sound drove into me a heavy anxiety. A realization that things weren't okay. The realization that wasting time imagining the brighter side will only leave you a sitting duck for the trouble that's present.

They're empty, Joey. Can't you see things aren't perfect. Times are a changin', son.

The Areca Palm in the corner. The Pothos that hung down over the side of the brass stand. The African Violets. All the plants that I never took interest in. Plants Mother cared for daily. Shined the leaves. Pulled off dead pieces. Fed and watered on a tight schedule. Jesus, they were all gone. The pots stood in place – empty and shining and hollow.

The drill screamed again.

Momma ain't cleaning up the pieces any more. You're all alone, kiddo.

There was a knock at the door. I turned my head and saw shapes of colour broken in the glass of the side window. Waited for another knock. Frozen in place. Helle Bishop's large head moved toward the window. It was broken into shapes in the glass, but I knew it was Helle. She moved away from the glass and knocked on the door again.

The drill screamed.

I ran up the steps two at a time.

At my bedroom door I couldn't hear my old man's voice. His one-sided conversation had finished. I gave it time. Waited a few minutes. Kept my breathing quiet so I wouldn't miss him. Helle tried the door again and gave up. She gave up for that day and all the other days. I didn't see her near the house again. She didn't come by to speak with Mother after that.

Once in a while my old man would just shut off. That was usual. But he wouldn't go quiet for long. Just gave me enough quiet to let the fear sink in. *He's behind you, kiddo. Don't look now.* Then the machines would start up. The screeching whirl of his drill or the maddening thump of his hammers would let me know he'd got to the basement. Or his voice would break into the air like a ghost from nowhere. Maybe yell like he'd brought a knife down on his knuckles. The rains of spring had brought the blessing of a bad cold. He coughed with a frequency that reassured me he wasn't in my closet. *He's in the bathroom, Joe. He's down the hall. No, he's in the basement now. Up in the attic, kiddo.* He didn't have the ability to sneak around. The cough sounded off like a foghorn. Came when I needed it.

I'd spent most of the day in my room looking through books. Flipping through the newspaper and trying to sleep. Sometimes sleep came. I'd nod off and come to with a jerk like someone had hooked me up with a bolt of electricity. Laying there, fresh from sleep, was the worst of it all. What did I miss? He could be anywhere now. So I listened and waited. Nothing came back to me. The house had died.

It was in times like these that I considered most the idea of braving the rain and heading to Dean's place. It was the rain that was keeping me in my old man's house. It'd shut the school down for almost two weeks that year. The roads flooded and the buses couldn't make the rounds. With the extra time off I found I didn't need school. I thought more freely outside its walls. But I did need to get away. Dean's place was the only option. The trouble was facing his mother. I didn't know her all that well. Still had a fear that she'd ask questions about my family. Didn't

119

know how much Dean had told her about my parents.

His dad beats him pretty good. His mother sits in her room and cries her head off. Joe thinks she's going to kill herself one of these days. After that his dad'll probably . . .

Just thinking about Dean and his mom talking about my family got under my skin. It's always easy to look in on a situation and wonder how come it can't be fixed. Dean came from a good family. He'd only tasted the sweet side of life. Folks like him can't get a handle on the difficulty of breaking a bad mould.

Before long I couldn't bear the silence. My throat felt raw while I took small breaths. I laid there and listened and heard nothing on the other side of my door. I knew I couldn't afford to come down with something. My old man's cough played on my mind. The thought of asking Dean's mother to take me to the doctor gave me a weak feeling. *You're better than that. You're no pussy. You're not like Dean. Harden up, Joe. Keep it together.* Hopped from the bed and walked out into the hallway. Only this time I didn't listen at the door. Just went out like I'd entered a place where I was welcome. Followed the pain in my throat and the popping in my ears. Had to get something before it got worse. Opened the door and out I stepped. Never had a warning someone was out there. Never gave a warning that I was leaving my room. Both of my feet stood firm on the middle of the hall carpet before I realized my mistake. Couldn't even decide if I should go back. Never had the time.

A few feet away from me stood my father. He looked shocked. Looked caught and tired. He held both of Mother's thin wrists with his right hand. His left arm curved round her, bracing her weight. Squeezing at the side to keep her from falling. I hadn't seen my mother for more than a week. She looked like she'd aged a lifetime.

'Get out of the fucking hall,' my father said. His words crunched inside his throat. He started to cough. It got deep in his chest and made a loose wet sound the more he hacked. My stillness at that moment didn't come as an act of defiance. It came for the same reason deer get cut down on the highway.

120

They see the cars coming and hear the horns and the tyres screaming. It's that second of shock that lasts for hours. Awed. Bewildered. I stood there, stunned by the sight of what my father held in his arms. The frail woman hung without a breath. She still held some resemblance to my mother, but it wasn't her. Mother had left that thing. She'd slipped out of that skin long ago. She'd escaped in all the screaming of her fits. Got out while everyone looked away.

'Things alright?' I asked. Mesmerized and frozen by the sight of Mother's empty shell. Her limp figure curled to the side like a bag of bones. Leaning in over my father's heavy arm. His hand holding her side had turned white from the pressure on his fingers. I half expected her feet to be off the carpet with the grip he had. A disappointment rumbled inside me when I saw the slippers touching down with each step.

'Trouble your middle name, hotshot?' Father coughed again. His eyes remained focused on my mother's jaw.

'Just making sure she's all . . .'

'See the problems?' he yelled into my mother's ear. 'See all the things I'm dealing with? The boy's . . . For chrissake, Clarisse. You're not even here!'

Mother's eyes shifted. Left, then right. Straight and down. They flipped everywhere, but never up. She looked like she was sleeping. Just like she was caught up in a really intense dream. Her eyes scanned the whole place, but never found me. Then she stared down one last time. Both eyes aimed straight into the floor. She saw all the steps she hadn't stepped yet. Like it didn't matter where she'd been, but she still wanted more than anything to know where she would end up. That's the way Mother always had been. It's the safest way around a man like my father, look to the future and hope for the best.

I retreated to my room and sat on the floor. My old man continued down the stairs, pulling my mother along with him. He didn't speak any more. His feet fell hard against the steps, but Mother glided. While listening to them I riffled through the pages of the newspaper. I wanted to find something to take my

121

mind away, if only for a moment. Looked for dramatic stories, pictures, headlines. I needed something to replace the sight of my mother, that image of empty skin over my old man's arm.

The pictures didn't catch me. The words didn't mean anything. They all looked smaller and blacker than ever before. That day I needed another accident on Grant's Road. I looked for the pictures of the busted car, smoke rising into the dented trees. Maybe another house fire. Anything would do, but I had to have a disaster that involved some other family. News of tragedy, of people in trouble. Something in the world had to be happening that made my family appear as small and blank as the words of the page. It stared at me and still it took me time to find it. It could've been the ringing in my ears, the buzzing sound of shock that hadn't yet died away.

It could've been the sound of my mother screaming. She'd started again. While my old man struggled to push her arms into a coat she screamed. Full lungs exploding. Like he was trying to get a plastic bag over her face.

'Last chance, Clarisse.' He sounded out of breath, riled up and violent. 'Give me your arm.'

An article on the top corner of the page caught my eye:

They're Coming Back. Cicadas Return

I thought of Helle Bishop telling mother about Mrs Murtache. She'd said something about the cicadas. *She strung them up like popcorn on a Christmas Tree.* But these things . . . The article told about the cicada. They came to town every seventeen years making an appearance that rivalled any plague. *Prepare yourselves for the return of the cicadas.* They arrived in massive numbers and chewed the crops of farms. Caused a nuisance to travellers in city centres. This was the seventeenth year and they were coming our way.

The article seemed to glow from the page, emerging from the other columns and building a space of its own. My breathing picked up. My heart pounded inside my chest and felt like it could break through my ribs. I'd been leaning forward against my hands. Hovered over the paper in a half-press-up. With my arms shaking so bad I had to lean back, coming up on my knees. There was no picture. Couldn't see what they looked like and that played on my mind. A story like that needed something, no matter how small. It deserved to be seen.

They emerge in swarms of hundreds of thousands. Emerge from what appeared to be both ground and sky. They destroy. On that day I got enough information about the cicada from the article. Knowing they were due made me think ahead. But the more I thought about the cicada the more I wanted an image. A black and white or a sketch, just something to accompany the writing. There was no face with the name as it was. My father had a small collection of books in his den. Near a painting of Jesus on the cross was a shiny set of encyclopaedias. I waited until he got Mother into the car. She'd stopped screaming somewhere along the way. Never knew when she'd quit, but she'd given up while I read the article. Could have been that my old man had done something to her to stop the noise. But it was quiet down in the house. His car started and I breathed easy. The garage door went up and he pulled out.

In those volumes I found the first picture of a cicada.

Red, round eyes set high on top of a thick black head. It was a beast of an insect. The body was long, almost two inches. With wings of thick clear plastic. They could cut the air and propel it forward. A squadron just like it trailing behind, millions of them combining in flight. Moving through the sky like a spreading inkblot. *The sound they must make. The buzzing. The chattering. Like a chainsaw.*

The insect exceeded what I had conjured in my own head. It was the power behind my thoughts for weeks after. The book had said they were known for their sounds, their songs. In large numbers their chorus could grow to drown out almost all other noise. I read about the cicada in all the books I found at the library. Looked through the papers most days worried that I'd find an article about a missed year. Some fuck-up in nature would

123

cause the insects to pass us by. The bad winter may have killed them off or the rains may have suffocated them in wet ground. *Sorry, folks. The seventeenth year has been missed. Better luck when the cycle returns.* Instead I found confirmation that they were on their way, it was only a matter of time.

They came in numbers that couldn't be counted. They brought noise that drowned out all other sound. They disrupted towns. But the most important thing came in the end when they returned to the soil. The cicada lived underground for seventeen years. Kept hidden in the darkness. Waited and grew until they found themselves ready to fly. After all that darkness they came into the light. They burst to life. In the thousands they appeared and in the masses they erupted.

Chapter Thirteen

All those days of fighting grew less frequent when the weather grew fierce. I wasn't as valued a commodity as the dry warmth of home. The hospitality of the MacDonald's on Main and Fourth. The cheap cinema seats or the bowling alley over in Kinnaird Plaza. Those who bumped my shoulder in the school hall walked in a different direction from me when the spring rains began to fall. After the bell rang I was free to walk where I chose. Just kept out in the rain and made a slow march home. Out where no one else wanted to be. Most times I headed off to sit under the bridge where I put my feet in the water. Listened to the chaos of the rain in the trees. All the noise in the forest drowned everything else away. I was alone at last.

That year the storms fell hard. The winter saw La Niña make an appearance. I heard about the worst storms from Maureen and from Mr Banks in his science class. By mid-March more than twelve inches of rain and hail fell in the area. Companies closed because of all the flooding and sent their employees home. People were stranded and had to wait for help inside their cars. The streets were lined with stalled vehicles, cars too low to keep the engines dry. Images on the news showed the local town in chaos. I watched it all from inside, part of it on the television in our family room. When news came that companies were closing I dressed in my jeans and raincoat and headed over to Dean's.

The rain in the city areas wasn't as dramatic as in outlying towns. In Maritime we got it like a monsoon. Walking to Dean's the wind caught me strong enough to push me from the path. I fell a few times too, slipping up on the mud and going down hard. It took me twice as long to get where I was going that day. Covered in slicks of mud and dog shit. The wind blew cold and the rain felt like it was dripping off ice cubes. My teeth were knocking together when I finally rang the Gillespies' doorbell. Dean's mom answered it.

'Joseph, what in God's name are you doing?' she yelled. She pulled me inside. I tried to keep myself over the front rug, but I was off balance. My right foot landed flat on a tile. It would've been less dramatic if I'd stepped on a bar of wet soap. An up-and-over kind of thing happened before there was any chance to use my arms for balance. I hit the floor and yelled something obscene. Dean's mother was too shocked at my falling to catch the words I'd let fly. If she heard it she never made a mention of it.

'Sorry,' I offered anyway.

'I keep meaning to buy a bigger rug. Dean's forever going down on those tiles.' She leaned down. 'You hurt yourself, darlin'?'

'No,' I said. 'No, ma'am. I'm fine.'

'You just sit there and get out of your coat. You'll need another pair of jeans too.'

'Oh,' I said. I kind of felt lost at that moment. The streaks of mud ran up my leg, thick in parts with blades of grass hanging off. 'My only pair.'

'Nonsense, Joe.' She headed off toward the kitchen. Before she was through the door she turned her head. 'I'm sure these I washed the other day are yours. Dean Gillespie's not a child who wears Wranglers.' She came back in with a pair of jeans in her hand. They were folded over and still had the store tag hanging off. She had a towel over her shoulder.

'His butt's too big for these. He's a Levi's man.'

'Those aren't mine,' I said.

She cocked her head to the side and pushed the jeans forward. I took them from her and gritted my teeth.

'When you've got changed just leave those you're wearing on the rug. Dean's down in the basement playing games.' She pulled the towel from her shoulder and handed it over to me. Then she was off to the kitchen before she finished. 'Watch yourself on those tiles, Joe. Don't want you falling over and doing some damage.' Her voice trailed around the corners of the house. It was easier to speak with her when she wasn't in the room with me.

'Thanks for letting me in,' I said.

'Don't be silly, Jo-Jo. You're always welcome here.'

I expected her to swing her head around the corner to check on me. Keep a watch on me while I took my coat off. Stripping from my gear in the foyer was awkward. I kept an eye aimed toward the kitchen while I pulled at my boots. It was a struggle to get them off without flinging mud and water. I managed in the end and slid my jeans down before pulling the new ones on. Then walked away from the rug and left everything piled together. The wet already dripped from the carpet onto the tiles. There wasn't anything I could do to fix it. So I went down into the basement.

Dean leaned over the pool table. He'd set some figures on the centre of the green felt and rolled the cue ball to knock them down. When I walked through the small hallway at the bottom of the stairs he looked up at me. Then he looked back down without saying anything. He pulled the eight ball from the corner pocket and rolled Spiderman over. The ball came back off the cushion and got him again.

'Hey,' I said. Fell into the sofa that pressed up against the far wall. Dean didn't say anything in reply.

'You seen all the problems from the rain?' I asked. 'It's all over the television.'

'No. I haven't been watching any TV,' he said. 'Bad?'

'Yeah. They're sending everyone home. Businesses downtown. Shops. Said there's going to be a bunch more before the day's up. Flooding, I mean.' I was crushing one of the pillows in my hands. I'd let up and before it gained its shape I'd crush it again. They had these expensive kinds of pillows. Ones that you could feel the feathers inside.

'Your dad coming home then?' he tossed the cue ball and knocked down a couple more figures. He jumped onto the table. Set his knees on the wood surround. Bent across to set the figures back up.

'Yeah, I guess.'

'Your mom at home?' he asked.

'Yep.'

In a stupid voice like he didn't believe me he asked: 'So he brought her home then?'

I nodded. Dean hopped down from the table and made a grunt when he hit. He shook his head and had this smile on his face. It was that smile he used when he wanted you to tell him he was right. That gloating I'm-a-clever-sonofabitch face that he knew aggravated me like nothing else.

'He brought her home,' I said.

'Didn't pull a bag over her head and dump her over a bridge?'

'Fuck off, Dean.'

'You're always suspicious, Pullman. Those ideas of yours aren't normal. Your dad's a mean guy, yeah, but he's no killer.' I nodded like I agreed and he kept on going. 'So where'd he take her? Doctor? Pharmacy?'

'Don't know.'

'Wasn't the bottom of a lake, anyway.'

I wanted to crash the white ball against his cheek.

'It was a dream . . .'

'Yeah, I hear you. One of your premonitions.' He laughed and then kicked a foam ball. It flew across the room and knocked a stack of cassettes off the top of a stereo. He nodded his head like he'd meant it. 'She still screaming?'

'She was this morning. When the rain started coming down

128

harder she went quiet. Didn't hear anything when I left to come over here.'

'Think she's alright?'

'I don't care.' I crushed the pillow. Half wished it was Dean's head.

There wasn't much of a break from the rain. Three days after the first fall came another shower. This time almost six inches dropped on Maritime. Dean's mom had let me stay a few nights but I left when the second bout of storms dumped a ton of water on the 25th. I got home to find my father sitting in the family room. His face looked long and grey. He smelled sweaty and looked unshaven. He watched me with dead eyes. Thick red eyes. He wore cut-off khakis and a v-necked t-shirt.

'Where you been, Joe?' he asked. His voice was deep, even though he was speaking quietly.

'I stayed over at Dean's a couple nights,' I told him. 'His mom didn't think it was a good idea for me to go out. Not in the storm. The way it was, I mean.'

He looked away from me. His eyes focused in on the front window. Outside the rain fell in a diagonal pattern, heavy enough to make the Bishops' house across the street look like an unfinished oil painting. My father aimed his eyes back at me in true hunter fashion. The right side of his mouth came up a little when he stood in front of me.

His left hand shot out. He caught my cheek with a slap. It stung like mad, but was aimed to wake me up more than set me down. I took a step back and set up on my toes. Bounced a few times to get my legs ready. It all came natural. I'd practised it so many times before.

'Beat up a nigger and think you can take me?' my old man asked.

'No sir.'

'Why you bouncing, Joe?'

'Just . . .' Never got it out. Whatever I was going to say didn't have chance to leave my lips.

His right hand shot up from his side and caught me on the

chin. Teeth came together and head snapped back. Something popped on the inside, something deep in my neck. Felt it and heard it. Another jolt and my head went left. Then another thump against my jaw and I hit the floor. Before I opened my eyes my knees had come up to my chest. I'd balled up like a dog that'd just been hit by a car.

'Remember this,' my old man said. Standing over me with his finger pointing at my swelling face. 'Always remember this.'

He stepped over me and went into the kitchen. I listened while he unfastened the locks on the door. Metal sliding over metal. The clicking of the lock coming together again. Waited until he'd went down into his basement. Waited for him to switch on the fluorescent lights that made a humming noise when they warmed up. Then his machines came on. Saws and drills – they all played part in my old man's symphony.

While the engines of his machines spun – while he laughed that laugh loud enough for me to hear him over his orchestra – I watched the basement door. The handle with the ghosts of his fingers smudged against the polished brass. Chips of wood he left standing when he cut the squares for his latches. But most of all my eyes focused on the locks.

They're Yales, Joe-boy. Brand new silver shining Yale locks. Four locks for four keys, kiddo. Just like the ones dangling from your old man's key ring.

Rolled onto my side.

Ever want to see what he's got down there, Joe-Joe? May be something you need to know about. Might just be something real important.

'Get out,' I breathed. The words came from me and I wasn't able to hold them in. Wasn't able to control the smile that stretched my mouth. Even with the pain it sparked in my swelling cheek. No way to hold it back.

Then, over the whines and rattles of his tools, he yelled up to me. He yelled and I was on my feet in an instant. The pain bounced around in my head. I started for the foyer, straight for the stairs. Reached the bottom step when he yelled again. The same words as before, just as angry and excited as the first time.

'No,' I whispered back as I took the steps. 'No.'

Halfway up the stairs I could hear her. Mother's voice rambling words out a million miles a minute. The sound of her voice rolled in sentences, one after the other. She hadn't finished one before starting the next. What came out was a stream of sound. By the time I got to the top step I wanted to leave again. Get out of the house, back to Dean's where his mother never screamed. Where his father sat quiet on the porch and read the paper. But they were out, gone to a movie or a restaurant. Maybe both. That lucky asshole Dean was safe with full guts and a smile. But there wasn't any place for me to go.

I went into my bedroom and took off my jacket. Dropped it and the Wrangler jeans on fresh newspapers. They were heavy with rain but I couldn't bring myself to wring them out in the bath. My jaw felt unhinged. My neck was going stiff.

They'll dry soon enough, Joe. Sit back and listen to that rain.

It hit the house in waves. It came in a rhythm that made things okay. For that moment, laying on my bed, my life became normal. Mother would scream out once in a while, but the rain was loud enough to dull her voice. The sound of the storm outside made everything in the house grey. The sounds went dull. Colours faded. Even the air seemed to turn heavy.

Then it stopped. The rain quit and Mother fell silent. The entire house was still. The machines in the basement rattled and spun, then they died. For a few minutes everything was how it should have been all along. The colours returned. Sounds of the birds outside made it in through the hazy windows. I fell asleep a few times. Mother was always there to wake me if I got too deep. Her screams cutting into the air. Breaking into my dreams. She was still good for something. She reminded me how tired I was. She reminded me how bad things could get.

Then I thought I heard my father speak. Saying the same words he spoke while I lay bent on the floor. Only this time he wasn't excited. There wasn't the anger in his voice. He was just speaking to me, giving an instruction like a normal father might give his son.

131

Come down here, Joseph. I need to show you something.

'Oh, fuck.' I held the pillow close to my face. 'I'm not hearing you. Can't hear you all the way down there.'

By the end of the month the rain had stopped. It left a wet ground that broke easily under foot. Water filled the streets where the rain gutters had filled with debris. My old man went back to work and the newspapers started arriving again. I read an article about a cripple, some old guy over in Endicott City, who went crazy during the storms. He didn't have any family and no neighbours close enough to check in on him. They never called it cabin fever, but they didn't have to. Headlines were enough. *Stranded Man Kills Himself During Floods*. I couldn't get him out of my head. He'd died on his own – he had no one. I made an entry in my journal – a kind of personal obituary for another guy who fell through the cracks.

March 27, 1987. Curtis Lowell in his wheelchair. He cut his arms with garden shears. Evidence that he tried to stop bleeding. Bled too fast. Never fast enough.

It was something I could never completely understand. The human mind can't get to grips with solitude. Can't take the isolation and confinement. Must have been more than the storm. It's easy to use nature as an excuse. He just couldn't take the quiet. Maybe it was the riot of his thoughts that made him cut so deep. Whatever it was he couldn't take all that time on his own.

I craved that quiet. The drumming of my thoughts mixed in with the long stretches of nothing. My mother came from the same mould as the others. She came from the ones that died. There was something in her that went weak when no one else was around. Dean was the same as my mother, that's the way I saw it. But I never told him that. He could never have handled it well coming from me.

132

When classes started up after the floods Dean stuck close. He spoke less than before. I was dominating the conversations for the first time. He listened and nodded. It was clear he was hearing less of what I had to say. He'd shut off that much after the rains came. He was closing up and somehow that made him easier to speak to. Better to be around. Any friends he'd made before the break lost interest in him, found he wasn't the same kid. He didn't like to talk to the other students because they hated him. He didn't like to talk to me because he was becoming weak. That spring, coming back from the flood break, I watched out for Dean. I was his saviour.

There were days when my father stayed off work. He'd call in and tell them my mother was suffering again. From his side of the conversation I took it the people on the other end gave him sympathy. He'd nod his head and keep up the sad act until he came off the phone. Then he'd get back to things. Back to the basement and back to his tools. He'd take Mother food and fresh bottles of whatever she was drinking. Then he'd go back to the basement and fire up the noise again. While he was down there Mother would cry. She'd let out these moans and follow them up by sucking in air. Other times she'd laugh. It was just like she'd heard the funniest joke in the world. After she laughed she'd talk aloud. Chattering away like there was someone in there with her. Someone in her room, sitting at the end of her bed. There wasn't anyone else in the house. Sometimes I lifted the telephone to see who was on the other line. Nothing. Always met me with a dial tone.

Chapter Fourteen

Dean left Maryland to visit relatives during the few weeks we had for spring break. He was the only person I wanted to tell about the cicadas. About the articles. I'd held off to that point. There was part of me with a plan to keep it away from him until they came. Then I'd be able to tell him everything. But it didn't make sense to keep it back. That kind of anticipation can only be bottled up for so long. I needed to tell him. Give him the heads-up on what was coming to town.

Before April had been and gone that year Mother was sent away. My old man had loaded her in the car one afternoon. He came home the next evening, alone. He walked up the stairs slower than he usually did. I waited in my room, listening to him moving. He stopped in front of my door. It was a moment that seemed to scream, although everything was silent and still. He spent the rest of the day in his bedroom. I stood in the hall for a while that day. Listened like there was something to hear. Wondering if the sound coming from behind the walls was laughter.

He's done it, kiddo. He's tied her up just like you said he would. Weighed her down and dropped her in the river.

It was an idea that didn't upset me like I thought it should.

The next day I was standing at the kitchen sink watching the neighbour's kids playing in the back yard. Holding a glass of water, half full with the ice floating. The cubes clinking against the sides of the glass. The muscles in my forearm were shaking. Lifting my left hand and splaying my fingers the glass felt heavy. Full of lead and cement and . . . Each digit vibrated, all in a rhythm of its own. Raising the glass to drink I kept an eye on the children. A boy and a girl who looked so innocent. So fragile and vulnerable. They looked uninterested in what was happening with the rest of the world. Didn't know that their place in it was worth a big dark zero.

'I've told you 'bout that,' my father grunted moving all the way into the kitchen.

I knocked the rim of the glass against my front teeth. A sharp, cold jolt of pain shot through my head. The water burned my lips. Bit at my tongue. Held a mouthful of water and lowered the glass. I kept my eyes closed and swallowed hard.

'Yessir.' I turned from the window and leaned myself against the counter top.

My father sat down at the kitchen table. He crunched up his large frame and looked hopeless. For a long moment he stared at me. The skin around his eyes looked like it had started the process of dying. He blinked and rolled his head in circles like he wanted to get rid of a crick in his neck. The bones popped loudly, but he didn't seem to notice. When he focused on something outside I let out my breath. The pain inside my lungs became more intense.

My old man crossed his legs at the ankles. His shoulders hunched and his head dropped low in front. His arms went limp with his hands clasped together and dangling between his knees. Without a shirt I could see that his skin had started to look old. His once taut muscles had retreated behind layers of flab. The moles covering his arms no longer appeared light in colour and were now sprouting thick black hairs. They looked like a thousand wounds against his pale white skin. As always he knew I stood watching him. His head turned slowly with

135

his eyes aiming at me. They centred off on my eyes like the barrel of an old tank. I looked away.

'You're not in here today.'

'Yessir.'

There was a moment when I considered staying. Just to finish my water. I may have lifted the glass to my mouth. The sound of the ice shaking and chattering stopped. Took a second to look at my hand. I'd raised it and opened my fingers. Staring for a moment into the lines on my palm. My hand looked as still as a rock and felt twice as strong. I could sense my father's stare. Could see him in the wide haze from the corner of my eye. He may have been rocking slowly. The first glistening drops of sweat bubbled up from the centre of my hand.

'Get out of here, Joseph.'

I turned and set the glass of water in the sink. Slid away from the counter and turned so my back wasn't to my father for any longer than I could help. If he had moved, even slightly, I would have taken off. Snakes coil before they strike. They try to look threatening. They wait for you to move. They give you a chance to get away. If you don't take that chance they'll get you.

Spent my time outside. Walking round Westchester first. Then off into the forest. I sat under the Killing Tree for most of the day. When I needed a change I walked around and looked for dead animals. Those I found got stuffed in the pouches on my belt. On good days I found six or more. That day I didn't find any. With Dean being away I spent more time searching for the animals. The week he was away I found twenty-two and buried them all in a single grave. It was easier to keep track of the stock in case Dean didn't believe me.

It was only a few days after my mother was sent away that I first wondered if she would ever return. She'd never protected me. Never stopped events from taking place and only warned me after I'd already suffered. But with her away there was no telling what my father was capable of doing. There was no way to gauge how brutal he would be. If I met him in the hall or if he stopped me on the stairs he might start up and never stop. He could do whatever he wanted without her around. What would get him to stop?

Just go down, Joseph. Just fall!

Would that be enough?

I found myself listening more and moving round the house less frequently. Took more time to consider where I was in the house and where my old man might be. Like it was a game of chess played against my father. Only this game wasn't friendly. There was a real fear of making a wrong move because I only had one chance.

Mail arrived in late morning. With Dean away I found myself leaving the house later than usual. There was no hurry getting to the Killing Tree before him. No rush finding animals to push into the ground. So I'd stay in bed and listen to the sounds of the house. The air conditioner kicking on, pushing cool through the vents in the ceiling. Toilet flushing in my old man's room. Floorboards crackling under the weight of feet. This sound travelled up the hall and down the stairs. Then there was the lock hanging from the kitchen door. It scraped while my father jiggled the key in. Then he went down and the machines came to life.

I'd sit on the bottom step waiting for the mail. The figure of the fat guy who brought it moved up to the door in a quick waddle. The metal box hung outside, next to the door. The hinge creaked when he pulled up the flap and slipped the envelopes inside. He'd waddled away again before I opened the door and brought the letters in.

Each letter connected the house to somewhere outside. Like the statement from my old man's bank and a letter from the Internal Revenue Service. I'd scan through the names and addresses, looking for one to me. There was never a letter with my name. Still, the places the letters came from were as important. There was a letter from the University of Oklahoma once. It was addressed to the guy who owned the house before my father. That was the farthest a letter came. Usually it was all in-state. Bills and notices, mostly. All of them addressed to my old man. Some were yellow envelopes with red stripes across the top. *Urgent Attention Required*, they said. *Final Notice*. I'd set them on the top of the pile that was mounting in the dining room. They never moved. None of them ever moved.

I went through the ritual again. Check for my name and when it wasn't there checked the addresses of the senders. One of them caught my eye. The letter was slipping away from the bundle. Couldn't hold them all, they spread out like a poker hand. The return address was to a hospital in Virginia. I took hold of the green envelope and let the rest fall away. Not an envelope at all, but a brochure. Addressed to my father. *Information at your request*, it read.

As I walked down the hall toward the kitchen I stared at the brochure. It was with the same interest that I paid the black and white photograph of the woman in the psychology book. *You took her to a hospital in Virginia*, I thought. *Drove her out and dumped her in a loony bin.* Packed away and removed from my father's home like a dog that couldn't be trained. A fucking puppy that pissed in the corner one too many times. Only there would be no one to come along and collect her. No second chance with a family that would take her in and pat her on the head and tell her things were alright now. She was broken and old, and alone.

I found out about my mother from the return address on an envelope. She was at Leichter House, a Division of Health facility in the state of Virginia. Figured it was probably the most efficient way to learn about it. I have never been a person who can believe all the things I'm told. I have to read it, usually a few times before it sinks in. That's not to say that I believe everything that I read when I'm done. It's just that I have time to consider the things that I'm reading. When people speak to you they don't shut up so you can drift away in thought. They keep going on and on and on. That's why so many people can lie during conversations. They talked over your confusion. It's why I choose to trust only the things that I read.

There was another piece of mail from the same hospital. The same coloured envelopes came every couple of days. The envelopes changed shape and size, but they were all the same hospital, sterile green. One of the green envelopes arrived a few days after the first. I dropped the other mail on the counter top. Used a finger to pull the flap open and went through the contents. With all the mail piling on the dining room table I felt safe to look. There was still the cold feeling running up my back when I pulled the folded papers out. Still, I went ahead and looked.

From all the numbers on the invoice I figured my old man wanted his wife back. Back like old times, as good as new and twice as normal. The same lady, only in better condition than he had left her. As the weeks passed more mail arrived from Leichter House, also known as The Clinic. From one of those mailings I took a brochure. It was different than the first that I had seen. It looked new, the latest edition of the Crazy Freaks Review.

On the cover was a large white house, the kind my mother had always wanted to live in. The gardens were colourful. In the picture three people were walking on the green grounds. Looked like they were sneaking round the side of the house. None of them looked crazy, more like nurses or doctors. I figured they were models brought in for the shoot. Beyond the house and the open space of the gardens were trees, hundreds of trees. Some looked like they had blue leaves. The forest reached right up and surrounded the building. In one of the windows of the house was the shape of a person. The person was out of focus behind the tall pane of glass. They were behind the reflection of a bright sun. It was an image that haunted me. That person behind the window just stood there, in a house while the sun burned down. My mother looked out of windows when I was away. If I'd left the house and gone into the woods she'd stand in the window and look for me. Sometimes I could see her from the high oak trees. Other times the sun caught the window and she'd be lost, stripped away in the yellow blaze.

139

I slipped the brochure into my psychology book and placed it under the mattress.

Before I knew it school had started to wind down. Summer was coming and the heat of the weather and the promise of an end to classes changed Dean. He became more talkative. On his Easter trip to see family he'd collected a load of gifts. He had a lot to say although most of his conversations were simple and didn't hold much interest for me. Suppose the sound of another human voice was healthy. I kept quiet as he chattered away. Sometimes I imagined the swarms of cicadas that were readying themselves for warmer days. The sound of their digging and clawing at the soil drowned Dean out.

Dean didn't have much to say one morning. I was growing impatient, so I told him about the cicadas. The spring air was heating up and we were both walking the Angry Snake in knee length shorts. He didn't have a response to anything I'd been telling him. He seemed to listen as he pressed the buttons on his calculator watch, but I wasn't all that sure he understood. So I explained it all again, trying to make it simple for him.

I spoke fast because I needed to say something, anything. Needed to hear words – even if they were my own. Dean wasn't talking and that got under my skin more than usual. All the stuff that was going on and he wasn't talking. I left the house that morning with my old man still in the basement. He'd been down there all night and most of the morning. Came up and rattled the kitchen cabinets. Must have been looking for food that didn't exist. I waited until he'd gone back down to his workshop before I left my room. I'd found the envelope sitting on the kitchen counter top while getting ready to leave. Inside the envelope were numbers and a letter that began:

With Our Deepest Condolences,

Then there were numbers. From the pages inside the envelope I knew my mother was never coming home. I read quickly and took in as much as I could. My father was working in the basement. His drill was spinning deep into something. It whirled louder when it made it all the way through. He screamed. The sound of his voice came through the laundry chute. It sounded like his mouth was beside my ear. The drill went in again. Spinning and gnawing away. Before my old man screamed again I ran. Dean was already in the open space.

I watched Dean's face while we walked. He concentrated on that damned watch. Wanted to tell him what I'd just found. Needed to show him that life wasn't Gillespie-easy for everyone. He punched the buttons on his new watch. He worked it with his thumb and didn't say a word. My anger was building. My mind was wandering.

The letter.

Our deepest condolences.

My father –

'Clarisse! Oh, God!'

I needed other voices – even my own – to drown it all out. My old man's voice was still ringing through my head. Dean was in his shell so it was up to me to get rid of the screaming. I started talking. Watched the side of his head and started on about the first thing that came to my mind. It was the only way to keep from losing it.

'They only come in a seventeen-year cycle, Dean.' I held out my hands to show him how big an event the emergence would be.

'Yeah,' he replied. He looked annoyed. I'd interrupted him, whatever it was he was doing. Maybe he was counting leaves. Maybe he was trying to decide if he was going to ask his mom to make spaghetti or hamburgers for dinner.

'Seventeen years, Dean.' My hand balled up and I squeezed tight. *What the hell's wrong with you?* 'Christ, man. We weren't even born the last time they came through here. They'll be here in a month. Six weeks at most.'

Dean made the face that made me think of an old timer with sour dentures. He nodded his head.

'Why are you so happy about it?' he asked.

'First off, they're coming in the masses. Huge numbers. They crawl up from the ground. Been down there all that time. Hiding away. Can you imagine waiting seventeen years in pure darkness? They're coming out this year. Thousands of them. Millions even.'

'Okay.'

'Dean, you're not getting it.' *You're really pissing me off now.* 'If you could see them. They're big, man. And black as anything. They have these red eyes that're like completely round.' After I said this I found my hands curled into two Cs. Held them in front of my eyes to emphasize the point. Realizing what I was doing I felt like a fool. Used my hands to push my hair from my forehead. The sweat kept it back for a while. The more we walked the more the hair fell. I left it and waited for Dean to speak.

Dean kept a close eye on the path as we walked and I started talking again. Yabbering away like a lunatic. He wasn't moved when I spoke about the volumes they reached with their chattering. He wasn't impressed when I told him about the shells they pulled away from, the ones that look like empty armadillos. I went on and on about how the cicada inflated their wings for flight. After a while I stopped talking, just shut off. Tired of carrying the conversation and making out like I still wanted Dean around. We walked in silence until we reached the open space. He turned on the path that led to his house. I continued home, straight up the hill that led to Westchester Drive. Never looked back.

That night I found a spider trying to climb out of the kitchen sink. Took the time to stand there and watch while all its arms spun and found nothing to hold. Watched it get up the bend at the bottom of the basin before it slipped on the metal wall. It slid back down and started it all again. I moved the two cups out of the sink and set them with the rest on the counter. After spitting on my finger I held it over the spider and let small drops of spit fall. The spider would stop for a moment, raise an arm or two like it was wiping the white foam away. Then

142

it would try the wall again. It must have been in there for hours before I came along. Must have tried climbing out a hundred times. No success in all its effort. Growing tired of watching it I turned on the water and flipped the switch for the garbage disposal. The spider was washed into the drain hole with a small piece of carrot.

Down there in the darkness he was ground into nothing.

Chapter Fifteen

The concert at Wild Lake had been a small thing to occupy people's time. Members of the local council set it up to welcome the summer weather. The winter had been bad for blizzards and the spring brought floods. Both seasons locked the town in for a few weeks. The state roads were getting repaired around that time. Freezes during the winter months cracked the asphalt. The floods that followed took some chunks out of the blacktop. Only the two country roads could link people in Maritime to the outside world. The concert was organized while the roads were blocked and the work was done.

Other than the concert there wasn't much happening at all. So the venue was selected. The community centre sat near enough to the middle of town, just off the main banks of the lake. It gave everyone in town an equal chance to make it to the show. Even if the roads near their homes had been blocked off for the state crews to do their work, they could manage to walk.

Dean's mom called and invited me along. I'd picked up the telephone thinking it would be Mr Moon asking for my old man. When I heard Maureen's voice I felt the tight muscles in my back loosen up.

'Joe?' she asked.

'Yes ma'am.'

'It's Maureen, Joey. Dean's mom.'

'Yeah, I know . . . I mean I recognized your voice.'

She laughed. 'Sorry, hun. I'm so used to saying that. Never know when people're going to recognize my voice or not.'

'Okay.'

'Well, I'm calling to see if you're going to Lucille's concert at the lake.'

'No, ma'am. I didn't have any plans for it.'

'Would you like to go?'

'Haven't really thought about it.'

'Come with us,' she said. 'It'll be fun, darlin'. We know how you and Dean like Lucille.'

'Well, it's just . . .'

It's just you've got no idea. Your little precious has the hots for Lucille's sister. That mousy brunette. Same one with easy lips and fast-spreading . . .

'Your dad have you doing something?'

'Hu-uh.'

'Then be here by ten tomorrow morning. Bring a change of clothes if you're staying over.'

'Alright, Mrs Gillespie.'

'It's Maureen, hun.'

'Yes ma'am.'

'Oh, Joe. You're a card.'

She hung up the phone.

I turned up at ten. She let me in and I ate breakfast with the family. Dean's mom had made eggs and bacon and biscuits with white gravy to pour over top. She cleaned up and Dean's dad read the paper. Dean and me sat in the family room and waited. He was quiet. Kept looking up at me like he wanted to say something. When I caught him looking he moved his attention to something else.

'So you're going to see your girl?'

'Shut up, Pullman.'

'No big deal.'

'Leave it, will you?'

We walked to Wild Lake like most other people, taking the path through the open space behind the Gillespies' house. We came out on Bestview Terrace and walked up past the grocery store. After passing the library we got back on a path that took us toward the boathouse. Dean's parents were well ahead of us. Dean kept holding us back with his usual sliding-steps. When he found a puddle on the ground he didn't like to pick his feet up to step over it. He got around like a cross-country skier without the skies and a few months late for the snow.

'You miss your mom?' he asked.

'I don't know yet.' I spotted a big puddle just off the path. It had eyes. Someone had dropped a couple of stones in it. Maybe the stones had already been there when the rain came. I stepped off the path and gave the puddle a good kick. The water exploded in a spray and fell back to the path and soaked in. The puddle moved back into shape. The eyes hadn't moved, but the water rippled round them.

'What do you mean?' he kept his head down. 'You don't know if you miss her or not?' His hands stayed deep in his pockets.

'I haven't had time to really think about it,' I said shaking the water from my sneaker. 'I know she's gone. It's like sometimes I think she can still come back. If she wants to kind of thing.'

'But you know she's not coming back.'

'Yeah,' I said.

'So you should be sad already,' he told me. He used his sleeve to wipe his mouth. 'Maybe you're not gonna be sad.'

'Maybe.'

We walked. Dean's dad turned around once in a while. He had a polo shirt on with the collar pulled up over his chin line. He'd put on a driving hat, the kind I'd expect to see an English taxi driver wear. He'd brought it home from a business trip to Canada. He'd told me about Montreal. It was so far away and so different from Maritime that it had to be paradise. The details of what Mr Gillespie did while on his trip were shady, even for Dean. Dean knew he'd been gone for a while. A month or six weeks or something. But he didn't have a clue why his father had been up there. Dean could only tell me that his dad had met clients and sometimes it had been too cold to even breathe.

'Your dad likes his pipe, huh?' I asked.

'Mom doesn't. He's only allowed to smoke outside.'

'Think your dad's a spy?' I asked.

'No,' he shrieked. He'd always raise his voice if he thought something I'd said was amusing or insane. This time he didn't laugh or even snicker, so I took it he thought I was being weird again. He couldn't give a damn about jokes. He'd got himself in one of his moods.

'His hat looks goofy,' I mentioned.

'Yeah, I know.'

'He's real smart. Like the way you have to be to cheat people.' I nudged Dean with my elbow. 'He speak more than English?'

'Not that I know.'

'But he could. Maybe he's got connections around the world,' I offered. 'He's got guns in your house. Your place is rigged to go sky-high if his cover's blown. There's a body already in your basement. It's there to make everybody think he died with the rest of you in the fire.'

'Shut up, Pullman,' he grunted. 'Sometimes you're so full of shit your breath smells like a cow's ass.'

'You start talking then,' I said. 'I'm sick of you staying quiet all the time.'

'Go home then,' Dean said. He sounded mad. 'If you don't like me so much you should fuck off.'

He must have felt like he'd kept us far enough away from his parents to shoot off with the bad mouth. But he felt close enough to be protected. That's the kind of thing he did that got up under my skin. Really made me want to show him how bad life could be, just how bad it could all get. Had this urge to knock him in the jaw with a hook and before he hit the ground lay into his soft guts with a few good kicks. *Where's your momma now, Dean? Don't see your old man coming to pick up the pieces?* But I didn't have anyone else around. If I fucked things up with the Gillespies

147

it would've been just me and my old man. Dean had figured all this out. Must have spent his nights in his safe little house thinking of my old man working in the basement on something terrible. Wondering if when he walked into the forest the next morning I'd be there waiting, or if I'd ever show up at all.

We walked. Dean's parents took turns looking back at us. His father puffed at his pipe sending thick clouds into the air. I tried walking though the clouds, or just under whenever I could. The smoke smelled sweet and caught in my throat. It burned and made me want to cough. I swallowed hard and it went away. Maureen just looked back and held her stare for a few seconds at a time. She watched me while she walked with her chin pressed into her shoulder. She kept a hold of Mr Gillespie's arm. Her eyes made me feel uncomfortable so I did my best to smile and make her think I was having a good time. I'd agreed to come out for her sake. If I'd stayed home I figured she would've felt left out. Maybe she would've had a sense of loneliness or at least felt like she'd failed somewhere along the way. There's a kid who needs help, Maureen must have thought. If nothing else she may have felt sorry for me, knowing I'd be in the house with my old man. When she finally turned her head forward the pressure building up inside me started to ease off.

'Let's pick it up fellas,' Dean's dad called out. 'Hear they've got loads of food waiting. I'm not missing out on the sandwich wedges 'cause of a coupla slow pokes.'

'We're keeping up with you guys,' Dean called back.

'Fair enough.' Dean's dad started this exaggerated jog that made him look like an old man chasing somebody who'd just stolen his cane. We all laughed. He'd broken away from Maureen who went after him with her own awkward jog.

'Don't leave me with the baby,' she called after him. It must have been an inside joke. They all laughed with hysterics. Dean chimed in and they all forgot about me. They let me walk along in the background.

Step it up, kid. You came along for the ride. Ain't no leaving you behind now. Don't tell me this makes you feel . . . oh, hell, Jo-Jo.

148

You're a fuck-up, kid. This here is normal. This is how families are.
They smile. Odd as it seems, kiddo. They smile.

I walked along, keeping quiet. Staying small as I could. Disappeared into my confusion. All that happiness made me feel out of place. Made me feel like all my life I'd been kept in a closet.

Dean's old man looked back at me and smiled. I smiled back and things kind of went back to normal. Maureen latched onto Mr Gillespie's arm and they walked just the same as before. Dean and me followed, but we loosened up and made more distance between us and his parents. His dad kept doing this skipping thing and his mom laughed like she was really excited about something. They were just too right, for each other and with the world. Couldn't figure how different things had been between them and my parents. Walking along with Dean I couldn't help but wonder if it was me that changed it for my parents.

I started thinking about my father again. Felt bad that he sat in the house on his own. He had all that open space to move around in, but I couldn't help think he'd shoved himself in a corner of the house. Like maybe he was hiding. Don't know why I thought that and don't even know why I cared. The far corner in the dining room kept coming to mind. Behind the table where the light from the kitchen and the light from the family room missed an entire corner, the darkest place in the house. It was a good place to get lost. There he stayed, waiting for something. Part of me thought what he waited for would never come. That same part of me knew he wasn't waiting for my mother.

'Sorry, Dean,' I finally said. 'Just say something once in a while for Chrissake.'

'I'll talk when I got something to say.'

'Start thinking.'

We got to the lake and met up a lot of people the Gillespies knew. There were people from their street, people from the PTA that Maureen chaired at times during the year and people they'd met at other town gatherings. Maureen put her hand on Dean's shoulder and moved him around the crowd, telling pairs of these people how well he'd been doing at school. Mr Gillespie talked to people about his work, sales figures and profits and margins and other stuff like that. He looked over once in a while and gave me a wink. I felt better when he did that even though I didn't understand what he was talking about or what the wink was for. Even though he was from a different kind of family I figured he understood me. He had his wife and son and treated them a certain way, the way he thought was right. I got treated different from that and as long as I was round him he'd make it better for me. He'd make things alright for a while, whenever I was away from home.

All those people hanging round the lake that day must have thought what Mr Gillespie did for his family was right too, because they all wanted to see his family. They all wanted him to see their sons and daughters too. It was some kind of adult show and tell that I'd never been a part of. Never would have wanted to be.

'Earl,' a short fat man had said while shaking Dean's father's hand. 'Good to see you, bud. Looking real well. Yeah, real well.' Then, like an afterthought he said: 'Have you met my daughter? This is Linda, she's fourteen next month. Your son's about that age too, huh? Maybe they know each other. Linda goes to Hampden Academy too. Don't you, honey?'

What the hell's all this about? I'll show you my daughter if you show me your son. Same age, huh? They'll know each other. Maybe they can sneak off into the bushes together while we eat sandwich wedges and shoot the shit.

It was all so damned strange to me. Maureen walked Dean round the whole crowd and when she was finished she hugged him. Ruffled his hair and smiled like he'd just finished the New York Marathon in first place. What's so hard about being a kid like Dean? There was nothing difficult about liking a girl he'd never have the balls to talk to or running from a crowd of guys while they beat the crap out of your buddy. Maureen had asked me to tag along and be a temporary part of their family, but I didn't fit into anything they did. The wink Dean's dad gave let

150

me know he wanted me to stay. I kept my distance and let him talk with all those people, never made a move to be included. Maureen and Dean met up with him and they made the rounds mingling with other families. It was all too much at times and I just wanted to leave while they weren't looking. But I didn't have anywhere to go and I liked being near the lake. Besides there was food, so I helped myself. Really got into those finger sandwiches while the Gillespies talked away.

I'd finished a second plate when Lucille walked by with an entourage of adults all wearing matching blue jackets. Their jackets had a shield-shaped badge over the left breast, but I couldn't make out what the small letters spelt. One of the adults had a folded book of sheet music so I figured they were the band. It was a strange feeling seeing Lucille walking with adults following her like that, like she was leading them.

'There she goes,' Dean said. He'd left his parents without me noticing. He'd made it to my side without even making a noise. 'Thinks she's a big shot.'

'Guess she is kind of,' I told him. 'For Maritime anyway.'

'Who wants to be a big shot in a small place like this?'

I shrugged and folded my paper plate in half and then halved it again. Dean kicked at the dirt and drove his hands further into his pockets. He was still at it when I came back from tossing the plate into the wastebasket. Maureen kept looking over at me and then at Dean like she expected us to catch fire or something. It felt weird being so close to her, right where she could see us.

'Where's Gillian?' I asked looking around the crowd of people standing close to the water.

'Gone out on a canoe.'

'On her own?'

'Nah,' he said. 'With her cousins.' He sounded beat. I gave him a punch in the arm, but he didn't even flinch. He turned and started up the path toward the boathouse and I stepped up to follow him. Maureen was watching us and craned her neck to make sure I knew she'd seen us leaving, so I waved and she waved back.

151

We walked around for a while standing next to people Dean recognized. They were people who recognized Dean and called out to him when we were passing by. Must have been impolite to ignore them 'cause Dean pulled his arm away hard when I grabbed it.

'Quit that, Pullman.' He sounded real agitated. 'I know him. He knows my dad.'

'So?'

'He's seen me. I've gotta talk to him. Just give him a minute.'

So I'd follow Dean and we'd stand around listening to the group of adults he didn't really know. Listening in on the conversations of people who didn't want to include us, neither Dean or me. Only way I could work it out was that we were part of a control game. The same reason people have dogs is the reason those men called Dean. They controlled him by simply yelling out his name. There's the Gillespie kid from the middle-class neighbourhood, I'll make sure his father's trained him well. So they called and we went, stood right up close and kept quiet, no one trying to bring us into the conversation.

We heard the usual small-town gossip. *Did you hear what so and so did to so and so? Oh, my, did I ever. I couldn't believe it at first. And if she thinks he's going to take her back after that . . .* We'd heard it all before, usually from listening in to Maureen talking with her friends at the house. I can only take so much of people talking about other people before I blow a gasket. There are too many Helle Bishops on this freaking planet. Finally pulled Dean away and he didn't struggle much.

We walked out to the end of the pier at the boathouse. The pier only stuck out over the water ten or fifteen feet, but it was far enough for the water to go black. The incline of the lake took a steep dip after a few feet of shallows. We stood there tossing leaves and pebbles into the water. Off in the distance the canoe Gillian had gone out in floated in place. It sat in the centre of the lake and bobbed slightly. They'd stopped paddling and just sat there like they were fishing, only there were no poles leaning over the side. Dean stared at the boat and seemed kind of lost. He stood there with the thumb of his left hand tucked into the front of his jeans. His right arm swayed at his side. Once in a while it came up to swat at the mosquitoes and flies.

'She'll be back in a minute,' I said. 'The concert'll be starting soon anyway.'

He looked at me like I'd said something in Japanese.

'Don't care when she comes back,' he said.

'No big deal, Dean.' I smiled real big and shrugged my shoulder. 'Liking her's cool, you know. I'm not giving you jip or nothing.'

'Whatever.'

He looked out at the boat again and sucked in his bottom lip. I'd gotten tired of that face of his, the I'm-thinking-of-getting-out-of-here face. To keep from getting all riled up I took a few steps to shore, got almost halfway up the dock when Dean made this sound. Not really a word, but close enough and it made me turn round. He was kind of dancing in place, to the left and then the right. He went up and down the end of the pier, never letting his eyes leave the canoe out there in the middle. I looked out and saw straight away what had got him worked up.

The boat was rocking from one side to the next. All three small figures inside the boat started yelling something, but it didn't make it all the way to shore. That far out we couldn't hear what they'd said. Dean cupped his hand over his ear as if that was going to make a difference. They yelled again. He put his hands out to his sides and shook his head. Looked more like a rock star enjoying the attention of a stadium crowd than a kid who couldn't understand what people in the boat were yelling.

'I can't hear you.' He said it like he was only talking to me, like the boat was floating at his feet.

I cupped my hands around my mouth and yelled with all the air in my lungs.

'What?' I felt like I'd just thrown a stone that had no chance of getting to the target. Still, that kind of helpless feeling is compulsive and I found myself yelling again. 'Can't hear you. What'd you say?'

We waited and the canoe eased from the rocking. The guy sitting in the front of the canoe stood and put his hands up to his mouth. Before he could even try to yell the boat tilted. He bent down and touched the sides of the canoe and it tilted even more, one way, then the other. It looked like a ride at a carnival. The water didn't splash, but the canoe and the people in it tossed round in a frantic way. Finally the guy who was still standing jumped out. With the weight shifted so suddenly the canoe went the other way. Kind of catapulted the others. We saw the bottom of the boat for a few seconds and when it came back up we could see it'd lost almost everyone. There was a girl still holding tight to the inside, but I didn't recognize her.

'Where's she?' Dean asked. 'Don't think Gillian can . . .'

A head popped out from the water. It was the guy and he broke through the surface and came out of the water to his shoulder, then sank back so only his head was showing. He started swimming toward the canoe with strong strokes. His paddling lasted only a few seconds. He started chopping at the water like mad after the girl still sitting in the canoe leaned down toward him. Her mouth moved, but it was hopeless to hear what it was that came out. Gillian's gone in, most likely. Either way, the guy in the water grabbed onto the side of the boat and pulled himself up. With the rim of the boat tucked into his armpit he twisted round. Looked at the water like he expected another head to pop up at any minute. He kept pulling himself out of the water as much as he could. When he slipped down he'd pull himself back up, but he was more concerned about what was in the water than getting himself into the canoe.

The girl in the boat yelled something to us. This time we got it.

'Help!' she screamed. Came across clear as a bell.

'Oh, God.'

Dean took off running and I followed him. We rounded the trees and headed down the path like a pair of foxes with hungry dogs following. Half expected Dean to yell when we got close to the adults but he didn't. He ran by the first group of families

154

standing under some trees. We passed the people who had called him to their side, because now the loyalty was gone. They stood eating burgers off paper plates, smiling the way wealthy people smile. When he shot by the second group I wondered if he'd lost his head. But he burst into the third crowd and busted that gathering up pretty well.

'Dad!' he yelled. Took him a second to get the words out. He took a breath. 'Gillian's in the water. Fell out of the canoe. Can't find her.'

'Who's in the water?' an old guy standing behind Dean asked.

'Gillian Wilcox,' I told him. 'She's in the lake.'

People scattered from the trees and ran to the edge of the water. Where they stood you couldn't see the canoe. A cluster of trees reached out on a jetty of land. The canoe sat in the centre of the lake straight out from the boathouse and the jetty kept the canoe hidden. I can't help but think that's the reason they stopped the boat there. They looked for privacy and they got it. The only trouble was that it was too much privacy for their own good.

A group of men ran up the path to the boathouse. Dean and me followed them, but weren't fast enough to keep pace. A couple of the bigger men jumped in the water straight from the pier and swam out toward the canoe. They didn't even dress down. One of the guys went in wearing his sports jacket and loafers. There was a load of other people standing around yelling at the girl in the canoe. The boy still held the side of the boat, but had his head resting against his arms. He'd stopped looking and just tried to hold on.

One of the men smashed down the wooden door of the boat-house. Didn't even ask for a key, that's the kind of panic that was going on. He and a couple other men got one of the orange lifeguard canoes out of the house and into the water. They paddled past the two men who were still making their way swimming out there. Sheriff Wilcox jogged up in straw hat and Hawaiian shirt. His cheeks had gone red from all the beer he'd been drinking. He yelled with the other men from the shore.

155

He staggered out a few steps into the lake and called for Gillian. Asked the girl in the canoe if they saw Gillian. It did no good.

The concert was cancelled.

The sun went down earlier than usual that evening. A storm was coming in and the clouds blocked out any of the evening light. The canoe and orange lifeguard boat lay against one another on the sand. The ambulance came and took the Wilcox cousins away. Hooked them both up to plastic masks that fogged up when they breathed. The girl was crying and the boy just looked round like there was something he'd lost. I tried to get him to look at me. I stared at him and waited for his eyes to meet mine, but they didn't. The ambulance doors closed and they were off.

Everyone left the lake that night when the rain started to fall. Everyone returned to their homes except for Gillian Wilcox.

They found her body the following afternoon.

Chapter Sixteen

The far wall of the English room was covered with student-made posters. My effort hung at an odd angle and I kind of liked the way it didn't match up with the straight line of the others. Against the other posters it stuck out. The colours I'd used to draw the flames of the explosion were from the brightest markers I could find. I'd copied the explosion out of a book. The picture had been a bomb going off during World War II. You could see people in the background running. The explosion sat just off-centre in the photograph. No matter how long I looked at that picture I couldn't tell what the bomb had hit. The caption on my poster read: A Family of Three Were Killed When This Bomb Landed. My poster was meant to depict a story about civilian casualties, one I'd read in *From the Vietnam Conflict*.

When I presented that poster and the report to the class the eyes of my fellow students just stared back. A few mouths hung open, but that wasn't anything like I'd expected. Since Gillian Wilcox's death during that past weekend people had changed. Some had gone soft and now went pink around the eyes when you spoke about anything tragic. A few of the girls in the class had known Gill well enough to be upset. They looked down at their desks and got lost in whatever memories were the strongest.

157

The rest were just using a dead girl as an excuse to complain. A pair of timid laughs came up from the back of the room and kind of bounced off one another. Mrs Rhodes stood against the back wall with her black-haired man-arms folded under her large breasts. She didn't make any attempt to stop the laughs and I hated her for that. Added it on to the long list of things that made me hate her already.

'Joseph, that's an interesting piece you have there. You spent a lot of time on it and that is very commendable.' There came a pause. Mrs Rhodes always paused when her criticism gears hadn't yet ground into place, so she gave them time to heat up. She was a bad machine. Her only purpose was to chew up students from the inside. The extra time she took meant that she was looking for the most economic way of calling me an idiot piss-hole.

'You will remember the assignment was to read a book,' she continued. 'A novel or something that interests you. By that *something* I meant poetry or a play. The poster is a fine piece. Morbid and barbaric. Possibly too much so. But I take it this did not come from a work of literature.'

'No,' I said. 'This comes from something else.' For a few seconds I hung my head. Aiming my eyes over to the table where the other posters and dioramas sat. All those posters took less time to prepare than a piece of toilet paper swiped between ass cheeks. I'd gone all out and taken a big swing. Three hours of drawing and pasting and writing with a random hope of getting the junior high English equivalent to hitting a home run. *Why the hell not, Joe. You've got nothing else to do. See what you get for it.* I could tell I hadn't even made it to first-base before she called me out. No chance in hell to even start running for it. I'd taken a big swing, a gamble and a half on that one. Figured that everyone could appreciate it. But the ball came down without clearing the fence. Mrs Rhodes stood there to catch it.

'What did it come from, Joseph?' her voice sounded tired. 'Where did you find inspiration for such a piece as this?' Rhodes' tired wasn't the kind of tired you get from staying up late and

158

reading and marking papers. Not the kind you get from spending too much time in the break room before coming to class. This tired came from telling Joseph Reginald Pullman on too many occasions that he'd screwed things up. He'd taken a chance and the chance didn't pay off. It was a tired that came from not being able to hammer some sense into his head like everyone else had been doing.

'I read a few books about war.' I cleared my throat.

After the words came out there was silence. While her eyes followed me I walked over and tossed my report on top of Catriona Bowers'. She'd read something by Dickens and drawn a picture of Big Ben and the Eiffel Tower. Rhodes had come down hard about architecture and the time Dickens wrote the book. Catriona cried it up in front of the entire class. Rhodes wasn't expecting me to do the same, we'd danced that dance before. There was going to be no tears from Joey's eyes on that day.

'What kind of books are we speaking about, Joseph?'

'Fact books.' Cleared my throat. 'Non-fiction. One about World War II. Different battles. A couple 'bout the Korean War.' I didn't want to talk any more. Didn't want to be standing in front of a class that didn't want me around. The eyes that had been staring at me started to look around the room, meeting up with another eyes. *Nice one, Pullman. Find a bridge, kid. Jump like a saint and make us all remember ya.* I just stood there like a cat in the circle of a pack of dogs. Remembered the one Drexler's white Alsatians picked apart while I listened from the backseat of my old man's Diplomat. Felt the pink scar over my left eye pulsing and the small hairs on my back prickling up. The goose bumps came up on my arms and I rubbed at them, but they were there to stay. Couldn't go back to my seat without Rhodes telling me to get back to the front. She'd belt out something like I don't believe you have finished the assignment, Mr Pullman. I'd left her podium before time had been called on many occasions. I took the failing mark and the humiliation of her nagging old voice with a sense of self-respect. My pride was pumping heavy with the anger that started to bubble up inside. Not wanting to lose it in class I did the next best thing and kept talking.

'Another couple about Vietnam. Books. Tunnel rats and Charlie kind of stuff.'

'Interesting, Joseph. But nevertheless you did not take part in the assignment did you? You skipped a major point. In doing so you neglected to complete the material and the criteria outlined.' If her nose had been the barrel of a rifle she had me dead in her sights.

'Look, I read a lot. Made this poster. The report's on your desk.' My hand flipped out before I knew it and made a motion. It came as a gesture that told her I didn't care any more. It may have been to ask in a demanding way to be seated, but I knew it came off looking like I was done with the whole thing. *No permission needs to be granted. I'll do it my way.* Whatever the hand signal was meant to accomplish it missed the target. Rhodes either didn't see it or didn't get it.

'That is not what I am interested in, Joseph. Do you believe that you took part in this assignment?'

I baulked 'cause there was no answer. Just stared at her largeness framed by the green board in the back of the room. All of the eyes in the twisting heads met me. Then they snapped off again. Came back, but never for long.

'Can I sit down please?'

'The question is not a difficult one, Joseph. If you wish to sit you can answer me without further delay.'

With my head spinning I couldn't keep track. Catriona Bowers had drawn an old English street on her poster. *Big Ben, my ass.* A rectangle with an egg shaped clock. The Eiffel Tower on the other side looked more like the Sky Needle in Seattle. The lines didn't look steady and the Londoners would've been better off as stick figures. She'd used a black marker on yellow board. *Where's the time in that?* I'd sat on the floor of my room. Dean's mom took a trip out to buy me all I needed for that fucking poster. She headed off to the grocery store one day just for a pack of ground chuck and bought a load of stuff for me. Especially purchased by my temporary mother for Rhodes' project. Maureen had asked because she wanted me to get by, to pass the class and move on. She wanted me to do well and get out of a bad mess. Maureen Gillespie wanted everything to be alright for Joe Pullman. Sweet Jo-Jo whose mother hung herself at a country estate for lunatics. A kid whose father's walking the same dark path as the dead psycho bitch. But the eyes in that classroom kept on me, just stared and saw the kid with dirty clothes and a busted face. They reached out and poked at me with those freaking eyes. Came right out and touched me all over. A single snicker turned to a laugh and that laugh had echoed. A moment later that echo filled the room.

'Quiet!' Rhodes' voice broke the noise and all the chaos. 'Do we have a problem, Mr Pullman?'

'I did what I knew to do.' My voice came out and didn't have control of where it went.

'And by this you mean?'

'I took what you asked and I did my best. Got books out of the library. Read those books. Every word on every page. Then I wrote about it and drew that.' Pointing to the wall where a dozen quick-drawn posters hung. I stared at Mrs Rhodes' belt. It was fake snakeskin with a gold buckle half-hidden under a hefty roll of gut.

'Your assignment was to read a novel or a book of poetry . . .'

'And I didn't!' my voice yelled back. 'I read about real things. Read about bombs. About Nazis. People doing real bad things to other people. Bad things we're not supposed to forget. Not supposed to talk about and not supposed to forget. All at the same time, Mrs Rhodes. What did I read? I read about a guy in Vietnam who went into a tunnel with a rope around his waist. When his buddies pulled the rope out the guy wasn't all there. You can keep the freakin' novels. You can chew your faggot-assed pages of poetry. I've read it before. It didn't get to me. These books got me. In a big fucking way.'

'I think it is time for you to speak with Mrs Nemecheck.'

'Can't handle me?' I don't know where that came from. It sounded good.

'I'll have your bag sent down.'

'Kiss my ass.'

I hit the door with the palm of my hand and sent the hinges vibrating. The science class stopped and heads turned to look at me. Couldn't help but smile, it just kind of came out all over my face. I'd snapped on Rhodes and there was everybody to see. Sitting in that class or outside that class, through the glass or sitting right there in Room 25 I gave a show that day. There was no going back and part of me knew I should have worried about consequences. *What's done is done, Joe. Enjoy it while it's there.* That's what I was trying to do, just enjoy that feeling while it lasted. That feeling of control and power, 'cause it never lasted for long. It's in your hands, then it's out of your hands and that's the way life goes. I had to learn early on that my hands are meant to be empty more than they're meant to be full. It's the way my family operated and there wasn't any way of changing it. Until that summer came along my hands never felt so much, and I wasn't willing to go back to the way things had been.

There wasn't any reason to detour on the trip to the office. Walked out of the arena, into the corridor and headed straight down the scarlet hall. Walked with my hands in the pockets of my jeans, passed the cafeteria. Half of the school sat in there eating their lunch and a few familiar faces looked up at me. No one waved in my direction. Even if they had I didn't have the intention of waving back. I thought about taking a piss before I got to the office, but I figured it was only excitement I was feeling. Would've probably just stood in front of the urinal and squeezed like mad for a couple drops. Nemechek had a habit of making me wait, just for the hell of it. I'd been caught out before, sitting in that office with nothing but the sound of the fish aquarium bubbling away.

Before I'd made it to the glass door the secretary looked up from her magazine. She stared at me the whole time, right up to the glass fronted office. Could never help wondering if she wished I'd turn down the hall to the music room. *Just once, Joseph, turn* I could almost hear her say. Maybe she thought I'd head to the wood-shop. The music room couldn't have been a possibility because I'd dodged the required music section of the curriculum. Suppose the faculty thought Joseph Pullman couldn't be trusted with a state-owned guitar. Shriver had banned me from the wood-shop after the incident with the lathe. Danny Bassett should never have put his hand so close. I swear to God, still to this very day, that I never pushed his fingers into that thing. No matter how sure he was that I'd grabbed his hand. For some reason he screamed my name and told them I did it. Kept at it all the way to the police, but no witnesses means no trial. You learn more in school than you get from the books they loan you.

'Howdy, there,' I said pushing open the door.

She kind of shook her head and there may have been a smile creeping up in the corners of her mouth. I dropped into the black vinyl couch and hoped the feeling wasn't going to leave me before I got in to see Nemechek. I was really wired and could sense that right then I'd take anybody in a fight. No telling what I could do, how far I'd take it before I stopped.

The secretary dropped her eyes into her magazine. Her pen wrote letters into the blank squares of her crossword. Smoke trailed up behind the blue partition backing up to her desk. Someone coughed and I made a guess who it came from. Found out that I'd got it wrong when Ned Cunningham came out with his worried look holding strong to his narrow face. When he saw me sitting there another deep wrinkle cut into his forehead.

'Joseph,' he said. 'You here to see me?'

'I don't need counselling today, Mr Cunningham.'

'Good deal,' he said and walked by. He went past the secretary's desk without saying a word to her. He didn't need any files and he didn't think the coffee pot should be rinsed so he left her alone. He left her to waste a little more air and fill in a couple more squares with letters. He shut the door to his office when he got inside. The sign on his door read: In Session.

'What have you done now, Joseph Pullman?' the secretary

asked. She didn't look up from her magazine and that came as a relief.

'Read the wrong things. Figure I didn't get the assignment right.'

Her shoulders bounced a couple times, but she didn't make any noise.

'How did you manage that?' she asked.

'Just unlucky,' I said. She laughed aloud, but not so anyone could hear it through the closed doors. 'Doesn't matter what I'd do. I'll just end up in here again.'

'Never ending.' She nodded.

Nemecheck's door opened up and she waved me in. That's a record breaking wait-time, I told myself. *Shortest all year. Give that bitch a medal.* Brushing past her I smiled a cool smile, best I could manage. Then I took a seat in one of the two chairs in front of her desk. Those chairs had more cushion in them than any chair I've ever been in. A luxury in a place that lacked anything good or even half-decent.

'What's happening, Joseph?' Nemechek asked after she'd shut the door. She walked around to the other side of the desk. She didn't look at me until she'd sat in her seat. Grabbed her hands together into one big fist and her fingers went white with the pressure.

'Read the wrong books, I guess.'

'That's today. This makes a dozen times you've been in here in the past three weeks. That's too much. Do you not think that's too much?'

'Yeah,' I said. 'I guess there's other people you need to see. Place is busy out there.'

All credit to her when she didn't get riled. I'd aimed for it and thought I'd got her dead to rights with that one, but she didn't bite.

'What can we do about this?'

We just watched one another for a minute or two. This staring competition hit something funny inside me and I smiled more than ever. It could have been the adrenaline or the tiredness or the absurdity, but I couldn't help the smile. The smile didn't come out on my face as big as I felt it inside. Never could have been that size, 'cause my face wasn't big enough. No chance in hell that I could have smiled as wide as I felt it. If I had it would've split my head in two.

'Do you find this amusing? Our meetings?'

'I didn't ask to come down here. I did what I needed to do for that project. Rhodes told me . . .'

'Mrs Rhodes told you.' Nemechek corrected me.

I took a breath.

'Mrs Rhodes told us to read a book. Like a novel or something. I read four books. 'Cause they were real. You know what I mean, fact books. Didn't like it so she sent me down here.'

'Did you act up in class?'

'Like how?'

'Did you raise your voice? Did you disrupt the class?'

'I was giving a presentation on the stuff I did for the project.'

'Then why are you here?'

'Ask Rhodes.'

'Mrs Rhodes.' We continued the staring match. I had a confidence to win the thing. 'That is a big part of your problem, Joseph. You don't like to take criticism. You seem to have a distrust for adults.' She blinked and still I held steady with dry eyes. 'Mr Cunningham agrees with me. We have spoken at length about you and your troubles. Your file has grown this year. It's become weighted with your lack of performance in classes. It has become thick with your aggressive behaviour.'

I started one of those slow yawns that I've never been able to control. It began in my throat and got to my jaw before I could keep it shut. With my jaw opening I tried to hide it behind my closed lips, but it didn't work.

'Your disrespect for authority has gone too far.'

My right hand came up and covered my mouth. The yawning made my eyes water so I wiped the wetness away. This had an effect on Nemechek. She softened like I'd never heard her soften before. She even cleared her throat with a more gentle grunt.

'I understand you're having . . .' she stopped herself. 'I understand you've had problems at home,' she said. A pain started in my chest when she said that and it came up in a fast motion and caught in my throat. All that energy buzzing round inside of me dissolved and disappeared. Suddenly I was empty and weak and alone. Looking up at her I could see she hadn't expected me to react. My head dropped on cue and I wanted to get lost in something. Needed to get back in the forest and sit on the bridge. Lay on the soil under the branches of the Killing Tree.

'It's hard to lose a parent,' she said.

She didn't hit the nail square on the head. I wasn't even sure she was swinging the hammer at all. The air in my lungs came out with a slow and steady stream. *Someone who used to live in my father's house died. But it wasn't my mother. Looked close enough, but it wasn't her. Trust me. It wasn't Mother he took away. What they found hanging from that tree in Virginia wasn't Mother. She left long before.* It was all there on my tongue to say it. Come right out and tell her the way it was.

'Yeah,' I said. I wanted to keep her going. But she didn't stay quiet for long.

'How's your father been?'

'Tired,' I said. Maybe too quick.

'How has he been to you?'

The question came too deliberate and straightforward. It came in a formal way like she and Cunningham, the limp prick, had come up with questions to ask. My name should've been tagged on to the end of the question. *How has he been to you, Joseph? Does your father touch you, Joe? Do you feel as if home is no longer a safe place, Joe-Joe?* Even without her saying my name she'd made it clear I needed to answer. And quick.

'He's all right. Fine. He's just tired.'

'Is he working again?'

How's she know the old man stopped working, Joey-boy? If that gets back home before you . . .

'Joseph?' Nemechek said.

I didn't answer. That energy was all gone away now, took away

166

the competitive edge I'd had for a while. Hadn't just blinked during a staring competition, but I closed my eyes altogether. I'd seen all I needed to see and now I just wanted darkness. I needed to curl up somewhere and close my eyes and wake up when it was all over, when everything had changed. Hearing her talk to me didn't help my case. It hurt knowing outside the streets were empty. Knowing that all these clones inside with their schedules would walk out at five and be home for dinner by half-past. All the students with their uninterested faces would run and laugh at three thirty and I'd be lost as I ever was.

Nemechek left the office. I leaned back in the chair and closed my eyes.

She woke me half an hour later with the sound of her car keys. She handed over my school bag. One of my classmates had brought it down at the end of period. I looked up at Nemechek and she pursed her lips and breathed slowly out her nose. Then she said something that frightened me, something that cut right to the bone.

'I'm taking you home.'

Chapter Seventeen

The 'For Sale' sign stuck out of the grass at an odd angle from the centre of our yard. Nemechek pulled her car up into the drive. The garage door was closed. *Thank Christ for that.* Nemechek cut the engine and held onto the steering wheel while we both looked at the house. It was like we'd just driven down a highway that ended at the side of a cliff. There was nowhere else to go, but she wasn't willing to turn around just yet. So she stared ahead at the two-storey white colonial. Mother's dream house, until we moved in. It looked so big from the car, so much a waste.

Nemechek hit the button that unfastened her seatbelt.

'Let's see if your father's in,' she said.

'Let's leave it.'

'That is not an option, Joseph. I did not bring you home to save you from the walk. We are here to settle something.'

'What're you trying to settle?' I asked.

'The trouble.'

'Let me ask you one thing,' I said. Didn't look up when I started because I never planned to get out of the car if Nemechek went first. I couldn't see her going up to the front door without me at her side. 'If you knew something would cause more trouble than good would you still go for it?'

'What kind of trouble are we talking about, Joseph?'

'A kind that can get worse. A kind that's bad already, but can get so there's no going back.'

'Does your father hit you?'

'Jesus,' I breathed and gripped at the knees of my jeans with both hands.

'Does he hit you?' she asked again.

'Who doesn't?' I looked up. She just stared at me, her eyes right on mine and all of a sudden she didn't seem all that bad. She looked like a normal woman that I might pass in the street. She looked like any of the other well-dressed ladies that watched from the banks of Wild Lake the day Gillian Wilcox drowned. She wasn't perfect and she wasn't immovable. She was a middle-aged woman who got paid for sorting out problems and I was at the top of the week's agenda.

'Who hasn't taken a shot at this face?' I wasn't angry any more, but she still looked like she wanted to get out of the car. 'If it wasn't my old man it'd be Desmond Walker or Mookie Carlyle or any of the rest of them. I'm a target. Coming round here only makes it flash a little brighter.'

She went quiet for a while.

'Would it help if I . . .'

'It'd help if you backed off. Give me a few days' suspension. Drop in a detention once in a while. Do what you have to do. But keep my father out of it. This isn't where you belong. This is way out of your area. Out of your league.'

'That is the kind of thing that keeps you in my office,' Nemechek started.

'And it brings you to my father's home?'

'It is your home too.'

Her eyebrows lifted. Then she went quiet.

'I'll see you tomorrow,' I said. 'Probably in your office again.'

I got out of the car and walked to the front door. Nemechek pulled her Honda Civic away and was up the top of Westchester, turning right onto Grant's Road when I went inside.

I found my father perching on a wooden stool next to the

169

kitchen table. A dry mug sat on the table in front of him. Brown stains of coffee painted the sides. He turned his head to look at me. His jaw line looked more defined than usual. He'd dropped a lot of weight and his ribs were showing. The skin around his eyes had swollen up thick and turned purple.

'I'm moving,' he said.

He turned his head and looked into the mug. I stood in the doorway for a moment, keeping silent and staring at the side of his head. A part of me wanted him to twist around with the force of a cyclone and collide with me. Wanted the heaviness of his fists to fall on my head. But he remained still and the weight of the silence felt devastating. We stayed like that for a while. I waited for him to speak or move, give me some kind of a sign. Stood so I could've reached over and touched his pale shoulder. Could've put my hand on his head. Could've smashed a row of knuckles against his nose, anything to bring on a response. It never came because the longer I waited the quicker my energy evaporated.

My father's head hung and his arms went limp from the elbows and lay dead on the table. One at each side of the empty mug. I left him in that weak position, curled over and looking out the window, watching nothing. Walked up the stairs and slipped under the covers of my bed. That night sleep didn't come easy, but it came.

That night I dreamed about my mother. She lay in a shallow grave under the wooden deck. The dream started and I found myself looking out of my bedroom window. Could hear noises growing louder and moving closer. A chattering that broke on occasion to a scratching sound. Sometimes there came a thumping sound like soft hands against wood. The chattering started to build and from below my window the deck spread out like a lake in shadows. Somehow I fell down to it, crashing in what couldn't have been a jump or a hard fall. Before I hit something took me, it felt like I was floating in water and it brought my feet to the ground without noise. Following the chattering I crawled under the deck.

170

There I found my mother.

The grave wasn't deep enough to hold her body. A sheath of dirt covered her and created a silhouette of her arms and legs and breasts. Thin layers of the dirt fell away the closer I pulled my body to be near her. I found her eyes closed. When I tried to reach my hand out to touch her face my arm wouldn't stretch. That floating feeling came back and I couldn't get near her. Her dead skin shed a cold wave that touched my fingers. The longer I stayed near her the colder I became. Tried to back out of the darkness and found myself farther under the deck than I'd remembered crawling. Tried to turn around and the walls of earth moved up around me. Found myself in a tunnel that opened into a cavern. My mother lay in the centre of the opening. Thick pale roots grew up from the foundation of the house and ran close to her arms and legs.

I struggled to get out when the chattering grew louder. The sound came from the distance at first. It came in an almost thundering roll. Growing louder as it got close. Moving. Moving. Pulsing. When the sound made it to my ears it became more of a shrill. Mother's face moved like she wanted to smile. The closer the chattering got the more her lips twitched and her cheeks moved.

Something began writhing under her skin, pressing shapes into her face. Her mouth began to swell and deflate. As her lips parted the sound grew louder. The chirping and the screams swam out and into the black air. I moved back and found myself still caught in the tunnel. It closed in. Got to my knees and moved back. My hand went into wetness. It slipped. Reached out to regain my balance and touched my mother's face. Her head turned at the neck and I saw her eyes had been eaten away. Tried to take air. The smell of decay rushed into my nose. Pressed against the wall I watched my mother's face, thinking it would come back to life. As the first of the cicadas crawled from her opened mouth I tried to scream. From my lips came rushing silence.

I woke with my back pressed against the wall. The covers spun

171

around my legs and it took me some effort to get them free. Struggled with deep breaths trying to focus my eyes in the darkness. Wiped the sweat away from my forehead and ran my tongue around the inside of my mouth knowing I wouldn't be able to leave my room for water. With the heavy breathing the copper taste in my mouth grew worse. Started thinking of the kitchen and it seemed so far away. My eyes began to focus and things weren't where they should have been. The dresser I thought I'd pushed against the door sat in the centre of the room. The door looked almost shut, but the strip of soft light showed it'd been opened slightly. Let my breath go without sound and tried closing my eyes.

Waiting in the dark for sleep to come, I couldn't concentrate on anything. There was nothing in my memories that I could go to that made me feel safe. I thought about the pile of leaves that sat eighteen feet below my window. Tried to remember the dirty joke Oscar Lewiston had told Dean and me at the creek. *These two nuns are riding bicycles . . .* I didn't understand what made it funny but I'd laughed anyway. We'd all laughed and slapped the sand with open palms. But in the darkness of my bedroom where nothing appeared familiar anymore I couldn't feel safe. I wondered if there would be other times when I could sit with Dean and Oscar at the creek bed.

Something moved in the corner. It hid in the corner beyond the window, just past the silver haze streaking through. It pressed into the shadows as far as it could go. It was too big to keep from the silver light. All of it couldn't fill into the darkness all at once.

Maybe ask the boys what's so funny about the joke. Maybe if they'd tell it to you again. Let you hear it one more time, kind of thing . . .

Rolling over I made a moaning noise. I tried to make it sound authentic, close to sleeping. Angled my head so it fell in the shadow and stared back at the thing in the corner. Through narrow eyes I watched the dark space and waited for the thing to breathe again. My legs felt paralysed and my stomach bunched up and my lungs burned behind my ribs. Wanted to pull my feet up close, but that thing in the corner would grab them.

Closed my eyes and began to count again. This exercise got me to sleep so many times that year. Sometimes the counting helped, but sometimes it wasn't enough. I'd always been convinced that people who die without knowing the end is near go with ease. At that moment I counted so I wouldn't know how close I lay to the shadows in the corner. Counted till I'd fall asleep and never know what had happened and move on to some other place.

Kept counting. Ten-one-thousand. Eleven-one-thousand. Twelve-one-thou . . .

The thing moved. It made a dull noise, nothing powerful, but it stopped my counting cold. I let out a quick breath and the thing stopped. Opened my eyes a fraction more and from the blackness I saw a shoulder emerge. In that silver line of light the shadow peeled away from other shadows. Just like it was coming out of water the figure grew from the dark. With the shoulder came the arm. A neck emerged and then a chest and the head. The sight of my father moving away from the black corner shot a bolt of lightning through my body.

My muscles went tense.

He came to the foot of my bed, stood in silence and stared down at me. He looked into my eyes that I narrowed into thin creases. *How hidden are your eyes in these shadows, Joe? He can see you watching him.* His arm came up and I closed my eyes.

Wait for it, Joe. Here comes the big one and you're awake to feel it.

My lungs felt too full and my ribs burned. Small, sharp jolts ran through me. They danced over my skin while I lay there . . . waiting. My body anticipated where his first punch might land. Tightened all my muscles and kept steady as a rock. His silence kept me guessing what part he would be aiming for first. Then his feet moved over the carpet. Muscles tightened more until they felt like they'd tear to shreds.

Then there was nothing. No breathing. No feeling that he was over me. Through the slits of my closed eyes I saw the shadows. Nothing but empty shadows.

173

He'd left my room and I was still frozen. He left without noise and he took my breath with him. The sound of his feet dragging over the carpet let me know he was going away. He was heading down the hall. I had to concentrate to hear that faint sound of my old man walking. The pulsing of blood drummed inside my head. *Wait for it, Joe.* Oh, Christ, he was still in there with me. He was still in the corner and I'd just lost it for a minute. Wanted so bad for him to be gone that I thought it all up. Made up the whole thing, even that sound of his feet. He's still down there, at the bottom of the bed and he's reaching down to . . .

His bedroom door shut with a painful thump. I got out of bed and my legs felt like I'd walked twenty miles, they shook at the knees. Shook so much they hurt all the way up to my hips. In the dark I found my pocket knife on top of the dresser. It was between a 2-litre bottle of Pepsi I'd half-filled with pennies and a copy of *Pet Sematary*. Opened the blade of the knife and went back to the bed, thinking I was going to fall before I got there. I hid the knife under my pillow and used my hands to rub my legs.

The rest of the night went slow. Watched the door for hours, went cold when the house made a creak or the air conditioner kicked in. I fell in and out of sleep. Each time I came awake in a spasm. Just like Mick Drexler's dogs had found another cat to tear apart and they were doing it right there in my room. So I'd lay there and imagine him breathing in the black corner. But my old man no longer stood there waiting. With the sun rising and pushing yellow heat through my window I started feeling safe again. The shadows had all been burned away and the room was empty. Pushed the dresser against the door and fell asleep. It didn't take long before the dreams started.

A black man dressed in hospital greens was dancing on a bridge. Oscar was there, his legs dangling over the side. They were both the same length and I wanted to ask him how he'd been fixed. But I couldn't speak. Somehow I couldn't find the slightest bit of breath. The black man danced away but there was no sound. The creek moved in small rapids. Kicked up white foam where it cut between rocks. Sounded louder than usual like there had been a heavy rain. But the heat was cutting into me. I took a knee like a boxer hit with the big punch. My breath just wasn't coming, even when I tried to suck in with all my might. Then I looked up at the bridge. Oscar and the black man were watching me. They were staring with all they had and laughing like they'd gone mad.

It's all good, they yelled. I couldn't hear them. Their mouths shaped into the words, but nothing came out. *It's all good.* And then they laughed. Opened my mouth wide to suck in or yell, anything. Then I fell toward the ground, only it wasn't solid. It was moving. It was a moving floor of leaves and underneath was a darkness I couldn't stand.

I woke with a gasp and sweat dripping from my brow. The red numbers of my alarm clock glowing 9:08. Kept under the covers for another half an hour, maybe more. My fingers gripped the pocket knife while I listened for movement. After finding the courage I walked to my bedroom door and waited for any sounds. Something to let me know if my father was in the hallway. In the weeks leading up to that night my old man couldn't stay still. He paced constantly, up and down the rooms. Then he'd go to another part of the house and pace there. Sometimes he'd rake the walls with his fingers when he walked the hall. He'd smashed all the plates on the kitchen floor and left the pieces. That morning there were none of the sounds that made his presence known. There were no coughs and no scratching sounds. There wasn't even the noise of his drill.

I waited and listened. When I was sure he wasn't waiting for me I opened the door and walked down the stairs. Took them one at a time easing my weight onto each step. At the bottom I heard his voice and my spine turned to ice just like it was ready to crack. *He's on to you, Joe. He's got someone in the house. They're talking about your trips into the forest.* Then the voice hit something clean and clear that dropped me where I stood. *He's got that Nemechek bitch in the house.*

175

Right there on the bottom step I was in the loneliest place in the world. I wrapped my arms round my knees and waited to hear Nemechek's voice. Waited for her to ask my father about the abuse. Maybe she'd give him a chance to make things up to me before she called the cops. Maybe she'd brought the cops with her. A couple of boys in blue with a social services suit to escort me out of there. That was enough to get me on my feet. Still, I couldn't go in there. Couldn't just walk into the kitchen and give myself up.

What the hell're you waiting on, Jo-Jo? This is your chance, darlin'.

I almost went. That voice in my head almost came just in time to start a run that wouldn't stop until I'd got behind the toughest sonofabitch in there. But that would've caused more trouble than I'd ever encountered.

My old man started talking again, sounded almost like there was a laugh in his voice. His words kind of bounced like they did when he and my mother used to talk about buying expensive things. He'd talk and then stop in mid-sentence. After a few seconds he'd get going again. The more I listened to him the more things started to piece together. It's like standing and staring at a picture and it slowly comes to mean something. There was only my father's voice coming from the room. Waited and listened hard, almost trying to will that other voice to take over when my old man stopped. That damn voice never came. I was listening to the stop and start of a telephone conversation. Leaning against the banister at the base of the stairs the energy had left me. While I listened to his half of the conversation I tried to make out who held the phone at the other end. My breath was lost in an instant when he spoke my mother's name.

'Clarisse,' he said. There was a pause and his hand came slapping down on top of the counter. 'Yes, but . . . you can't just . . .' It was the first time I'd heard my father plead with her. His voice became brittle and the words fell to pieces as he spoke. After a long silence he let out a loud breath. He sounded like a swimmer who'd been under water too long.

'He's fine.' Pause. 'I know and I did.'

There was a series of other sounds coming from the room that made me wonder if my old man was crying. Heaving sounds and a wet kind of sniffling. He'd always been a powerful man, never giving me anything but reason to believe he was harder than life. He lived in my mind as a creature of purpose, one with few emotions. He roamed inside my head until I couldn't act unless I'd considered my father's face. Until I'd remembered the weight of his hands crashing down on me. He cleared his throat, an effort that took several attempts.

'He's only a boy!' my father finally yelled. The sounds of his breathing, heavy and strained came from the room. That sound of my father losing his strength came to me. The weakness seeped out of him like a ghost. I listened to him breathing and I imagined that ghost sitting down on the bottom step. Looking up at me with tired eyes. *Can't hurt you like this. Go get a look at him. Go see for yourself how pathetic a man he is. Better do it before time's up.*

I slid my feet over the hardwood floor and came to the doorway leading to the kitchen. The shutters angled slightly open and I looked into the gap. My father faced away from me, his bare back striped with three pink scars on his shoulder. His tall frame hunched forward. His hand held the counter, balancing his weight, while his legs crossed at the ankles. He held the handset in one hand and stared at the floor. There was something inside me that asked to go back. Just head to your room and ram the dresser in front of the door. I was frightened looking into the room. Not because of my father appearing so detached, so lame and weak compared to what he had once been. The fear came because I knew there was no one on the other end of the telephone. Not Mother. Not Nemechek. Not anyone.

There'd never been a telephone in the kitchen. There was no outlet for phone lines in that part of the house, never had been. The old-fashioned, black rotary dial box sat on the counter. The phone line hung, wound up in a rubber band, dangling over the edge of the counter top. The frayed end of copper wire splayed like a fan.

177

Slid myself back to the foot of the stairs, careful to make no sound.

'Yes, I know it's best, dear.' There it was again, that half-dead voice that almost sounded like my old man's. 'I'll make sure he hears your name.'

I climbed the stairs without making the slightest noise. Dressed quick as I could manage with my hands shaking as bad as they were. Had to rub the shakes out of my legs again and then went out of the house faster than I ever made it before. Didn't listen at the door for my old man before I left my room. Just went for it, eyes wide and mouth open. Got to the front door not knowing if my father would try to stop me. My heart pounded inside my chest. The pulsing blood carried adrenaline to my cheeks, made them feel like I'd marched a hundred miles in a blizzard. Outside the air was hot and the wet grass glistened under the bright sky. I ran into the open space and hid among the oaks. Never spent long behind one before it felt unsafe, then I'd move to another.

The sun had fallen and turned the blue sky to deep purple before I started a walk back to the house. Climbed into a tall oak and watched him through the kitchen window. Don't know if he ever set the telephone down that day. He still held it in his hand when I climbed down that night. Before I went inside the house I collected a dozen armfuls of leaves and piled them beyond the railings of the deck. The small mound was waist high before I'd finished. Looking up at the side of the house I wondered if I'd done the right thing. Imagined myself falling from my window and hoped I'd built the pile in the best spot. It was never going to be enough to take all my weight, but I needed to know it was there. I'd jump quicker that way.

I'd started to dread the thought of my father's house again. Liked the idea of it being sold, but no one who went in to look at it came out all that interested. It was a big place with five bedrooms. Seemed a mansion while I lived there with my mother around. There was always a room I could go that was far enough away from her. The house stood in the dark shade from the trees that surrounded it. The shutters had started to rot away and the shrubs were struggling, untended to since the last freeze came and turned them brown.

During those first days of summer I hid in the front garden. Laid down in the blades of grass, overgrown and sagging with the weight of their seeds. In the mornings I'd wake before the sun and leave the sweat-stale smell of my bed for the long green blades. Then I'd walk into the open space and kick pine cones and throw stones at trees until I'd dried off.

Chapter Eighteen

Rumours travelled round town like they were carried by the wind. The day after Gillian Wilcox drowned people all over Maritime were in agreement that she'd been murdered. Word got out that someone had stolen all the lifejackets from the boathouse the day before. With Gillian never learning to swim she didn't have much of a chance once she'd hit the water. When a kid dies in a small town it's not always easy to put it down to an accident. Sometimes it helps the pain to have a person to blame, however irrational the claim. There wasn't anyone to suspect for the theft of the lifejackets, or the loosely connected death of the sheriff's daughter, so the rumour machine built one, or built on an old one anyway.

'Bet it's those damn Grits again,' Dean told me.

'What's that?'

'Who stole the jackets from the boathouse.'

'Never heard of 'em.' I looked out at the lake. The water was flat and smooth and was only ever broken when a fish came up to take something from the surface. 'Either way, Dean, she would've gone without one.'

He didn't want to hear me.

'They're travellers,' he said. He was still withdrawn and

wouldn't talk about Gillian if I started up on the subject. Like most things Dean was fine to talk about the tough subjects only when he could choose them.

'Dad calls them American Gypsies.'

'Like I said. Never heard of 'em.'

He was quiet for a while and I thought that was the end of it. We watched while an old couple walked up to the edge of the lake. They set a bouquet of flowers down on top of all the others that had been collecting from earlier visitors. Watching them build onto that mountain of carnations must have hit something in Dean. He must have had a memory of Gill that he couldn't handle sitting down. He hopped up and started walking in the opposite direction from the memorial. I followed him, but kept my distance thinking he might start crying. Walking next to Dean when he broke down would've made me look just as much a pussy as he was.

'Come on, Pullman,' Dean yelled over his shoulder. His voice had that rubbery sound like he'd gotten himself all choked up. 'I got something to tell you.'

That caught my attention enough to forget about him going soft. Figured if he did get wet round the eye I could make him harden up somehow. Pulled up next to him and stuck my hands deep in my pockets.

'What're you telling me about?'

'Grits have been around for a while,' he said like he was out of breath. With the pace he was walking it was no wonder. He went on with his story like he didn't want to stop. 'Travel in and out of the area. Maritime. Columbia. Denholm. Dad says they're roamers.'

'Nomads.'

'Let me talk, Pullman.' He sounded edgy. I kept quiet thinking it would be better for him to talk than for him to have the time to remember Gillian again. 'They've been coming round for years. Decades even from the sounds of it.'

He took a deep breath. He sucked in so much air that his chest rose out in the front. Then he let out the breath through his puckered lips. He turned his head and looked at me like he wanted to say something, but couldn't find the words.

'They kidnap kids.'

'Huh?' I said.

'The Grits. They take kids and do stuff to them.'

'Kind of stuff?'

'Don't know. No one likes to talk about that part of it. I've heard they bury them alive when they're done.'

'Jesus,' I said.

'If a kid went missing round here the town would shut down.' He let out a laugh that made me wonder what he had on his mind. It was one of those laughs that comes without you knowing about it even being there in the first place. Like when you think of something funny, right out of the blue. Or when you think of something so devastating you have to laugh just to get yourself to believe that it wasn't you who thought of it.

'Maritime doesn't lose its kids,' Dean said. He looked at me with this really sincere face, like he wanted me in on a secret. 'But if it did, people would start up about the Grits.'

After that day by the lake I hadn't seen Dean for a while, a few days anyway. I'd been dealing with my old man and his telephone calls to a dead woman. I'd been dodging an encounter with him, thinking that meeting up in the hallway or the kitchen could have been the end of it all. Dean had been with his parents, of course. They went to church with a load of other families and paid their respects and lit candles in memory of Gill. Maureen didn't invite me to that one and there was part of me that hated her for not calling. It was the only time I'd hoped she would phone. But it was the moment of realization, the kick in the pants that only reality can bring with that much force. I wasn't part of their family. I had my own and it was broken and the only person who had the ability to change that was me.

Dean was at the bridge the day after Gillian's funeral. He got there before me so when I came up on him I figured he was in a slump. *So they get your girl in the ground alright? You and your*

182

folks have a good time without me? You know Gillian sucked off a senior on the Lincoln football field last season? Christ, the things that were going on inside my head while I was walking up the creek bed toward the bridge. The more Dean stared at me the more these comments kept coming in.

'Hey, Dean.' I climbed the embankment and slipped a few times before making the top. 'You okay?'

'Yeah. Just kind of tired.'

'That's cool, I guess.'

'Not really.'

'Got any more to tell me about the Grits?'

'No.' He lowered his head and spat into the water. 'Wasn't them anyway.'

'Lifejackets you mean?'

'Yeah. Kincaid needed them for a camping trip. He's the leader of some scout thing.'

'Mystery solved,' I said.

He smiled and nodded his head.

'Think the Grits are real anyway?'

'Yeah. They're out here in the woods. Somewhere out here.'

'Know where?'

'Got an idea.'

Me and Dean knew most of the forest. From the open space it branched out into two thin lines of trees for a while. These lines only spanned about three hundred yards. That may seem like a lot, but when there are houses bordering each side the noise makes you aware of suburban life. That kind of civilization can be damning if you're out there to escape it all.

With such a narrow distance between neighbourhoods these two lines of forest seemed like they went on for miles. To the left the line of trees lead to Grant's Road. Past Grant's there was another forest, bigger than the one Dean and me called our own. That other forest always looked like it held more darkness than it should. Me and Dean mainly went right at the open space. That line of forest headed out toward Wild Lake and Packson Valley. It was a good long walk to get to Packson Valley but we

183

went sometimes. It's still known round these parts for the streams out there. The fishing's good and the deer in the valley are all good sized, or so I'm told. It's in the Maryland State guides for the Farmer's Markets, but that kind of stuff doesn't pull the kids. It didn't give us a calling to trek the four miles to get there. We went because it got us away from Maritime, away from my old man.

This one morning in May Dean told me he wanted to head left. He didn't make many decisions so when he got a notion for something new I let him lead. We started walking with our heads down. Both of us watched the ground and neither of us felt up to saying much. Before we got to the Angry Snake Dean pulled out a packet of Big Red chewing gum. We stood under a tree while he divvied it out, a couple pieces each. The cinnamon burned at my gums more than it usually did. I made a lot of noise sucking in some air between my teeth. The sucking came half in an effort to cool my mouth and half to emphasize the severe discomfort.

'Your dad's not letting up is he?' Dean asked.

'No.' I touched a couple of fingers up to my right eye. The brow had swollen up since that morning, but the blood had dried quicker than expected. For that I felt kind of disappointed. Dean seemed easier to lead when I sported heavy wounds sponsored by my old man's knuckles. It was easy to look at Dean like he was a retarded lamb when I dripped blood. He went shy and quiet when I showed up looking like a Grant's Road crash victim. Could do anything and say anything to him and he'd just take it. He must have been rolling it over and over in his head that my old man could tear him apart.

'Should call the cops,' he told me. Didn't even look at me when he spoke, just kept his eyes on the path ahead. 'Your dad's a freak, Pullman. One of these days he's not gonna let you up.'

'Yeah. Call the cops,' I laughed. 'Where'm I gonna go then?'

'Where you gonna go when he sells the house?'

'Hell if I know.'

'Then tell somebody, Pullman. Christ. Get some help while you still can.'

Truth is I'd thought about all that stuff. Over the past evening I'd given it plenty of damn thought. With my old man holding a handful of my hair while he drove the knuckles of his other hand into my ribs. I'd run through the scene while he rocketed in another shot.

Phone ringing a half dozen times. Tired voice picks up the other end. '9-1-1 dis . . .'

Before the voice finished talking a fist connected with my cheek.

Some part-time dispatcher repeats her greeting: '9-1-1 dispatch. What is your emergency, please?' She's not all that interested, anyway.

– This is Joe Pullman. My father just beat the hell out of me. I need help.

Hold the line, please.

He'll be back any minute. Send a car. Send someone.

Hold, please.

Trouble was I couldn't even convince myself that the person answering the call would take it serious. I'd been passed up for help by all the teachers and faculty since I started school. They got paid by the same local government as the asshole taking the 9-1-1 call. *Hold, please. Just fuck it . . . I'll take care of it myself.*

My old man came in with another punch. Never saw it coming. I'd been sliding to the side. His hand scraped against my left temple. Then his knuckles crashed into the wall behind me. I picked up on his agony after he let go of my head. Opened my eyes to see him bend down. Almost on his knees, squeezing his wrist. *Hold the line, my ass.* I rolled over thinking he was going to pull me back. When I'd made it to the hall I figured his hand must've been busted real bad. Still waited for him to even things up when I got to the top of the stairs. Locked in the bathroom rinsing my cut mouth – waiting for him to hammer the door in. Instead I heard the drills kicking on down in the basement. Then his other tools came on, one after the other. He had them all playing his own personal symphony.

I looked over at Dean who wasn't man enough to look me in the eye. Sucked in some more air. The cinnamon started biting at my gums like a school of piranhas had been let loose in there. My tongue eased off with the burn, but that cut was small. The top gum still fired up at times. The cut there was more of a gash, opened up by the first big right hand my old man had thrown.

'Why're you doing that?' Dean asked.

'Doing what?'

'That sound . . . that hissssst thing.'

I just looked at him with my eyes all screwed up. It's the way we questioned things, Dean to me and me to him. We were blunt and to the point, but it wasn't always easy to take. After you've spent the night stuffing worn socks in your mouth to easy the bleeding you don't need some skinny runt giving you stick.

'With your mouth.' He pointed to his own pouty lips. 'That sucking thing,' he said. Used his index finger to draw circles in the air in front of his lips. Kept at it for a few seconds like I hadn't understood him before.

'Mouth's burning like it's on fire.'

'Still. It's kind of annoying.'

'So are you,' I said. 'Fucking asshole prick.'

Things went quiet again.

'Lose teeth this time?' He looked excited. He sounded excited too.

'No.'

'Lemme see. Come on, Pullman,' he said. Now he looked at me. Had this smile on his face. 'Lemme have a look.'

We stopped and he faced me. I gave in and opened my mouth and there we stood in the middle of the Angry Snake for a few minutes. Dean inspected me with his mouth open as much as I'd opened mine. He kept moving his head around while I stayed still. When he'd had enough he stepped back and made a whistling sound. Then he shook his head and did that thing with his eyes, made them real sincere.

'Doesn't look good.'

'What?' I asked. 'Worse than before?'

He nodded. 'Seen your gums?'

'No.' My stomach felt like I'd just hit the first drop of a theme park roller coaster. My head went light dizzy and for a minute I got worried that things weren't all that right. Maybe my old man had done something that I'd need to get fixed. I'd have to go back to Dean's place and ask Maureen to take me to see some doctor. First explain to her that I'd fallen down the stairs and then give the same freaking story to the hospital and maybe the cops. Stuff got bad for a few seconds. If they were going to take me away they would need to take me for good. None of this take him for a night and then back home tomorrow. My old man wouldn't be too happy to have me home after a night in the county lock-up.

So what've you been saying now, son?

I looked up and saw Dean standing there in front of me, smiling one of his my-parents-get-me-to-the-dentist-every-six-fucking-months smiles. That look got my back up even more than before.

'If you liked what you saw so much,' I said, 'maybe I should give you the same.'

The smile faded from his face like a melting candle. That smile was completely hidden when he walked away. The back of his head bounced in front of me like an easy and inviting target. We walked through the water tunnel that cuts under Grant's Road. Something about that day made it feel like a good time to be out there. Under the leaves of the forest, out and away from everybody that didn't want us around.

Halfway through the tunnel Dean found a rat. It'd been chewed up pretty good, probably by other rats. Maybe it'd been eaten by other rats from its own rat family. Dean flicked the thing with his shoe not expecting anything more than a light, dead weight. When it flinched and tried to turn itself over he almost filled his Levis. I was bent over, coming through the tunnel behind him. He backtracked and stuck an elbow into my ribs. There was too much pain for me to come down on him straight away.

187

I backed aside and Dean went past. He left the tunnel for a minute, but came back with a branch.

'Dickhead,' I said. It echoed in the tunnel. 'That's a bad place to hit me.'

'Sorry.' He didn't sound like he even cared. He didn't give much notice to the fist I'd balled up, waiting for him. 'Just needed to get something to kill it.'

I let him past and watched him beat the rat round the tunnel. He smacked it with the stick and it barely moved. It rolled in the shallow water and made like it was going to dart off. Then Dean shoved the stick under it and flicked it forward, toward the other opening of the tunnel. Along the way he swatted at the thing like crazy. It must have taken ten minutes to get through the tunnel. When we came out the other side Dean dunked the rat in the white and yellow foam collecting below the run-off. Then he speared it in the side and sank the thing to the bottom of the stream. He held it there until it stopped moving. When he'd finished he let it float up and flicked it with the stick to the opposite bank.

'Remember where it is,' he told me. He'd played himself out, taking the game farther than he'd wanted to go. He stood there with the branch in hand, almost out of breath. 'I'll get it on the way back.'

Then he went ahead and hacked at anything in his way with that wet branch. I followed and lagged behind at times. When I don't know where I'm going I can be stubborn. It's the way I've always been, I guess. When your father has a heavy hand you have to maintain a silent kind of stubbornness. It's made me an undesirable companion to many people, I guess, including Dean. Still, Dean always came back for more. I always took him in.

We'd made it to Fuller's Mark when we finally stopped. Fuller's Mark is a ruin that's supposed to be from Civil War times. I'd asked Dean's father about it on a few occasions and he just shrugged. I didn't have anyone else to ask so I just believed what I'd heard from people my own age. Fuller's Mark was just another suburban myth coming back to haunt Joseph Pullman. Even so I kept the more elaborate stories aside, thought about them until they played like movies in my head. There were rumours that the Mark had housed witches back in the day. Some people talked about a guy who killed his wife and then ate her skin to the bone. I liked to hear all the stories, but I couldn't believe them. Not when I stood there looking at the thing, looking at the Mark.

The bricks had been knocked down to almost ground level. The wooden planks that covered the floor remained in place for the most part. They'd gone brittle over the years and some had fallen in with the weight of snow and rain. Dean and me tried to dig for stuff a few times, but of course didn't find anything. Kept expectations high, somehow we always found a way to do that. Even though we always came up with a big fat nothing.

On these digs we'd spend a few hours, just milling round the place. Hacking at the ground, sifting through soil. Didn't get up to much with any real commitment. The first half-hour we'd be all for it. We spread out to cover more ground. If one of us came up with something that looked worth the time the other would be right there. We had it all covered *fast as a flash*, Dean used to say.

'I want a bag of money,' Dean always claimed. It never failed. 'I want a million bucks in unmarked notes.'

'It'll be old money, dumb-ass,' I'd tell him.

'Just the same as new. Got dead presidents on it still.'

Oz, on the few times we let him come with us, would keep his mouth shut for the best part of the day. When he did talk Dean made him wish he'd kept his mouth closed.

'I'm gonna find a musket,' Oz had a habit of saying. 'One of them long sniper kinds with the flip-up sights. I'll find a sword too. I betcha. I'll get a sword that's worth more'n any bag of money you find.'

'You find a sword,' Dean told him, 'I'll use it to cut you in half, gimp.'

'How're you gonna do that if I cut your hands off first, Gillespie?'

I let them fight. Most times I got so deep in thought that I didn't even hear them. They had their wishes and wanted everyone to know about them. I stayed silent and kept it all to myself. While they fought I drew the Fuller's Mark site in my journal. Whenever we dug I drew a hole and shaded it in. Dean had dug in the same spot a couple times, but I never called him on it. If I had he would've known I'd kept track and maybe then he'd have figured my journal was more than just for show. While digging I kept thinking about dead slaves. Slaves trying to get up north who suffered for the mistake of passing through Maritime. Fuller's Mark stood as a safe house from what I understand. Mr Brudzinski spoke about it in his history class. Fuller's Mark must have always been full. According to Brudzinski Maritime was lily white in those times, and the only safe house in town was a hidden house.

In my dreams Fuller's Mark fell to fire. The dreams came during nights following the visits we made. The more time we spent there, the more soil I dug and the more detailed the dreams became. Some of the dreams were intense while some came and went leaving me with almost nothing to remember. I'd wake up knowing they'd been, but there wasn't anything that stayed behind to haunt me through the day. Most of the time I saw things that made me rethink it all. Those dreams burned into my brain like the black and white pictures of my father's book. Even with the images of those people screaming I could shake them off easy enough if I tried, but the smell always lingered. The smells in my dreams are always stronger than what I experience in the waking hours. The smell of the burning slaves caught in my throat, so strong it came back during the day. That smell and that burning seemed more than real.

Inside Fuller's Mark the floor planks had been bending and breaking over the years. Every time me and Dean went to the Mark he'd pull up another plank to check for snakes. Before we left the plank would be back in its place. The snakes we found got beaten into the soft soil with sticks. Some of them got away after all the commotion, beaten but still alive.

I'd been trekking along with expectations of spending the afternoon at Fuller's Mark. Dean came up on it with so much energy, swatting at the bushes and branches he passed with that damned stick. Figured he was ready for a day of digging. Then he turned round and waited for me to catch up and I saw he had this look on his face. Truth was I didn't feel like digging that day. Walking up the paths I kept thinking about dead slaves. Felt kind of cold in all the sweating knowing that people could have died at the Mark. Couldn't help but wonder who it was that set the place on fire, if it was one of the slaves or someone they never expected.

'We're gonna find Grits' Cave,' Dean said in his hardest voice. He stared at me with this uncaring look on his face.

'Fine,' I told him.

He sat on the highest part of the Mark's fallen brick walls. I came up and started kicking a few layers of dirt away before covering them over again. After a few minutes of silence Dean got up and started walking again. I followed and kept swiping at my face to keep the sweat from falling into the fresh cut on my forehead. It took a while to get through the thickets that lined the ravine. We'd never gone that far before because it was outside of the safe zone. The neighbourhoods stopped and the forest opened up past the ravine and spread far and wide. This is where civilization ended and the great wild wilderness began.

We both kind of stalled for a while. Looking across the dried-up stream we couldn't tell how far the ravine stretched. Brush and trees had grown on each side. They kind of came together at places and looking down into it made the thing seem only a dip in the ground. We both knew it was a small valley, at least that's what we'd been told. Like anything else we weren't sure how much of all this was myth and legend.

Having my suspicions I tossed some rocks. Dean followed my lead and each of the stones we threw went into the thicket on the other side. They didn't make much noise when they hit bottom. We looked at one another and nodded like we didn't know the answer to a question we both wanted to ask. One of us made the decision to go on and the other followed. I can't remember who went first.

Past the thick vines the trees opened up so we didn't have to go sideways to get through any more. Further on they thinned out again. The ground started getting moist and water soaked into the soles of our shoes. The realization was slow to come to both of us that the ground didn't look like ground any more. Our socks had filled up with water before we figured out that we had come upon floating ground. It wasn't forest soil we stood on any more.

'This is kind of weird, Pullman.'

'Yeah, it's moving. The ground I mean.'

'I know what you mean. Weird.'

Only a few trees dotted that part of the forest. It looked like a field where a house should have been standing. Below the sparse branches lay a covering of leaves, too many leaves to have been dropped by the trees that still stood in the area. I looked over the landscape trying to catch sight of the trunks of fallen trees. There was nothing sticking out of the ground, nothing making a hump in the flat land.

'Look at them moving,' Dean said watching the ground.

'Yeah, I see it.'

With our sneakers half-sunken in sludge we stood side-by-side. In front of us the ground of leaves looked too soft. The movements were small, but enough to notice. I took a stick and jabbed it into the leaves a few feet away. Although I gave it a heavy stab the surface didn't break. The stick didn't go through the leaves. Pulled the stick in and broke the thick part, bending it over my knee. I tossed it in and it hit the top with a heavy slapping sound. The movements of the leaves were bigger where the stick landed. For a second or two there was a swaying move-ment, then it all returned to the easy motion. It was a motion you could almost miss if you weren't looking for it.

'Like it's breathing,' Dean said.

'What's breathing?'

'The ground.' Dean walked away, but I stayed put. Part of me wanted to get away from the shifting leaves, but there was something about it. Something familiar, like I'd experienced it before.

Dean didn't go far, he'd just walked far enough to find a rock. He came back and tossed it out to where my stick had landed. The rock busted the leaves and sent water shooting up. The noise it made could have doubled for a shotgun round fired somewhere in the distance. It was a sound that came in two parts. First a dull heavy sucking sound and then a louder whoosh with the spray lifting into the air. Water came out of the small hole the rock made in the leaves.

'Think it's deep?' I asked.

'I don't want to chance it.'

'Don't know what's in there anyway.'

'Snakes, probably. What else we got?' Dean knelt close to the leaves. Just in front of him the ground shifted so he pressed at the leaves with his rat stick. The leaves stuck together, but where the stick touched they sank. When he let off they came back up. Dean straightened himself and started a fast walk away and this time I followed him.

We walked a long path around the edge of the moving ground. While we walked we watched the leaves. Under the surface was darkness. Anything could get lost down there. When Dean chose a new path I kept up with him. Still, I kept looking back. Had to make sure the surface wasn't broken.

Dean led us into a line of trees that bunched in parts so heavy we had to twist sideways to get between them. The ground felt solid after those trees and before long we found a path. It came close to the edge of the marsh, but was real soil. We followed it with the floating leaves shifting at our side.

It wasn't long after the moving ground that we heard the voices. Something drove us to keep going deeper into the forest. Dean slowed his lead and when I caught up he stopped and grabbed at my arm. I pulled away before he could get a grip.

193

Up ahead the trees spread out and there was something that looked like a tent in a clearing. I turned to find Dean standing like an idiot just staring at me.

'Come on, Dean.'

'Shut up, Pullman. That's the place. They're going to . . .'

He ducked like he saw something or someone. I ducked with him and twisted so I could see what it was that freaked him out. There was nothing up ahead. Just trees and beyond there was a tent. Dean caught up with me and pressed in too close. His arm rubbed up against me so I elbowed him hard in the chin. He looked hurt, but more in a shocked sense than anything else.

That hit got him moving forward, like it jolted him into action. He pushed branches aside with a panicky fast-motion. I came up behind him and if he heard me he didn't make an effort to slow down. We got closer to the voices and the clearing and the tent. Dean stopped pushing branches aside and froze up when he was about to reach the tree line. He stared ahead with his mouth half open. I came up behind him and almost pushed hard to move him forward. But I stopped when I saw what he saw.

Two guys walked around the camp, but from where we stood I couldn't tell if we knew them. Didn't ask Dean what he thought, but he looked like he wanted to turn and run home. Head back to Momma and those big pitchers of lemonade. I brushed by him and knocked his hand away when he tried to stop me. If it had been adults I'd seen I would've gone back, never would've gone for it. Dean had told me bad things about the Grits. But that was Dean, a middle-class kid with a safe life. What the fuck did Dean Gillespie know about a gang of travelling killers?

I got to the edge of the clearing where the tent stood. The two guys had their backs to me so I couldn't make out the faces through the leaves. Dean came up behind me without making a sound. He put a hand on my shoulder and I shrugged it off. One of the guys in the clearing wailed a kind of laugh and the other yelled out and I became intoxicated. Feeling nothing bad could happen to me I took a step forward and Dean went for me again. He stood at my side and made a motion toward the trees behind me.

'Get back home to Momma,' I said and ran through the tree line. Dean ducked back and wedged himself in hiding. Out of sight and out of mind, I didn't care. The voices in front of me came from guys my age. They were out of their depth just as much as Dean and me. With that kind of thought going through my head I stepped quicker, almost jumping into the opening of the camp.

'What the hell, Pullman?' I heard one of the boys yell. The voice reached me before I'd even got through the tree line. Didn't think I'd gotten close, but the guy reached out a fist and connected with my chest. Even one of J.D.'s quick-fire punches could break you. Running into it only doubled his strength.

'Take it easy,' I breathed. Pushed a hand over my left breast where he hit me. Tried to hold in the pain, but it burned in deep. I bent down unable to catch my breath and grabbed my knee with the other hand.

'You can't run up on people like that an' expect a smile, dick cheese. Think before you fall, Pullman,' J.D. yelled. With his face a few inches from mine he gave me a good look at his blue eyes. I didn't stare back, just looked up and then away again. Then I caught sight of the can of Budweiser J.D. held in his hand. Saw the blue streak Ernie's t-shirt made when he ran toward the tree line. Dean squealed just after Ernie dove behind it.

'Leave him alone. It was my idea,' I called out. J.D. connected another fist. This time it landed square on my arm. His punch came out fast as a flash of lightning and made a hell of a jolt, felt it down in my ribs. My arm went numb from fingers to shoulder.

Goddamn.

I kept quiet.

Dean came flying through the tree line. I've got a feeling his thrust into the open space came on his own steam. People had a tendency to move quicker when Ernie got that temper of his heated up. Dean hit the ground but didn't stay down long enough for any dirt to stick. He got back to his feet with his hands never leaving his sides.

Ernie came into the clearing and charged toward Dean who lifted those two skinny arms like he knew how to use them. I'd told him before not to raise them unless he planned to take up a fight, but I guess he forgot about that in all the excitement. Dean told me later that it was a safety first, kind of thing. *He's gonna hit me no matter what.* He was right about that. Ernie walked right into that fighting stance of his and caught Dean with a straight right. *Fast as a flash.* Dean's nose took the shot and his specs flew off.

'Oh, God,' Dean screamed into his hand. 'My nose's broke. I'm bleedin'.'

'The hell're you runnin' up on?'

'Ern, cool it, will ya.' J.D. turned his attention to me. I was flexing my hand hoping that the sharp pains would go before I needed to fight. He gave me this look like he didn't understand when I stepped back and rolled my shoulders a few times to loosen up my chest.

'It's cool,' I told him. Hoping to buy some time.

'What're you doin' out here?' J.D. asked.

'Just out for a walk. No big deal.' I backed away and kept flexing my hand and rolling my shoulders. J.D. let his head fall back and made this laugh.

'Think I'm going hit you or something?' he asked me. 'I scare you, Pullman?'

'It's just my arm's numb.' I closed up my fist and let it out again. The feeling started coming back, but my chest was tight as hell.

J.D. turned and walked toward Dean who was crouched near a rusted oil drum. He was blowing his nose and streams of blood and snot were falling into the sand. J.D. got up to him and set a hand on his shoulder.

'Okay, man?'

196

'No. 'ell no, man.' He sounded like he had a bad cold.

'Ern, why not get his glasses?' J.D. stood there with Dean spitting into the sand and blowing out more lines of blood. Ernie came over with the glasses and held them out without much of an expression. Dean took them from him without looking up. His shoulders sank when he saw the glasses.

'Lens's busted.'

'That'll teach you.'

'Ern, cut it out.'

J.D. sat next to Dean and took a look at the glasses when Dean finally let them go. He couldn't fix them and checked with me to see if I could do anything. Although the lens wasn't busted the plastic frame was cracked so the lens kept falling out. We all figured it was a wasted effort putting it back in. Dean sat with his head held back until the bleeding stopped. Then he put the lens in his pocket and set his glasses on his swollen nose with soft hands, like he was wiring a landmine.

'Think you'll survive?' J.D. asked.

'Yeah,' Dean told him. 'But my mom's gonna be pissed off about the glasses.'

'Forget about that,' J.D. told him. 'How's the nose?'

'Sore.'

And that was the end of that. Ernie was kicking through a pile of cans near the red tent and acting like something over there was really interesting him. I figured he was just kind of embarrassed for laying such a heavy shot on Dean. J.D. would've broken bones if he'd chosen my face for a target, but that wasn't his style. Ernie had a tendency to get caught in the moment. He was quick to laugh and quick to fight and either way he decided to go was an extreme.

'This Grits' Cave?' Dean asked J.D.

'You seein' a cave? Them lenses not workin'?' Ernie yelled.

'Never mind,' Dean said. He dropped his head again and spat something into the sand. Sitting there with his glasses cocked at that angle he sounded as beaten as he looked.

'This the Grits' place anyway?' I asked. Dean looked up at

me and I could see he didn't want to be there any more. He wanted to be at Washington Pond or anywhere on our side of Grant's Road. To Dean the familiar paths and streams didn't seem dull any more. He tilted his head toward the line of trees he'd just flown through. He wanted to say good-byes and hit the trail. *Thanks for the memories and the broken nose, fellas.* He would've been content to run like mad, but he couldn't do it without me by his side.

I shook my head while looking at him and he spat into the sand.

'This is it. Nothing more'n a dumping ground,' J.D. said. He sounded almost proud. 'No Grits. No bones. No cave.' He stood up and brushed the butt of his slacks before putting his hands on his hips. He wore the sleeves of his t-shirt rolled up to show off the high curves and definition of his arms.

'First time bein' here?' I asked. Dean rolled to the side and stood and walked past me. As he went by he threw an elbow that landed against my ribs.

'Uh-huh,' Ernie grunted. 'Figured it'd be full of all the stuff people'd been tellin' us. Figured we'd find a couple Grits if nothin' else.'

'What would you've done if you found them?' I asked.

'Fuck knows,' Ernie replied and shook his head.

'Who're they anyway?'

'Bums. Junkies. Hobos,' J.D. said. 'Anybody without a home and everyone with secrets. They come and hide out here.'

Ernie walked to a stump where a large brown grocery bag sat. He stuck his hand in the bag and pulled out a silver can of beer. I watched him with as much interest as I'd watched anything before. He broke the tab and put the can to his lips and tilted it up. His throat bulged out and his head dropped farther back. When he came forward he took the can away from his mouth and crushed it in his grip.

'You alright?' he asked before belching.

'Fine,' J.D. said nodding his head.

Ernie tossed his empty can at the metal barrel. The can hit

the side and fell onto a pile of empties that collected round the barrel.

'Get me for littering?' Ernie asked.

'See Wilcox around?' J.D. replied, lifting his arms out wide. 'Will who?'

The brothers laughed and I wanted to join in, but couldn't bring myself to make that much of a connection.

Chapter Nineteen

The cicadas could never have been too early. It seemed that one day there was no sign of them. Then the next they appeared. The morning they came I woke to find one bumping against the glass of my bedroom window. Without feeling excited I sat up and watched it. I'd expected myself to be filled with some sense of elation, some kind of fulfilment. When they finally showed I found myself tired. I felt lost and tired and confused, like I'd been waiting for something to come that would change everything. While the cicada bumped against the glass the sound of my father's drill was making its rise and fall sounds in the basement. The bruises J.D.'s hands made had spread yellow and purple on my arm and chest. Nothing had changed. The cicadas had arrived and I was still Joseph Reginald Pullman, son of Richard and Clarisse Pullman of Tallahassee, Florida. Displaced and beaten and tired of imagining that some fucking natural cycle was going to change what I already had.

I'd anticipated their arrival for so long that what I felt was like relief. Only this was a relief without an expectation that things would get better. *Here they are, Joe. Now you know that everything's not all that bad. Some things that are meant to happen still happen.* They'd shown up and come when they were due and for that I was relieved. When I'd needed them they came. In all of the uncertainty that surrounded my family, my life, the cicadas were a constant. If only in my thoughts they were something to maintain structure.

I sat on my bed watching the cicada hitting against the glass until the sun raised high. Dressed and walked down the stairs one at a time, careful not to make any noise that would arouse my father's attention. In the kitchen I found a glass jar under the sink and used a hardened dishtowel to wipe away the fluids coating the sides. Could still smell the chemicals so I rinsed the jar with water. Didn't give it another wipe with the towel after the sound of my old man's drill cut off. The noise coming up from the basement had been rising through the laundry shoot like the sounds of a steam train powering through a tunnel. Then it all went dead. I listened for a second or two until my old man started talking. *Come here, Joe. I've got something to show you.* I went outside with the wet jar in my hand.

The cicadas jumped and flew round the shrubs in the front garden. Hundreds crawled on the pavement near our fallen mailbox. Some had already broken from their orange shells. Others hadn't shed to let their wings out. They moved slowly over branches of shrubs and trunks of trees in a beetle-crawl.

I collected seven of them in the jar. Five had their wings and two were still in their orange shells. Twisted the lid on and shook the jar like mad. Their large bodies crackled and thumped against the sides of the jar. I felt it in the palm of my hand as they collided against the metal lid. When I stopped shaking them I put the glass to my ear and felt the vibration of their wings flapping round inside my head. In that small space they crawled over one another looking for a way out. In the grass they spread and moved until they had made it away from one another. They scattered and became wanderers in the great wide open. In my jar they huddled together and they looked confused. They should have been accustomed to being so close and confined. Instead their black faces and red eyes looked angry. Seventeen years underground should have prepared them for life in a glass jar.

Almost two decades pressed down by dark soil with nowhere to go. But they never expected to be caught, not when they set themselves free. I played a part in an evolution the cicada had never prepared for and that made me feel powerful.

After giving the jar one last shake I dumped it over and spilled the cicadas into the grass. They staggered away and disappeared into the long blades. Some righted themselves quickly and used big plastic wings to take off. They had an unsteady flight, like giant bumblebees. They didn't fly in a straight line, but went everywhere. When they flew low I swatted at them, but the effort came without much effect. I missed every time I tried, but couldn't bring myself to care.

Of the first fifty I caught in the jar only one died. It was an accident and at first I felt ashamed that it'd happened. I'd been careful at first to catch only one cicada at a time. Made sure the captives settled to the bottom of the jar before bringing in another. But as the hours passed I felt a need to catch more. There were so many of them that catching one at a time seemed pointless. With a dozen or so in the jar I shook it and listened to them cracking against the inside of the glass. Waiting for them to settle down I knelt low near the crumbling azaleas of my old man's garden. Hundreds of them held on to the azalea bushes lining the porch. I scooped a few into the jar, but didn't do it quick enough. *You're never fast enough, Joe.*

'Fuck off, Mother.'

One of the captive cicadas took a chance and went for the escape. I closed the lid too quick and the metal on glass cut the head from the body in an instant. I'd been kneeling on a paving stone and the black head landed on the slab. It was too light to make a sound. It sat there on the path like a seed, small and pathetic. I stood up straight and kicked the head with the toe of my sneaker. It caught under the rubber sole and was crushed in a black line on the cement.

There were twelve buzzing cicadas in the jar and a body that lay twitching on the bottom. I gave the jar one last shake before unscrewing the lid. Tossed them all out and the dazed squadron took to the sky and scattered. They swarmed for a moment like they were thinking of attacking the monster that captured them. But they valued their freedom and broke apart and disappeared. I looked at the ground and found the headless torso. It'd fallen into the mulch beside the pavement. It lay with legs to the ground and looked ready to walk away.

Towering over it I felt that surge again and squished it with my shoe.

Dean came around later that week, spent a few days away after going home with a broken nose. He walked up into the cul-de-sac with new black frames on his taped nose. I'd been catching cicadas, but stopped when I saw him walking past the Rosenthal's place. The shade under my father's oak tree was a cool place to wait for him to make his way up the street.

'How's it going, Dean?'

'Alright, I guess.'

'Nice glasses.'

'Yeah,' he said. 'Mom's wanting you to tell her what happened.'

'What did happen?'

'Ran into a lamp-post. We were trying to get away from some dog.'

'That's the best you could come up with?'

'I broke my nose, Pullman.' He looked annoyed already. 'I had to come up with something like that. I'm not like you where I can say some kid kicked my ass and that's that. She'd have called everyone until she found the guy.'

'She can't believe that kind of story.'

'No, you're right.' He shook his head. 'She thinks it was you.'

'Huh?'

'You haven't been round for a while so she thinks we've been fighting. Arguing and stuff. When I got back the other night she asked me if you'd done it.'

'That's bullshit, Dean.'

'She didn't ask if it was you really. She just said, "what's he done?"'

'What the hell?'

I turned away from him and started toward the house. There he was telling me about his mother thinking I'd busted him in the face. He told me she'd asked what I'd done. He wasn't telling me about the things he said. All the stuff he told her to make her believe I didn't do it. Instead he come up with the lamest excuse for a broken nose. How many people run into lamp-posts trying to get away from a dog? I wanted to drive a few knuckles into his nose and bring fresh blood.

'It's cool, Pullman. She's wanting you to come over this week for dinner.'

'So she can grill me about what happened to your face?'

'No, man. She's just worried.'

'About what?'

'About you I think. About what you might be up to.'

We caught more cicadas and shook them up in jars before setting them free. As with all the things we did together we grew tired. We got bored of shaking them up and letting them go. Wasn't long before we took a break. My old man's house was no good. He'd been making more noise in the basement, working on something important. He yelled out like someone was with him. I didn't want Dean to see him that way. So we walked back to Dean's house. His mother greeted us at the door and didn't make like she was annoyed at me being there. She sat us at the kitchen table and fed us snacks and poured glasses of fresh lemonade. But she'd started to look at me with her head to one side. The day had started winding down and the sun broke into purple and red streaks in the sky.

'What've you been up to lately, doll? I haven't seen you for a few days.' Dean's mother stood over me with the empty pitcher clutched in both hands. Her breath smelled like the mints she always ate. They disguised the stale tang her cigarettes left behind. But they were only strong enough to make the stale tang minty fresh. When she smiled at me I could see the dark brown glaze that formed in spaces between her teeth. She got too close at times, that day closer than usual.

'Just been outside really.' I looked away after I spoke hoping to divert her attention away from me.

'He's killin' the cicadas round his house,' Dean said.

I kicked him under the table. He made a hurt look, but I didn't kick him all that hard, not like I wanted to. Didn't break anything anyway.

'Protecting your dad's place, huh?' Maureen asked.

'I s'pose.' I kept my eyes away from her. It wasn't aimed to make her think I wanted to ignore her. It was my shy look that usually got her sympathy. She spoke to me with a gentle voice if she thought I felt uncomfortable. Dean told her everything that happened with my family and she seemed pleased to fill in where my mother should have. She'd filled in where Mother never had and now couldn't ever try.

'He just likes catchin' 'em in his jar.' Dean shoved a chocolate chip cookie into his mouth and tried to bite down. It was too much and he ended up spitting most of it back into his hand. Maureen slapped the back of his head. He'd told me his mother could hit, but seeing it for myself I didn't feel impressed. It didn't look like anything worth mentioning after it'd happened. At that moment I couldn't help but wish he'd experienced one of my father's slaps. He would've been thankful for his mother then, thankful for her soft hands.

Dean recovered as soon as Maureen's hand returned to the pocket of her shorts. He stared at the crumbs that piled like an anthill in his hand. After a few seconds he placed his mouth over the hill and tipped his head back.

'Are you collecting them?' his mother asked.

'No, I catch 'em and let 'em go again.' I found it hard to look her in the eyes when I spoke. This time I made contact, but I felt uneasy. After Dean told me she thought I'd busted him up Maureen didn't seem all that gentle any more. I wondered if Ernie's straight right had ruined my surrogate mother. Sitting there I had this feeling like I'd done something wrong. She made me feel uncomfortable, even then while she acted kind toward me. There seemed to be an expectation, one that I hadn't lived

205

up to. It's like she wanted me to be something I couldn't have been and she'd realized it. Not in a million years of trying could I have been like her blue-eyed boy. It seemed like she waited for the change for the better to take place right there, each and every time she looked at me.

'Killed a couple though,' Dean muttered. A spray of cookie dust shattered into the air. 'Dead as dead as dead.'

'Dean, you know better. We taught you better than that. You don't see Joseph doing that kind of thing.' She turned and set the pitcher of lemonade down on the table and left the room. For a minute I sat and watched the slices of lemon float round the top of the pitcher. The sound of the vacuum cleaner filled the air. The dog came into the kitchen in a hurry and settled itself under my chair. Every time the sound of the vacuum came close to the kitchen door the dog nuzzled my leg. I reached down and patted its nose, but I raised my hand before it could lick my fingers.

'Why do you want her to hate me?' I asked. Looked at the bubbles of condensation sliding down the side my half-empty glass.

'Don't know.' Dean didn't look up at me and when I turned to get out of my chair he flinched.

'It's not about Gillian?'

'Don't think so.'

I walked outside thinking about climbing the oak tree. We hadn't even touched the fresh pitcher of lemonade Maureen had made. It wasn't like me to leave free food when it was set out. Dean followed after a minute or two. I'd got to the oak and found the trunk played host to some cicadas. They were still in orange shells and none of them looked ready for wings. Some of them climbed using small arms to hoist themselves higher and higher. After a while I found one round the other side of the tree trying to transform. A small crack had opened up in the middle of its back. Under the shell it wiggled and pushed trying to break free. Through the crack of the shell I could see the white bug. Thought about telling Dean how they come out white.

How they take hours to turn black. Come out like weak maggots and change into black beasts. That's all it takes – just hours and they aren't weak any more. Dean stood with his hands behind him. He'd looked at the cicadas, but never gave them the attention I thought they deserved.

I got bored watching the cicada struggle. It took too long to come out and change and with Dean hanging round like that I was losing my head. Thought about throwing a kick to knock it off the tree. Bounced round with my hands up like those Chinese guys do in kung-fu movies. I was ready to snap out my leg when I saw all the spots on the bark. They kind of flashed all at once and brought my leg to the ground again. There was an army of small orange shells. I stopped bouncing

The cicadas held onto the tree with their crab-like arms. I started counting them but stopped after I reached forty, maybe fifty. There were too many and I didn't figure I could count them without missing one or counting another twice. Instead I leaned in and plucked the cicada that struggled most with the shell. It gave a good fight while trying to hold the bark. It could only hold for an instant before it came away. I examined it, watching it clawing at the air. It moved its head and the body twisted in a crazy dance. Inside the orange shell it moved and jerked and felt wild in my fingers. I showed it to Dean, but he just sucked his teeth and screwed up his eyes.

'Looks like a flea,' he said.

'Yeah,' I replied. 'A real big flea.'

Dean moved closer. I fought the urge to force the cicada forward and make him jump in surprise. He was taking an interest in the thing. He showed the interest I'd wanted him to take earlier that year. When I'd first told him about the cicadas after his trip he'd been too absorbed in his new watch. Just before Mother went away he had been too surrounded by his family to share in my discovery. Before she'd died, before my mother swung from the tree, he had almost ignored all the information I'd collected about the cicadas. All that time I'd spent alone, reading about them just so I could tell it all to Dean. And he'd ignored me. He'd played with his calculator watch and made out like I was losing my mind.

Now you got him, Joe. Now he's ready to hear what you've got to say.

I pushed the cicada at Dean's face and got it a few inches away. He stared at it with his nose wrinkled and his top lip peeled back. Before long I got tired of holding the thing. Waited until he'd leaned in closer and tried to get a better look before I moved away. Dean had some kind of suspicion about the cicada. It's like he knew it brought some kind of a danger to the town. It's like he understood that with it came his family's last good summer.

'Here,' I said, pushing the cicada closer to his face. 'Just take it.'

He stepped back and said: 'I don't want to touch it.'

I couldn't hold it any longer. Turned from Dean and took a step, dropping the shell to the ground. As it fell I brought my foot up before it made the grass. There came a small crackle of sound when the cicada made contact with the rubber toe of my sneaker. We both watched the broken cicada arch high in the sky and disappear into the leaves of the oak tree. I looked at Dean and we both smiled. He didn't object when I pulled another orange shell from the tree. This one held on tighter than the last. Imagined it'd watched what I'd just done and it was scared as hell. This energy filled my legs and arms and I had to concentrate so my fingers wouldn't crush it. Thinking the insect feared me gave the same rush I got from fighting. The thing knew I'd intended to send it for a final flight. Once I had it away from the tree I offered it to Dean. He shook his head because he didn't want to hold it.

'Drop it on my foot,' he said. 'I betcha I can kick it farther than you.'

'Keep dreaming.'

Dean got close to me and I dropped the cicada to the ground. He took a swipe with his foot and caught it dead on his toe. The orange dot took off like a rocket. We laughed loud and slapped hands after losing sight of where it had gone. The night kept getting darker. The sun fell fast, but it didn't feel like it was closing me in, not that night. We kicked more of those orange shells into the top shadows of the trees. We laughed and we slapped each other's hands. We cleared the oak tree and had to search for more.

Chapter Twenty

My old man's pay stubs stopped arriving in the mail. They'd been delivered in a long narrow envelope with a PO Box in DC as a return address. They were the only envelopes my father opened. Of all the mail I'd left on the dining room table. He'd stopped driving to the office by the end of March. Since then he'd spent his time in the basement. All his time down there hammering and drilling and worst of all laughing that new laugh of his. I know almost nothing about what he did while he was down there. He used tools that made the house shake. Sometimes the lights would go dim. There were a few nights when all of the power went out. On those nights I could hear my old man's voice through the laundry chute, talking wildly.

I slept with my knife under my pillow, gripping it so tight in a fist my fingers felt like they would separate at the knuckles. Sleep didn't come easily. Figure no one can blame me for that. Even with the dresser shoved against the door I didn't feel at ease enough to drift off. *He got through that shitty little trap before, Joe. What stopped him that last time? What kept him from slitting you ear to ear?* When sleep did come I woke with every noise. No matter how slight the sound might have been I was up. There was none of that open-eyed, laying in silence kind of thing any more. When I woke I was sitting up with my knife aimed into the darkness. Sometimes I'd be so wired that I took a few swipes. It wasn't that I felt afraid of what might come. Just feared I might not see it before it got me.

It was around this time that the mason jars showed up scattered round the house. They'd be sitting on end tables or counter tops and on the floor beside sofas. Each of the jars smelled of chemicals that made the lining of my nose burn when I sniffed them. Every time I came across one of the jars I took it to the kitchen and placed it in the cabinet under the sink. With every jar I replaced another went missing. The more times this happened the more disturbing it became. My old man continued setting them out, leaving them in different rooms of the house. What his purpose for this was I never found out. I kept playing his new game, replacing his acid stinking glass jars back inside the cabinet. It went on and on until the end of it all.

My father had taken to old habits, drinking his alcohol again. The bottles were stacked in the corner of the kitchen. Empties lined up next to the new ones that he set side-by-side like toy soldiers. They kind of looked like a row of trophies. Each day there was another empty in the line. Then six fresh bottles would appear from out of nowhere and sit on top of the refrigerator. If the empty bottle didn't show up one day there were two appearing the next. My father became consistent in his habit. His only companions came in the form of Jack Daniels, Jim Beam and Johnnie Walker. Father spoke to these three in the basement and he sang with them. I listened to it all through the metal laundry chute and it sounded like they had a hell of a time.

It was necessary for me to match my father's schedule. Doing so turned out to be as easy as stealing empty bourbon bottles from the guy who drank them. I got up and headed out early every morning. My body clock found a fresh pulse of energy with the break of the sun. Each morning I got up before my old

211

man and I made sure as hell that I was back in my room that evening while he was still working down below. At night I locked the door to my room with a pair of sliding bolts I nabbed from Li'l Mel's Convenience. Found myself more afraid since my mother had died. Not really afraid of my father, though that feeling was still there too. But I'd started to fear my mother. Like she'd come into my room the way she did when she was still alive.

The premonitions started around this time. Images of what my father built in his workshop that flashed up now and again. I say premonitions because they always came to me as dreams. The dreams were dark and I felt cold even after I'd broken out of sleep. The smells were overwhelming, like the scent of what coated the inside of the mason jars. Just as strong as the smell of the burned dead slaves from Fuller's Mark. That smell followed me when I searched the house. It took a while before I figured out that I was looking for the small things my old man built. The small things that now hid in the corners of the house. That clicked when they moved. I had a sense that alone they were nothing, but my father made hundreds of them, thousands maybe. Together they could come out all at once with their clicking sounds and bring madness.

My dreams never lasted long enough to bring total clarity. Never woke knowing everything and at times I'd just sit there on my bed with a lost and empty feeling. The creatures he made scattered and huddled in shadows. The clicking noises gave them up, but I could never find them. I'd followed the sound and come right up on it, but they'd be gone. Before it was over, before I had one in hand, they started going quiet. One after the other they'd shut off and then there were only a few left. I'd never have the chance to get them before my father came looking for me. I'd hide from him in the shadows, pressed back into the same shadows as his creations. He never found me, but Mother always knew where I hid. She came up from the basement at night and she could always find me.

These dreams were short-lived. All of the things happened at once and it all finished as quickly as it started. The creatures my father made clicking that damn noise and Mother slumping toward me with her face hanging. The smell from the mason jars stuck to the inside of my nose and burned me. It all came in a heavy wave, senses and fear heightened until they were ready to break open. Always woke in a sweat, gasping for breath and checking that I lay alone. Nothing with me in the darkness. No clicking. Stayed as calm as my breath would allow me to be while my lungs pumped air in and out. Chest felt like it'd been crushed. If there'd been someone in my room I would've wanted to seem strong.

They never attack the strong ones, Joseph.

Dreams came more often than I like to remember. If they weren't every night then they came close to it. They were something that I kept from Dean. Most things I was alright to speak with him about and he'd listen. Most of the time. Later in the summer he stayed distant, like he was getting lost in his own mind. But he sat there and for the most part that's all I've ever needed. I could tell him about the way my mother screamed on her bad days and probably even told him about the jars my father started leaving around the house. He liked to hear about those things, sometimes getting really anxious for me to tell him. Wasn't shy about showing all that excitement. He would prop himself up and smile at me when I got to the things he thought were *freaky*.

'What do you think was wrong with her?' he asked one day.

'What do you mean?' A surge of anger welled inside me. He had no right to speak about my mother like she died without value to anyone. I'd started talking, thinking he'd just kick back and listen and nod his head once in a while. Instead, in true Dean Gillespie fashion, he got in there and picked my family to pieces. In a single sentence he'd lowered my mother to the young and lost that still had a chance. Before I'd shown him how mad it got me he'd go to another question. He knew how I was and he knew what he needed to do to stay safe. Get me thinking of something else, something less painful. Something

213

less maddening so I wouldn't lose it. He did it a lot, that recovery of his. Still, he went after my mother because she fascinated him.

He knew it ate at my nerves and made me ready to break him. Still he pushed me sometimes. He tested the ropes and the ropes were never far from snapping. That day he pulled at the rope without fear. He stared at me like he'd done nothing wrong. Like we'd just been talking about another kid. Some kid from our school who we hadn't seen for a while. Who'd gone off the rails. Someone like Billie Tait who got hit by a Chrysler her aunt was driving. Billie never came back and neither did my mother and Dean didn't let Billie's dying go quietly.

'You know,' he started up again. 'Why'd she scream?'

'Couldn't tell you. She just did. It's not like I can ask her.'

'Yeah, but you gotta have some idea. She just wouldn't start cryin' for no reason.'

I waited for a minute or two and took a few deep breaths. He started looking at the leaves of the trees. Searching for the birds that hid from us up there, but could still look right down on our heads. He hid himself from my eyes, because he knew I could use them to cut him to pieces. They hurt him and he didn't like me knowing just how much.

'She just had bad days.'

'But you have to know something.' He picked his nose. Didn't even take it serious, the idea of my mother within the conversation. All the business about my mother was second-hand to him, used shoes. 'You guys have all the stuff she left behind.'

'We guys don't have anything. My old man's got her stuff.'

'Can you get to it?' He looked interested, too freaking interested for my liking.

'Kiss my ass, Dean.'

We stopped talking for a while and just kept watching the trees.

'Your dad still going out at nights?' he asked.

'Yeah. Last night's the first time in a few days.'

'You ever wish he'd never come back?' He stopped looking at

214

the leaves and stared at me again. It felt like it was my turn to look away and so I did.

'I don't know. Think if I wished he'd stay away something bad might happen.'

'Like he wouldn't come back?' Dean asked.

'No,' I sighed. 'Like he'd know I wished he'd keep gone.'

'What, like he's psychic?' Dean laughed loud.

'Shut up, dickhead.' My voice was pulsing with anger and it stopped Dean's laughing. He kept his eyes on me for a minute like he was waiting to see if I was joking. Then he gave me that dumb look of his that showed he was upset.

'I just meant . . .' He trailed off like he always did when he couldn't think of a way to fix his mistakes.

'You don't know what he's capable of, Dean.'

Dean looked at me again and his eyes looked sad behind those new glasses of his.

'What is he capable of?' he asked.

'I haven't figured that out yet,' I told him. 'Something bad's all I know.'

Somewhere around that conversation Dean and me made an unspoken pact to stop talking about Mother. After that he'd ask me about her once in a while, but that was about it. Wasn't like when she was first taken away. Back then all he wanted to know was how she was doing. Wanted to know if I'd seen her in the hospital. His idea about my relationship with Mother was based on the one he had with Maureen.

Dean must have spent a lot of time considering what it would have been like for me. Probably spent a few long nights in his room, under fresh washed sheets, thinking about it. Maybe even dumped all my trouble onto his family while he laid there with a light on. Knowing Dean so damn well I figure he probably cried like a bitch when he got to the best part. The moment in his personal nightmare when poor old crazy Maureen was getting shipped to a nuthouse.

'You got letters from her?' he asked me one evening while up in the oak tree in his parents' back yard. We sat there watching

Maureen through the kitchen window, wiping the dinner plates in the sink.

I shook my head and kept watching his mom wipe like it's all she ever wanted to do.

'Drawings maybe? Poems?' He kept going on. I guess Dean had this romantic idea that my mother was painting her way to good health. She'd been stuck in front of a canvas with all these brushes and colours in that dumb little head of his. Before he knew it she'd be coming home and Joe'd have his momma back. Loads of art and a new brain to match and from then on it was happy fucking days again. Dean knew jack shit about what goes on in the lives of real people.

Want to know what happened, Dean? Well, so do I! That'd be more fucking relief than I think I could handle. Now take a minute to imagine something . . . Imagine what it's like to listen to some lucky prick smiling and laughing about my mother's death. Get that in your head and while you're at it think about the letter from the funeral directors . . . 'Our deepest condolences', my ass! How would you feel about seeing the charges for the removal of her goddamned body before you even knew she'd fucking died! What a way to see the old bitch go, huh?

'She'll probably cut her wrists while no one's looking,' I told him. He didn't like that and told me so. But as it turned out I wasn't far off target. She must have went looking, but couldn't find something sharp enough. But there was a rope and that's all Mother ever needed.

After we'd sorted the limits about my mother Dean kept his mouth shut most times. Still, he slipped up and that's fine for a while. He wanted to know about all the formalities that came with losing someone. He still had both sets of grandparents, mom's and dad's. Both my parents lost theirs early in the marriage, before I was even born. I cut him slack when he was curious most times, but he could cross lines and get comfortable too quick.

With Mother dead Dean wasn't shy about asking if I'd seen her body in the morgue. I punched him in the ribs so hard it frightened me. Trouble is I didn't want to stop there, not with just that one punch. He'd gone to the side and I almost grabbed him to hold him up. He dropped like a lead weight to one knee so I stood over him. Grabbed a handful of his hair and turned his eyes up to me while I balled up the other fist. I really yanked his head back and let out this scream. With his eyes wide and filling with water I yelled into his face:

'Don't you ever speak about my mother!'

I had to run. Just to get myself away from him before I'd snapped all the way. Don't know how far I would have gone, but at that minute I think I could've gone all the way. Maybe I could have done it right there on the bridge. With my hands balled to stones and my body lit with adrenaline I could've ended him. Instead I threw his head back and before he'd landed on wood planks I'd made a fast stride. Never looked back, just kept thinking I'd found part of myself that I didn't ever want to find again.

For a while that punch and threat was all it took to keep Dean off the subject. He still tested the ropes, just to show me he was still interested in case I wanted to tell him something. There were times he eased into the questions that touched his curiosity most. If we were close by his parents, in his house or walking somewhere with them, he felt safe. He'd fire off questions about my mother's illness and sometimes her death. That safety he felt round his parents is one I never completely understood. I'd get him alone again and he knew that.

The further into summer we got the less I worried about Dean's curiosity and the more I worried about my old man. I worried about his mind and his intentions. As the summer moved on I made all efforts possible to keep safe. Secured my bedroom, first with that lock and then the dresser pressed tight against the door. Before I'd lay down on my bed each night I even scattered objects around the floor. It'd stopped my mother when she was alive and I figured it would've slowed my old man down. Also made it a ritual to replenish the pile of leaves below my window. There was always the chance I'd need to jump.

Made no difference how much time I spent stacking leaves on the pile, it still looked small. It would never have been enough to stop me if I had fallen from the second floor. Couldn't have taken the weight of an infant, let alone a kid my size. But it gave me peace of mind and at that time there was nothing more valuable than thinking there was a way out. Even now, when I think back to that summer I can only remember wanting to be far enough away where I could sleep. Close my eyes for the entire night and not wake up holding a knife in my hand. But that summer I never got to a safe distance, not until the cicadas were almost gone.

By this time in late June Dean and I had killed too many cicadas to keep any kind of accurate tally. I'd chosen the plastic baseball bat as my means of extermination. Dean had borrowed an old tennis racket from my old man's garage. We'd pledged not to clean the guts from the tools of our trade. As the insides of the insects hardened and fell off there came a fresh layer from broken shells to be added. Dean now found it easy enough to take hold of the bugs. Sometimes he'd get himself wired up in a wild frenzy from swinging the racket at flying cicadas. He'd look so demented with fury when he couldn't kill them all that he'd grab at them with his free hand. The cicada he caught was wingless in an instant. Then he'd send it airborne one last time, courtesy of a size six Converse sneaker.

We spent all of our days searching through the branches and leaves of trees and shrubs. They were sanctuaries for the cicadas. If we weren't searching for more cicadas we were in Dean's house cooling off, taking breaks. Listened to Maureen in another room jabbering away to her parakeet. Singing with it through that crazy collection of tunes it knew. The bird seemed too intelligent to be real. It could whistle a load of songs and spoke in Maureen's voice and laughed like Dean's dad in a rubbery cackle. It even seemed to cut into conversations at the perfect moment. I thought the bird was something amazing. Never been around an animal like that bird, but Dean didn't think of it the same way.

On one of our trips to Washington Pond Dean told me something frightening. He'd got this idea, as he called it. But, it was more of an urge than anything else.

'Can't get it out of my head, Pullman.'

'What's that?'

'This thing. It's kind of like anger I guess. But I'm not angry really. Know what I mean?'

I laughed.

'You're going tough on me.'

'Come on, Pullman. You're . . . mean sometimes.'

'So?' I told him. Wanted to laugh 'cause it was happening already. He was picking at me. Talking about me in that direct way. It's like staring, but without his eyes.

'You know. Like really . . .' He peeled his lips back and clenched his teeth. His face turned deep red and he held his fists out. Looked like he was going to lose it. Just snap and come at me. Then he let it go. He breathed out and looked at me like he was really excited. 'Like that, you know. But not 'cause anything's happened.'

'Shut up, Dean.'

'Don't get freaked out,' he said. 'I'm just sayin' it's kind of like that. I'm feeling that way sometimes.'

'Why're you telling me?'

''Cause it's not normal,' he said and then paused to blow air through his teeth again. 'Probably not anyway. I don't know, Pullman. It's kind of weird is all.'

No matter how weird he thought that feeling was he couldn't stop it from coming back. I didn't tell him that. But I knew it too well. That's the worst part about having these things running round in your head, they always come back. They can always find you and tap in when you need them the least.

'So you're mad.' I shrugged. 'Who gives a flying fuck about that?'

But he wasn't done coming out with it all. Hadn't come clean on what was going on inside his head. All that stuff that was really working at his nerves.

219

'Sometimes I want to kill something more than insects.'

'So that's the trouble.' I laughed, even though I didn't think it was funny. 'That's what's in your head.' I kept walking and smiled a smile to hide the ideas that were doing a quickfire routine on me. He kept on speaking and I listened, not hearing a hell of a lot of what he was saying.

Now you're in the shit, Joe. Where's this gonna lead?

Sometimes I laughed at him, maybe too hard. He'd melted down into himself when I really started going into hysterics. It took a while for him to build back up, but he always came back again. Out in the woods he'd build back up quicker than usual.

'Come on, Pullman. Those bugs don't even bleed.'

I gave him a look. Told him he was an idiot without even saying a word. But I didn't laugh. He'd just come back and it was too early to melt him down again.

'Fine,' he said.

'Come on, Dean. They get that yellow shit all over the racket when you hit 'em. What about their guts on the bat?'

'It's not red.'

'So.'

'Blood's red, Pullman. That stuff on the bat is . . . it's just insect guts. It's different.'

'How?' I asked and started a laugh.

'It just is!' he yelled. It was loud enough to cut the laugh out of the air. Loud enough to keep me from trying to start it up again.

'Alright.'

We walked for a while without talking. When we came under the big oak we stopped. I pulled at the thick bark and tossed what came away into the clearing. The pieces disappeared into a patch of thick ferns.

'You have a conscience?'

'Kind of a question is that?'

'But you worry about things you've done,' he said.

'Hell no.'

220

'What about when you get angry?'

'I get angry. So what, Dean? Jesus Christ. You're coming at me heavy all of a sudden.' I started walking away and he hopped over the leaves so he could keep up with me.

'It's just I was talking with my dad about stuff. About getting angry.'

'I don't care.'

'He told me about conscience and anger. Said something about one is always outweighing the other. Trouble starts when . . .'

'Cut the psychology, man. What the hell?'

'I'm trying to understand!'

'What? What is it?'

'This angry thing . . .' He made his hands like he was indicating himself.

'It's not anger,' I kept walking.

'So you've got that feeling too?'

'Yeah, it's not always there though. You can probably switch yours off easy.'

'Christ, Pullman, I'm not a psycho or anything.' Couldn't help but feel he was trying to convince himself. 'It's there and then it's gone. Then it's back and . . .'

'It been staying? That feeling?'

He stared at me a while. When I looked away he shook his head.

'Dunno,' he said. 'Yours?'

'Hard to say. Like I told you, it's not always there.'

We came to the creek bank. I picked up stones and started throwing them toward the water. Then at the wall of soil the creek was cutting away. Watched the sands slide into the creek below. Before long we were throwing the stones with all we had. They sank into the soft soil and made perfect, round holes. We made explosive noises with our mouths that sent spit spraying into the air.

'We need something more than insects,' Dean reminded me. 'That's what I think sometimes.' He hefted a large stone and threw it at the bank. It smacked and tumbled down into the water. A slide of earth fell into the water with it, making a gulping splash. The more stones we threw the harder we threw them. Before long they were disappearing into deep black holes.

'Come on,' Dean yelled and tossed one side-armed. It dug deep.

'That's what I'm sayin'!' I yelled back and sunk mine.

We were breathing heavy. Throwing rocks so fast most weren't even hitting the creek bed. They were flying off into the trees. Off into the ferns on the other side. It didn't matter where they went. It was a release.

'Damn, I could kill something,' Dean said.

I looked over at him. He'd worked himself up. Behind his glasses his eyes were wild. Sweat dripped down his forehead. It fell into his eyes and he didn't even blink.

'Yeah,' I told him.

'Something bleeds.'

'Yeah. Something big.' I turned away from him and tossed a stone, but the earth didn't move. The stone stuck in the dirt and it was like time froze.

He tossed another stone and more soil fell into the water.

'Think a cicada knows when it's about to die?' he asked.

'Does anything?' I looked at him when I said it. He stood still for a minute and looked at me. It's like he was thinking about it. Like he was considering that thought more than anything I'd ever told to him before. Wondering if I knew more about it all than I was letting on.

I turned away before he could break the stare. Kept quiet and searched the bank for better stones. Got a few steps away from Dean with the secret hope that he'd forget what he'd been saying. Walking away from him I felt an uncertainty and sensed him watching my back. Things were uneasy in the world and it felt like I'd started sinking into a hole that didn't have a bottom. Felt myself getting trapped and I didn't like the idea of being buried before I took a last breath.

'We should kill the bird.'

When he said it I stopped. Facing away from him I made

myself feel disconnected. Could feel pulsing in bright red across my cheeks. Burning under my skin and my pores swelling up on my arms. If it wasn't the words he spoke it was the sound of his voice, but it made my guts sink deep. His intentions sounded real and he sounded too energized to be putting on a show. He only got that way when he needed backing. He needed me to hop on for the ride and join in his game.

You take the legs, Joe and I'll get the wings. Now pull hard as you can. Stretch this freaking thing like you mean it.

'What bird?' I asked. My chin aimed to the trees above.

'Mom's bird.'

Hearing him say it hurt in a way I hadn't expected. Maybe it was just the way he said it. He sounded so sure about the whole thing. Like he'd been planning it for a while. Like he'd only been working up to telling me what he had in mind. I felt my decision would be final and so I stalled. I made it all like I was walking round considering something as important as the sun rising. Go along with him and kill the bird, or let it live. Trouble is it wasn't the bird I kept thinking about. Maureen kept coming into my head, filling up lemonade glasses and handing me jeans with the labels still attached.

'What do you think, Pullman?'

Couldn't think and that was the trouble of it all. The bird was singing that damn song and laughing Mr Gillespie's rubbery cackle and there was Maureen with a fresh pair of jeans. *I'm sure these I washed the other day are yours. Dean Gillespie's not a child who wears Wranglers. By the way, Joe, don't kill my birdie.*

'Come on, Pullman. Is it a go?'

Had trouble thinking of what I was supposed to do or what to say so I let out a scream. This yell that hit up from the middle of me and exploded out like lava. It came out loud in a mix of wild energies and it poured into the air in a surge of all my aggressions. Same as I felt when the cicadas first arrived. It merged all the things that'd happened and all the things that lived and died.

'You want to!' Dean yelled back.

Turned round on the soft sand and when I looked at him he stood there smiling. His teeth looked too white and too clinically straight. Behind the dust-layered lenses his eyes shined black and bold. That look frightened me. It stared at me. I saw that it had changed. He'd become a new kid, one with a purpose.

'We got so much out here,' I said extending my arms to the sides.

'And?'

'There's hundreds of birds, Dean.'

'Not the same.' He was shaking his head like he was real excited. He had this smile on his face. 'The animals out here don't . . .' He aimed that smile at me like I was in on the joke, but hadn't realized it yet. 'They're not the same.'

'Alright.' I said this so he knew I wasn't convinced. Said it like I intended to follow it up with a question. For a second he waited, but then he screwed up his face in frustration. Flapped his arms and slapped his legs hard enough to make a noise. Then he spun on me and pointed a bony finger at my chest.

'That bird drives me crazy, Pullman. Makes me nuts.'

'How?'

'It just does. I wanna off the thing.' He dropped to a crouch and picked something up. Made that awkward motion of his and threw it. Another rock hit the bank and made a perfect circle, adding to the other black dots. This time all the dots connected somehow and the side of the bank fell into the water.

'I wanna break its freakin' wings.'

We stayed at the creek for the rest of the afternoon. It felt both exciting and frightening out in the woods. We talked about upping the ante, but not always about doing it with Maureen's bird. I wanted so badly to appear in control and offer a new angle to his idea. A new angle that would show I didn't feel scared by the old one. But I'd filled up with so much apprehension inside that I couldn't hold it in. I didn't want to take his mother's bird away. She had an attachment to it, some kind of spiritual thing that I didn't understand. Couldn't figure how a person could have that kind of connection with an animal. That

224

day we stayed away from his house. He wanted to go back, but I kept him outside. In the woods it was alright to be primal. At our age it was acceptable. In the woods killing was necessary, just to survive.

Chapter Twenty-One

More people came to look at my old man's house. I watched
them from the trees across the road. Kept hidden in the line of
maples that separated the Shaws' property from the Bishop's
place. All the people that came to look at my father's house
looked far too normal to live in it. They arrived in shiny sedans
driven by people in suits that needed special cleaning. Some
spent a long time in the house, but most were only in a few
minutes or so. Those people that took the quick view came out
all excited and shaking their heads.

'I can assure you that the basement is furnished,' one of the
estate agents said.

'What's with the locks on the door then?' her client asked.

'I'm sorry I don't have an answer for that.'

'Who's going to buy without seeing it all first?'

'Again, I don't have an answer for that.'

They weren't shy people, those who came and went. Some
came out and spoke loudly about the smell and the bottles and
the letters on the dining room table. Others just shook their
head and smiled a nice-try-but-we're-not-buying-that kind of
smile. They were good to watch, see the reactions of normal
people to a dysfunctional home. With the telescope I could see

them passing through the front rooms. When I couldn't see them any more I worried they'd been going through my things.

Each time the cars left, taking the visitors away, I returned to the house. Ran through an inventory of all my stuff. Looked through my drawers and through the bins in the bottom of my closet. Always made sure the book was still under my mattress first. Everything else had an importance but failed to compare to that book. I had a need for it and for the photographs it contained.

Figured out what happened with my old man's job. It was something I found out on my own just as I had always done. When I passed him in the hall he'd sometimes nudge me out of the way. Caught me with a punch once in a while. Still had a shot on him. Even with all that weight dropping away. Other times he'd stare at me. Just look down on me with his glassy eyes. When he got like that I froze up. Found it the best thing to keep myself from running away.

After Mother passed away I'd started listening carefully to the sounds my father made when he worked in the basement. Through the metal laundry chute I could hear him moving and working. The chute cut down inside the centre of the house, hidden behind the walls. Started in the basement and ended on the second floor just outside my bedroom. It was metal and carried sound clear as a phone call. Carried everything from voices and laughs to drills and wood saws. I'd listen with my ear pressed against the cold steel flap-door. If I knew my father was in the basement I felt at ease when walking around the house. It was a terrible feeling when he went silent. All the time I couldn't tell where he was I felt that unease coming back again. Couldn't help but wonder if he was hiding again. So I'd listen in the chute where the metal carried sounds through the house. I could hear almost everything.

Coming home one evening I checked the chute for sounds of my old man. He was moving something heavy across the cement floor. I listened for a while, but couldn't figure out what the thing was from its sound. So I gave up and went for a glass of water. There was a white cloth in the sink. Where it dripped bubbles of red water were collecting.

'What've you done now?' I whispered.

I headed for the stairs and took them one at a time so I could listen to him moving. He'd started to laugh that new laugh and I was alright with him being down there. At the top of the stairs I looked in his study. The big brown desk cut through the centre of the room and on it was the phone. Next to it the red light flashed on the answering machine. My old man kept the machine clear. Hadn't seen a message flash since Maureen had invited me for dinner. I went in and hit the green button on the machine and didn't worry about lowering the volume.

'Hey, bud,' the man's voice said. From just that I'd recognized Mr Moon's cool tone. The hinted southern drawl warmed the words and made him sound smooth. 'Just callin' to check on you and Joseph. Liz's asking about you both. She's wantin' me to let you know you're both welcome over here anytime you'd like. Anything you need. Have a cookout or somethin'. If you're needin' some time on your own we'll take Joe for a night or two.' He paused. I wiped the sweat from my palms onto the thighs of my Wranglers.

'We hope you're okay,' he finished. 'Hope you're both coping well. God bless.'

I deleted the message and went to my room. Wondered if there were people who would come to the house for me. Someone who would knock on the door with interest in helping me out and not just show up to help my old man. Someone who would ask if I was alright and not give a damn about my father. In the dark I tried to think of the people who might wonder where I'd gone if things went bad. Couldn't think of anyone who'd take the time out to check. Spend part of their day to come over and see if I was still breathing. Dean's mom might talk to her friends about me, but she'd probably never visit.

The list of people stayed with that one name and Maureen was still a long shot. Everybody else could go and burn for all I cared. Realizing how alone I was made me wonder if I'd ever

228

get out of the hole I lived in. Opened the long blade in my pocket knife and set it across my palm. Sank the blade in deep and hated myself for causing the pain. Hated myself even more for having no one to care that I'd done such a fucked-up thing.

It was the first time I'd done anything like that before. Never had the urge to mark myself, but right then it seemed like a good thing to do. I felt alone and vulnerable and there was no danger around to kick my head into gear. My old man was down in the basement singing his songs with Jack, Jim and Johnnie. With him sounding so lame I needed to do something myself to get that spark going. Something to jump me out of the rut and bring me back to life. The slice the knife made in my skin went deep into the meat of my hand, but the pain held back. Almost kept away all together except for a burning around the edge of the wound. With the blade of the knife I opened the flap of skin and let blood drain onto the cover of a comic book. After a while I tried to stop the bleeding with an old sock. Ended up having trouble 'cause I'd gone so deep.

There were a few moments of panic when I imagined myself dying on the floor of my bedroom. The cut was small, but I'd stuck the knife in with my own hand. Dying like that had to be the weakest way to go. I went back and revisited that sad short list of people who may or may not mourn my dead body. The name of the only person who may care popped up and the rest was empty space. I laid back and pulled my elbow close to my ribs. My arm stuck straight up and kept my hand floating right there in front of me. The pulsing was getting deeper and spreading. To keep from thinking about the pain I closed my eyes and thought about the bridge and the creek and the wind. I thought so hard that somewhere in all that pulsing and water and wind I fell asleep.

That's when Mother came back all in a rush. She sat alone under a Shady Oak bordering the grounds of the Leichter House gardens. Wondered if she'd heard her own neck snap in the fall. She may have changed her mind at the last minute. When her feet could find nothing to stand on, after they'd already kicked away the aluminium folding chair. There may have been a moment of panic.

Oh, shit. What happens now? Where do we go from here?

I woke in a dark room and it took a few minutes for my eyes to adjust. The sound of my father's tools still buzzed and rattled in the basement. The door to my room stood open and I lost a moment's breath when I remembered the cloth in the sink. Slid off the bed and closed the door, slid the bolts. Pushed the chest over the floor using a shoulder instead of two hands. The pulsing in my hand was worse than before.

Took off the strip of cloth I'd wrapped round my hand. Sat on the bed and looked at the wound like it wasn't even connected to me. It was like an open mouth, pink on the inside without teeth. When the line of blood started to darken in my palm it turned to gel. It had gone solid round the lips of the cut. The later it got that night the more that wound would pulse, the pain grew intense. The burn ignited and spread to the flesh deep inside my hand. Kept drilling down until it felt like I'd never move my fingers again. The throbbing made me worry that I'd be left with a continuous pulsing, something to remind me of a weak moment. My quickness to react without thought had always been my downfall. Still, I figured a throbbing pain is nothing compared to a snapped neck. I may have laughed while sitting there in the darkness. Remember thinking it was funny at the time.

The pain cut through the centre of my hand. Squeezed my wrist and the pain was more intense. I kept thinking of my mother. Felt denied of an opportunity, but couldn't decide just what that opportunity was. Couldn't decide if I had just become addicted to worrying about stuff I couldn't control. All the trouble that appeared in my life had become too much a part of me. *Snap out of it, Joey. Now you're causing trouble for chrissakes. Snap out of it. Just stirring a load of shit ain't nobody gonna eat.* It's like I thrived on the bad moments. Lived in a house with a man who didn't speak to me. Son of a lunatic who chose to string herself from the limbs of a tree. I'd been captured inside a world my family had built for me. One they'd constructed for me with moments of uncertainty and the nagging of fear.

While I considered all the things that had gone wrong I bound my hand. Strapped it up in fresh torn fabric of Fruit of the Loom underpants. Then curled myself into a ball on top of the bed with my knees pulled to my cold chest. I breathed in deep. Huddled into the corner and pulled my knees in hard as I could. The sheets had started smelling like stale sweat weeks ago. I'd taken them off and pushed them into the closet with my dirtied clothes. The smells seeped through the louvred doors and filled the room again. The heat outside made the smell worse. With my chin pressed firm against my knees I fell into a deep sleep. It didn't last for long, but then it never did.

Outside of my room there was a banging sound. Came loud and heavy and jolted me. Went to the door and listened and there was silence. I raised my hand so it was just in front of my mouth and I blew on the cloth. Couldn't feel a thing on the cut, but it helped. Then halfway up the hallway wall the sound came again. The small square metal door of the laundry chute carried an echoed blast. Took a minute to get the dresser away from the door. Then the bolts gave me a fight. My hand wasn't working like I needed it. The pulsing came and they were shaking. Both my hands were shaking.

Bang.

It came again and I waited. Breathed and gripped my wrist with the good hand. Squeezed it like mad until the blood came in and the pulsing grew so bad things round me went calm. Got the door open and went into the hallway. It was dark and silent except for the quiet laugh that was coming from the wall. Silence all round, except for an echoed whisper of a laugh that came through the laundry chute. The chute door was hinged at the top and the springs screeched when it was pushed open. During most nights I woke up to the sounds that echoed in the chute. That night the sound was louder than it had ever been.

While my old man worked I'd sit up in bed listening. Made myself wait, holding off on sleep to make sure he stayed down

231

there. When I knew he'd sunk deep into his trade I'd walk to my door and open it and listen. At the metal flap I waited for something to tell me what was happening. Any sound that gave me an idea of what he was building with all those tools, all that noise. But it was all the same noise and all the same tools that lit up the quiet at night. I couldn't find the energy to imagine what it was that took up all his time. What he experienced in the basement that made him so angry and so driven.

Music played on a radio at a low volume. He kept it in the background, away from the chute. Could make out a voice singing here and there and sometimes there was a piano. My father's voice would cut in once in a while, but he didn't sing. He talked to himself. No matter how hard I strained to figure out what he said it just wouldn't reach me. His voice came in a tone too deep to travel. Wasn't clear by the time it got up to me. His words didn't make it through the metal chute with the ease of the music and of his tools – the sound of a hammer, the pulsing rhythm of his saw. Over and over again until the wood fell to the ground. It banged against the cement floor and echoed through the house.

Waiting in the silence was painful. It hurt even more as I stood there thinking about the nights when the screams of the saw and the whining of the drill pulled me from sleep. With my shoulder pressed against the wall the smell of cigar smoke came through the chute. Then the silence was broken with metal scraping against the cement floor, chains maybe. Then the links of metal fell and a dead calm dropped into place. I waited at the metal flap, patient and still. My hands slicked with perspiration, one gripping a wrist and the other pulsing like mad. Bare feet felt cold and stiff. No motion or sound came from the chute and I turned to walk away.

'I am not to blame!' my father yelled.

Took a breath that made my lungs stretch to their limits. Backed away from the metal flap and waited for my old man's head to press through it. *Here's Johnnie!* His voice exploded. Loud and echoing through the house. His head felt near, like he breathed behind the walls. I stayed still and feared more than ever that he knew I was there, watching and listening. All of a sudden he knew I'd been there all along. All that night and all the nights before. The times when he worked while Mother was still alive and when . . .

'This is not right!' he called into the chute.

I stood at the flap listening to him panting and gulping at the air. Another moment of calm fell. The gasps of my old man's breath broke the quiet.

'Are you listening?' he said in an almost calm voice. 'I am not to blame.'

Something in his voice made me think my father spoke to someone else. If not someone with him, someone he thought may be near by. Close at hand and almost near enough to touch. I leaned closer to the flap to listen for another voice. Could hear my father take a drink. He swallowed loud and the sucking sound he made rose up the chute. The popping sound when his lips came off the bottle. The chute picked it up. The sound touched my ear and I wanted to push the flap open, almost worried that I was missing something. I knew there was more to hear. But the springs would have given me away. Waited and let go of my wrist and rubbed my hand against my shorts.

Father coughed and I stared at the carpet covering the hallway floor. Thought of the marks my feet might leave in it. Wondered if my old man would know I'd stood near the flap. He'd know I'd been listening and he'd need to keep me quiet. I stepped away and saw the shape my feet had pressed in the pile. I rubbed at it using one foot and stepped back again. Repeated that retreat all the way to my bedroom door. Before moving all the way back into my room he screamed. My old man screamed loud as his lungs would allow.

'You are listening to me!'

I made it through the door of my room and shut it behind me. My hands and knees shook while I slid the bolts and pulled the chest of drawers in place. It all took so much damn time. Did my best to do it all without any sound, but my nerves kicked in. Speed and fear mixed into this awkward dance that finished

233

when the furniture blocked my father's entrance. It had been quickness and haste before silence at that moment. With the door barricaded I went back to my bed. My hand throbbed more than before and now the fabric felt damp where it had gone dark. I lay on my back and set my hand on my chest. The feeling of the warm wetness was as close to comforting as I could have hoped. Even with my old man yelling through the chute.

When he stopped I kept on guard, holding the knife in my good hand. Sometime that night I fell asleep.

When my father worked in the basement he moved in bursts. There were fragments of sound followed by long silences. He would come up from the basement taking the wooden steps slow and heavy. I stayed out of the way when he made it to the door entering the kitchen. He'd come up for food or he'd leave his drinking glass on the counter top. He'd find another and return to the basement. Always locked the door with a key behind him. He'd installed locks inside and outside the basement door. Bolt locks, like the ones I stole from the Li'l Mel's Convenience were on the kitchen side. Sometimes I wondered why he had so many locks. Too many just to keep me out. Made me wonder if he planned to keep someone in.

His drinking glass smelled like floor cleaner. His fingers made smudges on the sides of the glass, marks in bronze coloured soot that clung to the side. I imagined slicking the rim with poison. But then I never believed I could deal with the reality of my father's death. Not if it came by my own hands. That would've been haunting and would last long past the moment he'd gone. Round that time I still couldn't get Mother out of my head and she'd gone without my help.

My old man and I lived in the same house and I like to think we shared memories of my mother. Although we never spoke and there were moments of fear when I was around him the thought of my old man dying was close to being painful. It could have been that I realized being alone would cause problems. Had this kind of freedom that came in the absence of family. Existed to roam without answering to anyone. Dean told me so many times that he didn't like to think about his mother dying. But then he grew frustrated when she demanded to know where he'd been or where he was going. Every time we left the house he'd make up a place. Never told her the real reason for him leaving or where it was he'd be. Still, the lies satisfied her and made her feel some kind of comfortable. Could never really decide which was more pathetic, Dean's situation or mine.

The day after the chute incident I'd been gathering leaves, throwing them onto the pile below my window. My father's neighbour came out of the house next door. Her kids didn't follow her like they usually did. Most times it's like she'd connected one to each leg on an invisible string. She walked through her sliding glass door and stepped onto her back deck. Would've made the effort to hide, but she clocked me straight away. She waved and I did the wrong thing by offering her a small nod of my head. Meant it as a gesture that showed I acknowledged her without wanting any company. It must have been a poor effort. She walked down the four steps that connected the deck to a line of seashell steppingstones. When she got close I thought about kicking at the pile of leaves to make them less obvious.

'Hey, Joey. Haven't seen you around in a while, kiddo.' She had a nice smile with clean teeth and fresh pink lips. Her blond hair was pulled from her forehead and was held in place by a pair of white sunglasses. Standing there looking at me she kept pulling her shirt away from her chest. Trying to cool herself down she flashed a load of skin. Made me feel something start to kind of well up inside me.

'I been busy.' Wiped my hands clean on my shirt.

'You finish off school okay?'

'Yeah, I'm all done. For the summer anyway.'

She looked up into the trees that sheltered my father's back yard. Over the Malcolms' house the sky opened up. They'd had a tree service cut most of the big trees down the summer before. Their back yard was filled with the wide stumps of the fallen oaks. The Malcolm kids used one of the stumps to lean on when they were drawing outside. It was covered in pastel coloured marks made by their fat sticks of chalk. Looked like oversized crayons and never seemed to leave their hands.

Ruth would sit on her deck reading her books while she kept an eye on the kids. From the high trees on the open space I could see into the Malcolms' backyard. Oscar Lewiston took a couple shots at the kids with his pellet gun. Don't know how close he'd come to a hit, but I never took him up on an offer of a chance.

'C'mon, Pullman.' He'd push the gun toward me.

'Leave it alone, Oz. I'm busy.'

'Get your eyes off the lady and take a shot at her kid.'

'Don't feel like it.'

'You're a pervert, Pullman.'

'What's so fucking funny, gimp?'

'Hey, take it easy.' That got him. That kind of thing always got him. 'It's just you're always watching her.'

'So? What's the point?'

'Just kind of weird how you're always . . .'

'You're not doing something for the good of the people, Oz. Taking pot shots at a couple kids isn't exactly noble.'

'Fine, Pullman. Leave it.'

I almost shoved him out of the tree. But the woman on the deck was standing now. She'd stood sometime while we were talking. One of the kids was crying, and Ruth stood there with her hands on her hips. Then her face went all concerned before she kind of hopped over to the kid. She had his arm straight out and ran her fingers between the shoulder and elbow. Through the telescope I could see she was really excited. She got in close and looked at his arm and then she looked up and our eyes met. She stared straight into the lens of my telescope and waited like that.

'I just don't understand why you . . .'

'Cut it out, Oz. She's got us.'

'Huh?' he said.

She kept a hold of the kid's arm and stood all the way up.

'Oh, man. She's got us.'

But then she looked down at the arm and ruffled the kid's head before they went inside. For a while I watched the back door of the house and waited for her to come back out. Maybe she'd bring neighbours or one of Sheriff Wilcox's guys would come out with her. They'd stand together and she'd point us out. That would be the end of that after the cop took me home to my old man.

'She gone? Can't see her.'

'Put the gun down, Oz. Jesus lover. Want them to see you doing that?'

'The scope's all I got, Pullman. I wanna see too.'

'There's nothing to see. Just get down.'

So we did. Before we made the grass Dean came running up in a low crouch. It's like he'd seen guys do in war films. The brand new Pumpmaster pellet rifle he carried worked with the image.

'See that?' he asked.

'See what?' Oz asked.

'Got that kid. Twelve pumps and . . .' Dean made this popping sound with his mouth. It was lame considering he'd used it to describe putting a pellet in a kid's arm.

'No way,' Oz said. 'Probably got stung or something.'

Either way I'd had enough. I'd had enough of them talking. I'd been filled up to the limits with Oz talking about his missed attempts all afternoon and now there was Dean at it. Superstar Dean who just shot my old man's neighbour kid while he rubbed chalk into a tree stump.

'No, man. Perfect shot. Straight in the arm.'

I shot a hand across and swatted the gun out of Dean's hand. He looked at the gun and then up at me. He looked like he was about to say something so I came in with a left hand and thumped his chest. He stumbled back and I went for him. He fell into the bushes and I fell on top of him. Straddled him like a horse and held my hands over him ready to start dropping shots. He used his to cover up.

237

'Holy shit, Pullman. What the?'

'That's my old man's neighbour, you fuck up.' I dropped a right and it caught him on the shoulder. 'What comes next? When she gets an idea about what just happened? Who's she going to come see then?'

'Get off.'

'I'll send her to your house, Dean. I'll tell her that you took the perfect shot. *Shoulda seen it . . .*' I did that popping sound of his to show him how freaking lame it was. Wanted to show him how freaking lame he was.

'Get off me, Pullman.'

A left dropped on his chest. It hit dead centre and cracked against the bone. He made this squealing noise and tried to roll under me. I stood up and he went to the side and held both hands to his chest. He almost cried like a damn girl.

'Shoot your own neighbours next time.'

I walked home thinking the cops would be parked in the cul-de-sac. The circle was empty and so I walked up the street to Grant's Road and down to the bottom. Spent the rest of the day looking for body parts from the latest wreck. A Beetle that didn't make the turn.

Ruth lowered her head and looked at the pile of leaves I'd made. She frowned like she wanted to ask, but didn't think it would be right if she did. Gave me a smile that felt reassuring, kind of like she understood.

'Cleaning the place up for your dad?'

'Yeah. Kind of I guess.'

She touched her chin with two long fingers. Bit her lower lip and moved at the hips.

'Your scars are starting to fade,' she said. 'If they keep going at that rate you won't have them for long.'

I nodded without saying anything.

'Still, if they stayed they'll only give you more character. More than you already have.' She laughed at me. 'And you got a lot of character already, Joe.'

She watched me with too much patience, like she was waiting for me to speak. The longer I stood there the more I felt obligated to say something. My mind started kicking up a list of things to say. It came up with an inventory of things that sounded good and some that sounded bad. *You have nice kids. The sky's too blue. I can see your nipples through your shirt. You've gotta be the only person in town doesn't realize your husband's been screwing Cedric Fielding's older sister for the past three months.* I fell deeper into thought, or trying for thoughts anyway. Then I got a feeling like my old man was standing in a window. *I'm watching you, Joe. What're you telling that horny bitch about me?* I wanted to turn around and look at the house. Searching for something else to say became a lost cause.

He's changing, Joe. He ain't the same guy. He's getting worse.

I stood with my mouth open and no words coming out. No words even getting close to finding a way out.

'Are you alright?' Ruth asked.

When I looked at her again I found her face had moulded into an expression of concern. Felt my own face dissolving from the pained look I took on when I got caught out for dreaming. Gritted my teeth, annoyed at having been lost in thought. Angered that she'd watched me when I hadn't realized she'd been staring.

'Sorry,' I said. 'Just thinking.'

Without giving me a moment to recover she fired a shot.

'Missing your mom?'

'No,' I said too quickly.

Ruth straightened and looked away at nothing in particular.

'I didn't want to say anything,' she said without looking back at me. 'I know it can be . . .'

I felt bad for the woman. She looked young and innocent and she'd come over on a clear day trying to connect with an awkward kid. Figured that her maternal instinct made her speak words of comfort to those in need. But I didn't need her comfort. Just like I didn't miss my mother. Just wanted to finish the pile of leaves. Get them all mounted up and ready so I could sleep later that night knowing. Finally wear off some more of my tiredness by knowing that I had some place to fall.

Your old man's in a window, Joe. He thinks you've just spilled the gravy to his pretty little neighbour. Oh, what's that? Thinks you've let fly about the thing he's made in the basement.

All of this started revolving in my head and I still felt pity for the woman.

'Sometimes I miss her.'

I think I said it in a calm voice. It may have sounded convincing because Ruth looked at me and grinned like she was glad I'd told her. She didn't show any teeth – it was a universal grin of understanding or misunderstanding. One of those grins you offer when someone speaks to you and you didn't hear what they'd said. When you don't care enough to ask for it to be repeated. The words came to me – *sometimes I miss her* – as I thought of the hours of blackness in the middle of the night. The times I lay in bed and my mother's body would hang above me, pieces falling down. A dark sky towering over her, opened up in my ceiling. It's a scene that plays as if she'd never been found. Her skin turned grey and peeled away from withering muscle.

'It's good seeing you're doing okay, Joey.' She started back to her house before she even finished her sentence. I watched her until she disappeared through the glass doors. I turned to the pile and kept mounding on armfuls of leaves. When I'd got it over waist high I walked away. With my bag tossed over one shoulder I ran to the open space. Didn't look back. Never even glanced at the windows of my old man's house. It felt good to leave him behind with his eyes watching me.

My running figure fading into the distance.

Chapter Twenty-Two

The incident with Oscar Lewiston wasn't an accident. It was a situation that could've been stopped, maybe. But we got to that point where you have to drive forward. That place you cross where you can't go back after you've got there. Oz could be living a good life if things hadn't gotten out of hand. It was a strange time for Dean and me and the whole town seemed a strange place. That summer changed us. Even the whole year leading up to the summer was a build-up to the hot days where we fell apart. Never saw it while it was happening, but it was full of so much tension. It brought so many things out of me and Dean that we never expected. There were parts of our personalities that had been kept silent. Evil parts of us came to light when the air grew warmer. Oz was a mistake.

Dean came to the house early that day. He knocked on the door and ran away before it was opened. My old man answered it. I stayed silent when I heard him yelling into the street.

'Who's knocking on my fucking door?' he yelled. 'Goddamned assholes, all of you. Taking your coward-fucking turns with the knock-and-run! What're you gonna do when I'm here to catch you? What then?'

Someone yelled back, but it was the voice of an adult. My

241

father spoke to the man and went calm pretty quick. He'd change like that at times if he had to. It was a thing he was good at doing. It was something that came naturally to him, like he really couldn't help it happening.

I listened in and got a few pieces of his conversation. Neighbourly stuff about what had just happened. They stood on the porch and spoke and smoked a cigarette and everything kind of calmed down. Mick Drexler spoke in his drawl and my old man laughed the old laugh and they got into a conversation about Ford trucks. They went on about small and medium sized models while I pulled my jeans on and slid my head into a t-shirt.

'My F-150's prob'ly 'bout the best there is,' Mick told my father. 'Got an 8 in it and man she's got all the stuff. My daddy called it shit'n'git. Mojo scoot. Hear what I'm sayin'?'

I got to the bottom step and passed between my old man and the door. He leaned back and caught me there for a second, but moved off before I fell.

'I'll be damned,' Mick said. 'How's things with good ole Joe Pullman?'

'I'm fine as ever, Mr Drexler.'

'The Stapps've been askin' for ya. Beatrice thought she saw you up Meadows way.'

I shrugged: 'Don't know where that is.'

'Up Grant's Road.' He spat into the bushes. 'Other side of the woods where the duct runs out to the old ravine.'

Oh. Out to Grits' Cave . . .

'Still can't place it.' I shook my head.

'No big deal.' He smiled. Brown flakes of chewing tobacco stuck between his yellowed teeth.

'Get outta here, Joe.' My old man didn't pull the punches, even with Mick Drexler around. Calm and dead toward me as he ever had been. He dangled his key ring from his right hand. Had a bad moment while he rattled the keys. Wondered if it was a signal that he knew something was different. Something was missing.

'Lose yourself,' he said.

242

'Yessir.'

'You and that buddy a yours off somewhere new?' Mick asked.

I shook my head and turned to go.

'What buddy's that?' my old man asked.

Spun back round to answer him, but he wasn't asking me.

'Kid with glasses.' Mick took a moment to chew on the clump of tobacco in his cheek. He spat into the bushes before he finished. 'One just knocked on your door. Took off that way.'

My old man stared at me and I couldn't hang out to take it any more. Ran for the forest and got to the end of the street when my old man yelled something. Didn't look back and didn't slow down. Never heard what it was he yelled. Even when he called it out a second time. I got past the oaks and took the hill on the seat of my jeans. Hit a few rocks but only felt the pain after it was all over. It's like my old man was right behind me, running like a wolf. Couldn't feel like I was getting any farther away, no matter how fast I ran.

Dean met me half way to the open space. By the time I saw him hiding behind a tree at the edge of the clearing he was slick with sweat. He was breathing heavy with his hands on his knees. When I'd started my run he'd taken off with his and come the long way around. He'd been watching me from the Malcolms' back garden. It was the normal thing for him to do. The days he saw my father he told me he didn't feel right. There was something about my old man that Dean couldn't get his head around.

'Your dad gives me the creeps, Pullman. Really freaks me out.'

'Think about what he gives me,' I told him.

'It's what I mean. You're dad's not right.'

'Neither am I.'

'That's kind of freaky too.'

I'd laugh it off, but I knew what he meant. Dean wiped at his glasses with his shirt when we got to the open space. The sweat from his shirt left streaks on his lenses. By the time he finished and pushed them back on his nose he'd be pulling them off to try again.

243

We bypassed the Killing Tree. The sun was coming down hard, burning streaks of light through the canopy of leaves. Made the forest seem less dangerous with all that gold. At the creek Dean took a branch and poked at the crawfish that walked like space creatures over the rocks. They were all too quick for him to stab. At first he didn't make a good try to smash them. It was a time waster, but after a while even time wasters became challenges to Dean. Before long he was jamming the stick into the water like he was God with lightning. When he'd finished with one pond we'd move to the next. Each pool lay farther upstream than the last. Pieces of shattered crawfish floated slower than we walked. While he started hunting the next spot parts of shells from the last passed us by.

I stood on the bank pointing out crawfish he'd missed. It seemed like a pointless game to me, wasted too much energy. So I stood there pointing while chewing on a fresh piece of branch. I'd peeled the bark away and sucked at the sweet taste. It was green on most places, but where I was sucking it went tan. Spat everything out thinking it might be bad to swallow.

Dean kept going at it, but the sun was catching up with me. My head felt tired and light so I knelt down. Kept watching him stab at the water and everything it held within. Before long kneeling wasn't enough so I laid down in the sand.

'Jesus, they're everywhere. How many of these damn things are there?' Dean asked and jabbed the branch into the water like he wanted to probe for the centre of earth. The stick he held broke on a rock and threw off his balance. He went forward and made a big splash. The water got deep in some areas of the ponds and Dean had found one right where he went in. Even with his right arm straight out his head dunked under. It wasn't that the water was deep as the length of his arm, it just slipped when he touched for the bottom.

'Good one, killer,' I said.

The sand felt too cool on my back. Didn't want to sit up and from that angle I could see Dean was flopping around. If he'd been trying to catch the things in a net he'd probably have taken it easy trying to get out. But he'd been hunting them with a stick, digging in for the kill, and that had pumped him up. His nastiness had set in and with it came a dark side to Dean that was magnified. He was real wired up and coiled tight as a spring. He'd been that way before.

After he'd killed Maureen's bird he had a few bad days. After all the excitement of stretching the thing until it came apart he'd found a low point. Felt guilt like no other person I've ever known. Even if it was something minor he did he'd be chewing on it for days. He treated his parents most times like they were a couple of priests. He told them all kinds of stuff he'd done, some-times with me and sometimes on his own. That confession time he had with his parents really didn't sit well with me. I didn't know what he'd been telling them. More important I didn't know just how much he'd made out like I'd driven him to do it.

His mom and dad would get all holy once in a while from what he told me. *How do you feel about that? Do you think you were right in what you did? How do you think you should make up for it, Dean?* Most often they let him off, asking him to take some time and think about what he'd done. Without fail he'd be bright as gold to them for coming clean. But there were things he didn't tell his parents. These were the bad things. These were the burn in kiddie-hell type ugliness that he'd never dream of telling his momma. Things like the crawfish and her precious little para-keet for starters. This nastiness scared him when he thought about it. After the frenzy was over and he had time to consider it all, look at it with a cooled-off head. When all the cracked shells had floated away down stream and all the white feathers were stuffed in the Killing Tree's soil.

While he was down there struggling in the water he must have got that thought. It must have come floating into his head like a thundercloud. He thrashed about and got to his knees. Then he tried to stand and slipped up, dropped like a boulder down into the water again.

'Them crawfish ain't gonna be too happy, boy,' I called out in my best Florida slang. It's what he was thinking while he

245

worked himself in the water. When his head came up and his legs started spinning over the slick rocks I could see the panic. His arms pulled out of the water so quick he tossed his weight back. Half in the water and half out sprawled on the beach. He pulled himself the rest of the way up like a car driving on ice.

'Holy shit,' Dean breathed. 'They're all in there. Under that cover. I felt a couple.'

'They're watching you, Dean. Here comes another of their cousins. You're not a popular kid in those waters.' I tipped my head back and laughed. Dean didn't see the funny side. Like in an afterthought he put his hands up to his face and felt around. His face hung in a daze for a second before I'd figured it out.

'Your glasses,' I said.

'Dammit.' He looked back at the water. It was thick brown with all the mud he'd pulled up from the bottom. To Dean it must have looked like a shape in the dirt. Water and land blended together in a thick brown soup. His eyes saw nothing but shapes of colour without his glasses.

'I can't find my glasses in that.' He sounded worried and hurt and scared.

He just stood there, looking into the water. I figure he wasn't seeing much with his eyes as screwed up as they were. He'd really squinted them up to help focus on the few things he was able to make out. There wasn't much use for me to stand up just then. The water takes a while to settle. With more of the stream flowing down it kicked up the mud that already floated round.

'This is so wrong,' he said.

'How's it wrong? You slipped up. Your glasses are in the water. I'll get 'em back. Just take it easy.' I closed my eyes trying to make things look effortless. Dean started kicking at stones from where he lay in the sand. He muttered about something and I laughed enough for him to see I wasn't affected by his trouble. The glasses fixed his eyes and made his dysfunction function. Without them he was only half right and that made him need

246

me more. I stayed put, sat in the middle of a thin shard of sun. Took it all in as cool as I could so he'd understand.

'Thought I heard you guys.' The voice came out of nowhere, like the last song of the morning popping into your head halfway through the day. Annoying and constant and no chance in hell it's going to ever leave you alone. I looked at Dean and he came back at me with the same, only his eyes were still screwed up.

Oz came out from the tree line and walked to the edge of the bank on the other side of the water. He stood on a level a few feet higher than us. From where I lay it was like watching a scene in a film. A cowboy arrives to shoot a bunch of corrupt Indians that have been terrorizing a mining town. The sun glowed behind him. It wasn't really Oz, but his silhouette and that was better than the real thing, any day. He had his pellet gun in his right hand, leaned up against his shoulder. Had his weight on the short leg, only the silhouette version of Oz didn't look as lame as the real McCoy. It just looked like he was relaxed, weight resting on a bent knee.

'Heard what? I didn't hear anything,' I said and lowered my eyelids again.

'Funny, Pullman,' Dean said.

'You fell in?' Oz asked.

'What's it look like to you, gimp?'

'Might be a gimp, but I'm dry.' Oz walked down to where the creek narrowed. He jumped and hit the rocks like he almost always did. Came down hard and off-balance. The rifle went down and made a racket when it bounced over the rocks and landed in the sand. Oz tripped up on a stone and dropped to his knees on the bank. He got up quick and looked at Dean. Then he looked over at me, but I didn't acknowledge him.

More concerned about the rifle Oz didn't notice the piece of glass stuck in his leg. Just a small thing, but it looked sore. He checked the barrel of his rifle was still straight before picking up his shoe that'd come off in the fall. When he put it on it made a squelching sound. He didn't have chance to care because he caught sight of the glass. I didn't say anything to him then, but I thought it was something when he pulled it out and tossed it in the water. He didn't even flinch, just wiped the blood away and more came in a thin red line. The gun looked good as new leaning next to him.

'Still dry, fatboy?' Dean asked.

'More than you, Gill.' Oz knew that name worked Dean up something rotten. Oz'd call him Gill as short for Gillespie. Dean didn't like it 'cause Oz always said it in a girl's whiney voice. If he really wanted to wind Dean up he'd pucker up his lips after he said it. But the name took on a different meaning after Gillian Wilcox died in Wild Lake. Dean had feelings for her – more than he liked to admit. Oz knew this so he'd dropped the nickname after Gillian had died. What made him come out with it at the side of Washington Pond, when Dean was mad as hell already, I'll never know. Oz had a bad sense of timing. The Gillian connection may have slipped his mind. He may have said it thinking Dean was blind and defenceless. He didn't take into consideration that nature makes up for faults by giving strengths in other areas. Dean's strength was memory and silence and patience. Mix that with an eagerness for revenge and you could have yourself problems.

'Oz, make yourself useful.' I'd covered my eyes with an arm. The warm air and the sound of the leaves moving overhead had intoxicated me. 'Feel around in there for Dean's glasses.' With my free hand I pointed out the pond.

'Not my problem.'

'It'll be your problem if you want it.' Dean was almost growling.

'Make it.'

'Look,' I said. Sat up on my elbows and felt a rush of blood to my head. I was tired, and getting kind of angry. The day had no plans and no direction. My body was telling me to relax and with all the mess there was no chance of that happening. Sitting there with all that chaos I started thinking about my old man. Started to wonder if he'd spoken with Mick Drexler any more about the kid who'd been knocking on his door in the mornings.

248

'Sooner we get the glasses the sooner we check out Grits' Cave,' I said.

Oz snapped his head round to look at me. 'What cave?'

'The Grits' place. It's on the other side of town.' I was talking a stream of crap and it was sounding good. 'Went out there with J.D. and Ernie. You know them. The brothers. Only got a few minutes in. Left all the flashlights and stuff out there. Ready for today if you'll move it.'

Dean didn't make a motion that he was willing to play along. He was that smart not too. More importantly he didn't give too much of a damn about the game. His glasses were in the bottom of muddy water and he had to rely on Oscar Lewiston to get them back. Must have been running in his head how much Oz would cast that one up. Dean wouldn't be able to talk about the gimp without getting the water episode thrown back at him.

'How'd you guys get to hang out with them?'

'Just do sometimes,' Dean said. He came out with it in a matter of fact way that made me almost smile.

'I want to go.'

'Figured you would. Get the glasses and we're off.'

To add some urgency I stood and started pulling my shirt on again. We hadn't planned on going back to the Grits' place. Me and Dean had talked about never going back there, but that day was different. The sun sent down fiery yellow streaks and the wind cut in cool when you needed it. That day the forest couldn't have been a place that held secrets or evils. But the Grits' place wasn't part of the same forest as Washington Pond. It was another forest altogether. Still, that didn't register, not while we stood there at the pond where it was calm. Couldn't help but hope that it would be calm everywhere. With that kind of thinking we decided to go to Grits' Cave.

Oz went into the water and kept checking back to see if his rifle was still leaning against the tree. He didn't waste any time moving his hands over the rocks. He kicked up a load of mud in the process and made it harder on himself. Dean and me stood

249

with our arms folded. Watched from the bank with our usual irritable acceptance of Oscar being round.

'Be careful, Oz. Don't stand on 'em,' Dean said.

Oz move deeper and looked like he was walking on all fours. Then he got to the deep part where the water went up to his thighs. The closer he got to the other side the surer I was that he'd be going in. Dropping like a boulder same as Dean. I wanted it to happen because it would've evened things between him and Dean. We could laugh off the argument and head off with smiles. But that didn't happen. Oz somehow stood strong in the water. On land he could trip over a crack in the pavement. In the water he touched rocks and kind of stuck to them. Before long he was in the deepest part. His lower lip tucked up over his teeth. His eyes narrowed to slits and he stayed like that for a while. Then he changed the course of the day and found the glasses.

'Got 'em!' Oz came up and moved out without even a stagger.

Before the glasses had even been handed over Dean was asking for more help.

'Borrow your shirt to wipe 'em off?'

I held out the front of my Adidas top and waited for him to do his thing. Oz placed the glasses in Dean's waiting hand. Dean opened the glasses and rubbed the bubbles away with my shirt.

'You're welcome, Gill,' Oz said.

Dean looked at me. His eyes were screwed up still, but what he wanted to say was understood. *Ditch the Runt.* Dean cleaned the glasses off while Oz got his rifle. I stared up at the leaves and the sun breaking through them, hot as ever. Dean had his glasses back on and seemed eager to take off. Oz wouldn't have been able to catch us. We'd done it so many times before. But that day I decided not to run. Didn't want Dean to take off and have to come back. It's the type of thing that can break a kid's confidence. Before he'd made the move I nudged his arm. He looked up like he expected me to be counting off before the big race. When he saw I wasn't ready he kind of looked ready to give up.

'Let's get to the cave.' Didn't say it loud enough for Oz to hear me. Dean gave me his mad look before I'd turned and gone up the bank. Headed off at full-pace and Oz started after me and grunted while he hoisted his weight against his rifle for balance. Dean passed him and evened up with me just like I'd planned. Dean needed to know what I was thinking without Oz getting wind of it. Dean came up next to me with his hands out in front of him. He was staring at me with big dark eyes.

'Cool it, Dean. I've got something to keep the day going.'

'Look, Pullman, we agreed. That place's not right.'

'Yeah, that's why we're taking him.' I tossed a thumb over my shoulder.

'Hey, wait up you guys,' Oz called out.

'Just keep his hopes up about it. He'll be disappointed as he ever was. Then me and you split.'

Dean laughed and shook his head and said: 'What then? Leave him to find his way back?'

'Just the plan,' I told him.

Me and Dean kept up the same speed so we were alone and ahead of the gimp. Dean liked the plan judging from the smile he had on his face. Hadn't seen him smile that big since the first time we'd looked at the middle pages of his old man's Penthouse.

'Hurry up, Oz,' Dean yelled over his shoulder. 'Gotta get there 'fore it's too late.'

'Too late for what?' Oz already struggled to keep his breath in rhythm.

'Too late to check their traps.' Dean could lie so well at times and I couldn't help but smile at him. He gave it back so much bigger and better than mine.

'How're we gonna be too late for that?'

'The Grits come out of the cave just before dark. You don't want to be there when they show up.'

Oz huffed and puffed, but he was no big bad wolf. He struggled to keep close behind us. Dean kept looking back and waving his arm to urge him on. He'd give me reports that weren't loud enough for Oz to hear. *His face's real red now. Looks like he's gonna explode. Ever noticed how much he bends with that limp. Man he's a sucker and a half. He's not gonna make it, Pullman.*

'C'mon, Oz,' Dean called back now and again. 'We're almost there.'

When we made it to the camp my legs felt like I'd run a marathon. The last time we'd walked to the camp the trip had been staggered. It was a stop and start kind of thing. We made the three miles in a series of short bursts. This trip came in one single journey that in the heat seemed package sized extra-large. Walking into the camp didn't seem as extreme an event as I'd anticipated. With the warm air and the sun coming down the place was tame. Still, the legend of the Grits kept the tingles of fear passing over my shoulders. Me and Dean looked into the woods around the camp. Neither of us saying what we were looking for, but we made a show of it for Oz. Dean's face told me he was apprehensive and maybe it wasn't all that much acting for him. There are too many hiding places in that forest. That deep in, away from towns and road, it was more possible for one of those places to be hiding a terrible thing.

'Don't fucking tell me this is the cave,' Oz said circling the same spot on the clearing.

His face glowed red in patches. His chest grew then fell and he circled. He held the gun with the barrel pointed at the ground. Even if he'd wanted to point it at us I don't think his arms had enough strength to lift it.

'What's wrong with it?' Dean laughed.

'It's not a cave.' Oz hit one of the support poles with the barrel of his rifle. It let out a high-pitched ping sound that echoed. 'It's a tent.'

'What's your problem?' Dean walked over to Oz with this cowboy swagger. I expected him to just stand there staring at him. Expected him to get up close and ask for the fight without talking. When Dean closed up his hand into a fist I held my breath. It's like my body started preparing for a fight. Getting all pumped up and ready for a fight I was about to be involved in.

Dean swung a solid punch. His hand hit Oz below the left eye and it made a slapping sound. Oz went stiff 'cause he didn't

252

see it coming. The next punch followed without warning and jabbed in from the left side. Then a right to the head. A left to the unguarded side of Oz's neck. The rifle hit the dirt before Oz lost his legs. Dean landed a knee to the gimp's balls before Oz went for one of the poles. His hands came out with the fingers splayed. Looking for anything to keep him up. He went halfway down but held himself from going the rest of the way. Shook like he was cold and sweat ran down his forehead and he blinked it out of his eyes. Dean bounced around. His arms pumped with energy he'd never felt before.

'Stop it,' Oz said. His voice was loud for a kid that'd just experienced his first good beating. Loud for a kid who'd just had his balls crushed. I'd keep quiet after my beatings. If they came from my father or the hands of guys at school I kept my mouth zipped. Lay low and let the guy breathe it out of his system.

No sense in sparking a fire that's dying out, Oz.

Standing behind Dean I could see that maybe I didn't fit in with the norm. Thought maybe Dean was coming to the other side too. All that time his parents had spent raising a good little middle-class sucker had found a drain. If Maureen had been out there to see her precious Dean . . .

Dean went in again and started thumping the gimp. He came in swinging with his face red. His teeth clenched so damn tight the muscles in his jaw bulged. Oz kept himself up by holding on to that post. Dean worked his punches into the head. Didn't even think to lean down and go for a body shot. He wanted that knockout. That all important dull thump that I'd been after. He rocked Oz with a couple heavy shots before the gimp lost hold of the post and hit the deck.

With arms over his head Oz left his gut wide open. Dean's Converse sneakers made the paste-white rolls a target. After Dean landed a few Oz dropped his arms to cover up. Target practice went back to his head. Dean leaned in with a few punches. He got crouched down low and dug in. He looked like he was skimming stones over a pond. His arm came way up and then he'd swing it down in a big arc. Oz's head rolled to the side with the

253

punches. Dean stood back up for kicks when his arms got tired. Before he finished up Oz'd stopped moving.

'How's that, Ozzie? Want some more?' Dean danced around. Hovering over Oz he started searching for another target.

'Take it easy, Dean.' He didn't hear me. He didn't hear anything but the blood pulsing in his ears. The rhythm in his head kept the energy in his hands. I'd felt the energy and I'd danced the dance. Dean hadn't finished. Figured there wasn't much I could do just then to stop him. It was Dean's moment so I stood back out of the way holding my elbows.

'Call me Gill. C'mon, Ozzie. I don't hear you talkin' now!' Out came Dean's strength. That quiet memory that made him so dangerous. That complete and total recollection and eagerness for revenge. He composed himself and breathed at the pond when Oz cut in. Dean stood there on the beach, blind and lame and the gimp started in on him. *Call me Gill.* He must have said it a thousand times walking to the camp. He must have gone back over that anger the whole three miles. Must have reminded himself the reason for that anger. *Call me Gill.* But, I'd never heard it. His anger and his revenge was something he kept to himself.

He laid a boot up against Oz's ribs. Came in hard with a full swing of his leg. There was a cracking sound when the boot went in. Oz didn't move.

Chapter Twenty-Three

Dean's mother called a few times that week. First time she'd phoned since inviting me to the concert at the lake. Her messages made the red light flash on the answer machine in my old man's study. I'd listened to them a dozen times. Her voice burned holes in my stomach. I had a feeling that she'd held off calling because she thought I was some kind of an omen. I was the Gillespie family's raven. Still, she'd started calling again after Dean did that bad thing to Oz.

Maybe he's told her about this one too, Joe. Confessions time . . . I'm a sinner and it's been too fucking long since my last beating. Maybe he's told her about everything. How he'd kicked Oz's teeth in with the toe of his new Converse sneakers. Maybe she's got his story covered and she's needing you to get yours on the same page. Needs you in on the game in case the cops come knocking. But what about the day after the beating, Joe? Does she know about the day after . . . and all the things you and Dean did to Oz the day after . . .

'Joe, baby. It's Dean's mom. Maureen Gillespie, hun. I'm just calling to see if you're alright, doll,' she said. 'Dean tells me you're fine and all that. We sure do miss you round here. Haven't see you for a bit. Just want to make sure you're hanging in there. Stop by, okay?'

255

That's the kind of message she left. I tried telling myself that it was genuine concern in the sound of her voice. Wanted to make a quick dash to see her. Knew the food would be good and ready and she'd be willing to make what wasn't there. Still, I couldn't leave the house. It's not like I worried about getting caught while away. It's more like I worried someone would come when I couldn't defend myself. So I stayed and sat tight and waited for my time to come. While I waited that week a few of the neighbours brought food. I ate it most of the time sitting on the bottom step. Watched the frosted white glass window by the front door.

People still came to the house for those few months after my mother'd killed herself. They rang the doorbell and looked through the glass panels. Most of the faces looked always hopeful that someone might answer. Sometimes they caught me sitting on the stairs. I'd got spotted walking through the hall a few times. Halfway to the stairs on my way up or at the bottom step on the way down, they got me. So I just kept still while they watched me. There was no place to hide. It seemed a better option than running for cover. On the other side of the door faces just hovered like they'd caught sight of me. If they didn't see me the faces still hung there. Can't tell for sure what they caught, but they came close to the glass and cupped hands around eyes. Frosted white didn't let much through from my end. I'd tested it a hundred times just to keep on the safe side.

Most of the time folks gave up and went away. I never opened the door in all the months they came. No matter who stood on the other side I just sat there and watched them just like they watched me. I didn't even move when some of them waved before heading off. After they'd gone I'd open up and bring in what they left behind. Some of those people left plenty.

Beatrice Stapp stopped by at the beginning of the week and left roasts in flimsy foil containers. Valerie Drexler dropped off mounds of baked foods. Almost all of them were too sweet and white dog hairs stuck out from the cling-film covering the stuff. Still we ate them and didn't leave much to throw away. Me and

256

my old man ate everything they left behind. Never ate it together, but I made sure that he got his share. My father took it like it was from Santa Claus. I'd eat what I needed and set the rest on the kitchen table. Next morning the plate would be empty except for a few crumbs or smudges. Never saw my old man take his share. I started it and my father finished it and that was alright by me. When he took his food I knew that he was still around. Even with the tools quiet most days the empty plate told me that my old man still existed.

Leonidas Murtache left the best food. He'd come by more often than most and drop off buckets of chicken he'd picked up from the drive-thru. There was a Kentucky Fried Chicken just outside of town. Sometimes he'd write a note on a spare napkin. Pen ink scratched over the Colonel's face. The notes weren't much, but they came to mean more as I saw less of my old man.

Hang in there, boys. That kind of message can mean a lot.

Times get better.

God, I hope so.

Leonidas never rang the bell. He'd just leave the bucket and walk back across the street. By then he'd started to slump with his weak spine. The bend in his back curled him over like he carried a ten-ton cross on his shoulders. He pressed his hands so hard into his pockets that the fabric of his pants faded where his knuckles rubbed. The skin on his face turned as ashen as the cigarettes that crumbled from his lips. His cough started to sound like rocks breaking.

When I saw him walking toward the house with another red and white bucket in his hands I thought about opening the door. Since they'd found Oscar I hadn't left my old man's house. I stayed close to the door hoping the food would keep arriving and the police would stay the hell away. Our cupboards had gone to waste and never been replenished. Old food had left behind spots of mould and fungus. Black patches of fur marked the empty shelves of the fridge.

The local radio station gave reports about a boy being found. Said he'd been located in a place called Delaware Glenn. The

257

name of that place didn't mean anything to me at first. Then the announcer started talking about a clearing used by local high school students to drink beer and smoke marijuana. They didn't give the boy's name but they called him a local. Said he'd been missing for a few days and that an anonymous call tipped off the police. A k-9 patrol found the boy naked and tied to a post. Reports said he was suffering from hypothermia at the time of his rescue. The report told of the kid's wounds *suffered in a brutal and savage attack*. One of the reporters from a Baltimore television station said the kid was *indecently assaulted*. Police were calling out for anyone with information.

Part of me stayed calm and it was easy enough to convince myself that some other kid had been given the same as Oz. The local missing kid isn't Oz at all, I kept saying to myself. He'd been home for days. He was sitting with his dad watching basketball and eating popcorn. Playing the Atari and drinking an RC Cola. Still if the kid was Oz and the police had him in a safe place why didn't he talk about me and Dean? He must have said something by then. He'd had a full twenty-eight hours to cough up the goods on us. The media don't always give away all the information. They need to hold things back so the police can sneak in and nab the bad guys. I sat waiting and hoping my name hadn't been added to a law enforcement shit list.

From the bottom steps I could see everyone coming up to the house. They were just shapes in the windows, but those shapes let me know someone was on their way. They couldn't see me from the sun reflecting against the glass. I left the bottom step and walked through to the front room. Stood behind the curtain and looked out past the window frame. Watched the street for a while and wondered how many people knew what we'd done.

I kept a close watch on the tall, bent figure walking down Westchester Drive. He kept to the side of the road and took long slow steps. Walked like he still carried that cross. Leonidas looked up a few times along the way. But he'd looked down to the road fast as a flash. The sun's reflection came with the brightness of a frozen bolt of lightning. When he made it to our drive I wanted to get to the door. Imagined opening it up wide and smiling at the old guy. Giving him a wink while I took the bucket from his hand. Maybe I'd say something to him that would make him come more often. But I couldn't move. Something kept me frozen. Kind of like I feared him and pitied him all at the same time.

He stood at the frosted white window and bent down. I'd left the curtains and got to the foyer and stood there at the door. Heard him moving on the other side. Still, I couldn't bring myself to open it up. When he stood again my face met his in the frosted window. He caught sight of me, my shape anyway. We looked at one another for a second. The glass was bubbled out in places and it distorted his long face. Took away his features, but I could always tell Leonidas from his chin. It hung low, like a horse. The glass must have reduced me to circles of dull colour. Broken my face into the obscure shapes of eyes and hair. Knowing that made the moment bearable, but it still lasted too long.

He finally tapped the panel with a swollen knuckle. It made a hard sound that cut through me. Before turning away he opened his hand in a wave that looked more like a peace offering. I left it a few minutes after he'd dissolved into the white frosted glass. Gave him just enough time to get across the street. Time to head off back toward his house and disappear from the street. Then I opened the door and pulled the bucket to my chest.

Got the foil wrapping off and ripped a chunk of meat away from a bone with my teeth. The grease was still hot and melted into my lips. That burn brought me back to life. It sparked part of me that needed to know I was still alive.

'Can't finish all that off on your own,' a voice called out.

I looked over as Dean came crawling out from under the azaleas. He'd found a small space at the bottom of the hedge. Must have moved in early and been there for hours. He sat himself up, crossing his legs and swatting at the dirt covering his knees. He had a smile on his face that made me think the news about the boy maybe wasn't real. Like I'd picked up a radio station from out of town or something. Some other place called Maritime had a lost kid. A story broadcast far and wide about a lost-and-found-beat-to-shit kid just like our Oz. The kid had a limp and one leg shorter than the other, but it wasn't Oscar Lewiston. It was all just a sick coincidence that played off like a bad joke.

'First thing I've eaten since Wednesday,' I told him. Let the foil drop from my hand. My stomach made loud noises so I swallowed and chewed more meat from the bone.

'Celebrating?' Dean grunted while standing up.

'What's to celebrate?'

'Oz's coming home.' He smiled just enough to make him look as scared as I felt.

'So that kid they found,' I swallowed the chunk of greasy meat. 'Oz.'

'Oh, yeah,' he said. 'Spent a few days at Columbia Medical Centre. They kept it quiet for a while. Now it's all over the news like they just found him.'

'How'd you know so much?'

'With a mom like mine?' his shoulders bounced. 'I know everything before it even happens.'

'They coming to get us?'

'Probably not. He's in bad shape.'

'Bad enough to keep him quiet?' I asked, looking at the chicken bone.

'I listened in to mom talking with one of her friends.' He looked up at me and clarified. 'That nurse friend. Big jugs and stuff.' I nodded to let him know I followed. He went on: 'She said he still can't talk. Can't even think all that great from what people are saying.'

'What are people saying?'

'Hasn't said a single word since they found him.' Dean moved closer and craned his neck to look into the bucket. 'Like a fucking vegetable.'

'Jesus, Dean.' I kept my head down and turned for the door. 'How long'll that last? His . . . you know.'

'Better be a long freakin' time. We'd get in a serious mess for this one, Pullman. Adult time probably.'

'Dammit.' My guts rolled and I breathed through my nose to keep from puking up the chicken. 'He's gotta keep quiet.'

'More than quiet.'

'For your sake,' I said.

'You too, hotshot.' Then he just stared at me. Looking up from the bucket I met his eyes with my own cold stare. I chewed the rest of the meat away and tossed a leg bone at him. It hit his chest and fell into the bushes.

'Go home, Dean.' I backed into the house and started closing the door.

'We better go see him.'

'Tomorrow,' I said.

'Whenever,' Dean replied. 'But the sooner the better.'

Chapter Twenty-Four

I knocked on the door with Dean standing at my side. We'd both just looked at the nameplate for a while. The plate was brass and shining. We breathed and tried to settle ourselves without talking to each other. I felt like I'd just run a marathon. My breath wasn't coming easy and my medicine head was coming back. Dean's chest raised so heavy it moved his shoulders. He kept rubbing his hands together. Then he'd shove them in his pockets. He'd pull them out again and start rubbing them together. He ran his fingers through his hair and stuffed his hands back in his pockets. I folded my arms to keep from looking just as much an idiot.

That nameplate was shining so damn bright.

Lewiston.

On the walk over we kept pretty quiet. We didn't make a plan of what we'd say to Oz. Or what we'd say to his old man for that matter. Whoever opened the door would be alien to us. We'd expected recognition in a way since most of Oz's family had seen him with us. His old man would pick us out of a crowd and that's the kind of thing that was playing on my mind.

How much does this guy know about you, Joe? Maybe Oz has learned to talk again. Maybe his old man's on the phone to Wilcox right now. Of course he could be ready to deal with you on his own . . .

Couldn't help but think that maybe we'd walked ourselves into the middle of a trap. We'd get bound up and they'd take us away in the light of television cameras. That would bring an end to the story and end of life with my father. It would bring an end to it all. Didn't seem all that bad all of a sudden. How bad could it be for a couple of kids who stepped off the deep end one day and busted up a gimp? But we'd gone back. That's the most terrible thing.

Could've left it as a beating, Joe. Didn't have to . . .

Didn't think about the best way to ask Mr Lewiston to let us into his house. We just left that morning with a pair of shy smiles and hoped for the best. One thing came for certain – even though we didn't talk about it – if Oz looked bad we wouldn't break down. We wouldn't exchange any worried looks while we were round him. None of those shaky stares that make you look guilty. Never a chance for tears that day, no matter how scared we felt. I hadn't said anything to Dean, but I knew he could keep things in. When it came to secrets that could screw up the rest of his life I figured him to be safer than a gold coin in Fort Knox. He had a future as part of a middle-class carbon copy family of his own. He came from good stock and didn't want to screw things up.

We'd met in the open space and took the long way around. After backtracking to Potter's Drive we came up Duponte Circle and down Oz's road – Carlton Lane. We made stops to collect cicadas from the bushes. Ligustrums lined Carlton. Orange cicada shells hung from the leaves like hundreds of empty fruit skins.

We'd picked up a bunch of them that had gone through the change. They'd stayed close to the shells while their wings stretched and went solid for first flight. After pulling off the limp wings we dropped their bodies onto the road. Kicked them until they broke apart. Crushed them into the asphalt so they looked like they'd never existed. Even that late into the cicada summer the noise hadn't died much. On good days you couldn't hear the traffic coming. That constant chatter took over the sky. That buzzing sound they made got right inside your head.

I had to knock a second time and may have buzzed the door-bell right after. First knock didn't bring anything. No sound of footsteps and no one shuffling inside the house. The third knock was heavy, like I meant it. The door went in and took a gust of wind with it. Swung wide in one big sucking motion. It came quick like he knew something important had arrived. *Special order for Mr Lewiston. Parcel delivery of your son's kidnappers.* With the door open Mr Lewiston stepped out like he'd meant to run into the streets. I took a step back and bumped into Dean kind of heavy. He tumbled over the dead Boxwood bush and landed on the lawn. He rolled onto his back and straightened up his glasses.

'What do you want?' Mr Lewiston asked. He looked over my head and into the street.

'I came for Oz. Wanting to see how he's been doing,' I said. My voice came out loud. 'We came, I mean.' Threw a thumb to where Dean lay on the lawn. 'To see if he's okay and all.'

'He's not okay,' Mr Lewiston said. His eyes looked small behind the lenses of his glasses. He let out a breath and scratched the top of his head. His fingernails left red lines on his bald scalp. Those red lines stayed there, like he'd dug them in deep. His fingers scratched at the side of his face.

'Sorry to bother you,' I said.

'You guys seen any kids buzzing?' he asked. He moved to the side and looked up the street. 'Buzzing the goddamned bell and running off. Bunch of cowards. At a time like this.'

'No,' I told him. 'Haven't seen . . .'

'Little pricks,' he muttered. 'Every damn day. Buzzing every goddamned day since Oz's been gone.' His voice started breaking. His eyes were red and looked tired. It's the kind of state a man should never have to find himself in. There was part of me that thought he looked weak. Then there was part that understood him too.

I turned to walk away.

'Look . . . Joseph, right?' he asked. 'You're the Pullman kid.' His fingers moved to touch the wrinkles beside his left eye.

They stayed there while he looked at me. Stared like he'd remembered something. Probably something Oz told him. *Hey, Dad, I was out today with the Pullman kid. One with the busted-up face.* Mr Lewiston recognized me. He knew who I was and that wasn't usual. Scared the hell out of me.

'Yeah.' I faced him again.

'Ozzie's been through a lot. He's on medication that makes him sleep.' He went back to rubbing the red lines on his head. His fingers moved over the bald skin, looking for something. Had a hell of a lot of interest in something that didn't exist any more. 'Right now he's not the kid you know. Or knew even. Not my kid either. He's someplace else.'

'Can we see him?' Dean asked. He'd stood without me noticing. Somehow he'd made it to my side again.

'I don't think so.' Mr Lewiston looked at Dean like he had a vision. Like what he saw wasn't something he wanted to be close by. Didn't want to be up close and personal with what little boy blue had become. Whatever Mr Lewiston saw while looking at Dean froze him for a second. It puzzled him and cut deep lines in his brow. It was a bad moment and it lasted a few seconds. Lasted a few seconds that seemed like hours. Then we all just broke out of it like stepping out of a car that'd just ran through a crowd of children. Our eyes searched around for something else to take our minds off the moment. No one made a motion to move and so we just stood there looking at the dead plants sticking up from the soil.

'We'll come back when he's better,' I said. 'Maybe in a couple weeks.'

Mr Lewiston almost smiled. It looked strained and thoughtful. He was a sad man who was smiling. I don't know what made him even try.

'Do that,' he said.

When he shut the door Dean pulled me away. We walked to the end of the road without talking. The path leading to the open space from Carlton Lane had half a dozen rubber plants lining it. Big things that grew like giants and stretched high and

wide. I pulled off a heavy leaf and started breaking it into pieces.
Kept working at that leaf while we walked. Broke the small pieces
even smaller. Dropped them behind me. Just like I was making
a trail to find my way back.

'Man,' Dean laughed. 'I thought he had us. Figure he knows.
Oz gave it up. He's just waiting for the right time. Yeah, he
knows what we did.'

'Got that feeling too.' Broke up the leaf again.

'He probably wonders if we're coming back for him.' Dean
hopped a couple times and held his hands up like a prize-fighter.
'Come back to finish Oz off or something like that.'

I tossed more leaf to the pavement.

'See how he looked at me?'

'Yeah,' I said.

'Didn't like that smile I gave him, huh?'

'What?'

Dean stopped and punched my arm.

'What's that for?' The leaf fell to the ground and my hands
rolled into stones.

'Let's go back and see him.'

'What smile?'

'Forget that, Pullman. Let's go back.'

'How're we gonna get in, Dean?'

'We're not.' Dean smiled too big again. 'Just going back for
a look. Check in on him. Through a window if it's all we can
get.'

'Why?'

'You don't want to see what I did?' he asked.

'I already have.'

'Not everything, Pullman.' Dean opened his mouth wide and
let out a high-pitched laugh. It came out loud enough to make
me think he'd bring attention our way. Didn't see anyone round,
but still, I didn't want to be there any more. Not standing out
in the open with Dean. Not outside on my own. Couldn't go
home to my old man and his fucked-up house.

You've got lost somewhere along the way, Joey-boy. This summer's

266

been somethin'. Never thought you'd have no place to go, huh? Well, kiddo, betcha never thought it'd get like this.

When Dean walked away I didn't follow. He kept turning round and waving me on. Really started to get my head pounding, all that flapping of his arm. Calling me up like an animal kept hitting at my nerves. The cicadas chattered and they buzzed and flew close by my head. I stood there between the line of rubber plants and the oleander hedge. The cicadas moved in close to me. Dropped by and almost touched my face before they went back up. The more I listened the more the cicadas' song sounded like something that I needed to hear. It grew louder as Dean made it to Carlton Lane. He disappeared from the trail and I made sure he was gone before I turned away. Walked home and went to my bedroom where I listened for my father who wasn't home.

Kept my eyes closed while in bed and imagined Oz. That's the only way I wanted to see him. Imagined him the way he was before the scars. The fat kid with the short leg before he went silent. In my head he didn't give me that look. He didn't ask me for help and his hands didn't shake. I made him like new again and before I fell asleep things got better. Oz wasn't the kid they'd found out in a place called Delaware Glenn. Some other unlucky sucker walked into a world of hurt. Some travellers that the local people called the Grits came into Maritime. They'd caught this kid stealing from their traps and got him good. Oz got busted up when he fell over on his way back from our trip. It had nothing to do with me and had nothing to do with Dean, just a bad step on a bad leg. It was some other kid they found. A real unlucky sucker, 'cause the Grits got him good.

I may not have slept that night. Sat up listening for the sound of my old man coming home. Waiting for his car to pull into the garage. Anticipated the doors slamming and him yelling up to me. Prepared myself for his heavy and uneven footsteps on the stairs. His shoulder dragging against the wall all the way. Couldn't help but wonder if he'd recognized the difference – the weight of a missing key. Wondered when he'd see that only one

267

of the shining new Yale keys was still on the ring. Gripped my pocket knife hard and waited. Prepared myself for morning to come.

It's all gonna change, kid.

The cicadas started their song before the sun even came up.

Yessa. It's all good.

Chapter Twenty-Five

Next day I walked to Dean's house. The sun was already reaching the centre of the sky. The wind blew in blasts of hot air. Yellow beams baked down through the cover overhead and pressed at my shoulders. Under the canopy of leaves the sun felt hot. Even the thickness of the forest couldn't stop the summer from burning. Out there the heat had a chance to spin around on the back of the wind. When the heat got in the forest it didn't have a way to get back out.

I felt weak and kind of lame that morning. Laid in bed for a long time, too long really. Listened for the sound of my old man. He didn't come home that night and I'd stayed up and listened with all I had. Occupied myself with stupid games. Counted the cicadas I'd killed from memory. Drew a picture of Fuller's Mark in the shadows on my ceiling. I'd done everything to keep ready for my old man coming home. I never heard a sound that whole night. Not a single creak in the house. But the silence wasn't a good thing. It wasn't reassuring. I couldn't bring myself to leave my room in case he'd somehow come back. In case he'd never left at all. So I tried to sleep and when I couldn't I walked from wall to wall. Then I'd lay down again.

The sun took a long time coming up that morning. Maybe it

always lifted that slow, but I'd never been up to watch it happen. I watched the window leaking dew. Watched the drops bead up and tackle one another for a while. I got up and walked from wall to wall again, but I couldn't settle in. Waited at the door of my room and listened. Tried to remember if I'd fallen asleep. Recall any glimpse of a dream, but there was nothing. It took a few minutes, but I became convinced that my old man never came home.

I left the room and walked down the stairs. Stood in the foyer listening. The house was dead. Outside the street was yellow with mist and sun. The birds had started to sing, but they were still tired. I left the house through the sliding doors in the kitchen. The air was cold and it turned my arms to gooseflesh. There was no wind. Branches didn't sway. Leaves didn't rustle. The forest was dead – and inviting as ever.

The air was still cold when I went back inside. In my room I stripped from the t-shirt and jeans. Pushed them far back into the corner of my closet. Thought about stuffing them in my backpack. Considered taking them along to the Gillespies' later in the day. Bundle them with other clothes and get Maureen to wash them clean. But that wasn't going to happen.

Stood naked – watching out the window. Looking at the trees and the sun burning through them. Then I went to the bed and laid down. Something was different now. Pulled the quilt to my chin. Tried to settle myself. Went back to counting dead cicadas. Didn't get far before I fell asleep.

Woke to the sound of my father walking down the hall. His heavy steps came close to my door so I pulled my knees to my chest. Grabbed hold of the pocket knife and stayed silent. He stood at the top of the stairs for a while that morning. He stood just outside my door. Watched the brass handle and willed it not to spin. If it had the twin bolt locks and chest of drawers stood sturdy to keep it shut. Hoped it would buy me enough time to jump anyway. When he finally walked down the stairs he went in a rush. His feet pounded through the hall when he reached the ground floor.

He opened and slammed the cabinets in the kitchen. Then he unlocked the basement door and went down the stairs. The sounds that came up from his workshop echoed through the laundry shoot. They were faint, but if I concentrated I could almost tell what my father was doing. There were the usual machines. Trying to visualize what he was doing I closed my eyes. Waited for him to yell up to me. I fell asleep while he was walking around his workshop.

When I woke again the light had opened far and wide. Things seemed to glow and everything outside had a glaze of yellow. Sweat made my arms shine and beads covered my chest and legs. Dripped from my brow and fell into my eyes and pressed my hair down on my head. I dried off with the quilt from my bed. Dressed quickly and waited at my bedroom door. When I was sure my old man was still in the basement I slid the chest of drawers away from the door. Swatted back the bolts and took several deep breaths before running the stairs. Left the house and never looked back. Made it to the open space on pounding legs. Once under the trees I waited in the shade to collect my breath and let the sweat roll away.

The daily rounds didn't seem important that day. I hesitated with the idea of checking the Killing Tree. After walking the Angry Snake a half-dozen times I'd stared to worry. *Someone's gonna see you, Joe. They're gonna see you and know you're a bad kid. See you've got a bad head.* That voice cleared up any lingering uncertainty and so I made the trek to the clearing.

The tree looked bigger than usual and the grass was too green in places. Righted the headstones that had fallen and did a search of the grounds. Found three birds and a snake in the clearing. I wasn't able to find the strength to dig a hole. At the base of the Killing Tree there was a small tunnel. It was covered by the thickest root of the tree and went too deep for the light to touch the bottom. Me and Dean took turns figuring on what lived down there. We couldn't think of any animal brave enough to make it a home. Wasn't anything could handle living in the base of the Killing Tree. I looked into the hole one last time and got

271

myself so worked up that I could almost see a pair of eyes.

Dropped the birds and that snake down into the hole. Fed those eyes that I couldn't imagine weren't real. The bodies landed close to the opening but didn't go down. It's like they tried with what little they had left to keep from going all the way in. Used the toe of my sneaker to kick the bird and the snake. That'd stayed up. They went in and afterwards it seemed the right thing to do. Let the hole swallow them up and take them down close to the eyes. Kick them into the blackness and let them fall and fall.

Walked to Dean's house after the Killing Tree, but didn't take the main path. Coming to the bridge I jumped on the slats that had yet to break. The thing made noises like it would crack and fall to pieces. Still, it felt hard and sturdy as a castle of stone. Under the bridge the water flowed clear and fast. Stayed long enough to spit into the water a few times. Watch the white foam of my spit float away in the current. It went a long ways, much farther than I'd expected. Then it broke apart like smoke and dissolved into nothing. Things like that made me feel alive.

After all of my wanderings that day I came out onto Dean's street. Walked up between a couple houses and came out halfway down the road from his mother's place. I walked toward the house with the eyes of an elderly couple aimed at me. Nothing they could have done to stop me. There wasn't an ounce of anything they had to offer could harm what I'd become. I kept my head down and my shoulders curled forward. Hands in the pockets of my shorts. Felt both palms going moist like I was worried about something. Kept having to wipe them dry without taking them out of my pockets. Just rubbed away inside my pants until they'd dried off. Those old folks must have figured I was practising the five-knuckle shuffle. Can't remember if I looked over at them, but I'd like to think I did. Like to think I smiled while I rubbed myself dry.

When I came to Dean's yard I cut across the lawn. Walked to the front door and knocked harder than I needed to. I'd got myself worked up and really thumped at the door with a tight fist. All at once that feeling came on even heavier. It was the same feeling I got when standing on the porch looking at the shining brass nameplate on the Lewistons' front door. That worked up, anxious feeling came on so fast I couldn't find anything to focus on. Could still feel the neighbours' eyes focusing on my back.

Listen up, Old timers. Listen up good. I'm gonna cut your . . .

The door swung open but went slow and didn't take the big sucking wind I'd been expecting. Maureen smiled down on me and made like she was going to say something. But she didn't after all and bit her lip instead. She looked big in the doorway. Standing a step above me she seemed like a giant. She wiped her hands under a dishtowel marked with a faded map of the United Kingdom. Her head tilted and she continued to chew lightly at her lower lip. I felt odd standing like that below her. But she just kept chewing her lip and standing in the doorway looking at me with that sideways stare. It's the way she always met me at the door, same smile and same look. She always did it just like that before she stood aside to let me walk in the house.

Oh, look at the lost boy. Poor beaten, broken boy. Best let him in, I s'pose.

Her hand would fall on the top of my head while I passed her by. Her voice would call out to Dean who would never answer her back. She'd tell me to make myself at home. She'd leave us a while. She'd give us time to do our strange things that strange boys do. Then she'd feed us so we could keep doing those strange things some more.

Go right on in, darlin'. You know where he is.

But this time she just stood a step above and looked down at me. I waited and she waited. Neither of us seemed to have a clue what to do next. One of those quirky moments where time kind of stands still. It's your turn isn't it? No it's gotta be yours 'cause I don't have a clue where I'm going.

'Hey, Joe-Joe,' she said leaning to one side. 'What's going down, doll?'

'Nothing,' I said. Her eyes made it hard to look at her when

273

I spoke. Wanted to look at her but couldn't get my eyes to meet hers. Her smile was a million miles wide and wrinkled up the sides of her face. Her mouth kind of shook at the corners. Like she wasn't all that sure what was happening was really all that funny. Like she was running through the situation all over again because it may not be funny at all.

'Dean with you?' she asked.

'No,' I said wishing I'd stayed at the bridge and spent the day spitting into the water.

'He said he'd be out with you when he left this morning.' Cleared her throat and frowned down at me with her head still to the side. 'You guys did meet up this morning?'

'Haven't seen him.' I shrugged my shoulders. 'Should I?'

'Didn't you have plans? You two going off some place to fish.'

'Right.' Made my eyes like I'd no idea what she was talking about.

'Well, didn't you?'

'Probably just forgot,' I told her. Chewed on my fingernails and looked off toward the porch where the old people sat. They weren't watching me any more, but I still felt that burning of eyes coming from somewhere.

She straightened up all of a sudden and I backed away. Thought maybe she was coming out. Had that look like she wanted to go for a run or something. That look people get when they've got an idea to act but haven't decided if it'd be worth the trouble.

'Maybe I was supposed to meet him at Wild Lake.'

'Maybe's not a good thing, baby.' She didn't really say that to me, but to herself. Sounded like she was repeating something she'd heard a long time ago. Something said to her during a bad time. Brought a feeling back all of a sudden. An old saying that all at once became important and full of meaning.

'Yeah.' I turned and walked off the porch. 'I'll go find him.'

'Bring him back here for lunch,' she called after me. 'Ham and cheese. I'll make some brownies too.'

Waved a hand over my shoulder and took off running. Under

the trees I felt easy again. Never stopped pushing my legs until I got out of sight. Out of Maureen Gillespie's sight and away from the old folks sitting on their porch. Kept rolling my legs out in front of me. Pumping my feet at the ground like mad. *Going fast as a flash. Ain't that right, Dean. Fast as a* . . . I got to Washington Pond in a hurry. My thighs burned and nausea started kicking in deep inside my guts. I took off my shirt and started rinsing it in the water. Splashed up the cool water and rubbed it over and over. Rubbing it on my chest and arms like I'd seen dark women do in National Geographic magazines. Checked the water over to make sure it was clear before I started. Made sure there wasn't anything coming off me while I rubbed like mad. Started to feel like I was getting back to normal. Kind of felt clean but stood there brown and gritty from the stream mud. Draped my shirt over a bush and while it dried I lay back on the cold sand. Closed my eyes and listened to the cicadas sing. Chattered and buzzed until they filled that empty forest and made it so I wasn't all that alone.

Wanted to sing back but didn't know how.

When my shirt felt dry I pulled it over my head. Walked back to Dean's house with more confidence. My skin felt dry from the creek grit that caught between my clothes and skin. Came out between the same two houses and turned up the street toward Dean's. The old people had left the porch swing and gone in. Maybe they'd taken the Cadillac for a spin up the state road for an easy ride up memory lane. They could've gone in to do what married people do. Whatever moved them from the porch swing was alright by me. They could keep that cold stare for the next idiot who walked on by. I didn't want any of it and wouldn't have reacted well if I'd seen it again.

My knuckles rattled the Gillespies' door. This time I did it with more force. Really laid my knuckles into it. Hit it hard enough to take a slit of skin from my middle finger. Rap-tap-tap. Could've buzzed the doorbell, but felt like hitting out instead. The dog barked and got louder while it made its way to the door. Its claws scratched at the tiles when it came sliding to a stop just on the other side. Maureen called it back as sweet as she'd ever spoken to it. Had a tone in her voice that sounded like she didn't expect trouble to come knocking. I lowered my head before she'd even opened up.

'Joseph,' she said. Cut off her voice almost before she finished my name.

'Dean come back?' I asked.

'He's not with you?' Her eyes kind of bulged out bigger and bigger while she watched me.

'Been looking all round the woods for him,' I said. 'He's not in the usual places.'

She looked over my head and out into the yard behind me. Her hands came out from under the dishtowel. Fabric fell limp and hung wet and heavy. She kept it tucked into the front of her skirt, but it kind of dangled. She rubbed her hands against her blouse. Left wet marks like tyre skids. When she cleared her throat I wanted to move close to her. Get right up near and touch her somewhere. She frowned at the thoughts going on inside her head. Just stared past me and went all serious for a minute. Didn't look down at me and when I moved she just kept shifting her eyes away. She couldn't bring herself to look at me. She just stared straight ahead. She looked for something out in the big old nothing.

'Where's Dean?' she asked. She'd gone real serious and wanted me to know it. Her voice told me she'd had enough of the joke and wanted Dean to get his sorry ass in the house.

'I thought he'd be here by now.' Did my best to sound worked up. Wanted to sound worried, but not overexcited. 'Can't figure where else he'd be. Went to the pond. Up the creek. Followed it out to Grant's Road. No sign of him. Must have come back by now . . .'

'No, baby,' Maureen said. She raised a fist and bounced it in front of her mouth. Tapped away like it helped her think. The skin under her eyes started swelling. 'He went to your house early this mornin'. Took his net with him. Said you both were going to the creek. Then maybe on to something else.'

276

I only shook my head.

'He wasn't at the lake?' she asked.

'Don't know.' Put on my real serious eyes and shook my head.

'You told me you checked the lake.'

'No ma'am. Just the creek.'

Here we go, Joey.

Her face went red. It came in splotches that continued down her neck. Kept spreading until they'd come out round the split of her cleavage. Looked too red over her pale skin. Marked so deep red in places they looked like burns.

'That what you two were planning?' Her voice sounded strained. The corners of her mouth kept pulling up before falling down again. It all reminded me of a plane that'd lost power. Reminded me of a plane full of a hundred families that had no chance of clearing a mountain.

'Yes, ma'am,' I said. 'But I didn't wake up 'til late today. He never came to the house. I'd have heard the doorbell.'

Her face went kind of elastic and kept changing. Stretching, folding and twisting before coming back together again. Dean told me about Maureen being an emotional person. He'd said bad things seemed to affect her quickly, but standing in the doorway I couldn't read her. I watched close, but couldn't tell what I was seeing. She moulded her face into too many expressions in that short space of time. Her hands moved in front of her breasts and she looked like she wanted to turn one way and then she'd go the other. Finally she leaned down toward me. She grabbed at the door jambs to hold herself from falling onto the porch.

'Dean!' she screamed. 'Dean!' Her words came like gun shots. Sound of her voice froze the wind that hid inside my lungs. I crouched slightly when she screamed out. It came as a reflex. Like dodging a punch or lifting my legs when a kick's coming. I'd got myself prepared to take a swipe from a sword that came too fast to dodge. Her voice was just as sharp as anything I'd ever felt before.

I waited and she waited and the silence surrounded us. The

wind blew and the leaves in her apple trees ruffled. We waited for a response that never came. She ran back into the house. Standing on the porch I turned and looked out to the street. The old people across the road came out of their house. Made it back on their porch and the old man held onto the white banister. Maybe they'd some kind of radar for trouble in the neighbourhood. For a minute I almost got myself believing just that. Almost made them out to be something special. Then the curtains blew in through the screens in their windows.

Had the windows open the whole time. Musta been listening out for you, Joey-boy. If it ain't their eyes they're burning you with it's their goddamned ears.

The old man leaned hard against the porch rail. The old lady crossed her arms and stood close to her man. Their eyes kept aimed my way.

Standing in their line of fire I felt kind of hopeless. Stepped into the house and stood in the foyer listening to Dean's mother speak. She went on and on. Talking to no one in particular, the animal maybe. The dog came out of the family room and sniffed my shoes before waddling away again. I followed it a few steps and saw Dean's mother sitting on the sofa. She sat trying to tie the laces of a pair of tennis shoes. Her fingers looked like they were working too fast to be doing any good.

'It's fine, baby,' she told the dog. It'd come in and got up under her arm while she worked at her laces. 'I'll be back in a minute or two.'

Her words seemed like something you'd say if you felt calm. But they came out in a way that made me think she wasn't all that together. She didn't have enough breath for the words when she spoke. Her fingers got all tied up while she played at the laces. The laces came together in the end. She brought both hands up together and placed them over her mouth. She stood and turned with this fast military move. When she saw me standing in the doorway she stopped cold. Her mouth hung open and her eyes looked heavy. She came rushing toward me so I moved to the side. She headed out the door, not even speaking

278

a word as she went. I followed and shut the front door behind me. The dog barked and pawed at the wood from the other side.

Maureen ran off the porch and landed on the lawn. Headed out toward the woods like she knew where she was going. I jumped the steps of the porch and hit the cement walkway hard. Ran after her and caught up before she'd made it to the path. She walked toward the open space. Kept a good clip going, but wasn't running any more. She'd started an excited walking skip thing. Guess she was too anxious and full of worry to walk. Wanted to get there, but frightened she'd get there too quick. She headed down the dirt trail with exaggerated high steps. Ferns grew up on each side of the path and whacked at our legs when we passed them. I kicked back while Maureen didn't even notice.

She kept on calling his name.

'Dean!' she yelled. 'Dean!'

Took my turn and started yelling with her. It wasn't until I yelled that I felt like something very bad had taken place. It all felt like a blank up to that point. Going through the motions of something that wasn't all that real. It was kind of like a walk-through for something that may have happened. It wasn't all that difficult keeping up with Maureen. Wasn't tiring out at the pace she was walking. It was just another walk for me. Hanging out with a woman who'd been a kind of mother to me for a few months. I'd just been out for a stroll until my lungs coughed out his name. It had been a simple thing that Dean's mother had blown out of proportion until that moment. Up to that point it was nothing but an overreaction. I'd almost expected Dean to walk out from beside the house laughing in his awkward way.

I got you. What a freakin' joke. Look at your face, Pullman.

Kind of expected to see him walking up the path with his net slung over his shoulders. But yelling his name, screaming so loud my throat burned, made it all frightening and real. At that point the chances of Dean rushing up with a smile on his face went down the Killing Tree's black hole. The further we walked down the path calling for him the more I expected nothing but bad.

'Oh, Dean. Dean, baby.' Maureen was muttering away to herself. She'd stopped yelling and was walking and looking and chattering away. 'Where are you, Dean?'

It only gets worse. Ain't that right, Joe-Joe?

We were far along the path. Almost made it all the way to the open space. Maureen was out ahead of me so I could think. She kept on going, driven by something powerful. She had hope and expectation that things would be okay. Even when she'd got herself that worked up she'd been able to find something inside to keep going. Continue the search until you find what you're looking for. She'd started after Dean and she wasn't going to stop until she'd . . .

Then she came across it. Way out ahead of me she'd come across part of it.

Dean's chances of being found and brought home headed south. From the sound of Maureen breathing I figured she'd found something she recognized. I almost didn't want to look. Jogged up to Maureen's side and leaned in to see over her shoulder.

Ain't all that lucky today, buddy boy.

Maureen crouched with her hand reaching for a piece of fabric. She'd stopped like she'd come to the end of a cliff. I'd hovered behind her and got this tight feeling in my lower guts. Wondered why she was taking so long to grab it. When her hands started shaking I wanted to give her a kick in the ass. Wanted to move her to grab that piece of blue nylon. Just like she'd heard my thought she reached down and picked it up.

'Dean's rain jacket,' she whispered. 'Made him wear it this morning.'

'Man.' Don't know why I said it. It just kind of came out when I thought she needed someone to acknowledge her. That tight feeling was getting lower on me.

'Wasn't even raining this morning. Still made him wear it.'

'Sure it's his?' I asked.

Got a fire going on in your shorts, Joey-boy?

'Of course I'm sure it's his!' she screamed at me. She knocked me a few steps back when she stood up. Before I'd even got my balance she'd turned on me. 'I made him wear it, Joseph. I told him to put it on.'

'Sorry.' Stepped back again and that tight feeling had faded away.

With the fabric in her hand Maureen started to shake again. She walked all round that area of the path a few times more. Stepped in through the ferns and looked through the branches and leaves. She pulled back the thicket that grew in a wall further back. Marched out a ways from the path just to find more blue nylon. Stuck her hand in and spread apart the thorns and vines and all. Her head swung round, looking for something. Anything that would keep that search going. Her hope and expectations burned out when the scrap of raincoat turned up. She needed Dean. If not Dean, she needed a sign that he was okay. She'd exhausted one side of the path until there was nothing else to see. Followed her when she moved to the other side. She went through it quick and I followed the path she made.

When she slowed down the search I'd gone back to the path. Stood under a sun that felt hot enough to melt me to the ground. Licked at my lips a few times and thought about the pitchers of lemonade Maureen had served up. Drops of water falling down the side, collecting others as they fell. Came out of that thought when Maureen's feet slapped at the path. Came right up on me and almost blocked out the sun. First time since seeing her in the doorway of the house she towered. She looked strong and incredible in her anger. I'd never expected to see Maureen Gillespie become so frightening.

'Where is he?' she said. 'What's going on?'

Looked up at her and didn't need to fake it any more. I wanted to help, but could do nothing. Putting her mind at ease wasn't something I could've done. She wanted her son and I couldn't give him to her. No one could've helped her the way she needed to be helped. She was looking for something that wasn't there. Even if it'd been there that close she would've never wanted to find it. This seemed all too terrifyingly clear to me. As I stood

281

in disbelief it was all rushing in. All of the things that'd happened already. *It's out of control now, kiddo. Just look at her . . .* It was so clear to me. With my shoulders wet and cold I watched Maureen search. I stood as a confused young man thinking how wrong everything had become. Knowing I could have predicted all of the things that had yet to take place.

Maureen stepped away from me and stared at the grass off the side of the path. Her head rose up slowly and she focused on the leaves overhead. She stared into all of that green. So many layers of green it covered the sky. It held us in.

'Dean!' she yelled. 'Come back here!'

The forest felt empty and cold. With the sweat boiling on my brow I walked to Maureen's side. Placed a hand on her shoulder and all at once that tight feeling was back in my belly. She jumped away and twisted round on me. She swelled up and stuck out a fist between us. In her fist was the blue nylon from Dean's rain-coat. She shook the fist at me. She grew taller and wider with each strained breath.

'Where in God's name is he, Joseph?'

I shook my head.

'Wish I could tell you,' I said. 'But I can't.'

Chapter Twenty-Six

The days were growing hotter. The sun never seemed to be entirely willing to burn itself out. Clouds dried up and disappeared into the blue sky. All of their moisture was sucked out before it had a chance to fall. It could have been a good summer. May have been the best summer Maritime had seen in a hundred years, but no one noticed. People in the town went blind to the weather when Oz went missing. Even after he was found they didn't find a renewed interest in the heat or the sunshine. They never had a chance to recover before Dean went. Either didn't have time to recover or thought laughing in the sun wasn't the right thing to do.

After Dean went missing I spent more time alone. Being by myself in the forest I had time to think about things. Started to realize that Dean had just filled empty conversation. After he'd gone the voices I'd collected in my head took care of that space. They came back like they'd never really left. Started talking to myself on trips into the forest. Spoke out loud sometimes, not caring who heard me. There weren't good odds on someone coming up on me while I searched the forest for animal carcasses. The trips made to the Killing Tree became more frequent. The remains of the larger animals got dropped in a new area. I'd marked it off with large sandstones.

The first morning without Dean round I walked along the creek bed. Checked in Washington Pond for crawfish. Took out my journal and marked up what I found:

Washington Pond. 2 BD. 16 June AD.

After writing it down I couldn't help but wonder if AD was for After Death or After Dean. Maybe it stood for both, but it didn't register until after I'd written it down.

From the pond I took the creek bed to the bridge. Sat with my legs hanging over the side. Leaned back and set the journal down and laid my head on it. With the heat falling so heavy I felt tired. Wasn't sleeping much at nights with my old man being so quiet. Never knew where he was any more. He'd left early in the evening, but the exact time I'm not sure. There was still light in the sky and the cicadas were still singing. Neither had called it a night and shut off to the darkness.

The breeze pressed up against me and made the heat disappear at times. In those times I fell asleep listening to the chattering. The water cutting under me wanted to carry me off somewhere and if it had been deeper I would've gone in. Instead the bridge and the wind took me away. Dreamed of Dean for a while. He was in a canoe with Gillian Wilcox and he smiled that told-you-so smile that cut in me deep. His face changed when the storm came and then he was too far out to make it in. Storm pushed him farther away from land. He tried to yell to me and I could hear him fine. Shook my head and cupped hands round my ears. He yelled louder and I heard him so clear and still shook my head. Gillian laughed and stood to flap her hand at me. Before my hand made it high enough to wave back the canoe tilted and they went into a wave.

Woke with a jolt saying Gillian's name.

After the dreams got bad I kept awake. Kicked my legs over the side of the bridge. The wood creaked like it was ready to fall to pieces, spilling me down into the creek. Looked down thinking the fall wouldn't make a difference when I spotted the snake. A copperhead coiling backward on the sand while trying to fit a salamander down its throat. It twisted and manoeuvred like it was trying to get away from the water. Took a stone from the pile Dean and me left on the bridge. Hit near the snake and it froze. Stared at it for a long time and felt this power going through me. It was a good feeling, like I'd become part of the forest. I'd become one of the animals. That snake never knew I was there and the rock was a warning. It took it and moved back in a slow coil. Took another rock from the pile.

Sound of feet moving through leaves came from the far side of the creek. The shuffling sound grew louder until a red shirt came out from between a couple of trees. J.D. stood there with his sleeves rolled up to show the muscles in his arms. He was sweating chewing on a blade of grass. Moved round between the trees and was looking kind of anxious. Looked like he wanted something but not sure what it was.

I tossed the rock and it hit at his feet. Fluffed up a leaf and he didn't even notice anything happened. The next stone caught him in the leg. Didn't mean to throw it all that hard, but something came over me. Felt my face going red when he hopped round and aimed his eyes at me. Yelled a few things that I didn't catch because of my own voices.

You're on a roll, Joe. How much trouble can a kid stir up in a season?

'The fuck's 'at for?' J.D. lowered his foot to the ground and rubbed at his shin. 'Tell me you're not wantin' the shit kicked straight out your head.'

'Meant that to hit the ground.'

'Well, you missed, Pullman. All this ground and you missed.'

'Guess I didn't aim.'

Hell with that, Joe. Got him square on.

'Maybe you aimed too good.'

He started toward the bridge. Figured if he got to me that quick he'd still be too upset for any good. Needed to slow him down. Needed to keep him from getting to the bridge at all.

'You'll want to come over this side of the creek.'

285

He looked up and squinted into the blade of light that cut down on him.

'And why's that?'

'Your side of the bridge's falling in.'

He kind of growled and took a few steps toward the creek. Got up on the line of sand and hopped down from the grassy bank. Hit the sand, sank a few inches before turning toward me again. Caught him looking at my legs dangling over the side. May have got in his mind this idea of pulling me down from the bridge. Grabbing hold of both ankles and yanking like mad. Pulling me down into the creek so he'd have an easy time holding me under water.

That snake's looking hungry, Pullman. May get real angry if your buddy walked up on it. Walked up and interrupted him.

'There's an easy place to jump cross this way.' Pointed to where the creek narrowed and went deep. 'Not much of a jump from there.'

He kept walking up toward me. Kept eyeing my legs and I kept swinging them to bring him on. The snake coiled back and pressed itself under a root of a tree. The root stuck out of the sand like a black bone. Other than that black bone there was no place for the snake to go. Banks of sand were all high round that part of the creek. He was stuck down there with J.D. who was coming with mad steps.

'Don't get you, Pullman,' he said. 'Out here on your own all the damn time.'

'So're you.' *Two more, Joe. Two more steps.*

'Not the same, man. You're a diff . . .'

He never got it out. Whatever he'd planned didn't have the fragment of time to get from his brain to his mouth. The copperhead jumped when he stepped out near it. Jumped out fast as a flash and bounced off J.D.'s right leg. He hopped back and went into the water. Splashed like crazy but didn't go down. The snake backed away and made another jump that didn't get far. More of a warning than a drive to sink in his teeth, but enough to say he wasn't finished.

'I'm bit!' J.D. yelled out. 'Jesus Christ, I'm bit!'

'Got ya?' I'd brought my legs back up on the planks and was standing again. Leaned over the side and looked down at them. The snake turned and tried for the grass. It went for the slope with all the speed its body could find. Almost had it the first time, but came back down when the sand crumbled away. After the fourth attempt it settled in and coiled up tight. No chance of making the forest again so it'd have to fight.

'Hit me on the leg,' J.D. said. 'Right up and sank in my leg.'

He wasn't talking to me. He'd moved to the far side of the creek to get the water separating him from the snake. He watched the thing until he was up on the opposite bank. Held onto the side and raised his leg out of the water. Stood with his leg hiked up and his foot set on the embankment. Kept running his fingers over his right calf while he spoke, too quiet for me to hear him.

'Need to get to a hospital. It'll probably kill you.'

He said something back but it didn't get to me.

'Started swelling up yet?' Walked up the bridge to get a better look. The way he was standing I couldn't see his leg or the dots the fangs made when they went in. Couldn't see the blood or the blue thickness of his dying skin. Only saw his back and the red shirt with his sleeves rolled up.

'It burn yet?'

'Just what the hell's so goddamned funny, Pullman?' J.D. dropped his leg through the surface of the water. Made a splash that went high and wide. He spun round and saw the snake. Then he looked up at me. Could see in his eyes that he knew. Wasn't okay with the idea of being set up. Didn't like the way I'd called him into the place where he'd been bit.

'I'm not . . .'

'Get rid of the smile, asshole.'

'I'm not smiling.' But I felt it. Felt that tightness in my cheeks and the air on my teeth and tongue.

How can a guy get to smiling that big without even knowing about it? What's happened to you, Pullman? Get it together, man. Get rid of the smile.

'Get that fuckin' thing off your face!' J.D. yelled out with all he had and it made me want to run. Made me want to get into the forest and hide before he had a chance to get a hold of me. 'Get it off, Pullman!'

'I'm trying. I swear to God I'm trying.'

'The hell's wrong with you?'

'I don't know. Look, I'm trying okay. Don't want to smile any more.'

May have been all the stress. That's the way I'd figured it after everything was over and J.D. was gone. Must have been the shock of that copperhead hitting against J.D.'s leg. Must have been the way he danced back into the water. Even the way the snake backed away and went for him again. Could've been the idea that I'd planned something to happen and it'd happened. I'd seen a way out and it'd worked. J.D. didn't get to my legs to pull me off the bridge. He'd forgot about the stone that'd hit his leg. Now he was in the creek bed with a snake and a leg full of poison.

'Real fucked up.'

'It's not me. It's not my fault.'

'Yeah. You're not to blame.'

Something cold ran up my spine when J.D. spoke those words. My old man's voice came back and rattled inside my head. His voice echoing through the laundry chute.

It's not my fault. Do you hear me? I'm not to blame.

'Never got me, anyway.'

'Huh?' I asked him.

'Didn't break skin. Never got the teeth in.'

J.D. never took his eyes off the snake while he spoke to me. I never took my eyes off J.D. all the time he watched the snake.

'So you're okay?'

'Good as ever. Madder than hell.'

He dropped his hand into the water and pulled out a rock. Took a quick aim and fired a shot at the snake. Landed the rock close enough to get the snake moving. It unravelled itself and went for the forest again. Faster it moved the more it slipped back. Before it had come down to the beach again J.D. had launched more stones. He dropped in and picked them off the bottom of the creek. Never gave himself time to straighten all the way up. He tossed them while curled over ready to pull the next round from the water.

'Got him!' I yelled down. 'That one's got him.'

He threw so many rocks that a few hit the target. Opened up a cut a few inches from the snake's head. It was a cut big enough to see the pink of muscles under the plastic skin. Must've injured the snake good because it coiled up tight on the sand bank. It tried to make a hissing noise but the limp salamander stopped most of the noise coming out of its mouth.

'Keep going, man,' I told him. 'Hurry up before it gets away.'

J.D. moved in the water until he'd stood up a few yards away from the snake. It sensed his approach and slid back. Mouth chewed at the salamander like it wanted to get it down quick. Figured the thing to be trying to spit the lizard out. Still it looked like the damn thing didn't like the idea of missing a meal. Not even with a storm of stones falling down on it.

'Copperhead.' J.D. breathed heavy while he stood there looking down at the snake. Breathed heavy like he was getting himself ready to start all over again. Breathing heavy like he was buying time for the thing to get the hell away.

'Yep. And a big one too.' Wiped at the sweat that ran into my eyes. It stung like acid.

J.D. crouched and took a final breath before he pulled up more rocks. I took a deep breath and held it in my lungs. It's the way I did when I'd watched Dean and Oz taking shots at the Malcolms' kids. J.D. made himself a machine and fired stone after stone. They hit and kicked up sand and disappeared. He came in with a few that cracked against the snake and sparked it to life.

'Take it, J.D.'

'Shut it, Pullman.' He took a minute to look at me. In all the excitement I'd hoped he forgot about the stone I'd hit him with. I'd hoped he let go of my calling him into the snake's path. But that look he gave me told me that he was dealing with a snake. It told me when he was finished he had something else to deal with.

He crouched when the snake started moving again. More stones came up and rolled off his spinning arms. They burned off through the air and sunk into the sand. Then he got it. He pulled up a stone the size of a baseball. Round and shining with the water it was the perfect weapon. He brought his arm way back and stepped into the throw. Before the snake could move J.D. brought his arm down. The stone came out of his hand and in an instant had connected with the snake's head.

'Hit it again,' I said.

My voice sounded almost bored, but my heart pulsed inside my chest. Pulsed hard and heavy and was almost painful. Enough to make my ribs shake and my head spin. Lungs still felt thick and weighted and full. Couldn't get enough air no matter how hard I tried.

J.D. fumbled with the stones at the bottom of the creek. Dropped down to one knee and dug in for the big rocks. Snapping back up with one in each hand. He almost lost his balance with his arm back to throw the first stone. His hands went out and righted his legs. He was filled to his neck with adrenaline. That first rock had connected and it did it for him. He was full of fire and wanted the flames to grow. He stepped onto the sand and leaned into the next throw. He got the snake again and while it rolled over itself he gave me a look. It told me to watch for the next rock to cut the damn thing in half. His lips parted in a smile. I'm not sure he knew he wore it.

'Got him now.' He tossed the last stone like he was juggling it in his right hand. Looked like he was testing the weight. Looked down at the snake and kept tossing and grabbing that stone in his right hand.

'He's all cut up and busted now,' I told him.

'About to have more of what he's already got.'

This time he didn't take aim. It's like he didn't need to aim any more. It was a fast move he made. Arm back and arm forward in a big arcing motion. The snake's slowing rolls jolted to a fresh wave of motion when the rock crushed it against the other stones that had started to collect. The pain drove a fresh wave of energy through slick skin. It flipped fast and moved over itself so quick it was hard to tell where one part stopped and another began.

'Finish him off, man.' Pushed my hands in my pockets. Got tired of wiping the sweat off my palms. Didn't want J.D. to see me getting worked up just watching him kill something.

'Yeah,' he said and stepped onto the sand and passed a few feet by the copperhead. He walked up the beach away from the bridge. 'Turn away, Pullman.'

I didn't ask why. Just turned away and gave him that moment. I heard the sound of water splashing into water. J.D. whistled a song I didn't recognize before clearing out his nose. Hocked up something from his throat and spat it into the creek. What came out made a splash.

'You're all right now,' he said.

When I raised my head again his hand worked on the zipper at the front of his shorts. It'd stuck halfway down and he was pulling with all he had to get it up again. He grunted and pulled at the thing and it fought him back.

'Want me to come down and get a rock?'

'No,' he said. 'Dang it! These freakin' shorts always get stuck.'

I'd made it off the bridge and was down in the creek bed before J.D. looked up again. Felt weird being that close to the snake after watching it from the bridge. J.D. and me were in a container with a poisonous snake. The banks of the creek dropped on both sides in small cliffs.

J.D. leaned down to pick a flat stone from the sand. Can't figure his eyes ever lost sight of the copperhead. Even while he was pissing into the creek he must have watched that damned snake. He walked back up the bank and edged in beside me. Elbowed me a few times like he was thinking of shoving me toward the copperhead. The snake rolled in slow motion and kept on slowing down. It struggled to wrap around itself but kept trying. J.D. lifted the stone to his chest. Took all he had to keep it up with both hands. He took a couple steps closer to the snake. Even with the weight of that stone he stood and watched the thing turn for a while. Stayed quiet while I watched his arms start to shake under the weight. Felt impatient and wanted him to get it over with.

'Drop it,' I said.

The stone fell and covered the snake. It landed in a couple inches of sand and made a heavy dull sound when it hit. A section of the snake's tail stuck out from under the stone. It came out like a finger and twitched. It kept shaking so much I didn't want to watch it. I'd turned and walked off, but didn't get far before J.D. came moving up behind me. He could be quick when he wanted to be. He was panting like he'd run a mile and tripped over the branches and shrubs while he tried to keep close.

'Let's find something else.'

'Not interested,' I said.

'What's that all about?' he asked. 'Way I figure it you could use a couple extra friends.'

'You figured things wrong.'

'Yeah? Looks like people round you are pretty fuckin' unlucky if you ask me.'

'Don't remember asking.' Kept walking faster hoping he'd trip over and slow enough for me to get away . . .

'What all happened with Oz?'

. . . walked faster and needed to get away . . .

'How much you holding back, Pullman?'

. . . *get out of here before he* . . .

'Know what happened to that Dean friend of yours?'

. . . *oh, Christ. Walk, Pullman. Walk until you've* . . .

'Kinda weird how all your friends are getting – '

Spun round in a quick motion and caught J.D.'s neck in my right hand. It felt soft and wide, almost too wide for my fingers. Gripped harder and he stumbled forward. Thought I had him good when his left hand flew up and caught me under the chin. Hard as brick and would've dropped me if I'd had nothing to keep me up. Kept hold on his neck and didn't let go. Squeezed his neck tighter and the throbbing in my jaw came on fast. A throbbing that came fast and felt intense.

'Want to be smart?' I yelled watching his eyes. They looked clear even with the way his face was turning red in patches. Felt dizzy but had to be strong so I shook my head like mad. Squeezed at his throat and went for him with my other hand. His eyes filled with water and the skin on his face turned shades of blue. He choked hard before his arms came up, but I had him. He kind of went limp before I let go expecting him to fall. He dropped his shoulder down and touched his neck with an open hand. But he never fell.

'Hell's wrong with you?' he wheezed. Sounded concerned but the look on his face showed something different.

'Forget it.'

He slapped me on my right temple with another left. The hand came in fast and hard. If it'd been closed I'd have been coming to on a pile of broken twigs.

'You're a nutcase, Pullman.' He got himself ready by cracking his knuckles. Knew how to fight and he'd beat bigger and badder guys than me. We were alone in the woods and he didn't have anything to hold him back.

'Get out of here, J.D.'

'People always told us 'bout you. Told us you're a freak. Heard your old lady was carted off to the friggin' loony bin. Didn't expect it'd happen to you too.'

I'd picked the wrong time to get worked up. Been good up to then at keeping the anger at bay when the tough guys came round. J.D. caught me when I'd gone weak on a bad day.

'Real fuckin' psycho,' he said.

'Sorry, man. I'm just . . .'

'You're lucky Ern's not here,' J.D. said. He started rubbing his neck again. He shook his head while his hand worked under his chin. 'He'd kick your ass two shades of black.'

I hung my head somehow thinking that made up for things. Somehow thinking it called quits to what I'd got started. Instead it made me an easy target. The punch came in without warning and I didn't even see it heading my way. With J.D. it never mattered if you knew a fist was coming or not. He had hands like sewing machines on full speed. I'd been lucky up to then and never had to fight him. He'd always stayed clear of me 'cause I'd given him no reason to bring it on. He only fought the guys that gave him a reason. Only knocked down the idiots that gave him an invitation. Now I experienced what people talked about. The legendary left from that quiet guy J.D.

His fist drilled into the top of my head. Coming in a ball of knuckles cemented together inside hard skin. The shot sent a message to my legs: stop working. I fell to the grass in a ball. Laid there like a dog that'd just tasted the chrome from a fast truck bumper.

'Get the hint, Pullman?' he yelled at me.

I looked up at him with a hand touching the pulsing centre of my scalp. My body felt numb and that feeling went in deep. Specks of yellow and red lights flew around behind my eyes. Tried to blink them away, but they wouldn't leave.

'Got it,' I tried to say. Don't know if it came out right or even came out at all. My first attempt to stand up failed. Something in my head had shifted. My balance favoured one side over the other. The second time I rolled over and made it to my knees.

'Quit dickin' around.' J.D. grabbed my arm and pulled me to my feet. He let go, but grabbed me again when I started swaying.

'Give me a second,' I said.

'To what?' he asked.

Didn't know what I needed time to do. Maybe just needed time to think about things and get straight on all the simple things. Name and place of birth and where I lived and . . . J.D. didn't give me the time to think. Didn't want me to get myself back to normal. He pulled me off the path and leaned me up against a tree.

'If you're lucky I'll keep all this away from Ernie,' he told me.

I tried to focus on him. Couldn't get his face in clear view.

'If you're out of luck, Pullman . . . Ernie's gonna have a party on you that you ain't never gonna forget.'

He walked away and I stayed put. Waited without the strength to speak or move. Watched him head off through the trees, wiping his hands over his neck. Trying to get the red lines to go away before he got back to the house. Before Ernie saw he'd had trouble and made for the source. Watched him all the way until his red shirt got lost in the forest. Didn't know which way he went and didn't have the energy to care.

After J.D. was out of sight I got back to the bridge. Hung my feet over the side and kicked my legs a while. My head was pounding and my jaw felt like a door half off its hinges. Leaned back and got lost in the breeze and the water. The cicadas came back from a break and started another song. They came loud and covered up most of the noise. Still had the wind and the water bringing that tired feeling again. I let it come and didn't take long before the dreams started up again. This time they started off bad and got worse.

A pack of dogs barked and sounded close by. Pulled myself up to the bridge and laid so I was hidden by the brushes and trees. Wet soil soaking into the seat of my jeans. Set a soft hand on my scalp and could feel the swelling had come on quick. The pain edged down round my head and licked at my cars. The burn fell further to the back of my neck. Moving my head from side to side I couldn't help but think J.D. had busted something. Maybe broke something off that I needed. The barks of dogs made me look up and forget my head.

'We'll need to check all this area again,' someone said. Sounded like it came from someone way off in the distance. Didn't think it'd make much of a difference so I pushed up with my arms and looked over the bushes.

'Take a team and start the other side of Grant's Road,' the voice said. 'Send them dog boys first.'

Sheriff Wilcox moved into view with some guy who was always in the papers. I'm almost sure he was the Chairman of Maritime Council or something like it. Sheriff Wilcox wore a blue t-shirt with a yellow star on his thick left breast. Vince Gibbs and most of the others in their posse wore plaid button-downs with khaki trousers. They all wore boots of some kind. They had leather-looking army boots and hikers and a few cowboy boots. Behind them came a second team of men. A couple of women were mixed in the crowd. Some had the same blue t-shirt with the star on the left breast. Most just wore street clothes. Volunteers.

The dogs barked again and I saw the pack of them coming round a clump of trees. Headed down a path toward the open space. The dogs dragged their police handlers along on long leashes. Their noses skimmed the ground. There must have been a dozen of those dogs. When one went left the others went with it. They had some smell in their noses that made them all excited. Must have had a real good smell of what they were looking for. No doubt in hell they were going to find it.

They're off, Joe. Ain't gonna be long now, boy.

The pain in my head disappeared when the dogs took a run at me. One came my way and the others followed. My legs froze up on me. Otherwise I may have taken off. That group of cops and volunteers looked hot under the collar. Sweat coming down their heads and making long dark shapes on their clothes. Thought about them opening fire when I'd started the run. Had a sense of what the bullets would feel like tearing through me. Hot and thick, taking parts of my guts with them on a super-sonic flight.

Must have got caught in that dream because the dogs were getting close. Got myself flat to the ground and held in a quick breath. Took in some dirt and wanted to cough it back up, but knew it'd give me away. Any chance I had of getting through this one was slim. No sense in being a weak fuck and coughing at the last minute. Game wasn't over until the dog took hold of my leg. Until one of the cops hopped on my back and another was stretching my arm too much to get cuffs on.

But one of the pack took a turn and headed off to the path. Made a commotion that got someone yelling: 'He's onto it fellas. We got something here.' Then they were off. The bloodhound gang turned up the path and headed after the leader. With all the dogs heading my way it was hard to tell what they'd got the smell of. I'd worn Dean's clothes before. Been to his house so many times over the past few months that maybe we'd picked up the same odour. It's not like my jeans and t-shirts were washed any more. Couldn't help but think they'd been after me 'cause I'd been spending too much time round him. Laid there in the dirt thinking it was almost a crime to know a kid that'd gone missing.

Then J.D. spoke into my ear. His words sounded so damned clear I even felt the heat of his breath on my face. Had to look to see if he'd snuck up on me.

Know what happened to that Dean friend of yours?

'Shut up, J.D.' Had the forethought to keep it to a whisper. Wanted to yell it out so I'd knock the voice out of my head.

Kinda weird how all your friends are getting –

Hit my head against the hard soil until the sparks of pain flashed up bright as fireworks behind my eyes. Raised my head to find my neck stiffening again. Pulsing in my head pounding harder and faster than ever. But the sound had gone back to normal. Cicadas singing in the trees right alongside the birds. Two creatures singing together until one eats the other and there's only one song left.

The group of men and dogs stopped up the path a hundred feet away from me. The sheriff directed the men and they split up. I kept low in the bushes while folks in the back group started looking round the place. Sinking down into the never more's what I was trying for. The sound of yelling men and barking dogs filled the air like thunder. Stayed put until the sounds all died off and the groups had faded away. The men fell silent and the dogs stopped barking. The sound of the wind was all I heard. The cicadas got tired of singing or the birds had eaten them all. Either way neither was making much of a sound. Or maybe they'd made so much noise the past month that I'd grown immune. Listened to the songs so much that they'd become a part of me.

297

I ran back to the house with all my energy filling my legs. Standing in the foyer I heard the sounds of my father's tools rising from the basement. The bottom step became my throne again. Sat there and watched while people passed by on the street. There were parades of people heading up toward Grant's Road with walking sticks and portable radios in hand. They were all real excited like they were part of something they'd never forget. Police and their dogs can wake a sleeping community up in a second. Every time they passed the house I expected them to come up the drive. Just like Leonidas had with that bucket of chicken under his arm. They'd come with their dogs and rifles leaned against their shoulders. Straight up to the door where they'd knock with all they had. This wasn't like sitting round after they'd found Oz. Dean wouldn't be hiding in the azaleas when I opened the door to get a delivery of food from the neighbours.

I waited and watched. Then I watched and watched some more. The moment would come when the police came up the path. When they'd knock on the door and not even ask if they could come in. When it wasn't really talking they wanted to do. They'd just come up the drive and walk right in.

It was only a matter of time.

Chapter Twenty-Seven

The police dogs I'd seen in the forest made the headlines of newspapers across the country. Early one morning they sniffed out a hand-crafted wooden crate. Took three men to pull the thing to solid ground. After the police were able to cut through the chains and break the metal locks they found it contained a dead kid. He'd been wrapped in a plastic bag and folded in half. He was wrapped up tight and strapped with silver duct tape. They gave most of the details on the evening and late night news channels. They never gave his name. But they told what the wooden crate contained. Knew that the naked kid inside it was Dean. Knew Maureen would've made that horrible sound of hers. Same one she'd made when she found that bird of hers on the step to her back door.

The crate had been sunk in bog land about a mile and a half on the other side of Grant's Road. This time the radio and television stations didn't delay their broadcasts. After Oz paved the way for kidnappings in the area a story like Dean's made for hot property, I guess. Bad things happened to two kids from the same small town. One goes missing and ends up found. *Hallelujah and a big pat on the back goes to* . . . The other kid goes missing and never makes it home. Made it even worse that he'd been cut up so bad.

Maritime went nationwide for all the wrong reasons. It's the kind of thing that creates a media frenzy. There was this vacuum in the town that sucked in local and national news vans. People from near and far started driving into Maritime to have a glimpse at what tragedy looked like. The stories of both Oz and Dean made the major networks on the same day. The day Dean's body was pulled from the crate. Within hours I was watching Maritime on CBS. Snapshots of the middle school showed on the screen. Wilcox gave interviews in front of the colonial looking court-house. People were stopped outside Li'l Mel's Convenience to speak with reporters about the boys. Felt kind of sick watching them standing in front of those boarded-up windows. *They're coming here next, Joe-Joe. Why the hell else would they be in front of Li'l Mel's with a camera? That was your place. The three of you.* Then they showed the bog field where they'd found the crate. *The place where the ground moved.* It came up on the screen and looked familiar, but not like I'd been there. It was a place that didn't hold a lot to recognize. But the ground kept shifting behind the talking reporter. Past the yellow police tape, men were in the bog. Fishing waders covered their legs. They jammed at the bottom with long metal rods.

When I got tired of the CBS reporters saying the same things I flipped to NBC. Didn't have cable, but figured it was on that too. The same scenes at different angles. Same backgrounds set off past different sober looking reporters. Same moving ground of leaves that made my guts turn when I looked at it.

Sheriff Wilcox's face showed up on all the big networks. His interviews got broadcast on syndicated radio shows all over the country. People way over in California must've got to know Wilcox's face. Must've heard his grumbling voice breaking up at times. The country got to know him as the small town lawman in charge of a desperate situation. I flipped from one of the networks to the next and got different sides of Wilcox's face. Even when it was the same live interview it looked different. It's like no one wanted to miss what the sheriff had to say. Reporters kept asking the important questions. Most of them kept me on the edge of the sofa while I watched. Wilcox's face changed from sad to thoughtful.

What condition is the body in? Was the boy killed in the forest or was he taken there after the crime? Do you have any suspects at this time? Do you expect to find other bodies?

'How many do you need?' I asked the television.

Wilcox kept his cool most of the time. Took the questions like a boxer takes punches, stuck out his chin and when they hurt he rolled with them. He came up with comments about the boy and the family. He seemed connected with the dead even though he'd still held onto the name. He spoke about the community. Talked about the attention the crime was bringing from the nation. He ducked and dodged until you'd forget what had been asked in the first place. Until everyone else had forgot what'd been asked too.

On one interview Wilcox spoke with tears in his eyes. Went on about the people of Maritime. How the stuff that happened had changed everyone in town. He called what happened to Oscar Lewiston *a terrible crime.*

Even looked into the camera and said: 'We're all prayin' for ya boy. Whole town's pullin' for you to get right again.'

He looked shaken when he spoke about Dean. Didn't give a lot of details about what they knew of the crime. Didn't update much at all. Went on with the usual line of *the investigation is ongoing.* Told how a local boy had been a victim of a *savage tragedy.*

The day they found Dean I heard it on all the radio stations. I'd been in bed still with the covers off. Kicked them away and they'd piled up on the floor. Sometime that night I'd pissed myself while dreaming. Woke to a cool sticky feeling and the smell of ammonia. Kept the radio on for company while I laid there naked. My underwear drying on the mound of clothes collected in my closet. Bruce Springstein croaked out something about working-class people. The speaker was bad and cracked with the guitar.

Then this thing that sounded like morse code broke in. Cut the crackling guitar off in mid-strum.

301

'We interrupt the regularly scheduled programme to brin . . .' that interruption was interrupted by the announcement.

'At eight forty-five this morning police in Maritime, Maryland located the body of a young male. The body is believed to be that of a teenaged boy. There is widespread speculation that the grisly find may mark the end of the search for missing Hampden Academy student Dean Gillespie.'

The guy speaking didn't sound all that shocked about the news. Could have smashed the radio with my bare hands while he rambled through the report. He was talking about Dean and there wasn't the slightest hint of sympathy in his voice. There was no emotion in his words. No sign that he'd read through the news and taken in the story before sending it over the air. Before I went for the radio I got things under control. Took a few deep breaths and told myself to cool it.

The guy gets paid for this kind of stuff. It's second nature to read what's handed over.

Struck me as kind of strange that Dean had been reduced to a Hampden Academy student. He was no longer a young man who had gone missing. No longer a middle-class kid from a good family who mourned the loss. He'd been connected with a shitty institution that drummed into its kids that the tough always win. It was a place that led lambs to the lions and then to the slaughter.

Can't connect a dead kid to a place like that. Now he's stuck there always.

'Police have secured woodland areas of Maritime where the discovery was made by law enforcement officers. Members of a dog-handling tracker unit of the local police force, accompanied by officers from Columbia Police Departments have been searching for the boy since Monday morning. The discovery comes as a shock to the community.'

Then Sheriff Wilcox came on.

'This morning, just before nine o'clock, officers of Maritime PD located the body of an unidentified male youth. Investigations are now underway. We will inform you of any further developments as they transpire. On behalf of the community I ask that

302

the privacy of the citizens of Maritime is respected. Cooperation from the media will speed our investigations.'

DJ with a cool deep voice came back on to finish up the report. I'd sat up on the bed while listening to Wilcox speaking. My chest was thumping so damned fast. Looked down and watched my ribs shaking with the pumping of my heart. My lungs were letting out breath as fast as I was able to gasp it in.

Didn't catch what the DJ said next. Maybe he was giving his wishes to the town. Maybe he came up with some words of advice or hope. It wasn't something directed at me so I'd lost it in a flashback of Dean's face. Afterwards I wondered if I should've listened to what he was saying. Maybe he'd come up with something important.

Get over it, kiddo. It wasn't directed at you anyhow.

And it wasn't directed at me. He'd been talking to a faceless audience. What he had to say wasn't like the stuff Sheriff Wilcox was saying. It wasn't like Wilcox's news of Dean's body being found. That was all directed at me. It was all aimed at my ears because Dean was with me all the time. We'd be remembered by everyone who'd seen us on the path. All those people we passed heading out into the forest. Someone was going to cough it up sooner or later. If Maureen didn't get there first it'd be a stranger or a neighbour.

Maybe you should check out that other kid. One always hung out with Dean. Kind of a weird fella. Got all these scars.

Dean and me stuffed a hundred animals into holes at the Killing Tree. Dean and me stole from that retarded fat girl at the Li'l Mel's Convenience. Dean and me took Oz to the deep forest and stripped away his innocence. Dean and me made news all the time and never got our names in the paper. He'd beat me to it. He'd made the headlines while I laid naked in a piss-stinking room.

Won't last for ever. They'll come for you too.

Left my bed and dressed before my pants had completely dried. Sat on the bottom step of the staircase. Watched the door with half-closed eyes. Went to the step straight after hearing the

303

news. Didn't move all morning and didn't let my eyes miss a single figure that walked past on the road. My old man came down the stairs. Drove a knee to the back of my head. Then he slid past me and finished the last two steps. He turned while I rubbed the pain in. Didn't give me any warning. Must've felt like he needed to remind me he was still around.

Looked away from his eyes hoping he'd just leave. Stared at the door hoping someone would come. Wondering if I'd get there to answer it. He took a long time watching me. Almost figured he'd got tired of the game. But he wasn't done. That knee didn't get the response he'd been looking for. He made a move like he was going to jump. I straightened and took the force of his kick in the centre of my chest. His bare foot bounced off the bone. I rolled to the side and curled up best I could. Never let my eyes lose sight of the door. That white frosted square of glass was too important. What he had to bring I didn't fear. That kind of reaction had died before Dean. He had nothing on me and he didn't even know it.

'Make me fucking sick. You're a mess. A stinking goddamned mess.'

'Leave me alone.' I tried not to whine the words, but that's what happened. That's how they came out. With the weakness exposed my old man's face lit up.

Here's Johnny!

'Smell like piss.' He leaned in and dropped a punch on my left arm. Another came down like a hammer on an anvil. Skimmed off my shoulder. Bounced onto my cheek. 'Still pissin' your bed? Still got that problem, huh?' More punches that brought more burning.

'Get off me!'

That's better.

'No wonder I can't sell this fuckin' hole!' Three punches from his right hand. All came down on my ribs. My bones pressed in, but popped back out after each shot. Sharp rods of pain went into my side. Lodged in the middle of my body. Pain that just kind of floated in my blood. It got everywhere inside me.

'Your fucking hands off me!' *Get it on, Pullman!* 'That's the last you'll lay!'

'Ain't fightin' niggers now!'

He tried a punch and I moved. Looked down and somehow had found my feet. Must've stood when yelling at him. Never felt my legs working to stand. Never felt the pain in my ribs until my old man stepped in with another punch. Took his fast shot. Caught a spark of pain. It brought an inferno that ran up my side.

'This all you've got?' Leaned against the banister and held on. 'Best of your life spent banging away at your son.'

'Shut your damn mouth.'

'Day after day.' There was a shake in my words. Not a shaking that came from fear. This one was a laugh. 'Night after night. You're alone down there 'cause no one wants you.'

Another punch and more pain.

'I'm all you've got.' Managed to keep the smile on my numbed face. 'Keep coming back for more.'

'For all I care . . .'

I finished it for him: 'I could go away like Mother.'

He jumped at me and got a hold of my legs. His teeth went in at the thigh. Took a grip I couldn't shake. My hands beat down on his head and neck. Rolled to the side. Kicked with my free leg. He kept chewing at the fabric of my jeans. Kept biting away at the skin underneath.

'I'll kill you!' I screamed. 'Swear to Christ I'll kill you!'

Now you've got him, kiddo.

Landed the heel of my foot against the top of his head. Felt like kicking at a tree stump. Connecting with something hard and sturdy. Only it cut him loose. My old man let go. His teeth ripped from my jeans. Two crescents of wet marked my jeans. Below the mark my skin pulsed. He stood himself straight at the base of the stairs. Looked up at me. Shoulders wide and bouncing with his fast breaths.

'Gonna kill me?'

'Take the smile off your face.' I tried to sound like J D. Tried to bring some kind of rough tone that'd make him jump on the inside.

'Enough talkin', kid.'

'You're pathetic.'

'You're wasting my life,' he said.

'It's what you get for having a son.'

'You're not my son!' Took a step toward me. Then he made out with that new laugh of his. Roared that laugh in my face. 'Bastard sonofabitch! You're not my kid!'

'Go to hell.'

And he went.

My old man was still working in the basement when the day started to happen. A group of people kept walking up and down the street. Their shapes slowed when passing our house. They never stopped, but the figures in the white glass made me wonder what they knew. Half an hour after the figures first showed a car pulled up. It was a big dark car. It pulled into the driveway. Four shapes climbed out of the car like they'd practised the move for years. Watched two of the figures get bigger in the window. Became clear the closer they got to the door. A dark blue uniform and a dark suit were coming up the path. Two figures stayed with the car. Stood like pillars outside the front doors. The bell rang and the sound of my old man's drill cut off. The radio he'd been singing to died out.

The figures didn't even look through the glass panels. It's like they didn't need to see if I was there. Like they already knew everything about me. Even knew I'd be there waiting. They knocked on the wood. Rang the bell a second time. They were angry knocks that sent fresh waves of flames through my ribs. Finally stood, my knees ached. My stomach closed in. Neighbours had forgot the food over the past few days. With all that was going on in the town no one had chance to remember Joe Pullman.

Sweat fell from my head. Beaded up on my arms. My hands felt like dead fish that hadn't gone dry. Mouth felt thick when I choked down an empty swallow. The door felt heavy. It took all I had to get it open.

'Hey,' I said.

It was a female officer standing closest to me. She looked at my face and made a clicking sound with her mouth. Then she smiled like I'd opened a bottle of champagne for her arrival. *Come in. Have a seat. Welcome to La Casa de Pullman. Beating will commence in quarter of an hour. Take your seat before the show. Ordearve anyone?* Still, the woman gave me this look. I'd seen it before once in a while. The nurses at Columbia Medical Centre had that look when Mother hauled me through the ER doors with a split tongue. Nemechek got that look too toward the end.

It was a look that said it all: *Check out the scars on this freak. Bet we can tell you where those came from. Bunch of kids on the playground, my ass.*

This lady cop understood what I was all about. She had this look on her face that told me she'd been round kids. Kids that'd seen the same, maybe even worse. Knew the kind of kid I was. Knew about the family I came from. She knew about the wanting to hide away. All this I figured from the way she stood there in the door with that look on her face. She didn't force herself in the house. She just smiled at me with her head to the side.

The guy standing by her could've done the shoving and the restraining. He could've grabbed me with a hand. Called an end to the game. Kept looking up at him thinking he's the one that'll decide what happens. He'll haul my ass away with my arm half busted from his struggle. The female cop'll give me the poutey stare while one of the two pillars outside flip on the sirens. But I looked at the woman cop again. Didn't feel like shit was hitting the fan. Didn't get the impression that I'd been hit with any dirty even if it had.

She just kept giving me that look: *I understand. You're Joseph Reginald Pullman and that's okay. I've heard about you from people. You're a real screwed up kid. You've got a bad situation here. Just want to talk about it. Thought we'd stop by and lend a helping hand.*

But that kind of thing didn't sit all that well with me. There wasn't a lot of help and charity coming my way. At that point I couldn't shove away the help when it arrived.

So why the two cops outside, Joe? Don't jump the gun. May be here to talk about Oz. Can't forget what you and Dean did to that poor asshole. There's also that small matter of Dean Gillespie in a box. By the way, Joe . . . he's dead!

'Hey,' I said again.

There was a smile coming up on my face. It seemed like a genuine smile even though it took a while to bring up the edges of my mouth. Didn't know the woman cop from Daisy Duke, but she made me feel alright somehow.

'Are you Joseph?' she finally asked. Must have grown tired of sharing smiles with me. 'Joseph Reginald Pullman?'

'Yes, ma'am.'

'Are your parents,' she started. Stopped and gritted her teeth in an exaggerated smile. 'Is your father home?'

'No,' I lied. 'Don't think he's back yet.'

'Can you tell me where he might be?'

'Wish I could.' Nodding my head I tried to hold back any expressions that might've made me a liar. Felt those expressions floating up to the surface of my face.

'He's away a lot,' I finished.

'Business?' she asked.

'Quit his job,' I said.

She looked at her partner who kept craning his neck around the door jamb. *Have a look, big guy. Ain't a thing in here but trouble. Welcome to come in and take all you want.*

'Could we come in? Have a talk with you, Joseph?' She kept her voice soft like a sponge and it soaked me up. Even after looking at her partner it didn't feel all that bad having cops around. Her partner was a tall guy with a build that could make a heavyweight boxer look like they'd missed puberty. Even with him there I felt I could trust her. Felt like she'd make right the wrongs of the summer.

I stepped aside and she followed the lead I'd made with my arm. Directed her like I was directing traffic. Walked into the front room and stood in front of the sofa at the window. The big guy stepped into the house and stopped dead. He looked

308

down at me and didn't offer a smile. Didn't give me the slightest damn wink to say *I'm with her kiddo. We're here to watch your back from here on out. Nothin's gonna get you now.* He'd come on business and didn't have time for niceties. I followed his partner into the family room. The big guy shut the door and started to walk toward us. Then he positioned himself in the archway between the foyer and the family room. Stood with his thick forearms crossed.

I sat down on the sofa. The female officer stepped forward from where she'd been standing. Ran a hand down the thigh of her slacks before sitting on the cushion next to me. She had a folder in her hands. A plain manila folder like Nemechek had filled with all my past convictions. The one the lady cop held was thin compared to Nemechek's. She brought it up and set it on her lap.

'My name's Officer Reese,' she said. 'We understand you were with Dean Gillespie quite a bit recently. Together most days from what I understand. Am I correct in understanding that you two were together a lot in the week before he went missing?'

'With his mother too.' It came out before I could think of what to say. 'We tried to find him before anybody else even knew he'd been . . .'

'That's right.' She nodded her head. Looked at me with her head tilted to one side again. Couldn't help but wonder if Maureen had been coaching her. *He hates when I do this. He may really break up if you ask about his mother, dear. Hung herself, you know. Ask him what made her go whacko. That'll send him over the edge for sure, darlin'. That'll really bring out the beast.* She bit her bottom lip until the red went white. Made a dent in the soft skin, but not so it'd hurt. Couldn't tell if she sat thinking or if she'd been interested in hearing what I'd had to say.

'I take it you two were good friends,' she continued.

'Yes, ma'am.'

'Did you spend a lot of time at Dean's house?' she asked. Then she opened up the manila folder. Pulled a pen from her breast pocket. 'Sleepovers and having dinner with Dean and his parents? That kind of thing going on much?'

'I went over there a lot. Maureen called me sometimes. Asked if I'd go over for dinner. Went to the lake for a concert with them. That's when Sheriff Wil . . .'

There you go, Joe-Joe. Drop yourself in line for three disasters in a single freakin' summer.

The woman cop didn't flinch. Instead she asked:

'Dean spend much time here? Come over for sleepovers. Dinner with your family?' She looked kind of shy for a minute and then added: 'With your father and you? Dinners with your . . .'

'In this house?'

'Yes. Here with you and . . .' she stopped again and started searching for the word. I helped her along so she could keep the ball rolling.

'My mother's dead,' I told her.

'Oh, right.'

She had a pretty face, but could never have been a movie star. Her expression was the worst piece of acting I'd ever seen. She'd known about my mother. There was no harm in that. Maureen came into my head again. Got to admit it was all playing on my patience at that moment. Maureen had spelled everything out and made sure my mother's death came into the conversation.

If you can get him to admit she's dead he'll break. He's got this thing when people talk about that crazy old bitch. My sweet little angel Dean used to ask about her. Just wanted to know about her cold dead body. Nothing too gruesome, understand? But he'd punch Dean. He'd really lay into him some days. Could've taken it too far, doll. Could've killed him if he'd taken the notion.

Dean's mom had made good notes on my trips to the house. Passed those notes to the Maritime Police Department. It showed in the way the woman cop spoke. The way she reacted to my answers. She knew what was coming so there was no shock. She wasn't walking into any dark rooms in this house. Figured she played it that way so I'd give up the game and start talking. Tell her about my dead mother. Talk about how things headed south after she'd died. She wanted me to spill the story about my life in the house. A life of dodging fast hands badly. This woman cop knew her job too well to be that incompetent at keeping information close to her chest. She probably knew how screwed up a kid she was dealing with. Give the dog a bone and see if he's going to bite.

Or where he'll bury it.

'It's just me and my father,' I said. 'Just us two in a big house.'

'And did Dean spend much time with you and your father?' She got back into the groove quick and easy. I gave her the pitch and she took a big swing.

'No,' I said.

'And why was that do you think?' Her head tilted again.

'Cause my old man was in the basement making something. When he's not down there he's beating me until I can't stand. Kind of figured bringing Dean into the mix wouldn't be all that friendly.

'It's a . . .' I started but stopped after running through the questions I'd already answered. The line of questioning wasn't about me as a suspect. They'd connected the Oz thing with Dean just like anyone and everyone in town. *Bet that Pullman kid's got something to say about all this. He's the link. He's the third. Used to hang out with them two all over town. He's the weird one with all the scars.* But she wasn't asking questions about where I'd been on that Friday night. Didn't ask what I was doing at Dean's house Saturday morning. Christ, I'd helped Maureen look for the kid. I'd walked the path. Searched for him right alongside his frantic mother. Called out his name and followed Maureen back to the house when she called for help.

'Well, it's . . .'

They'd brought me into the frame like I'd figured they'd do. But they'd put me on the list as a victim. They'd come by to see what connections I had with the other two. Why were my friends so unlucky? They wanted to find out if I was on my way to the same end. They wanted to see how close I'd got to Oz and Dean. Her eyes looked big and brown and I wanted to spill my guts.

'Joseph?'

311

'Dean was afraid of . . .' I didn't get to finish.

'Dean was afraid of a lot of things.' My old man's voice sounded like it came out of an intercom. His words busted into the air. Cut my voice right out of the sky. Loud words that bounced from the four walls. I twisted my head and there he stood in the archway. Barefoot and smiling right there next to the big cop. My old man looked so small standing next to that man. He looked so fragile and so goddamned weak.

'I'm Officer Reese,' the woman said standing.

'Hello,' my father replied. 'I'm Richard Pullman.' He looked at me and smiled.

'I'm Joseph's dad,' he said. 'Well, that's obvious to you people.' He laughed. I'd never heard him laugh with his face pointed at me. It sounded so loud. I wanted to hold my hands over my ears. Hated him for that sound he was making.

'So you know Dean Gillespie well, Mr Pullman?' Officer Reese asked.

When my father stepped into the room the big cop dropped his right hand. It landed on the handle of his black pistol. The gun moved in the holster. Even when my father stopped the guy's hand stayed there. He used his index finger to pop the strap holding the gun in. My old man didn't make any motion like he'd noticed the cop's weapon. Didn't even flinch at the idea the guy may want to use it.

Go on and do it, big fella. Drive a round in him while you got the chance.

'Yeah, I'd say I know Dean. Well enough anyway.'

My father moved around the centre of the room like he wanted to give a show. It's like he'd been ready to set off in a dance. A dance that would use up every foot of floor in the whole place. He was getting himself ready for something. Trouble was I didn't know my father well enough. Couldn't figure on what it was he'd been planning. Kept sliding his bare feet over the carpet. Moving sideways like he was really anxious about something arriving. Then he'd walk with his feet dragging his weight. He rubbed his hands together the whole time. Reminded me of a salesman ready to close a big deal. Made me think of a starving man in the dinner line. A desperate man about to . . .

'Don't get me wrong.' He finally went on while looking straight at the woman cop. Her smile was falling off the side of her face. 'Only know him as well as I know any of my son's friends.'

'Can you give me the names of Joseph's friends? Friends that you have recently had to the house, Mr Pullman?' She made like she was going to write a list.

'I don't understand . . .' My old man rubbed those hands like crazy.

'We'll be interviewing several people today. People connected with Dean Gillespie and your son. A list of his friends would be very helpful.'

'I'm certain they would, Joe,' he said. Looked at me. He'd started smiling again. There was something in that smile that made me go cold. Made me fear him more than I'd feared him since things changed. Like I feared him before I'd found pride. Before I'd taken Desmond Walker in that fight on the football field. He was a changed man standing there in front of me. I'd never seen him like that with his wide smile. Never heard that professional voice he was using. This was my old man's façade for the outside world.

This is how he gets through his days, Joe. This is the voice Mr Moon speaks to. This is the man people are worried for. This is the man who lost his wife. The other is the one who killed her. He'll be back for you, Joe. Better get it out while you can. Better tell these fucking cops your life story. Get it out! Tell it all!

'I'll get the list from you, Mr Pullman,' the lady cop continued. 'You do know your son's friends. Don't you?'

'He has so many . . .' That smile came back and his laugh was so adjusted.

'We've been told that your son is a loner.' The woman cop looked at me. Gave me another thing with her eyes that told me she hated that word. Loner. Just the same as coming out with it and telling me *it's alright. You're a social defect. It'll make you an outcast for the rest of your life. Dontcha know . . .*

313

'Joe?' my old man asked. 'A loner?'

'What is he afraid of, Mr Pullman?' the lady cop asked.

'Who? Joe?' My old man looked worried.

'No, Dean Gillespie,' she continued. 'You said he's afraid of a lot of things. What kind of things have you found him to be afraid of?'

'Being away from his parents,' my father said. The air went from my lungs. The big cop held his hand on that gun. I got myself believing that he'd started pulling it up with a slow hand. The metal of the pistol scraped against the hard leather holster.

'That's why he never came over here,' my old man said. 'Joe's always telling me how much a loner this Dean kid is.'

'Is that right?'

'Dean's the loner. Not Joseph. Dean's got the problem with . . .'

'You speak to your son about his friends?' The woman cop looked confident as much as she looked angry.

'Never shuts up about 'em,' he said. I watched my old man's face turning back into the real Richard Pullman. The man who held anger in his fists and dropped them like time bombs. The man who lost his temper when his kid spilled a glass of lemonade. Guy who kept the same kid home from school after the beatings. After making his face bleed from fourteen separate cuts. Same damn guy who beat up his neighbour in Tallahassee for cutting into his side of the hedge.

'Thank Christ he's only got a couple,' he said under his breath. 'Could never take any more of it.'

'And when was the last conversation you had with Joseph?'

'This morning,' my father said shaking his head. 'He rambles on about so much stuff. I have to switch off. Honestly. It'd drive you fuckin' nuts.'

'What were you speaking about this morning?' she asked him.

'Can't tell you.' He looked at me like he needed my help. Looked at me and asked with his eyes for something that'd pull him out of a jam. *I'll owe you one, buddy.*

Go fuck yourself, old man.

'Was it a long conversation?'

'No.'

'Are you aware that Dean Gillespie was found this morning?'

Listening to that woman talk about Dean made everything go cold. My old man's face grew a few inches longer. The colour sank into his cheeks. The dark round shapes of his eyes got even darker. He was left with nothing but the dirty canvas of grey skin. His chin hung limp and his lips shook. He reminded me of a fish out of water. Stood there looking for a last gulp of air while those hands kept rubbing.

'Were you aware that Dean Gillespie has been missing for two days?' the woman asked.

My father didn't respond. He stared at the woman cop with his eyes thick and pink. The blue circles of his iris had been taken over by two large black dots. Those two dots rolled around the room in search of something. They stopped when they found me.

'His body, Mr Pullman,' the woman continued in a louder voice, 'was found in marshland this morning.'

The black dots swelled. His ash coloured face surrounding them looked dead.

'Are you missing a watch, Mr Pullman?'

'A what?' My father snapped out of the trance. He turned his head to look at the woman.

'Gold Seiko,' she said. Her eyes never left my old man. She was looking for something. She was looking for some kind of a reaction. 'Inscribed. R.P. X C'

My father turned on me and asked again for that help.

'Don't have a gold Seiko,' he said.

'Have you had one in the . . .'

'No,' he said. His eyes were still on me. 'My watch is upstairs on the dresser. I could get it for you. But that's not gonna prove anything.'

He had his eyes on me again. Didn't speak, but I heard what he was saying.

'This watch wasn't a gift from your wife?'

'I'm through with this.' My old man stepped toward me. Turned his eyes on the woman cop. 'I'll have a lawyer in two minutes calling your headquarters. You're finished with this list of bullshit questions. Shut the folder and get the hell out.'

'Before . . .' I started.

'Shut up, Joe,' my old man said. Pointed at the woman's chest and said: 'Get out of my house.'

The woman cop stood from the sofa. The big guy in the archway took a step into the room. I wanted to stand, but my old man was in front of me. Couldn't get up without him knocking me back down. There was an opportunity to get out.

Stand, Joe. Get your ass off the sofa. Follow the cops and give them a story. Tell them what's been going down.

'Joseph,' the woman cop said. 'Is there anything you'd like to . . .'

'Get out of here, now!' my old man yelled.

'I'm not really thinking straight,' I said.

'Damn right about that.' My old man stepped forward. Got within striking distance. Punched the palm of his hand again. 'Haven't been thinking straight a while now, huh?'

The woman cop stepped closer. Put out a hand like she was planning on grabbing hold of my old man's arm.

'S'pose not,' I told him.

'What'd you tell that cunt from your school?'

'Don't understand what you're talking . . .'

'Mr Pullman.' The woman cop looked worried. She tossed the folder onto the sofa. Went to touch the holster on her belt. I looked at her gun and wondered if she'd get there fast enough. My old man made a choking sound. It was a weird noise that made me look at him. His mouth hung and his eyes stared down. He was looking at the sofa cushion next to me.

'That's not . . .'

Something got him all worked up. I followed his eyes and saw the photograph. Sitting on the sofa next to me. It was a polaroid snap. Recognized the moving ground in the picture. The cops in the fishing waders were gone. The yellow police tape hung

316

in the distance. Recognized the leaves and the trees. The place looked so grey. In the centre of the picture, half sunk in all the moving ground was a box. A hand crafted wooden box.

'That's not mine . . .' he said. 'How'd it . . .'

'You made that,' I said. *Now I got you, old man! Now you're on my time!* 'He made this!'

My old man shot a hand forward. I grabbed at the picture before he got to it. For the first time in my life I got there before my old man. Mother's voice came back into my head. *You're never fast enough, Joseph.* I pulled the picture to my chest. Held it tight and covered it with both hands.

'You made this!' I looked up at my old man and felt my face swelling up. Before his hands even touched me. My cheeks burned and my eyes went all blurry. 'He made this! Oh, Jesus Christ!'

'How'd you?' My father kept grabbing at the polaroid. Got a good grip on my fingers, but I wasn't going to let go. His eyes locked onto mine. The anger had turned desperate. He leaned in on me and almost whispered:

'That door's locked.'

'He made that box!' I yelled at his face.

'Shut up, Joseph,' he said. Grabbed at my fingers. Used all he had to pull my fingers away.

He's yours, Joe-Joe. Keep it going!

'He's got others downstairs,' I told the woman cop. She was right there at my old man's side. Doing nothing to stop him pulling at my fingers. 'Look. He's built . . .'

I looked at the big guy in the doorway. He had the gun up. Pointed dead on my old man. He yelled something out, but I didn't hear it.

'You sneaking fucking bastard!' my father screamed.

Think I yelled. *Shoot him! Shoot him now!*

First punch took the sight from my right eye. It came in and cracked against my skull. I fell into the sofa. Rolled for a minute and there was a loud chattering sound. Buzzing and screeching noise rolled up in a single explosion. It kept going off inside my

317

head. Couldn't think or feel or . . . Sharp pain over my eye. Hundreds of sharp pains connected on my head. Made my head burn. Opened my eyes. Still couldn't see. More burning from my face. That buzzing sound kept fading in and out.

. . . zzzziiisss uuuurrr ggggaaaaaammmeee . . .

Something was trying to come in through all that buzzing. Voice maybe, but couldn't get out of that feeling. Numbed and hurt and broken. Tired all over. The noise wouldn't let go. Couldn't break free from that sound. And the stinging pain from my head. There was a jolt with a burst of cold pain in my side and another. Light came in through the side of my vision. Another shot of hurt to my side. That light came even more in the corner of my eye. Tried to roll, but couldn't get away. Swung a hand out. Caught something, but not with enough edge.

'This your game?' My old man yelled. 'Like this game?'

I went out before the big guy got into the ring with me and my old man. Never got to see the punch he landed on my father's jaw. It took out a row of teeth. Hate myself for not keeping awake for that moment. For that one big punch I always wanted to land. For that punch that took my old man down.

A paramedic who smelled of rubbing alcohol cleaned me up. My neck was braced in a block of blue foam. My chest was strapped to the gurney. Didn't get a whole lot of what was happening. Lots of commotion. Lots of people yelling and speaking round me. The woman cop stayed with me. Kept leaning over and talking. Telling me everything would be fine. Her face looked young and her voice stayed soft the whole time. While they taped gauze over a few cuts on my forehead I told her about the cicadas. Told her about all the things Dean and me did to them. She didn't make like she felt shocked. She patted my hand. Told me things would be alright.

Before they loaded me onto the ambulance I looked at the crowd of people. They lined the street. In those faces Helle Bishop standing next to Beatrice Stapp. They were speaking and looking at me with soft eyes. Both could see me but neither waved or signalled. Mick Drexler held one of his alsatians on a short leash. It sat at his feet, big as a wolf. The Malcolm kids stood holding their mother's legs. All those faces watched me. No one made a sign. No one told me things were alright. No one smiled and there wasn't a hand to be raised among them.

You're convicted, Joe. That's the trial over, kiddo.

Rode in the ambulance alone. Just me and a paramedic who wouldn't speak. I was glad of that.

Chapter Twenty-Eight

From news bulletins I found out all the rest. My old man's finger-prints had been lifted from the bag Dean's body had been wrapped in. His hair was stuck to the tape that strapped the bag. That with the watch Dean held in his hand made a good case against my old man. He went to trial. They found him guilty and locked him up in the Maryland State Penitentiary. He's prob-ably still in there. Maybe he's already dead. Doesn't matter really. I've never asked anyone 'cause I don't want to know.

The state sent me to live with a foster family. The McLeans lived in Columbia. It's a city just outside Maritime that was far enough away to keep me from memories. Close enough so I could get back in case I needed to go back. The McLeans were nice people. Had two sons of their own. One boy with short brown hair and an army of freckles named Charles Vincent. His younger brother Gerard had olive coloured skin. The two didn't look much alike. Never learned Gerard's second name. That's the way it went for the years in foster care. You only get so much before they move you on.

The brothers were well behaved in front of their parents. They spoke in complete sentences. Strained with the effort to keep from slanging their words. Yessir and no ma'am came out by thought more than reflex. Couple times they coughed on foul language. Mr McLean always caught them when they did. He'd take them off to a room. They'd be in there alone for a while. Then they'd come back out. No bruises. No swelling. But there was a quiet time after those meetings.

He's smarter than your old man, Joe. Knows how to hurt without leaving a mark.

For the most part McLean seemed like a kind man. He sat with me during some of the evenings I lived there. When we spoke he'd use the same calm voice that Dean's father had used with me. Some of the conversations were pretty much the same as I'd had with Mr Gillespie. Only Mr McLean wasn't all that smart a man. He was an engineer and knew his trade. Other than baseball and television commercials he didn't keep a lot in store. Conversations hung close to what we'd experienced in life.

He wanted to trade his army stories for my beatings. I let him deal his hands. Listened to what it was like for him in South America. What the training was like for an army engineer. But I folded before I showed him my hand. He was always willing to try a new story the next time we met up. Something with more guts to tease out my secrets. He wasn't smart enough.

Still, Neil McClean had a genuine interest in my feelings. He asked about the changes I'd gone through since my mother passed. How I'd felt after my old man was arrested. He never asked me if I thought my father was capable of doing all those things to Dean. All the beating and cutting. Folding him up and stuffing him in that box. I knew it hid in the questions he asked me. But he never came clean and shot from the hip. *You think your old man killed your buddy, Joe?* What he wanted me to tell him stayed inside my head. It would've made a good topic for the parties they threw. But I never offered him the gift. If he'd only have asked I'd have delivered a bomb.

You know that foster kid we have staying with us? The one whose father killed that boy over in Maritime this past summer? Well, I was sitting on the porch with him the other night and over a Dr Pepper he tells me he knew it was going to happen. It was just a matter of

321

*time. The kid blew a fuse. One minute he's just sitting there all quiet
and dopey. Then the next minute – zing. He's off. He tells me all
about the things his old man had been up to in the basement. After
his mother died the old guy lost it. She was the one that swung herself
from the rope out at Leichter House, remember? Kid's lost. You can
just imagine.*

He'd have got some serious fishing out of that can of worms.

Still, that wasn't the big one. That's not the biggest secret of
all.

'Joe,' he said one evening. He had this serious look on his
face. Was still wearing his business suit when he met me in the
family room. He'd taken off the tie and opened up the top button
of his shirt. 'Mind if we go outside to the porch. I've got something to tell you.'

Wiped the sweat from my hands when I stood from the sofa.
Followed him through the kitchen to the porch. He shut the
sliding door after I stepped out. He took a seat and I followed
his lead. Dropped into the wicker chair across from him.

'It's about your old house,' he said.

I slid my hands over the knees of my new Levis. The sweat
left dark spots of wet. Mr McLean watched my hands and
frowned.

*He's got your ticket, kiddo. One short call and you're on your way
to . . .*

'Son, I'm not sure I want to tell you this after all you've been
through.'

'Is it sold?' I asked.

'No,' he said. Smiled an uncomfortable smile and cleared his
throat. 'It's burned down, son. It's burned to the ground.'

'Right.' Kept rubbing my hands. Rubbed hard as I could like
I was trying to get the smell of lit matches off them. Took a
deep breath and caught a throat full of burning leaves.

'How do you feel about that?'

'What's done's done, I s'pose.'

'I suppose you're right about that.'

After that we went quiet for a while. That's the way it always went. He'd try to get into my head. I'd block him before he found out anything important. Then we'd just sit there. I'd listen to him breathing and he'd watch me close. Watched me until I wanted to jump across that low plastic coffee table and punch his damn face in. But I just sat there and waited for the right time to leave.

I thought plenty during those times when just me and him sat listening to the crickets. He'd look at me for long periods of time. I'd get so uncomfortable that I'd start thinking hard about other things just to keep myself from going nuts. Sometimes I thought about Dean. I'd wonder if Oz would ever talk. Thought about the Murtache house falling to the same flame as my old man's place. Sometimes I thought about my mother. She was the lucky one after all. A lot of the times I thought about the cicadas. If I thought hard enough I could feel them rumbling under the ground. They'd been burrowing in. Dug tight in a hole. Waiting in their millions in the darkness. Tunnelled in for the long wait. They'd already started the beginning of their seventeen-year hibernation.

So had I.

Charles Vincent and Gerard changed when their parents went away. Being party people, Neil and his wife went away a lot. The boys took that time to play their games. They wanted to dig for the stuff their dad didn't have guts to find. They wanted to know if I'd seen my old man kill Dean. Gave a helping hand in the act, maybe. They asked me if Dean had been my old man's first victim. They'd heard about a guy in Chicago that killed a bunch of boys and buried them under his house. They couldn't sleep at night thinking my old man had done the same.

'We heard you talking to our dad, Joey,' Charles Vincent said. 'We heard your dad spent a lot of time in the basement. He put more down there? Shove dead kids in the basement?'

'I don't know.'

'What about the back yard?' Gerald asked.

'Couldn't tell you.'

'What happened to your friend's clothes?' Charles Vincent asked.

'Not a clue.'

Possibly the most terrifying thing they asked me came in a matter of fact way. Charles Vincent, the older of the two boys, sat close to me. Gerald stood behind him. His arms crossed over his thin and sunken chest.

'Are you like your father, Joseph?' he asked me.

'I don't know,' I replied. With all honesty. *I don't know.*

It's a question that plays itself over and over. I hear Charles Vincent asking me continually. Can smell the smoke from the cigarettes they both coughed on. Can feel the hard chair pressing against my back. Wood slats rubbing against my spine. They looked at me with wide eyes when I answered. They laughed just like they'd found the pages of a dirty magazine. They were trying to stir my emotions. That day they got what they were after. I sat on that wooden seat and looked at them wishing I had the strength to catch them in a glass jar. Shake it up until their heads broke and stained the inside red.

But I sat frightened. That year I'd found a voice in my head. That voice had spoken to me when I threw my fists at Desmond Walker. It chattered in my ear the day I watched Dean turn on Oscar Lewiston. That voice had lulled me to sleep when my mother died. It sang in harmony as Dean and I knocked life from the sky. It told me things would be alright.

Now you hold the scars, Joseph.

All the way home from the marshlands that voice spoke to me.

It's all good, it sang.

It didn't shut off until I'd buried Dean's clothes under the Killing Tree.

Acknowledgements

Special thanks go to an important group of people. I'll make an effort to express my gratitude by mentioning their names. It doesn't seem enough. Jeff Olma, Arnold Wood, Ms D Parker and Mark O'Connor – endured the early stuff. Janet Burroway and Virgil Suarez – encouraged on progress. Dylis Rose and Margaret Elphinstone – they knew Joe's tale deserved a novel. Stephen Gordon – read through the bad to get to the good. Bernard MacLaverty – saw something in the sidestore. Gill Coleridge – with all her patience helped set me on my way and watches over me still. Lucy Luck and the rest of the RCW crew – work behind the scenes in a big way. Robin Robertson had the guts to put the dark to the world. And Ellah Allfrey, what can I say . . . she knows that Pullman kid.

The author wishes to acknowledge the support of the Scottish Arts Council for the purpose of writing this book.